DETECTIVES 2

DETECTIVES 2

MISS CAYLEY'S ADVENTURES

GRANT ALLEN

HILDA WADE

GRANT ALLEN

COACHWHIP PUBLICATIONS

Landisville, Pennsylvania

2 Detectives: Miss Cayley's Adventures / Hilda Wade
Copyright © 2012 Coachwhip Publications
No claim made on public domain material.

Miss Cayley's Adventures, by Grant Allen (1899)
Hilda Wade: A Woman with Tenacity of Purpose, by Grant Allen (1900)

ISBN 1-61646-125-X
ISBN-13 978-1-61646-125-6

CoachwhipBooks.com

MISS CAYLEY'S ADVENTURES

HILDA WADE
EPISODES

MISS CAYLEY'S
ADVENTURES

THE ADVENTURE OF THE
CANTANKEROUS OLD LADY

On the day when I found myself with twopence in my pocket, I naturally made up my mind to go round the world.

It was my stepfather's death that drove me to it. I had never seen my stepfather. Indeed, I never even thought of him as anything more than Colonel Watts-Morgan. I owed him nothing, except my poverty. He married my dear mother when I was a girl at school in Switzerland; and he proceeded to spend her little fortune, left at her sole disposal by my father's will, in paying his gambling debts. After that, he carried my dear mother off to Burma; and when he and the climate between them had succeeded in killing her, he made up for his appropriations at the cheapest rate by allowing me just enough to send me to Girton. So, when the Colonel died, in the year I was leaving college, I did not think it necessary to go into mourning for him. Especially as he chose the precise moment when my allowance was due, and bequeathed me nothing but his consolidated liabilities.

"Of course you will teach," said Elsie Petheridge, when I explained my affairs to her. "There is a good demand just now for high-school teachers."

I looked at her, aghast. "*Teach!* Elsie," I cried. (I had come up to town to settle her in at her unfurnished lodgings.) "Did you say *teach*? That's just like you dear good schoolmistresses! You go to Cambridge, and get examined till the heart and life have been examined out of you; then you say to yourselves at the end of it all, 'Let me see; what am I good for now? I'm just about fit to go away and examine other people!' That's what our Principal would call 'a vicious circle'—if one could ever admit there was anything vicious at all about *you*, dear. No, Elsie, I do *not* propose to teach. Nature did not cut me out for a high-school teacher. I couldn't swallow a poker if I tried for weeks. Pokers don't agree with me. Between ourselves, I am a bit of a rebel."

"You are, Brownie," she answered, pausing in her papering, with her sleeves rolled up—they called me "Brownie," partly because of my dark complexion, but partly because they could never understand me. "We all knew that long ago."

I laid down the paste-brush and mused.

"Do you remember, Elsie," I said, staring hard at the paper-board, "when I first went to Girton, how all you girls wore your hair quite straight, in neat smooth coils, plaited up at the back about the size of a pancake; and how of a sudden I burst in upon you, like a tropical hurricane, and demoralised you; and how, after three days of me, some of the dear innocents began with awe to cut themselves artless fringes, while others went out in fear and trembling and surreptitiously purchased a pair of curling-tongs? I was a bomb-shell in your midst in those days; why, you yourself were almost afraid at first to speak to me."

"You see, you had a bicycle," Elsie put in, smoothing the half-papered wall; "and in those days, of course, ladies didn't bicycle. You must admit, Brownie, dear, it *was* a startling innovation. You terrified us so. And yet, after all, there isn't much harm in you."

"I hope not," I said devoutly. "I was before my time, that was all; at present, even a curate's wife may blamelessly bicycle."

"But if you don't teach," Elsie went on, gazing at me with those wondering big blue eyes of hers, "whatever will you do, Brownie?" Her horizon was bounded by the scholastic circle.

"I haven't the faintest idea," I answered, continuing to paste. "Only, as I can't trespass upon your elegant hospitality for life, whatever I mean to do, I must begin doing this morning, when we've finished the papering. I couldn't teach" (teaching, like mauve, is the refuge of the incompetent); "and I don't, if possible, want to sell bonnets."

"As a milliner's girl?" Elsie asked, with a face of red horror.

"As a milliner's girl; why not? 'Tis an honest calling. Earls' daughters do it now. But you needn't look so shocked. I tell you, just at present, I am not contemplating it."

"Then what *do* you contemplate?"

I paused and reflected. "I am here in London," I answered, gazing rapt at the ceiling; "London, whose streets are paved with gold—though it *looks* at first sight like muddy flagstones; London, the greatest and richest city in the world, where an adventurous soul ought surely to find some loophole for an adventure. (That piece is hung crooked, dear; we shall have to take it down again.) I devise a Plan, therefore. I submit myself to fate; or, if you prefer it, I leave my future in the hands of Providence. I shall stroll out this morning, as soon as I've 'cleaned myself,' and embrace the first stray enterprise that offers. Our Bagdad teems with enchanted carpets. Let one but float my way, and, hi, presto, I seize it. I go where glory or a modest competence waits me. I snatch at the first offer, the first hint of an opening."

Elsie stared at me, more aghast and more puzzled than ever. "But, how?" she asked. "Where? When? You *are* so strange! What will you do to find one?"

"Put on my hat and walk out," I answered. "Nothing could be simpler. This city bursts with enterprises and surprises. Strangers from east and west hurry through it in all directions. Omnibuses traverse it from end to end—even, I am told, to Islington and Putney; within, folk sit face to face who never saw one another before in their lives, and who may never see one another again, or, on the contrary, may pass the rest of their days together."

I had a lovely harangue all pat in my head, in much the same strain, on the infinite possibilities of entertaining angels unawares, in cabs, on the Underground, in the aërated bread shops; but Elsie's widening eyes of horror pulled me up short like a hansom in Piccadilly when the inexorable upturned hand of the policeman checks it. "Oh, Brownie," she cried, drawing back, "you *don't* mean to tell me you're going to ask the first young man you meet in an omnibus to marry you?"

I shrieked with laughter, "Elsie," I cried, kissing her dear yellow little head, "you are *impayable*. You never will learn what I mean. You don't understand the language. No, no; I am going out, simply in search of adventure. What adventure may come, I have not at this moment the faintest conception. The fun lies in the search, the uncertainty, the toss-up of it. What is the good of being penniless—with the trifling exception of twopence—unless you are prepared to accept your position in the spirit of a masked ball at Covent Garden?"

"I have never been to one," Elsie put in.

"Gracious heavens, neither have I! What on earth do you take me for? But I mean to see where fate will lead me."

"I may go with you?" Elsie pleaded.

"Certainly *not*, my child," I answered—she was three years older than I, so I had the right to patronise her. "That would spoil all. Your dear little face would be quite enough to scare away a timid adventure." She knew what I meant. It was gentle and pensive, but it lacked initiative.

So, when we had finished that wall, I popped on my best hat, and popped out by myself into Kensington Gardens.

I am told I ought to have been terribly alarmed at the straits in which I found myself—a girl of twenty-one, alone in the world, and only twopence short of penniless, without a friend to protect, a relation to counsel her. (I don't count Aunt Susan, who lurked in ladylike indigence at Blackheath, and whose counsel, like her tracts, was given away too profusely to everybody to allow of one's placing any very high value upon it.) But, as a matter of fact, I must admit I was not in the least alarmed. Nature had endowed me with a profusion of crisp black hair, and plenty of high spirits. If my eyes had been like Elsie's—that liquid blue which looks out upon life with mingled pity and amazement—I might have felt as a girl ought to feel under such conditions; but having large dark eyes, with a bit of a twinkle in them, and being as well able to pilot a bicycle as any girl of my acquaintance, I have inherited or acquired an outlook on the world which distinctly leans rather towards cheeriness than despondency. I croak with difficulty. So I accepted my plight as an amusing experience, affording full scope for the congenial exercise of courage and ingenuity.

How boundless are the opportunities of Kensington Gardens—the Round Pond, the winding Serpentine, the mysterious seclusion of the Dutch brick Palace! Genii swarm there. One jostles possibilities. It is a land of romance, bounded on the north by the Abyss of Bayswater, and on the south by the Amphitheatre of the Albert Hall. But for a centre of adventure I choose the Long Walk; it beckoned me somewhat as the North-West Passage beckoned my seafaring ancestors—the buccaneering mariners of Elizabethan Devon. I sat down on a chair at the foot of an old elm with a poetic hollow, prosaically filled by a utilitarian plate of galvanised iron. Two ancient ladies were seated on the other side already—very grand-looking dames, with the haughty and exclusive ugliness of the English aristocracy in its later stages. For frank hideousness, commend me to the noble dowager. They were talking confidentially as I sat down; the trifling episode of my approach did not suffice to stem the full stream of their conversation. The great ignore the intrusion of their inferiors.

"Yes, it's a terrible nuisance," the eldest and ugliest of the two observed—she was a high-born lady, with a distinctly cantankerous cast of countenance. She had a Roman nose, and her skin was wrinkled like a wilted apple; she wore coffee-coloured point-lace in her bonnet, with a complexion to match. "But what could I do, my dear? I simply *couldn't* put up with such insolence. So I looked her straight back in the face—oh, she quailed, I can tell you; and I said to her, in my iciest voice—you know how icy I can be when occasion demands it"—the second old lady nodded an ungrudging assent, as if perfectly prepared to admit her friend's rare gift of iciness—"I said to her, 'Célestine, you can take your month's wages, and half an hour to get out of this house.' And she dropped me a deep reverence, and she answered: '*Oui, madame; merci beaucoup, madame; je ne desire pas mieux, madame.*' And out she flounced. So there was the end of it."

"Still, you go to Schlangenbad on Monday?"

"That's the point. On Monday. If it weren't for the journey, I should have been glad enough to be rid of the minx. I'm glad as it is, indeed; for a more insolent, upstanding, independent, answer-you-back-again young woman, with a sneer of her own, *I* never saw, Amelia—but I *must* get to Schlangenbad. Now, there the difficulty comes in. On the one hand, if I engage a maid in London, I have the choice of two evils. Either I must take a trapesing English girl—and I know by experience that an English girl on the Continent is a vast deal worse than no maid at all: *you* have to wait upon *her*, instead of her waiting upon you; she gets seasick on the crossing, and when she reaches France or Germany, she hates the meals, and she detests the hotel servants, and she can't speak the language, so that she's always calling you in to interpret for her in her private differences with the *fille-de-chambre* and the landlord; or else I must pick up a French maid in London, and I know equally by experience that the French maids one engages in London are invariably dishonest—more dishonest than the rest even; they've come here because they have no character to speak of elsewhere, and they think you aren't likely to write and enquire of their last mistress in Toulouse or St. Petersburg. Then, again, on the other hand, I can't wait to get a Gretchen, an unsophisticated little Gretchen of the Taunus at Schlangenbad—I suppose there *are* unsophisticated girls in Germany still—made in Germany—they don't make 'em any longer in England, I'm sure—like everything else, the trade in rustic innocence has been driven from the country. I can't wait to get a Gretchen, as I should like to do, of course, because I simply *daren't* undertake to cross the Channel alone and go all that long journey by Ostend or Calais, Brussels and Cologne, to Schlangenbad."

"You could get a temporary maid," her friend suggested, in a lull of the tornado.

The Cantankerous Old Lady flared up. "Yes, and have my jewel-case stolen! Or find she was an English girl without one word of German. Or nurse her on the boat when I want to give my undivided attention to my own misfortunes. No, Amelia, I call it positively unkind of you to suggest such a thing. You're *so* unsympathetic! I put my foot down there. I will *not* take any temporary person."

I saw my chance. This was a delightful idea. Why not start for Schlangenbad with the Cantankerous Old Lady?

Of course, I had not the slightest intention of taking a lady's-maid's place for a permanency. Nor even, if it comes to that, as a passing expedient. But *if* I wanted to go round the world, how could I do better than set out by the Rhine country? The Rhine leads you on to the Danube, the Danube to the Black Sea, the Black Sea to Asia; and so, by way of India, China, and Japan, you reach the Pacific and San Francisco; whence one returns quite easily by New York and the White Star Liners. I began to feel like a globe-trotter already; the Cantankerous Old Lady was the thin end of the wedge— the first rung of the ladder! I proceeded to put my foot on it.

I leaned around the corner of the tree and spoke. "Excuse me," I said, in my suavest voice, "but I think I see a way out of your difficulty."

My first impression was that the Cantankerous Old Lady would go off in a fit of apoplexy. She grew purple in the face with indignation and astonishment, that a casual outsider should venture to address her; so much so, indeed, that for a second I almost regretted my well-meant interposition. Then she scanned me up and down, as if I were a girl in a mantle shop, and she contemplated buying either me or the mantle. At last, catching my eye, she thought better of it, and burst out laughing.

"What do you mean by this eavesdropping?" she asked.

I flushed up in turn. "This is a public place," I replied, with dignity; "and you spoke in a tone which was hardly designed for the strictest privacy. If you don't wish to be overheard, you oughtn't to shout. Besides, I desired to do you a service."

The Cantankerous Old Lady regarded me once more from head to foot. I did not quail. Then she turned to her companion. "The girl has spirit," she remarked, in an encouraging tone, as if she were discussing some absent person. "Upon my word, Amelia, I rather like the look of her. Well, my good woman, what do you want to suggest to me?"

"Merely this," I replied, bridling up and crushing her. "I am a Girton girl, an officer's daughter, no more a good woman than most others of my class; and I have nothing in particular to do for the moment. I don't object to going to Schlangenbad. I would convoy you over, as companion, or lady-help, or anything else you choose to call it; I would remain with you there for a week, till you could arrange with your Gretchen, presumably unsophisticated; and then I would leave you. Salary is unimportant; my fare suffices. I accept the chance as a cheap opportunity of attaining Schlangenbad."

The yellow-faced old lady put up her long-handled tortoise-shell eyeglasses and inspected me all over again. "Well, I declare," she murmured. "What are girls coming to, I wonder? Girton, you say; Girton! That place at Cambridge! You speak Greek, of course; but how about German?"

"Like a native," I answered, with cheerful promptitude. "I was at school in Canton Berne; it is a mother tongue to me."

"No, no," the old lady went on, fixing her keen small eyes on my mouth. "Those little lips could never frame themselves to 'schlecht' or 'wunderschön'; they were not cut out for it."

"Pardon me," I answered, in German. "What I say, that I mean. The never-to-be-forgotten music of the Fatherland's-speech has on my infant ear from the first-beginning impressed itself."

The old lady laughed aloud.

"Don't jabber it to me, child," she cried. "I hate the lingo. It's the one tongue on earth that even a pretty girl's lips fail to render attractive. You yourself make faces over it. What's your name, young woman?"

"Lois Cayley."

"Lois! *What* a name! I never heard of any Lois in my life before, except Timothy's grandmother. *You're* not anybody's grandmother, are you?"

"Not to my knowledge," I answered, gravely.

She burst out laughing again.

"Well, you'll do, I think," she said, catching my arm. "That big mill down yonder hasn't ground the originality altogether out of you. I adore originality. It was clever of you to catch at the suggestion of this arrangement. Lois Cayley, you say; any relation of a mad-cap Captain Cayley whom I used once to know, in the Forty-second Highlanders?"

"His daughter," I answered, flushing. For I was proud of my father.

"Ha! I remember; he died, poor fellow; he was a good soldier—and his"—I felt she was going to say "his fool of a widow," but a glance from me quelled her; "his widow went and married that good-looking scapegrace, Jack Watts-Morgan. Never marry a man, my dear, with a double-barrelled name and no visible means of subsistence; above all, if he's generally known by a nickname. So you're poor Tom Cayley's daughter, are you? Well, well, we can settle this little matter between us. Mind, I'm a person who always expects to have my own way. If you come with *me* to Schlangenbad, you must do as I tell you."

"I *think* I could manage it—for a week," I answered, demurely.

She smiled at my audacity. We passed on to terms. They were quite satisfactory. She wanted no references. "Do I look like a woman who cares about a reference? What are called *characters* are usually essays in how not to say it. You take my fancy; that's the point! And poor Tom Cayley! But, mind, I will *not* be contradicted."

"I will not contradict your wildest misstatement," I answered, smiling.

"*And* your name and address?" I asked, after we had settled preliminaries.

A faint red spot rose quaintly in the centre of the Cantankerous Old Lady's sallow cheek. "My dear," she murmured, "my name is the one thing on earth I'm really ashamed of. My parents chose to inflict upon me the most odious label that human ingenuity ever devised for a Christian soul; and I've not had courage enough to burst out and change it."

A gleam of intuition flashed across me, "You don't mean to say," I exclaimed, "that you're called Georgina?"

The Cantankerous Old Lady gripped my arm hard. "What an unusually intelligent girl!" she broke in. "How on earth did you guess? It *is* Georgina."

"Fellow-feeling," I answered. "So is mine, Georgina Lois. But as I quite agree with you as to the atrocity of such conduct, I have suppressed the Georgina. It ought to be made penal to send innocent girls into the world so burdened."

"My opinion to a T! You are really an exceptionally sensible young woman. There's my name and address; I start on Monday."

I glanced at her card. The very copperplate was noisy. "Lady Georgina Fawley, 49 Fortescue Crescent, W."

It had taken us twenty minutes to arrange our protocols. As I walked off, well pleased, Lady Georgina's friend ran after me quickly.

"You must take care," she said, in a warning voice. "You've caught a Tartar."

"So I suspect," I answered. "But a week in Tartary will be at least an experience."

"She has an awful temper."

"That's nothing. So have I. Appalling, I assure you. And if it comes to blows, I'm bigger and younger and stronger than she is."

"Well, I wish you well out of it."

"Thank you. It is kind of you to give me this warning. But I think I can take care of myself. I come, you see, of a military family."

I nodded my thanks, and strolled back to Elsie's. Dear little Elsie was in transports of surprise when I related my adventure.

"Will you really go? And what will you do, my dear, when you get there?"

"I haven't a notion," I answered; "that's where the fun comes in. But, anyhow, I shall have got there."

"Oh, Brownie, you might starve!"

"And I might starve in London. In either place, I have only two hands and one head to help me."

"But, then, here you are among friends. You might stop with me for ever."

I kissed her fluffy forehead. "You good, generous little Elsie," I cried; "I won't stop here one moment after I have finished the painting and papering. I came here to help you. I couldn't go on eating your hard-earned bread and doing nothing. I know how sweet you are; but the last thing I want is to add to your burdens. Now let us roll up our sleeves again and hurry on with the dado."

"But, Brownie, you'll want to be getting your own things ready. Remember, you're off to Germany on Monday."

I shrugged my shoulders. 'Tis a foreign trick I picked up in Switzerland. "What have I got to get ready?" I asked. "I can't go out and buy a complete summer outfit in Bond Street for twopence. Now, don't look at me like that: be practical, Elsie, and let me help you paint the dado." For unless I helped her, poor Elsie could never have finished it herself. I cut out half her clothes for her; her own ideas were almost entirely limited to differential calculus. And cutting out a blouse by differential calculus is weary, uphill work for a high-school teacher.

By Monday I had papered and furnished the rooms, and was ready to start on my voyage of exploration. I met the Cantankerous Old Lady at Charing Cross, by appointment, and proceeded to take charge of her luggage and tickets.

Oh my, how fussy she was! "You will drop that basket! I hope you have got through tickets, *viâ* Malines, *not* by Brussels— I won't go by Brussels. You have to change there. Now, mind you notice how much the luggage weighs in English pounds, and make the man at the office give you a note of it to check those horrid Belgian porters. They'll charge you for double the weight, unless you reduce it at once to kilogrammes. *I* know their ways. Foreigners have no consciences. They just go to the priest and confess, you know, and wipe it all out, and start fresh again on a career of crime next morning. I'm sure I don't know why I *ever* go abroad. The only country in the world fit to live in is England. No mosquitoes, no passports, no—goodness gracious, child, don't let that odious man bang about my hat-box! Have you no immortal soul, porter, that you crush other people's property as if it was black-beetles? No, I will not let you take this, Lois; this is my jewel-box—it contains all that remains of the Fawley family jewels. I positively decline to appear at Schlangenbad without a diamond to my back. This never leaves my hands. It's hard enough nowadays to keep body and skirt together. *Have* you secured that *coupé* at Ostend?"

We got into our first-class carriage. It was clean and comfortable; but the Cantankerous Old Lady made the porter mop the floor, and fidgeted and worried till we slid out of the station. Fortunately, the only other occupant of the compartment was a most urbane and obliging Continental gentleman—I say Continental, because I couldn't quite make out whether he was French, German, or Austrian—who was anxious in every way to meet Lady Georgina's wishes. Did madame desire to have the window open? Oh, certainly, with pleasure; the day was so sultry. Closed a little more? *Parfaitement*, there *was* a current of air, *il faut l'admettre*. Madame would prefer the corner? No? Then perhaps she would like this valise for a footstool? *Permettez*—just thus. A cold draught runs so often along the floor in railway carriages. This is Kent that we traverse; ah, the garden of England! As a diplomat, he knew every nook of Europe, and he echoed the *mot* he had accidentally heard drop from madame's lips on the platform: no country in the world so delightful as England!

"Monsieur is attached to the Embassy in London?" Lady Georgina inquired, growing affable.

He twirled his grey moustache: a waxed moustache of great distinction. "No, madame; I have quitted the diplomatic service; I inhabit London now *pour mon agrément*. Some of my compatriots call it *triste*; for me, I find it the most fascinating capital in Europe. What gaiety! What movement! What poetry! What mystery!"

"If mystery means fog, it challenges the world," I interposed.

He gazed at me with fixed eyes. "Yes, mademoiselle," he answered, in quite a different and markedly chilly voice. "Whatever your great country attempts—were it only a fog—it achieves consummately."

I have quick intuitions. I felt the foreign gentleman took an instinctive dislike to me.

To make up for it, he talked much, and with animation, to Lady Georgina. They ferreted out friends in common, and were as much surprised at it as people always are at that inevitable experience.

"Ah yes, madame, I recollect him well in Vienna. I was there at the time, attached to our Legation. He was a charming man; you read his masterly paper on the Central Problem of the Dual Empire?"

"You were in Vienna then!" the Cantankerous Old Lady mused back. "Lois, my child, don't stare"—she had covenanted from the first to call me Lois, as my father's daughter, and I confess I preferred it to being Miss Cayley'd. "We must surely have met. Dare I ask your name, monsieur?"

I could see the foreign gentleman was delighted at this turn. He had played for it, and carried his point. He meant her to ask him. He had a card in his pocket, conveniently close; and he handed it across to her. She read it, and passed it on: "M. le Comte de Laroche-sur-Loiret."

"Oh, I remember your name well," the Cantankerous Old Lady broke in. "I think you knew my husband, Sir Evelyn Fawley, and my father, Lord Kynaston."

The Count looked profoundly surprised and delighted. "What! you are then Lady Georgina Fawley!" he cried, striking an attitude. "Indeed, miladi, your admirable husband was one of the very first to exert his influence in my favour at Vienna. Do I recall him, ce cher Sir Evelyn? If I recall him! What a fortunate rencounter! I must have seen you some years ago at Vienna, miladi, though I had not then the great pleasure of making your acquaintance. But your face had impressed itself on my sub-conscious self!" (I did not learn till later that the esoteric doctrine of the sub-conscious self was Lady Georgina's favourite hobby.) "The moment chance led me to this carriage this morning, I said to myself, 'That face, those features: so vivid, so striking: I have seen them somewhere. With what do I connect them in the recesses of my memory? A high-born family; genius; rank; the diplomatic service; some unnameable charm; some faint touch of eccentricity. Ha! I have it. Vienna, a carriage with footmen in red livery, a noble presence, a crowd of wits—poets, artists, politicians—pressing eagerly round the landau.' That was my mental picture as I sat and confronted you: I understand it all now; this is Lady Georgina Fawley!"

I thought the Cantankerous Old Lady, who was a shrewd person in her way, must surely see through this obvious patter; but I had under-estimated the average human capacity for swallowing flattery. Instead of dismissing his fulsome nonsense with a contemptuous smile, Lady Georgina perked herself up with a conscious air of coquetry, and asked for more. "Yes, they were delightful days in Vienna," she said, simpering; "I was young then, Count; I enjoyed life with a zest."

"Persons of miladi's temperament are always young," the Count retorted, glibly, leaning forward and gazing at her. "Growing old is a foolish habit of the stupid and the vacant. Men and women of *esprit* are never older. One learns as one goes on in life to admire, not the obvious beauty of mere youth and health"—he glanced across at me disdainfully—"but the profounder beauty of deep character in a face—that calm and serene beauty which is imprinted on the brow by experience of the emotions."

"I have had my moments," Lady Georgina murmured, with her head on one side.

"I believe it, miladi," the Count answered, and ogled her.

Thenceforward to Dover, they talked together with ceaseless animation. The Cantankerous Old Lady was capital company. She had a tang in her tongue, and in the course of ninety minutes she had flayed alive the greater part of London society, with keen wit and sprightliness. I laughed against my will at her ill-tempered sallies; they were too funny not to amuse, in spite of their vitriol. As for the Count, he was charmed. He talked well himself, too, and between them I almost forgot the time till we arrived at Dover.

It was a very rough passage. The Count helped us to carry our nineteen hand-packages and four rugs on board; but I noticed that, fascinated as she was with him, Lady Georgina resisted his ingenious efforts to gain possession of her precious jewel-case as she descended the gangway. She clung to it like grim death, even in the chops of the Channel. Fortunately I am a good sailor, and when Lady Georgina's sallow cheeks began to grow pale, I was steady enough to supply her with her shawl and her smelling-bottle. She fidgeted and worried the whole way over. She *would* be treated like a vertebrate animal. Those horrid Belgians had no right to stick their deck-chairs just in front of her. The impertinence of the hussies with the bright red hair—a grocer's daughters, she felt sure—in venturing to come and sit on the same bench with *her*—the bench "for ladies only," under the lee of the funnel! "Ladies only," indeed! Did the baggages pretend they considered themselves ladies? Oh, that placid old gentleman in the episcopal gaiters was their father, was he? Well, a bishop should bring up his daughters better, having his children in subjection with all gravity. Instead of which—"Lois, my smelling-salts!" This was a beastly boat; such an odour of machinery; they had no decent boats nowadays; with all our boasted improvements, she could remember well when the cross-Channel service was much better conducted than it was at present. But *that* was before we had compulsory education. The working classes were driving trade out of the country, and the consequence was, we couldn't build a boat which didn't reek like an oil-shop. Even the sailors on board were French—jabbering idiots; not an honest British Jack-tar among the lot of them; though the stewards were English, and very inferior Cockney English at that, with their off-hand ways, and their School Board airs and graces. *She'd* School Board them if they were her servants; *she'd* show them the sort of respect that was due to people of birth and education. But the children of the lower classes never learnt their catechism nowadays; they were too much occupied with literatoor, jography, and free-'and drawrin'. Happily for my nerves, a good lurch to leeward put a stop for a while to the course of her thoughts on the present distresses.

At Ostend the Count made a second gallant attempt to capture the jewel-case, which Lady Georgina automatically repulsed. She had a fixed habit, I believe, of sticking fast to that jewel-case; for she was too overpowered by the Count's urbanity, I feel sure, to suspect for a moment his honesty of purpose. But whenever she travelled, I fancy, she clung to her case as if her life depended upon it; it contained the whole of her valuable diamonds.

We had twenty minutes for refreshments at Ostend, during which interval my old lady declared with warmth that I *must* look after her registered luggage; though, as it was booked through to Cologne, I could not even see it till we crossed the German frontier; for the Belgian *douaniers* seal up the van as soon as the through baggage for Germany is unloaded. To satisfy her, however, I went through the formality of pretending to inspect it, and rendered myself hateful to the head of the *douane* by asking various foolish and inept questions, on which Lady Georgina insisted. When I had finished this silly and uncongenial task—for I am not by nature fussy, and it is hard to assume fussiness as another person's proxy—I returned to our *coupé* which I had arranged for in London. To my great amazement, I found the Cantankerous Old Lady and the egregious Count comfortably seated there. "Monsieur has been good enough to accept a place in our carriage," she observed, as I entered.

He bowed and smiled. "Or, rather, madame has been so kind as to offer me one," he corrected.

"Would you like some lunch, Lady Georgina?" I asked, in my chilliest voice. "There are ten minutes to spare, and the *buffet* is excellent."

"An admirable inspiration," the Count murmured. "Permit me to escort you, miladi."

"You will come, Lois?" Lady Georgina asked.

"No, thank you," I answered, for I had an idea. "I am a capital sailor, but the sea takes away my appetite."

"Then you'll keep our places," she said, turning to me. "I hope you won't allow them to stick in any horrid foreigners! They will try to force them on you unless you insist. *I* know their tricky ways. You have the tickets, I trust? And the *bulletin* for the *coupé*? Well, mind you don't lose the paper for the registered luggage. Don't let those dreadful porters touch my cloaks. And if anybody attempts to get in, be sure you stand in front of the door as they mount to prevent them."

The Count handed her out; he was all high courtly politeness. As Lady Georgina descended, he made yet another dexterous effort to relieve her of the jewel-case. I don't think she noticed it, but automatically once more she waved him aside. Then she turned to me. "Here, my dear," she said, handing it to me, "you'd better take care of it. If I lay it down in the *buffet* while I am eating my soup, some rogue may run away with it. But mind, don't let it out of your hands on any account. Hold it so, on your knee; and, for Heaven's sake, don't part with it."

By this time my suspicions of the Count were profound. From the first I had doubted him; he was so blandly plausible. But as we landed at Ostend I had accidentally overheard a low whispered conversation when he passed a shabby-looking man, who had travelled in a second-class carriage from London. "That succeeds?" the shabby-looking man had muttered under his breath in French, as the haughty nobleman with the waxed moustache brushed by him.

"That succeeds admirably," the Count had answered, in the same soft undertone. "*Ça réussit à merveille!*"

I understood him to mean that he had prospered in his attempt to impose on Lady Georgina.

They had been gone five minutes at the *buffet*, when the Count came back hurriedly to the door of the *coupé* with a *nonchalant* air. "Oh, mademoiselle," he said, in an off-hand tone, "Lady Georgina has sent me to fetch her jewel-case."

I gripped it hard with both hands. "*Pardon*, M. le Comte," I answered; "Lady Georgina intrusted it to *my* safe keeping, and, without her leave, I cannot give it up to any one."

"You mistrust me?" he cried, looking black. "You doubt my honour? You doubt my word when I say that miladi has sent me?"

"*Du tout*," I answered, calmly. "But I have Lady Georgina's orders to stick to this case; and till Lady Georgina returns I stick to it."

He murmured some indignant remark below his breath, and walked off. The shabby-looking passenger was pacing up and down the platform outside in a badly-made dust-coat. As they passed their lips moved. The Count's seemed to mutter, "*C'est un coup manqué.*"

However, he did not desist even so. I saw he meant to go on with his dangerous little game. He returned to the *buffet* and rejoined Lady Georgina. I felt sure it would be useless to warn her, so completely had the Count succeeded in gulling her; but I took my own steps. I examined the jewel-case closely. It had a leather outer covering; within was a strong steel box, with stout bands of metal to bind it. I took my cue at once, and acted for the best on my own responsibility.

When Lady Georgina and the Count returned, they were like old friends together. The quails in aspic and the sparkling hock had evidently opened their hearts to one another. As far as Malines they laughed and talked without ceasing. Lady Georgina was now in her finest vein of spleen: her acid wit grew sharper and more caustic each moment. Not a reputation in Europe had a rag left to cover it as we steamed in beneath the huge iron roof of the main central junction.

I had observed all the way from Ostend that the Count had been anxious lest we might have to give up our *coupé* at Malines. I assured him more than once that his fears were groundless, for I had arranged at Charing Cross that it should run right through to the German frontier. But he waved me aside, with one lordly hand. I had not told Lady Georgina of his vain attempt to take possession of her jewel-case; and the bare fact of my silence made him increasingly suspicious of me.

"Pardon me, mademoiselle," he said, coldly; "you do not understand these lines as well as I do. Nothing is more common than for those rascals of railway clerks to sell one a place in a *coupé* or a *wagon-lit*, and then never reserve it, or turn one out half way. It is very possible miladi may have to descend at Malines."

Lady Georgina bore him out by a large variety of selected stories concerning the various atrocities of the rival companies which had stolen her luggage on her way to Italy. As for *trains de luxe*, they were dens of robbers.

So when we reached Malines, just to satisfy Lady Georgina, I put out my head and inquired of a porter. As I anticipated, he replied that there was no change; we went through to Verviers.

The Count, however, was still unsatisfied. He descended, and made some remarks a little farther down the platform to an official in the gold-banded cap of a *chef-de-gare*, or some such functionary. Then he returned to us, all fuming. "It is as I said," he exclaimed, flinging open the door. "These rogues have deceived us. The *coupé* goes no farther. You must dismount at once, miladi, and take the train just opposite."

I felt sure he was wrong, and I ventured to say so. But Lady Georgina cried, "Nonsense, child! The *chef-de-gare* must know. Get out at once! Bring my bag and the rugs! Mind that cloak! Don't forget the sandwich-tin! Thanks, Count; will you kindly take charge of my umbrellas? Hurry up, Lois; hurry up! the train is just starting!"

I scrambled after her, with my fourteen bundles, keeping a quiet eye meanwhile on the jewel-case.

We took our seats in the opposite train, which I noticed was marked "Amsterdam, Bruxelles, Paris." But I said nothing. The Count jumped in, jumped about, arranged our parcels, jumped out again. He spoke to a porter; then he rushed back excitedly. "*Mille pardons*, miladi," he cried. "I find the *chef-de-gare* has cruelly deceived me. You were right, after all, mademoiselle! We must return to the *coupé*!"

With singular magnanimity, I refrained from saying, "I told you so."

Lady Georgina, very flustered and hot by this time, tumbled out once more, and bolted back to the *coupé*. Both trains were just starting. In her hurry, at last, she let the Count take possession of her jewel-case. I rather fancy that as he passed one window he handed it in to the shabby-looking passenger; but I am not certain. At any rate, when we were comfortably seated in our own compartment once more, and he stood on the footboard just about to enter, of a sudden he made an unexpected dash back, and flung himself wildly into a Paris carriage. At the self-same moment, with a piercing shriek, both trains started.

Lady Georgina threw up her hands in a frenzy of horror. "My diamonds!" she cried aloud. "Oh, Lois, my diamonds!"

"Don't distress yourself," I answered, holding her back, for I verily believe she would have leapt from the train. "He has only taken the outer shell, with the sandwich-case inside it. *Here* is the steel box!" And I produced it, triumphantly.

She seized it, overjoyed. "How did this happen?" she cried, hugging it, for she loved those diamonds.

"Very simply," I answered. "I saw the man was a rogue, and that he had a confederate with him in another carriage. So, while you were gone to the *buffet* at Ostend, I slipped the box out of the case, and put in the sandwich-tin, that he might carry it off, and we might have proofs against him. All you have to do now is to inform the conductor, who will telegraph to stop the train to Paris. I spoke to him about that at Ostend, so that everything is ready."

She positively hugged me. "My dear," she cried, "you are the cleverest little woman I ever met in my life! Who on earth could have suspected such a polished gentleman? Why, you're worth your weight in gold. What the dickens shall I do without you at Schlangenbad?"

THE ADVENTURE OF
THE SUPERCILIOUS *ATTACHÉ*

The Count must have been an adept in the gentle art of quick-change disguise; for though we telegraphed full particulars of his appearance from Louvain, the next station, nobody in the least resembling either him or his accomplice, the shabby-looking man, could be unearthed in the Paris train when it drew up at Brussels, its first stopping-place. They must have transformed themselves meanwhile into two different persons. Indeed, from the outset, I had suspected his moustache—'twas so *very* distinguished.

When we reached Cologne, the Cantankerous Old Lady overwhelmed me with the warmth of her thanks and praises. Nay, more; after breakfast next morning, before we set out by slow train for Schlangenbad, she burst like a tornado into my bedroom at the Cologne hotel with a cheque for twenty guineas, drawn in my favour. "That's for you, my dear," she said, handing it to me, and looking really quite gracious.

I glanced at the piece of paper and felt my face glow crimson. "Oh, Lady Georgina," I cried; "you misunderstand. You forget that I am a lady."

"Nonsense, child, nonsense! Your courage and promptitude were worth ten times that sum," she exclaimed, positively slipping her arm round my neck. "It was your courage I particularly admired, Lois; because you faced the risk of my happening to look inside the outer case, and finding you had abstracted the blessed box: in which case I might quite naturally have concluded you meant to steal it."

"I thought of that," I answered. "But I decided to risk it. I felt it was worthwhile. For I was sure the man meant to take the case as soon as ever you gave him the opportunity."

"Then you deserve to be rewarded," she insisted, pressing the cheque upon me.

I put her hand back firmly. "Lady Georgina," I said, "it is very amiable of you. I think you do right in offering me the money; but I think I should do altogether wrong in accepting it. A lady is not honest from the hope of gain; she is not brave because she expects to be paid for her bravery. You were my employer, and I was bound to serve my employer's interests. I did so as well as I could, and there is the end of it."

She looked absolutely disappointed; we all hate to crush a benevolent impulse; but she tore the cheque up into very small pieces. "As you will, my dear," she said, with her hands on her hips: "I see, you are poor Tom Cayley's daughter. He was always a bit Quixotic." Though I believe she liked me all the better for my refusal.

On the way from Cologne to Eltville, however, and on the drive up to Schlangenbad, I found her just as fussy and as worrying as ever. "Let me see, how many of these horrid pfennigs make an English penny? I never *can* remember. Oh, those silly little nickel things are ten pfennigs each, are they? Well, eight would be a penny, I suppose. A mark's a shilling; ridiculous of them to divide it into ten pence instead of twelve; one never really knows how much one's paying for anything. Why these Continental people can't be content to use pounds, shillings, and pence, all over alike, the same as we do, passes *my* comprehension. They're glad enough to get English sovereigns when they can; why, then, don't they use them as such, instead of reckoning them each at twenty-five francs, and then trying to cheat you out of the proper exchange, which is *always* ten centimes more than the brokers give you? What, *we* use their beastly decimal system? Lois, I'm ashamed of you. An English girl to turn and rend her native country like that! Francs and centimes, indeed! Fancy proposing it at Peter Robinson's! No, I will *not* go by the boat, my dear. I hate the Rhine boats, crowded with nasty selfish pigs of Germans. What *I* like is a first-class compartment all to myself, and no horrid foreigners. Especially Germans. They're bursting with self-satisfaction—have such an exaggerated belief in their 'land' and their 'folk.' And when they come to England, they do nothing but find fault with us. If people aren't satisfied with the countries they travel in, they'd better stop at home—that's *my* opinion. Nasty pigs of Germans! The very sight of them sickens me. Oh, I don't mind if they *do* understand me, child. They all learn English nowadays; it helps them in trade—that's why they're driving us out of all the markets. But it *must* be good for them to learn once in a way what other people really think of them—civilised people, I mean; not Germans. They're a set of barbarians."

We reached Schlangenbad alive, though I sometimes doubted it: for my old lady did her boisterous best to rouse some peppery German officer into cutting our throats incontinently by the way; and when we got there, we took up our abode in the nicest hotel in the village. Lady Georgina had engaged the best front room on the first floor, with a charming view across the pine-clad valley; but I must do her the justice to say that she took the second best for me, and that she treated me in every way like the guest she delighted to honour. My refusal to accept her twenty guineas made her anxious to pay it back to me within the terms of our agreement. She described me to everybody as a young friend who was travelling with her, and never gave any one the slightest hint of my being a paid companion. Our arrangement was that I was to have two guineas for the week, besides my travelling expenses, board, and lodging.

On our first morning at Schlangenbad, Lady Georgina sallied forth, very much overdressed, and in a youthful hat, to use the waters. They are valued chiefly for the complexion, I learned; I wondered then why Lady Georgina came there—for she hadn't any; but they are also recommended for nervous irritability, and as Lady Georgina had visited the place almost every summer for fifteen years, it opened before one's mind an appalling vista of what her temper might have been if she had *not* gone to Schlangenbad. The hot springs are used in the form of a bath. "*You* don't need them, my dear," Lady Georgina said to me, with a good-humoured smile; and I will own that I did not, for nature has gifted me with a tolerable cuticle. But I like when at Rome to do as Rome does; so I tried the baths once. I found them unpleasantly smooth and oily. I do not freckle, but if I did, I think I should prefer freckles.

We walked much on the terrace—the inevitable dawdling promenade of all German watering-places—it reeked of Serene Highness. We also drove out among the low wooded hills which bound the Rhine valley. The majority of the visitors, I found, were ladies—Court ladies, most of them; all there for their complexions, but all anxious to assure me privately they had come for what they described as "nervous debility." I divided them at once into two classes: half of them never had and never would have a complexion at all; the other half had exceptionally smooth and beautiful skins, of which they were obviously proud, and whose pink-and-white peach-blossom they thought to preserve by assiduous bathing. It was vanity working on two opposite bases. There was a sprinkling of men, however, who were really there for a sufficient reason—wounds or serious complaints; while a few good old sticks, porty and whisty, were in attendance on invalid wives or sisters.

From the beginning I noticed that Lady Georgina went peering about all over the place, as if she were hunting for something she had lost, with her long-handled tortoise-shell glasses perpetually in evidence—the "aristocratic outrage" I called them—and that she eyed all the men with peculiar attention. But I took no open notice of her little weakness. On our second day at the Spa, I was sauntering with her down the chief street—"a beastly little hole, my dear; not a decent shop where one can buy a reel of thread or a yard of tape in the place!"—when I observed a tall and handsome young man on the opposite side of the road cast a hasty glance at us, and then sneak round the corner hurriedly. He was a loose-limbed, languid-looking young man, with large, dreamy eyes, and a peculiarly beautiful and gentle expression; but what I noted about him most was an odd superficial air of superciliousness. He seemed always to be looking down with scorn on that foolish jumble, the

universe. He darted away so rapidly, however, that I hardly discovered all this just then. I piece it out from subsequent observations.

Later in the day, we chanced to pass a *café*, where three young
exquisites sat sipping Rhine wines after the fashion of the country. One of them, with a gold-tipped cigarette held gracefully between two slender fingers, was my languid-looking young aristocrat. He was blowing out smoke in a lazy blue stream. The moment he saw me, however, he turned away as if he desired to escape observation, and ducked down so as to hide his face behind
his companions. I wondered why on earth he should want to avoid
me. Could this be the Count? No, the young man with the halo of
cigarette smoke stood three inches taller. Who, then, at Schlangenbad could wish to avoid my notice? It was a singular mystery; for I
was quite certain the supercilious young man was trying his best
to prevent my seeing him.

That evening, after dinner, the Cantankerous Old Lady burst
out suddenly, "Well, I can't for the life of me imagine why Harold
hasn't turned up here. The wretch knew I was coming; and I heard
from our Ambassador at Rome last week that he was going to be at
Schlangenbad."

"Who is Harold?" I asked.

"My nephew," Lady Georgina snapped back, beating a devil's
tattoo with her fan on the table. "The only member of my family,
except myself, who isn't a born idiot. Harold's not an idiot; he's an
attaché at Rome."

I saw it at a glance. "Then he *is* in Schlangenbad," I answered.
"I noticed him this morning."

The old lady turned towards me sharply. She peered right
through me, as if she were a Röntgen ray. I could see she was asking herself whether this was a conspiracy, and whether I had come
there on purpose to meet "Harold." But I flatter myself I am tolerably mistress of my own countenance. I did not blench. "How do
you know?" she asked quickly, with an acid intonation.

If I had answered the truth, I should have said, "I know he is
here, because I saw a good-looking young man evidently trying to

avoid you this morning; and if a young man has the misfortune to
be born your nephew, and also to have expectations from you, it is
easy to understand that he would prefer to keep out of your way as
long as possible." But that would have been neither polite nor politic. Moreover, I reflected that I had no particular reason for wishing to do Mr. Harold a bad turn; and that it would be kinder to
him, as well as to her, to conceal the reasons on which I based my
instinctive inference. So I took up a strong strategic position. "I
have an intuition that I saw him in the village this morning," I said.
"Family likeness, perhaps. I merely jumped at it as you spoke. A
tall, languid young man; large, poetical eyes; an artistic moustache—just a trifle Oriental-looking."

"That's Harold!" the Cantankerous Old Lady rapped out sharply,
with clear conviction. "The miserable boy! Why on earth hasn't he
been round to see me?"

I reflected that I knew why; but I did not say so. Silence is golden. I also remarked mentally on that curious human blindness
which had made me conclude at first that the supercilious young
man was trying to avoid *me*, when I might have guessed it was far
more likely he was trying to avoid my companion. I was a nobody;
Lady Georgina Fawley was a woman of European reputation.

"Perhaps he didn't know which hotel you were stopping at," I
put in. "Or even that you were here." I felt a sudden desire to shield
poor Harold.

"Not know which hotel? Nonsense, child; he knows I come here
on this precise date regularly every summer; and if he didn't know,
is it likely I should try any other inn, when this is the only moder-
ately decent house to stop at in Schlangenbad? And the morning
coffee undrinkable at that; while the hash—*such* hash! But that's
the way in Germany. He's an ungrateful monster; if he comes now,
I shall refuse to see him."

Next morning after breakfast, however, in spite of these threats,
she hailed me forth with her on the Harold hunt. She had sent the
concierge to inquire at all the hotels already, it seemed, and found
her truant at none of them; now she ransacked the *pensions*. At
last she hunted him down in a house on the hill. I could see she

was really hurt. "Harold, you viper, what do you mean by trying to avoid me?"

"My dear aunt, *you* here in Schlangenbad! Why, when did you arrive? And what a colour you've got! You're looking *so* well!" That clever thrust saved him.

He cast me an appealing glance. "You will not betray me?" it said. I answered, mutely, "Not for worlds," with a faltering pair of downcast eyelids.

"Oh, I'm *well* enough, thank you," Lady Georgina replied, somewhat mollified by his astute allusion to her personal appearance. He had hit her weak point dexterously. "As well, that is, as one can expect to be nowadays. Hereditary gout—the sins of the fathers visited as usual. But why didn't you come to see me?"

"How can I come to see you if you don't tell me where you are? 'Lady Georgina Fawley, Europe,' was the only address I knew. It strikes me as insufficient."

His gentle drawl was a capital foil to Lady Georgina's acidulous soprano. It seemed to disarm her. She turned to me with a benignant wave of her hand. "Miss Cayley," she said, introducing me; "my nephew, Mr. Harold Tillington. You've heard me talk of poor Tom Cayley, Harold? This is poor Tom Cayley's daughter."

"Indeed?" the supercilious *attaché* put in, looking hard at me. "Delighted to make Miss Cayley's acquaintance."

"Now, Harold, I can tell from your voice at once you haven't remembered one word about Captain Cayley."

Harold stood on the defensive. "My dear aunt," he observed, expanding both palms, "I have heard you talk of so *very* many people, that even *my* diplomatic memory fails at times to recollect them all. But I do better: I dissemble. I will plead forgetfulness now of Captain Cayley, since you force it on me. It is not likely I shall have to plead it of Captain Cayley's daughter." And he bowed towards me gallantly.

The Cantankerous Old Lady darted a lightning glance at him. It was a glance of quick suspicion. Then she turned her Röntgen rays upon my face once more. I fear I burned crimson.

"A friend?" he asked. "Or a fellow-guest?"

"A companion." It was the first nasty thing she had said of me.

"Ha! more than a friend, then. A comrade." He turned the edge neatly.

We walked out on the terrace and a little way up the zigzag path. The day was superb. I found Mr. Tillington, in spite of his studiously languid and supercilious air, a most agreeable companion. He knew Europe. He was full of talk of Rome and the Romans. He had epigrammatic wit, curt, keen, and pointed. We sat down on a bench; he kept Lady Georgina and myself amused for an hour by his crisp sallies. Besides, he had been everywhere and seen everybody. Culture and agriculture seemed all one to him.

When we rose to go in, Lady Georgina remarked, with emphasis, "Of course, Harold, you'll come and take up your diggings at our hotel?"

"Of course, my dear aunt. How can you ask? Free quarters. Nothing would give me greater pleasure."

She glanced at him keenly again. I saw she had expected him to fake up some lame excuse for not joining us; and I fancied she was annoyed at his prompt acquiescence, which had done her out of the chance for a family disagreement. "Oh, you'll come then?" she said, grudgingly.

"Certainly, most respected aunt. I shall much prefer it."

She let her piercing eye descend upon me once more. I was aware that I had been talking with frank ease of manner to Mr. Tillington, and that I had said several things which clearly amused him. Then I remembered all at once our relative positions. A companion, I felt, should know her place: it is not her *rôle* to be smart and amusing. "Perhaps," I said, drawing back, "Mr. Tillington would like to remain in his present quarters till the end of the week, while I am with you, Lady Georgina; after that, he could have my room; it might be more convenient."

His eye caught mine quickly. "Oh, you're only going to stop a week, then, Miss Cayley?" he put in, with an air of disappointment.

"Only a week," I nodded.

"My dear child," the Cantankerous Old Lady broke out, "what nonsense you do talk! Only going to stop a week? How can I exist without you?"

"That was the arrangement," I said, mischievously. "You were going to look about, you recollect, for an unsophisticated Gretchen. You don't happen to know of any warehouse where a supply of unsophisticated Gretchens is kept constantly in stock, do you, Mr. Tillington?"

"No, I don't," he answered, laughing. "I believe there are dodos and auks' eggs, in very small numbers, still to be procured in the proper quarters; but the unsophisticated Gretchen, I am credibly informed, is an extinct animal. Why, the cap of one fetches high prices nowadays among collectors."

"But you will come to the hotel at once, Harold?" Lady Georgina interposed.

"Certainly, aunt. I will move in without delay. If Miss Cayley is going to stay for a single week only, that adds one extra inducement for joining you immediately."

His aunt's stony eye was cold as marble.

So when we got back to our hotel after the baths that afternoon, the *concierge* greeted us with: "Well, your noble nephew has arrived, high-well-born countess! He came with his boxes just now, and has taken a room near your honourable ladyship's."

Lady Georgina's face was a study of mingled emotions. I don't know whether she looked more pleased or jealous.

Later in the day, I chanced on Mr. Tillington, sunning himself on a bench in the hotel garden. He rose, and came up to me, as fast as his languid nature permitted. "Oh, Miss Cayley," he said, abruptly, "I do want to thank you so much for not betraying me. I know you spotted me twice in the town yesterday; and I also know you were good enough to say nothing to my revered aunt about it."

"I had no reason for wishing to hurt Lady Georgina's feelings," I answered, with a permissible evasion.

His countenance fell. "I never thought of that," he interposed, with one hand on his moustache. "I— I fancied you did it out of fellow-feeling."

"We all think of things mainly from our own point of view first," I answered. "The difference is that some of us think of them from other people's afterwards. Motives are mixed."

He smiled. "I didn't know my deeply venerated relative was coming here so soon," he went on. "I thought she wasn't expected till next week; my brother wrote me that she had quarrelled with her French maid, and 'twould take her full ten days to get another. I meant to clear out before she arrived. To tell you the truth, I was going to-morrow."

"And now you are stopping on?"

He caught my eye again.

"Circumstances alter cases," he murmured, with meaning.

"It is hardly polite to describe one as a circumstance," I objected.

"I meant," he said, quickly, "my aunt alone is one thing; my aunt with a friend is quite another."

"I see," I answered. "There is safety in numbers."

He eyed me hard.

"Are you mediæval or modern?" he asked.

"Modern, I hope," I replied. Then I looked at him again. "Oxford?"

He nodded. "And you?" half joking.

"Cambridge," I said, glad to catch him out. "What college?"

"Merton. Yours?"

"Girton."

The odd rhyme amused him. Thenceforth we were friends—"two 'Varsity men," he said. And indeed it does make a queer sort of link—a freemasonry to which even women are now admitted.

At dinner and through the evening he talked a great deal to me, Lady Georgina putting in from time to time a characteristic growl about the *table-d'hôte* chicken—"a special breed, my dear, with eight drumsticks apiece"—or about the inadequate lighting of the heavy German *salon*. She was worse than ever: pungent as a rule, that evening she was grumpy. When we retired for the night, to my great surprise, she walked into my bedroom. She seated herself on my bed: I saw she had come to talk over Harold.

"He will be very rich, my dear, you know. A great catch in time. He will inherit all my brother's money."

"Lord Kynaston's?"

"Bless the child, no. Kynaston's as poor as a church mouse with the tithes unpaid; he has three sons of his own, and not a blessed stiver to leave between them. How could he, poor dear idiot? Agricultural depression; a splendid pauper. He has only the estate, and that's in Essex; land going begging; worth nothing a year, encumbered up to the eyes, and loaded with first rent-charges, jointures, settlements. Money, indeed! poor Kynaston! It's my brother Marmaduke's I mean; lucky dog, *he* went in for speculation—began life as a guinea-pig, and rose with the rise of soap and cocoa. He's worth his half-million."

"Oh, Mr. Marmaduke Ashurst."

Lady Georgina nodded. "Marmy's a fool," she said, briefly; "but he knows which side of his bread is buttered."

"And Mr. Tillington is—his nephew?"

"Bless the child, yes; have you never read your British Bible, the peerage? Astonishing, the ignorance of these Girton girls! They don't even know the Leger's run at Doncaster. The family name's Ashurst. Kynaston's an earl— I was Lady Georgina Ashurst before I took it into my head to marry and do for poor Evelyn Fawley. My younger brother's the Honourable Marmaduke Ashurst—women get the best of it there—it's about the only place where they do get the best of it: an earl's daughter is Lady Betty; his son's nothing more than the Honourable Tom. So one scores off one's brothers. My younger sister, Lady Guinevere Ashurst, married Stanley Tillington of the Foreign Office. Harold's their eldest son. Now, child, do you grasp it?"

"Perfectly," I answered. "You speak like Debrett. Has issue, Harold."

"And Harold will inherit all Marmaduke's money. What I'm always afraid of is that some fascinating adventuress will try to marry him out of hand. A pretty face, and over goes Harold! *My* business in life is to stand in the way and prevent it."

She looked me through and through again with her X-ray scrutiny.

"I don't think Mr. Tillington is quite the sort that falls a prey to adventuresses," I answered, boldly.

"Ah, but there are faggots and faggots," the old lady said, wagging her head with profound meaning. "Never mind, though; *I'd* like to see an adventuress marry off Harold without my leave! *I'd* lead her a life! I'd turn her black hair gray for her!"

"I should think," I assented, "you could do it, Lady Georgina, if you gave your attention seriously to it."

From that moment forth, I was aware that my Cantankerous Old Lady's malign eye was inexorably fixed upon me every time I went within speaking distance of Mr. Tillington. She watched him like a lynx. She watched *me* like a dozen lynxes. Wherever we went, Lady Georgina was sure to turn up in the neighbourhood. She was perfectly ubiquitous: she seemed to possess a world-wide circulation. I don't know whether it was this constant suggestion of hers that I was stalking her nephew which roused my latent human feeling of opposition; but in the end, I began to be aware that I rather liked the supercilious *attaché* than otherwise. He evidently liked me, and he tried to meet me. Whenever he spoke to me, indeed, it was without the superciliousness which marked his manner towards others; in point of fact, it was with graceful deference. He watched for me on the stairs, in the garden, by the terrace; whenever he got a chance, he sidled over and talked to me. Sometimes he stopped in to read me Heine: he also introduced me to select portions of Gabriele d'Annunzio. It is feminine to be touched by such obvious attention; I confess, before long, I grew to like Mr. Harold Tillington.

The closer he followed me up, the more did I perceive that Lady Georgina threw out acrid hints with increasing spleen about the ways of adventuresses. They were hints of that acrimonious generalised kind, too, which one cannot answer back without seeming to admit that the cap has fitted. It was atrocious how middle-class young women nowadays ran after young men of birth and fortune. A girl would stoop to anything in order to catch five hundred thousand. Guileless youths should be thrown among their natural equals. It was a mistake to let them see too much of people of a lower rank who consider themselves good-looking. And the clever ones were the worst: they pretended to go in for intellectual companionship.

I also noticed that though at first Lady Georgina had expressed the strongest disinclination to my leaving her after the time originally proposed, she now began to take for granted that I would go at the end of my week, as arranged in London, and she even went on to some overt steps towards securing the help of the blameless Gretchen.

We had arrived at Schlangenbad on Tuesday. I was to stop with the Cantankerous Old Lady till the corresponding day of the following week. On the Sunday, I wandered out on the wooded hillside behind the village; and as I mounted the path I was dimly aware by a sort of instinct that Harold Tillington was following me.

He came up with me at last near a ledge of rock. "How fast you walk!" he exclaimed. "I gave you only a few minutes' start, and yet even my long legs have had hard work to overtake you."

"I am a fairly good climber," I answered, sitting down on a little wooden bench. "You see, at Cambridge, I went on the river a great deal—I canoed and sculled: and then, besides, I've done a lot of bicycling."

"What a splendid birthright it is," he cried, "to be a wholesome athletic English girl! You can't think how one admires English girls after living a year or two in Italy—where women are dolls, except for a brief period of intrigue, before they settle down to be contented frumps with an outline like a barrel."

"A little muscle and a little mind are no doubt advisable adjuncts for a housewife," I admitted.

"You shall not say that word," he cried, seating himself at my side. "It is a word for Germans, 'housewife.' Our English ideal is something immeasurably higher and better. A companion, a complement! Do you know, Miss Cayley, it always sickens me when I hear German students sentimentalising over their *mädchen*: their beautiful, pure, insipid, yellow-haired, blue-eyed *mädchen*; her, so fair, so innocent, so unapproachably vacuous—so like a wax doll—and then think of how they design her in days to come to cook sausages for their dinner, and knit them endless stockings through a placid middle age, till the needles drop from her paralysed fingers, and she retires into frilled caps and Teutonic senility."

"You seem to have almost as low an opinion of foreigners as your respected aunt!" I exclaimed, looking quizzically at him.

He drew back, surprised. "Oh, no; I'm not narrow-minded, like my aunt, I hope," he answered. "I am a good cosmopolitan. I allow Continental nations all their own good points, and each has many.

But their women, Miss Cayley—and their point of view of their women—you will admit that there they can't hold a candle to English women."

I drew a circle in the dust with the tip of my parasol.

"On that issue, I may not be a wholly unprejudiced observer," I answered. "The fact of my being myself an Englishwoman may possibly to some extent influence my judgment."

"You are sarcastic," he cried, drawing away.

"Not at all," I answered, making a wider circle. "I spoke a simple fact. But what is *your* ideal, then, as opposed to the German one?"

He gazed at me and hesitated. His lips half parted. "My ideal?" he said, after a pause. "Well, *my* ideal—do you happen to have such a thing as a pocket-mirror about you?"

I laughed in spite of myself. "Now, Mr. Tillington," I said severely, "if you're going to pay compliments, I shall have to return. If you want to stop here with me, you must remember that I am only Lady Georgina Fawley's temporary lady's-maid. Besides, I didn't mean that. I meant, what is your ideal of a man's right relation to his *mädchen*?"

"Don't say *mädchen*," he cried, petulantly. "It sounds as if you thought me one of those sentimental Germans. I hate sentiment."

"Then, towards the woman of his choice."

He glanced up through the trees at the light overhead, and spoke more slowly than ever. "I think," he said, fumbling his watch-chain nervously, "a man ought to wish the woman he loves to be a free agent, his equal in point of action, even as she is nobler and better than he in all spiritual matters. I think he ought to desire for her a life as high as she is capable of leading, with full scope for every faculty of her intellect or her emotional nature. She should be beautiful, with a vigorous, wholesome, many-sided beauty, moral, intellectual, physical; yet with soul in her, too; and with the soul and the mind lighting up her eyes, as it lights up—well, that is immaterial. And if a man can discover such a woman as that, and can induce her to believe in him, to love him, to accept him—though how such a woman can be satisfied with any man at all is to me unfathomable—well, then, I think he should be happy in devoting his whole life to her, and should give himself up to repay her condescension in taking him."

"And you hate sentiment!" I put in, smiling.

He brought his eyes back from the sky suddenly. "Miss Cayley," he said, "this is cruel. I was in earnest. You are playing with me."

"I believe the chief characteristic of the English girl is supposed to be common sense," I answered, calmly, "and I trust I possess it." But indeed, as he spoke, my heart was beginning to make its beat felt; for he was a charming young man; he had a soft voice and lustrous eyes; it was a summer's day; and alone in the woods with one other person, where the sunlight falls mellow in spots like a leopard's skin, one is apt to remember that we are all human.

That evening Lady Georgina managed to blurt out more malicious things than ever about the ways of adventuresses, and the duty of relations in saving young men from the clever clutches of designing creatures. She was ruthless in her rancour: her gibes stung me.

On Monday at breakfast I asked her casually if she had yet found a Gretchen.

"No," she answered, in a gloomy voice. "All slatterns, my dear; all slatterns! Brought up in pig-sties. I wouldn't let one of them touch my hair for thousands."

"That's unfortunate," I said, drily, "for you know I'm going to-morrow."

If I had dropped a bomb in their midst they couldn't have looked more astonished. "To-morrow?" Lady Georgina gasped, clutching my arm. "You don't mean it, child; you don't mean it?"

I asserted my Ego. "Certainly," I answered, with my coolest air. "I said I thought I could manage you for a week; and I have managed you."

She almost burst into tears. "But, my child, my child, what shall I do without you?"

"The unsophisticated Gretchen," I answered, trying not to look concerned; for in my heart of hearts, in spite of her innuendoes, I had really grown rather to like the Cantankerous Old Lady.

She rose hastily from the table, and darted up to her own room. "Lois," she said, as she rose, in a curious voice of mingled regret and suspicion, "I will talk to you about this later." I could see she was not quite satisfied in her own mind whether Harold Tillington and I had not arranged this *coup* together.

I put on my hat and strolled off into the garden, and then along the mossy hill path. In a minute more, Harold Tillington was beside me.

He seated me, half against my will, on a rustic bench. "Look here, Miss Cayley," he said, with a very earnest face; "is this really true? Are you going to-morrow?"

My voice trembled a little. "Yes," I answered, biting my lip. "I am going. I see several reasons why I should go, Mr. Tillington."

"But so soon?"

"Yes, I think so; the sooner the better." My heart was racing now, and his eyes pleaded mutely.

"Then where are you going?"

I shrugged my shoulders, and pouted my lips a little. "I don't know," I replied. "The world is all before me where to choose. I am an adventuress," I said it boldly, "and I am in quest of adventures. I really have not yet given a thought to my next place of sojourn."

"But you will let me know when you have decided?"

It was time to speak out. "No, Mr. Tillington," I said, with decision. "I will *not* let you know. One of my reasons for going is, that I think I had better see no more of you."

He flung himself on the bench at my side, and folded his hands in a helpless attitude. "But, Miss Cayley," he cried, "this is so short a notice; you give a fellow no chance; I hoped I might have seen more of you—might have had some opportunity of—of letting you realise how deeply I admired and respected you—some opportunity of showing myself as I really am to you—before—before—" he paused, and looked hard at me.

I did not know what to say. I really liked him so much; and when he spoke in that voice, I could not bear to seem cruel to him. Indeed, I was aware at the moment how much I had grown to care for him in those six short days. But I knew it was impossible. "Don't say it, Mr. Tillington," I murmured, turning my face away. "The less said, the sooner mended."

"But I must," he cried. "I must tell you now, if I am to have no chance afterwards. I wanted you to see more of me before I ventured to ask you if you could ever love me, if you could ever suffer me to go through life with you, to share my all with you." He seized my trembling hand. "Lois," he cried, in a pleading voice, "I *must* ask you; I can't expect you to answer me now, but *do* say you will give me at least some other chance of seeing you, and then, in time, of pressing my suit upon you."

Tears stood in my eyes. He was so earnest, so charming. But I remembered Lady Georgina, and his prospective half-million. I moved his hand away gently. "I cannot," I said. "I cannot— I am a penniless girl—an adventuress. Your family, your uncle, would never forgive you if you married me. I will not stand in your way. I— I like you very much, though I have seen so little of you. But I feel it is impossible—and I am going to-morrow."

Then I rose of a sudden, and ran down the hill with all my might, lest I should break my resolve, never stopping once till I reached my own bedroom.

An hour later, Lady Georgina burst in upon me in high dudgeon. "Why, Lois, my child," she cried. "What's this? What on earth does it mean? Harold tells me he has proposed to you—proposed to you—and you've rejected him!"

I dried my eyes and tried to look steadily at her. "Yes, Lady Georgina," I faltered. "You need not be afraid. I have refused him; and I mean it."

She looked at me, all aghast. "*And* you mean it!" she repeated. "You mean to refuse him. Then, all I can say is, Lois Cayley, I call it pure cheek of you!"

"What?" I cried, drawing back.

"Yes, cheek," she answered, volubly. "Forty thousand a year, and a good old family! Harold Tillington is my nephew; he's an earl's grandson; he's an *attaché* at Rome; and he's bound to be one of the richest commoners in England. Who are you, I'd like to know, miss, that you dare to reject him?"

I stared at her, amazed. "But, Lady Georgina," I cried, "you said you wished to protect your nephew against bare-faced adventuresses who were setting their caps at him."

She fixed her eyes on me, half-angry, half-tremulous.

"Of course," she answered, with withering scorn. "But, *then*, I thought you were trying to catch him. He tells me now you won't have him, and you won't tell him where you are going. I call it sheer insolence. Where do you hail from, girl, that you should refuse my nephew? A man that any woman in England would be proud to marry! Forty thousand a year, and an earl's grandson! That's what comes, I suppose, of going to Girton!"

I drew myself up. "Lady Georgina," I said, coldly, "I cannot allow you to use such language to me. I promised to accompany you to Germany for a week; and I have kept my word. I like your nephew; I respect your nephew; he has behaved like a gentleman. But I will *not* marry him. Your own conduct showed me in the plainest way that you did not judge such a match desirable for him; and I have common sense enough to see that you were quite right. I am a lady by birth and education; I am an officer's daughter; but I am not what society calls 'a good match' for Mr. Tillington. He had better marry into a rich stockbroker's family."

It was an unworthy taunt: the moment it escaped my lips I regretted it.

To my intense surprise, however, Lady Georgina flung herself on my bed, and burst into tears. "My dear," she sobbed out, covering her face with her hands, "I thought you would be sure to set your cap at Harold; and after I had seen you for twenty-four hours, I said to myself, 'That's just the sort of girl Harold ought to fall in love with.' I felt sure he would fall in love with you. I brought you here on purpose. I saw you had all the qualities that would strike Harold's fancy. So I had made up my mind for a delightful regulation family quarrel. I was going to oppose you and Harold, tooth and nail; I was going to threaten that Marmy would leave his money to Kynaston's eldest son; I was going to kick up, oh, a dickens of a row about it! Then, of course, in the end, we should all have been reconciled; we should have kissed and made friends: for you're just the one girl in the world for Harold; indeed, I never met anybody so capable and so intelligent. And now you spoil all my sport by going and refusing him! It's really most ill-timed of you. And Harold has sent me here—he's trembling with anxiety—to see whether I can't induce you to think better of your decision."

I made up my mind at once. "No, Lady Georgina," I said, in my gentlest voice—positively stooping down and kissing her. "I like Mr. Tillington very much. I dare not tell you how much I like him. He is a dear, good, kind fellow. But I cannot rest under the cruel imputation of being moved by his wealth and having tried to capture him. Even if *you* didn't think so, his family would. I am sorry to go; for in a way I like you. But it is best to adhere to our original plan. If *I* changed my mind, *you* might change yours again. Let us say no more. I will go to-morrow."

"But you will see Harold again?"

"Not alone. Only at dinner." For I feared lest, if he spoke to me alone, he might over-persuade me.

"Then at least you will tell him where you are going?"

"No, Lady Georgina; I do not know myself. And besides, it is best that this should now be final."

She flung herself upon me. "But, my dear child, a lady can't go out into the world with only two pounds in pocket. You *must* let me lend you something."

I unwound her clasping hands. "No, dear Lady Georgina," I said, though I was loth to say it. "You are very sweet and good, but I must work out my life in my own way. I have started to work it out, and I won't be turned aside just here on the threshold."

"And you won't stop with me?" she cried, opening her arms. "You think me too cantankerous?"

"I think you have a dear, kind old heart," I said, "under the quaintest and crustiest outside such a heart ever wore; you're a truculent old darling: so that's the plain truth of it."

She kissed me. I kissed her in return with fervour, though I am but a poor hand at kissing, for a woman. "So now this episode is concluded," I murmured.

"I don't know about that," she said, drying her eyes. "I have set my heart upon you now; and Harold has set his heart upon you; and considering that your own heart goes much the same way, I daresay, my dear, we shall find in the end some convenient road out of it."

Nevertheless, next morning I set out by myself in the coach from Schlangenbad. I went forth into the world to live my own life, partly because it was just then so fashionable, but mainly because fate had denied me the chance of living anybody else's.

THE ADVENTURE OF THE
INQUISITIVE AMERICAN

In one week I had multiplied my capital two hundred and forty-fold! I left London with twopence in the world; I quitted Schlangenbad with two pounds in pocket.

"There's a splendid turn-over!" I thought to myself. "If this luck holds, at the same rate, I shall have made four hundred and eighty pounds by Tuesday next, and I may look forward to being a Barney Barnato by Christmas." For I had taken high mathematical honours at Cambridge, and if there is anything on earth on which I pride myself, it is my firm grasp of the principle of ratios.

Still, in spite of this brilliant financial prospect, a budding Klondike, I went away from the little Spa on the flanks of the Taunus with a heavy heart. I had grown quite to like dear, virulent, fidgety old Lady Georgina; and I felt that it had cost me a distinct wrench to part with Harold Tillington. The wrench left a scar which was long in healing; but as I am not a professional sentimentalist, I will not trouble you here with details of the symptoms.

My livelihood, however, was now assured me. With two pounds in pocket, a sensible girl can read her title clear to six days' board and lodging, at six marks a day, with a glorious margin of four marks over for pocket-money. And if at the end of six days my fairy godmother had not pointed me out some other means of earning my bread honestly—well, I should feel myself unworthy to be ranked in the noble army of adventuresses. I thank thee, Lady Georgina, for teaching me that word. An adventuress I would be; for I loved adventure.

Meanwhile, it occurred to me that I might fill up the interval by going to study art at Frankfort. Elsie Petheridge had been there, and had impressed upon me the fact that I must on no account omit to see the Städel Gallery. She was strong on culture. Besides, the study of art should be most useful to an adventuress; for she must need all the arts that human skill has developed.

So to Frankfort I betook myself, and found there a nice little *pension*—"for ladies only," Frau Bockenheifner assured me—at very moderate rates, in a pleasant part of the Lindenstrasse. It had dimity curtains. I will not deny that as I entered the house I was conscious of feeling lonely; my heart sank once or twice as I glanced round the luncheon-table at the domestically-unsympathetic German old maids who formed the rank-and-file of my fellow-boarders. There they sat—eight comfortable Fraus who had missed their vocation; plentiful ladies, bulging and surging in tightly stretched black silk bodices. They had been cut out for such housewives as Harold Tillington had described, but found themselves deprived of their natural sphere in life by the unaccountable caprice of the men of their nation. Each was a model Teutonic matron *manquée*. Each looked capable of frying Frankfort sausages to a turn, and knitting woollen socks to a remote eternity. But I sought in vain for one kindred soul among them. How horrified they would have been, with their fat pudding-faces and big saucer-eyes, had I boldly announced myself as an English adventuress!

I spent my first morning in laborious self-education at the Ariadneum and the Städel Gallery. I borrowed a catalogue. I wrestled with Van der Weyden; I toiled like a galley-slave at Meister Wilhelm and Meister Stephan. I have a confused recollection that I saw a number of stiff mediæval pictures, and an alabaster statue of the lady who smiled as she rode on a tiger, taken at the beginning of that interesting episode. But the remainder of the Institute has faded from my memory.

In the afternoon I consoled myself for my herculean efforts in the direction of culture by going out for a bicycle ride on a hired machine, to which end I decided to devote my pocket-money. You will, perhaps, object here that my conduct was imprudent. To raise that objection is to misunderstand the spirit of these artless adventures. I told you that I set out to go round the world; but to go round the world does not necessarily mean to circumnavigate it. My idea was to go round by easy stages, seeing the world as I went as far as I got, and taking as little heed as possible of the morrow. Most of my readers, no doubt, accept that philosophy of life on Sundays only; on week-days they swallow the usual contradictory economic platitudes about prudential forethought and the horrid improvidence of the lower classes. For myself, I am not built that way. I prefer to take life in a spirit of pure inquiry. I put on my hat: I saunter where I choose, so far as circumstances permit; and I wait to see what chance will bring me. My ideal is breeziness.

The hired bicycle was not a bad machine, as hired bicycles go; it jolted one as little as you can expect from a common hack; it never stopped at a Bier-Garten; and it showed very few signs of having been ridden by beginners with an unconquerable desire to tilt at the hedgerow. So off I soared at once, heedless of the jeers of Teutonic youth who found the sight of a lady riding a cycle in skirts a strange one—for in South Germany the "rational" costume is so universal among women cyclists that 'tis the skirt that provokes unfavourable comment from those jealous guardians of female propriety, the street boys. I hurried on at a brisk pace past the Palm-Garden and the suburbs, with my loose hair straying on the breeze behind, till I found myself pedalling at a good round pace on a broad, level road, which led towards a village, by name Fraunheim.

As I scurried across the plain, with the wind in my face, not unpleasantly, I had some dim consciousness of somebody unknown flying after me headlong. My first idea was that Harold Tillington had hunted me down and tracked me to my lair; but gazing back, I saw my pursuer was a tall and ungainly man, with a straw-coloured moustache, apparently American, and that he was following me on his machine, closely watching my action. He had such a cunning expression on his face, and seemed so strangely inquisitive, with eyes riveted on my treadles, that I didn't quite like the look of him. I put on the pace, to see if I could outstrip him, for I am a

swift cyclist. But his long legs were too much for me. He did not
gain on me, it is true; but neither did I outpace him. Pedalling my
very hardest—and I can make good time when necessary—I still
kept pretty much at the same distance in front of him all the way
to Fraunheim.

Gradually I began to feel sure that the weedy-looking man with
the alert face was really pursuing me. When I went faster, he went
faster too; when I gave him a chance to pass me, he kept close at my
heels, and appeared to be keenly watching the style of my ankle-
action. I gathered that he was a connoisseur; but why on earth he
should persecute me I could not imagine. My spirit was roused
now—I pedalled with a will; if I rode all day I would not let him go
past me.

Beyond the cobble-paved chief street of Fraunheim the road
took a sharp bend, and began to mount the slopes of the Taunus
suddenly. It was an abrupt, steep climb; but I flatter myself I am a
tolerable mountain cyclist. I rode sturdily on; my pursuer darted after
me. But on this stiff upward grade my light weight and agile ankle-
action told; I began to distance him. He seemed afraid that I would
give him the slip, and called out suddenly, with a whoop, in English,
"Stop, miss!" I looked back with dignity, but answered nothing. He
put on the pace, panting; I pedalled away, and got clear from him.

At a turn of the corner, however, as luck would have it, I was
pulled up short by a mounted policeman. He blocked the road with
his horse, like an ogre, and asked me, in a very gruff Swabian voice,
if this was a licensed bicycle. I had no idea, till he spoke, that any
license was required; though to be sure I might have guessed it;
for modern Germany is studded with notices at all the street corners, to inform you in minute detail that everything is forbidden. I
stammered out that I did not know. The mounted policeman drew
near and inspected me rudely. "It is strongly undersaid," he began, but just at that moment my pursuer came up, and, with American quickness, took in the situation. He accosted the policeman in
choice bad German. "I have two licenses," he said, producing a
handful. "The Fräulein rides with me."

I was too much taken aback at so providential an interposition to contradict this highly imaginative statement. My highwayman had turned into a protecting knight-errant of injured innocence. I let the policeman go his way; then I glanced at my preserver. A very ordinary modern St. George he looked, with no lance to speak of, and no steed but a bicycle. Yet his mien was reassuring.

"Good morning, miss," he began—he called me "Miss" every time he addressed me, as though he took me for a barmaid. "Excuse *me*, but why did you want to speed her?"

"I thought you were pursuing me," I answered, a little tremulous, I will confess, but avid of incident.

"And if I was," he went on, "you might have conjectured, miss, it was for our mutual advantage. A business man don't go out of his way unless he expects to turn an honest dollar; and he don't reckon on other folks going out of theirs, unless he knows he can put them in the way of turning an honest dollar with him."

"That's reasonable," I answered: for I am a political economist. "The benefit should be mutual." But I wondered if he was going to propose at sight to me.

He looked me all up and down. "You're a lady of considerable personal attractions," he said, musingly, as if he were criticising a horse; "and I want one that sort. That's jest why I trailed you, see? Besides which, there's some style about you."

"Style!" I repeated.

"Yes," he went on; "you know how to use your feet; and you have good understandings."

I gathered from his glance that he referred to my nether limbs. We are all vertebrate animals; why seek to conceal the fact?

"I fail to follow you," I answered frigidly; for I really didn't know what the man might say next.

"That's so!" he replied. "It was *I* that followed *you*; seems I didn't make much of a job of it, either, anyway."

I mounted my machine again. "Well, good morning," I said, coldly. "I am much obliged for your kind assistance; but your remark was fictitious, and I desire to go on unaccompanied."

He held up his hand in warning. "You ain't going!" he cried, horrified. "You ain't going without hearing me! I mean business, say! Don't chuck away good money like that. I tell you, there's dollars in it."

"In what?" I asked, still moving on, but curious. On the slope, if need were, I could easily distance him.

"Why, in this cycling of yours," he replied. "You're jest about the very woman I'm looking for, miss. Lithe—that's what I call you. I kin put you in the way of making your pile, I kin. This is a *bonâ-fide* offer. No flies on *my* business! You decline it? Prejudice! Injures you; injures me! Be reasonable anyway!"

I looked round and laughed. "Formulate yourself," I said, briefly.

He rose to it like a man. "Meet me at Fraunheim; corner by the Post Office; ten o'clock to-morrow morning," he shouted, as I rode off, "and ef I don't convince you there's money in this job, my name's not Cyrus W. Hitchcock."

Something about his keen, unlovely face impressed me with a sense of his underlying honesty. "Very well," I answered, "I'll come, if you follow me no further." I reflected that Fraunheim was a populous village, and that only beyond it did the mountain road over the Taunus begin to grow lonely. If he wished to cut my throat, I was well within reach of the resources of civilisation.

When I got home to the Abode of Blighted Fraus that evening, I debated seriously with myself whether or not I should accept Mr. Cyrus W. Hitchcock's mysterious invitation. Prudence said *no*; curiosity said *yes*; I put the question to a meeting of one; and, since I am a daughter of Eve, curiosity had it. Carried unanimously. I think I might have hesitated, indeed, had it not been for the Blighted Fraus. Their talk was of dinner and of the digestive process; they were critics of digestion. They each of them sat so complacently through the evening—solid and stolid, stodgy and podgy, stuffed comatose images, knitting white woollen shawls, to throw over their capacious shoulders at *table d'hôte*—and they purred with such content in their middle-aged rotundity that I made up my mind I must take warning betimes, and avoid their temptations to adipose deposit. I prefer to grow upwards; the Frau grows sideways. Better get my throat cut by an American desperado, in my pursuit of romance, than settle down on a rock like a placid fat oyster. I am not by nature sessile.

Adventures are to the adventurous. They abound on every side; but only the chosen few have the courage to embrace them. And they will not come to you: you must go out to seek them. Then they meet you half-way, and rush into your arms, for they know their true lovers. There were eight Blighted Fraus at the Home for Lost Ideals, and I could tell by simple inspection that they had not had an average of half an adventure per lifetime between them. They sat and knitted still, like Awful Examples.

If I had declined to meet Mr. Hitchcock at Fraunheim, I know not what changes it might have induced in my life. I might now be knitting. But I went boldly forth, on a voyage of exploration, prepared to accept aught that fate held in store for me.

As Mr. Hitchcock had assured me there was money in his offer, I felt justified in speculating. I expended another three marks on the hire of a bicycle, though I ran the risk thereby of going perhaps without Monday's dinner. That showed my vocation. The Blighted Fraus, I felt sure, would have clung to their dinner at all hazards.

When I arrived at Fraunheim, I found my alert American punctually there before me. He raised his crush hat with awkward politeness. I could see he was little accustomed to ladies' society. Then he pointed to a close cab in which he had reached the village.

"I've got it inside," he whispered, in a confidential tone. "I couldn't let 'em ketch sight of it. You see, there's dollars in it."

"What have you got inside?" I asked, suspiciously, drawing back. I don't know why, but the word "it" somehow suggested a corpse. I began to grow frightened.

"Why, the wheel, of course," he answered. "Ain't you come here to ride it?"

"Oh, the wheel?" I echoed, vaguely, pretending to look wise; but unaware, as yet, that that word was the accepted Americanism for a cycle. "And I have come to ride it?"

"Why, certainly," he replied, jerking his hand towards the cab. "But we mustn't start right here. This thing has got to be kept dark, don't you see, till the last day."

Till the last day! That was ominous. It sounded like monomania. So ghostly and elusive! I began to suspect my American ally of being a dangerous madman.

"Jest you wheel away a bit up the hill," he went on, "out o' sight of the folks, and I'll fetch her along to you."

"Her?" I cried. "Who?" For the man bewildered me.

"Why, the wheel, miss! *You* understand! This is business, you bet! And you're jest the right woman!"

He motioned me on. Urged by a sort of spell, I remounted my machine and rode out of the village. He followed, on the box-seat of his cab. Then, when we had left the world well behind, and stood among the sun-smitten boles of the pine-trees, he opened the door mysteriously, and produced from the vehicle a very odd-looking bicycle.

It was clumsy to look at. It differed immensely, in many particulars, from any machine I had yet seen or ridden.

The strenuous American fondled it for a moment with his hand, as if it were a pet child. Then he mounted nimbly. Pride shone in his eye. I saw in a second he was a fond inventor.

He rode a few yards on. Next he turned to me eagerly. "This ma-chine," he said, in an impressive voice, "*is* propelled *by* an eccentric." Like all his countrymen, he laid most stress on unaccented syllables.

"Oh, I knew you were an eccentric," I said, "the moment I set eyes upon you."

He surveyed me gravely. "You misunderstand me, miss," he corrected. "*When* I say an eccentric, I mean, a crank."

"They are much the same thing," I answered, briskly. "Though I confess I would hardly have applied so rude a word as *crank* to you."

He looked me over suspiciously, as if I were trying to make game of him, but my face was sphinx-like. So he brought the machine a yard or two nearer, and explained its construction to me. He was quite right: it *was* driven by a crank. It had no chain, but was moved by a pedal, working narrowly up and down, and attached to a rigid bar, which impelled the wheels by means of an eccentric.

Besides this, it had a curious device for altering the gearing automatically while one rode, so as to enable one to adapt it to the varying slope in mounting hills. This part of the mechanism he explained to me elaborately. There was a gauge in front which allowed one to sight the steepness of the slope by mere inspection; and according as the gauge marked one, two, three, or four, as its gradient on the scale, the rider pressed a button on the handle-bar with his left hand once, twice, thrice, or four times, so that the gearing adapted itself without an effort to the rise in the surface. Besides, there were devices for rigidity and compensation. Altogether, it was a most apt and ingenious piece of mechanism. I did not wonder he was proud of it.

"Get up and ride, miss," he said in a persuasive voice.

I did as I was bid. To my immense surprise, I ran up the steep hill as smoothly and easily as if it were a perfectly-laid level.

"Goes nicely, doesn't she?" Mr. Hitchcock murmured, rubbing his hands.

"Beautifully," I answered. "One could ride such a machine up Mont Blanc, I should fancy."

He stroked his chin with nervous fingers. "It ought to knock 'em," he said, in an eager voice. "It's geared to run up most anything in creation."

"How steep?"

"One foot in three."

"That's good."

"Yes. It'll climb Mount Washington."

"What do you call it?" I asked.

He looked me over with close scrutiny.

"In Amurrica," he said, slowly, "we call it the Great Manitou, because it kin do pretty well what it chooses; but in Europe, I am thinking of calling it the Martin Conway or the Whymper, or something like that."

"Why so?"

"Well, because it's a famous mountain climber."

"I see," I said. "With such a machine you'll put a notice on the Matterhorn, 'This hill is dangerous to cyclists.'"

He laughed low to himself, and rubbed his hands again. "You'll do, miss," he said. "You're the right sort, you are. The moment I seen you, I thought we two could do a trade together. Benefits me; benefits you. A mutual advantage. Reciprocity is the soul of business. You hev some go in you, you hev. There's money in your feet. You'll give these Meinherrs fits. You'll take the clear-starch out of them."

"I fail to catch on," I answered, speaking his own dialect to humour him.

"Oh, you'll get there all the same," he replied, stroking his machine meanwhile. "It was a squirrel, it was!" (He pronounced it *squirl*.) "It 'ud run up a tree ef it wanted, wouldn't it?" He was talking to it now as if it were a dog or a baby. "There, there, it mustn't kick; it was a frisky little thing! Jest you step up on it, miss, and have a go at that there mountain."

I stepped up and had a "go." The machine bounded forward like an agile greyhound. You had but to touch it, and it ran of itself. Never had I ridden so vivacious, so animated a cycle. I returned to him, sailing, with the gradient reversed. The Manitou glided smoothly, as on a gentle slope, without the need for back-pedalling.

"It soars!" he remarked with enthusiasm.

"Balloons are at discount beside it," I answered.

"Now you want to know about this business, I guess," he went on. "You want to know jest where the reciprocity comes in, anyhow?"

"I am ready to hear you expound," I admitted, smiling.

"Oh, it ain't all on one side," he continued, eyeing his machine at an angle with parental affection. "I'm a-going to make your fortune right here. You shall ride her for me on the last day; and ef you pull this thing off, don't you be scared that I won't treat you handsome."

"If you were a little more succinct," I said, gravely, "we should get forrader faster."

"Perhaps you wonder," he put in, "that with money on it like this, I should intrust the job *into* the hands of a female." I winced, but was silent. "Well, it's like this, don't you see; ef a female wins, it makes success all the more striking and con-spicuous. The world to-day *is* ruled *by* adver*tize*ment."

I could stand it no longer. "Mr. Hitchcock," I said, with dignity, "I haven't the remotest idea what on earth you are talking about."

He gazed at me with surprise. "What?" he exclaimed, at last. "And you kin cycle like that! Not know what all the cycling world is mad about! Why, you don't mean to tell me you're not a professional?"

I enlightened him at once as to my position in society, which was respectable, if not lucrative. His face fell somewhat. "High-toned, eh? Still, you'd run all the same, wouldn't you?" he inquired.

"Run for what?" I asked, innocently. "Parliament? The Presidency? The Frankfort Town Council?"

He had difficulty in fathoming the depths of my ignorance. But by degrees I understood him. It seemed that the German Imperial and Prussian Royal Governments had offered a Kaiserly and Kingly prize for the best military bicycle; the course to be run over the Taunus, from Frankfort to Limburg; the winning machine to get the equivalent of a thousand pounds; each firm to supply its own make and rider. The "last day" was Saturday next; and the Great Manitou was the dark horse of the contest.

Then all was clear as day to me. Mr. Cyrus W. Hitchcock was keeping his machine a profound secret; he wanted a woman to ride it, so that his triumph might be the more complete; and the moment he saw me pedal up the hill, in trying to avoid him, he recognised at once that I was that woman.

I recognised it too. 'Twas a pre-ordained harmony. After two or three trials I felt that the Manitou was built for me, and I was built for the Manitou. We ran together like parts of one mechanism. I was always famed for my circular ankle-action; and in this new machine, ankle-action was everything. Strength of limb counted for naught; what told was the power of "clawing up again" promptly. I possess that power: I have prehistoric feet: my remote progenitors must certainly have been tree-haunting monkeys.

We arranged terms then and there.

"You accept?"

"Implicitly."

If I pulled off the race, I was to have fifty pounds. If I didn't, I was to have five. "It ain't only your skill, you see," Mr. Hitchcock said, with frank commercialism. "It's your personal attractiveness as well that I go upon. That's an element to consider in business relations."

"My face is my fortune," I answered, gravely. He nodded acquiescence.

Till Saturday, then, I was free. Meanwhile, I trained, and practised quietly with the Manitou, in sequestered parts of the hills. I also took spells, turn about, at the Städel Institute. I like to intersperse culture and athletics. I know something about athletics, and hope in time to acquire a taste for culture. 'Tis expected of a Girton girl, though my own accomplishments run rather towards rowing, punting, bicycling.

On Saturday, I confess, I rose with great misgivings. I was not a professional; and to find oneself practically backed for a thousand pounds in a race against men is a trifle disquieting. Still, having once put my hand to the plough, I felt I was bound to pull it through somehow. I dressed my hair neatly, in a very tight coil. I ate a light breakfast, eschewing the fried sausages which the Blighted Fraus pressed upon my notice, and satisfying myself with a gently-boiled egg and some toast and coffee. I always found I rowed best at Cambridge on the lightest diet; in my opinion, the raw beef *régime* is a serious error in training.

At a minute or two before eleven I turned up at the Schiller Platz in my short serge dress and cycling jacket. The great square was thronged with spectators to see us start; the police made a lane through their midst for the riders. My backer had advised me to come to the post as late as possible, "For I have entered your name," he said, "simply as Lois Cayley. These Deutschers don't think but what you're a man and a brother. But I am apprehensive of con-tingencies. When you put in a show they'll try to raise objections to you on account of your being a female. There won't be much time, though, and I shall rush the objections. Once they let you run and win, it don't matter to me whether I get the twenty thousand marks or not. It's the adver*tize*ment that tells. Jest you mark my words, miss, and don't you make no mistake about it—the world to-day is governed by adver*tize*ment."

So I turned up at the last moment, and cast a timid glance at my competitors. They were all men, of course, and two of them were German officers in a sort of undress cycling uniform. They eyed me superciliously. One of them went up and spoke to the Herr Over-Superintendent who had charge of the contest. I understood him to be lodging an objection against a mere woman taking part in the race. The Herr Over-Superintendent, a bulky official, came up beside me and perpended visibly. He bent his big brows to it. 'Twas appalling to observe the measurable amount of Teutonic cerebration going on under cover of his round, green glasses. He was perpending for some minutes. Time was almost up. Then he turned to Mr. Hitchcock, having finally made up his colossal mind, and murmured rudely, "The woman cannot compete."

"Why not?" I inquired, in my very sweetest German, with an angelic smile, though my heart trembled.

"Warum nicht? Because the word 'rider' in the Kaiserly and Kingly for-this-contest-provided decree is distinctly in the masculine gender stated."

"Pardon me, Herr Over-Superintendent," I replied, pulling out a copy of Law 97 on the subject, with which I had duly provided myself, "if you will to Section 45 of the Bicycles-Circulation-Regulation-Act your attention turn, you will find it therein expressly enacted that unless any clause be anywhere to the contrary inserted, the word 'rider,' in the masculine gender put, shall here the word 'rideress' in the feminine to embrace be considered."

For, anticipating this objection, I had taken the precaution to look the legal question up beforehand.

"That is true," the Herr Over-Superintendent observed, in a musing voice, gazing down at me with relenting eyes. "The masculine habitually embraces the feminine." And he brought his massive intellect to bear upon the problem once more with prodigious concentration.

I seized my opportunity. "Let me start, at least," I urged, holding out the Act. "If I win, you can the matter more fully with the Kaiserly and Kingly Governments hereafter argue out."

"I guess this will be an international affair," Mr. Hitchcock remarked, well pleased. "It would be a first-rate adver*tize*ment for the Great Manitou ef England and Germany were to make the question into a *casus belli*. The United States could look on, and pocket the chestnuts."

"Two minutes to go," the official starter with the watch called out.

"Fall in, then, Fräulein Engländerin," the Herr Over-Superintendent observed, without prejudice, waving me into line. He pinned a badge with a large number, 7, on my dress. "The Kaiserly and Kingly Governments shall on the affair of the starting's legality hereafter on my report more at leisure pass judgment."

The lieutenant in undress uniform drew back a little.

"Oh, if this is to be woman's play," he muttered, "then can a Prussian officer himself by competing not into contempt bring."

I dropped a little curtsy. "If the Herr Lieutenant is afraid even to *enter* against an Englishwoman—" I said, smiling.

He came up to the scratch sullenly. "One minute to go!" called out the starter.

We were all on the alert. There was a pause; a deep breath. I was horribly frightened, but I tried to look calm. Then sharp and quick came the one word "Go!" And like arrows from a bow, off we all started.

I had ridden over the whole course the day but one before, on a mountain pony, with an observant eye and my sedulous American—rising at five o'clock, so as not to excite undue attention; and I therefore knew beforehand the exact route we were to follow; but I confess when I saw the Prussian lieutenant and one of my other competitors dash forward at a pace that simply astonished me, that fifty pounds seemed to melt away in the dim abyss of the

Ewigkeit. I gave up all for lost. I could never make the running against such practised cyclists.

However, we all turned out into the open road which leads across the plain and down the Main valley, in the direction of Mayence. For the first ten miles or so, it is a dusty level. The surface is perfect; but 'twas a blinding white thread. As I toiled along it, that broiling June day, I could hear the voice of my backer, who followed on horseback, exhorting me in loud tones, "Don't scorch, miss; don't scorch; never mind ef you lose sight of 'em. Keep your wind; that's the point. The wind, the wind's everything. Let 'em beat you on the level; you'll catch 'em up fast enough when you get on the Taunus!"

But in spite of his encouragement, I almost lost heart as I saw one after another of my opponents' backs disappear in the distance, till at last I was left toiling along the bare white road alone, in a shower-bath of sunlight, with just a dense cloud of dust rising gray far ahead of me. My head swam. It repented me of my boldness.

Then the riders on horseback began to grumble; for by police regulation they were not allowed to pass the hindmost of the cyclists; and they were kept back by my presence from following up their special champions. "Give it up, Fräulein, give it up!" they cried. "You're beaten. Let us pass and get forward." But at the self-same moment, I heard the shrill voice of my American friend whooping aloud across the din, "Don't you do nothing of the sort, miss! You stick to it, and keep your wind! It's the wind that wins! Them Germans won't be worth a cent on the high slopes, anyway!"

Encouraged by his voice, I worked steadily on, neither scorching nor relaxing, but maintaining an even pace at my natural pitch under the broiling sunshine. Heat rose in waves on my face from the road below; in the thin white dust, the accusing tracks of six wheels confronted me. Still I kept on following them, till I reached the town of Höchst—nine miles from Frankfort. Soldiers along the route were timing us at intervals with chronometers, and noting our numbers. As I rattled over the paved High Street, I called aloud to one of them. "How far ahead the last man?"

He shouted back, good-humouredly: "Four minutes, Fräulein."

Again I lost heart. Then I mounted a slight slope, and felt how easily the Manitou moved up the gradient. From its summit I could note a long gray cloud of dust rolling steadily onward down the hill towards Hattersheim.

I coasted down, with my feet up, and a slight breeze just cooling me. Mr. Hitchcock, behind, called out, full-throated, from his seat, "No hurry! No flurry! Take your time! Take—your—time, miss!"

Over the bridge at Hattersheim you turn to the right abruptly, and begin to mount by the side of a pretty little stream, the Schwarzbach, which runs brawling over rocks down the Taunus from Eppstein. By this time the excitement had somewhat cooled down for the moment; I was getting reconciled to be beaten on the level, and began to realise that my chances would be best as we approached the steepest bits of the mountain road about Niederhausen. So I positively plucked up heart to look about me and enjoy the scenery. With hair flying behind—that coil had played me false—I swept through Hofheim, a pleasant little village at the mouth of a grassy valley inclosed by wooded slopes, the Schwarzbach making cool music in the glen below as I mounted beside it. Clambering larches, like huge candelabra, stood out on the ridge, silhouetted against the skyline.

"How far ahead the last man?" I cried to the recording soldier. He answered me back, "Two minutes, Fräulein."

I was gaining on them; I was gaining! I thundered across the Schwarzbach, by half-a-dozen clamorous little iron bridges, making easy time now, and with my feet working as if they were themselves an integral part of the machinery. Up, up, up; it looked a vertical ascent; the Manitou glided well in its oil-bath at its half-way gearing. I rode for dear life. At sixteen miles, Lorsbach; at eighteen, Eppstein; the road still rising. "How far ahead the last man?" "Just round the corner, Fräulein!"

I put on a little steam. Sure enough, round the corner I caught sight of his back. With a spurt, I passed him—a dust-covered soul, very hot and uncomfortable. He had not kept his wind; I flew past him like a whirlwind. But, oh, how sultry hot in that sweltering, close valley! A pretty little town, Eppstein, with its mediæval castle perched high on a craggy rock. I owed it some gratitude, I felt, as I left it behind, for 'twas here that I came up with the tail-end of my opponents.

That one victory cheered me. So far, our route had lain along the well-made but dusty high road in the steaming valley; at Nieder-Josbach, two miles on, we quitted the road abruptly, by the course marked out for us, and turned up a mountain path, only wide enough for two cycles abreast—a path that clambered towards the higher slopes of the Taunus. That was arranged on purpose—for this was no fair-weather show, but a practical trial for military bicycles, under the conditions they might meet with in actual warfare. It was rugged riding: black walls of pine rose steep on either hand; the ground was uncertain. Our path mounted sharply from the first; the steeper the better. By the time I had reached Ober-Josbach, nestling high among larch-woods, I had distanced all but two of my opponents. It was cooler now, too. As I passed the hamlet my cry altered.

"How far ahead the first man?"

"Two minutes, Fräulein."

"A civilian?"

"No, no; a Prussian officer."

The Herr Lieutenant led, then. For Old England's sake, I felt I must beat him.

The steepest slope of all lay in the next two miles. If I were going to win I must pass these two there, for my advantage lay all in the climb; if it came to coasting, the men's mere weight scored a point in their favour. Bump, crash, jolt! I pedalled away like a machine; the Manitou sobbed; my ankles flew round so that I scarcely felt them. But the road was rough and scarred with water-ways—ruts turned by rain to runnels. At half a mile, after a desperate struggle among sand and pebbles, I passed the second man; just ahead, the Prussian officer looked round and saw me. "Thunder-weather! you there, Engländerin?" he cried, darting me a look of unchivalrous dislike, such as only your sentimental German can cast at a woman.

"Yes, I am here, behind you, Herr Lieutenant," I answered, putting on a spurt; "and I hope next to be before you."

He answered not a word, but worked his hardest. So did I. He bent forward: I sat erect on my Manitou, pulling hard at my handles. Now, my front wheel was upon him. It reached his pedal. We were abreast. He had a narrow thread of solid path, and he forced me into a runnel. Still I gained. He swerved: I think he tried to foul me. But the slope was too steep; his attempt recoiled on himself; he ran against the rock at the side and almost overbalanced. That second lost him. I waved my hand as I sailed ahead. "Good morning," I cried, gaily. "See you again at Limburg!"

From the top of the slope I put my feet up and flew down into Idstein. A thunder-shower burst: I was glad of the cool of it. It laid the dust. I regained the high road. From that moment, save for the risk of sideslips, 'twas easy running—just an undulating line with occasional ups and downs; but I saw no more of my pursuers till, twenty-two kilometres farther on, I rattled on the cobble-paved causeway into Limburg. I had covered the forty-six miles in quick time for a mountain climb. As I crossed the bridge over the Lahn, to my immense surprise, Mr. Hitchcock waved his arms, all excitement, to greet me. He had taken the train on from Eppstein, it seemed, and got there before me. As I dismounted at the Cathedral, which was our appointed end, and gave my badge to the soldier, he rushed up and shook my hand. "Fifty pounds!" he cried. "Fifty pounds! How's that for the great Anglo-Saxon race! And hooray for the Manitou!"

The second man, the civilian, rode in, wet and draggled, forty seconds later. As for the Herr Lieutenant, a disappointed man, he fell out by the way, alleging a puncture. I believe he was ashamed to admit the fact that he had been beaten in open fight by the objurgated Engländerin.

So the end of it was, I was now a woman of means, with fifty pounds of my own to my credit.

I lunched with my backer royally at the best inn in Limburg.

THE ADVENTURE OF THE
AMATEUR COMMISSION AGENT

My eccentric American had assured me that if I won the great race for him I need not be "skeert" lest he should fail to treat me well; and to do him justice, I must admit that he kept his word magnanimously. While we sat at lunch in the cosy hotel at Limburg he counted out and paid me in hand the fifty good gold pieces he had promised me. "Whether these Deutschers fork out my twenty thousand marks or not," he said, in his brisk way, "it don't much matter. I shall get the contract, and I shall hev gotten the advert-*ize*ment!"

"Why do you start your bicycles in Germany, though?" I asked, innocently. "I should have thought myself there was so much a better chance of selling them in England."

He closed one eye, and looked abstractedly at the light through his glass of pale yellow Brauneberger with the other. "England? Yes, England! Well, see, miss, you hev not been raised in business. Business is business. The way to do it in Germany is—to manufacture for yourself: and I've got my works started right here in Frankfort. The way to do it in England—where capital's dirt cheap—is, to sell your patent for every cent it's worth to an English company, and let them boom or bust on it."

"I see," I said, catching at it. "The principle's as clear as mud, the moment you point it out to one. An English company will pay you well for the concession, and work for a smaller return on its investment than you Americans are content to receive on your capital!"

"That's so! You hit it in one, miss! Which will you take, a cigar or a cocoa-nut?"

I smiled. "And what do you think you will call the machine in Europe?"

He gazed hard at me, and stroked his straw-coloured moustache. "Well, what do *you* think of the *Lois Cayley*?"

"For Heaven's sake, no!" I cried, fervently. "Mr. Hitchcock, I implore you!"

He smiled pity for my weakness. "Ah, high-toned again?" he repeated, as if it were some natural malformation under which I laboured. "Oh, ef you don't like it, miss, we'll say no more about it. I am a gentleman, I am. What's the matter with the *Excelsior*?"

"Nothing, except that it's very bad Latin," I objected.

"That may be so; but it's very good business."

He paused and mused, then he murmured low to himself, "'When through an Alpine village passed.' That's where the idea of the *Excelsior* comes in; see? 'It goes up Mont Blanc,' you said yourself. 'Through snow and ice, A cycle with the strange device, Excelsior!'"

"If I were you," I said, "I would stick to the name *Manitou*. It's original, and it's distinctive."

"Think so? Then chalk it up; the thing's done. You may not be aware of it, miss, but you are a lady for whose opinion in such matters I hev a high regard. *And* you understand Europe. I do not. I admit it. Everything seems to me to be *verboten* in Germany; and everything else to be *bad form* in England."

We walked down the steps together. "What a picturesque old town!" I said, looking round me, well pleased. Its beauty appealed to me, for I had fifty pounds in pocket, and I had lunched sumptuously.

"*Old* town?" he repeated, gazing with a blank stare. "You call this town *old*, do you?"

"Why, of course! Just look at the cathedral! Eight hundred years old, at least!"

He ran his eye down the streets, dissatisfied.

"Well, ef this town is old," he said at last, with a snap of his fingers, "it's precious little for its age." And he strode away towards the railway station.

"What about the bicycle?" I asked; for it lay, a silent victor, against the railing of the steps, surrounded by a crowd of inquiring Teutons.

He glanced at it carelessly. "Oh, the wheel?" he said. "You may keep it."

He said it so exactly in the tone in which one tells a waiter he may keep the change, that I resented the impertinence. "No, thank you," I answered. "I do not require it."

He gazed at me, open-mouthed. "What? Put my foot in it again?" he interposed. "Not high-toned enough? Eh? Now, I do regret it. No offence meant, miss, nor none need be taken. What I meant to in-sinuate was this: you hev won the big race for me. Folks will notice you and talk about you at Frankfort. Ef you ride a Manitou, that'll make 'em talk the more. A mutual advantage. Benefits you; benefits me. You get the wheel; I get the adver*tize*ment."

I saw that reciprocity was the lodestar of his life. "Very well, Mr. Hitchcock," I said, pocketing my pride, "I'll accept the machine, and I'll ride it."

Then a light dawned upon me. I saw eventualities. "Look here," I went on, innocently—recollect, I was a girl just fresh from Girton—"I am thinking of going on very soon to Switzerland. Now, why shouldn't I do this—try to sell your machines, or, rather, take orders for them, from anybody that admires them? A mutual advantage. Benefits you; benefits me. You sell your wheels; I get—"

He stared at me. "The commission?"

"I don't know what commission means," I answered, somewhat at sea as to the name; "but I thought it might be worth your while, till the Manitou becomes better known, to pay me, say, ten per cent on all orders I brought you."

His face was one broad smile. "I do admire at you, miss," he cried, standing still to inspect me. "You may not know the meaning of the *word* commission; but durned ef you haven't got a hang of the *thing* itself that would do honour to a Wall Street operator, anyway."

"Then that's business?" I asked, eagerly; for I beheld vistas.

"Business?" he repeated. "Yes, that's jest about the size of it—business. Adver*tize*ment, miss, may be the soul of commerce, but Commission's its body. You go in and win. Ten per cent on every order you send me!"

He insisted on taking my ticket back to Frankfort. "My affair, miss; my affair!" There was no gainsaying him. He was immensely elated. "The biggest thing in cycles since Dunlop tyres," he repeated. "And to-morrow, they'll give me advertizements gratis in every newspaper!"

Next morning, he came round to call on me at the Abode of Unclaimed Domestic Angels. He was explicit and generous. "Look here, miss," he began; "I didn't do fair by you when you interviewed me about your agency last evening. I took advantage, *at* the time, *of* your youth and inexperience. You suggested 10 per cent *as* the amount of your commission on sales you might effect; and I jumped at it. That was conduct unworthy *of* a gentleman. Now, I will not deceive you. The ordinary commission on transactions in wheels is 25 per cent. I am going to sell the Manitou retail at twenty English pounds apiece. You shall hev your 25 per cent on all orders."

"Five pounds for every machine I sell?" I exclaimed, overjoyed.

He nodded. "That's so."

I was simply amazed at this magnificent prospect. "The cycle trade must be honeycombed with middlemen's profits!" I cried; for I had my misgivings.

"That's so," he replied again. "Then jest you take and be a middlewoman."

"But, as a consistent socialist—"

"It is your duty to fleece the capitalist and the consumer. A mutual benefit—triangular this time. I get the order, the public gets the machine, and you get the commission. I am richer, you are richer, and the public is mounted on much the best wheel ever yet invented."

"That sounds plausible," I admitted. "I shall try it on in Switzerland. I shall run up steep hills whenever I see any likely customers looking on; then I shall stop and ask them the time, as if quite accidentally."

He rubbed his hands. "You take to business like a young duck to the water," he exclaimed, admiringly. "That's the way to rake 'em in! You go up and say to them, 'Why not investigate? We defy competition. Leave the drudgery of walking uphill beside your cycle! Progress is the order of the day. Use modern methods! This is the age of the telegraph, the telephone, *and* the typewriter. You kin no longer afford to go on with an antiquated, ante-diluvian, armour-plated wheel. Invest in a Hill-Climber, the last and lightest product of evvolootion. *Is* it common-sense to buy an old-style, unautomatic, single-geared, inconvertible ten-ton machine, when for the same money or less you can purchase the self-acting Manitou, a priceless gem, as light as a feather, with all the most recent additions and improvements? Be reasonable! Get the best!' That's the style to fetch 'em!"

I laughed, in spite of myself. "Oh, Mr. Hitchcock," I burst out, "that's not *my* style at all. I shall say, simply 'This is a lovely new bicycle. You can see for yourself how it climbs hills. Try it, if you wish. It skims like a swallow. And I get what they call five pounds commission on every one I can sell of them!' I think that way of dealing is much more likely to bring you in orders."

His admiration was undisguised. "Well, I *do* call you a woman of business, miss," he cried. "You see it at a glance. That's so. That's the right kind of thing to rope in the Europeans. Some originality about you. You take 'em on their own ground. You've got the draw on them, you hev. I like your system. You'll jest haul in the dollars!"

"I hope so," I said, fervently; for I had evolved in my own mind, oh, such a *lovely* scheme for Elsie Petheridge's holidays!

He gazed at me once more. "Ef only I could get hold of a woman of business like you to soar through life with me," he murmured.

I grew interested in my shoes. His open admiration was getting quite embarrassing.

He paused a minute. Then he went on: "Well, what do you say to it?"

"To what?" I asked, amazed.

"To my proposition—my offer."

"I— I don't understand," I stammered out bewildered. "The 25 per cent, you mean?"

"No, the de-votion of a lifetime," he answered, looking sideways at me. "Miss Cayley, when a business man advances a proposition, commercial or otherwise, he advances it because he means it. He asks a prompt reply. Your time is valuable. So is mine. *Are you prepared to consider it?*"

"Mr. Hitchcock," I said, drawing back, "I think you misunderstand. I think you do not realise—"

"All right, miss," he answered, promptly, though with a disappointed air. "Ef it kin not be managed, it kin not be managed. I understand your European ex-clusiveness. I know your prejudices. But this little episode need not antagonise with the normal course of ordinary business. I respect you, Miss Cayley. You are a lady *of* intelligence, *of* initiative, and *of* high-toned culture. I will wish you good day for the present, without further words; and I shall be happy at any time to receive your orders on the usual commission."

He backed out and was gone. He was so honestly blunt that I really quite liked him.

Next day, I bade a tearless farewell to the Blighted Fraus. When I told those eight phlegmatic souls I was going, they all said "So!" much as they had said "So!" to every previous remark I had been moved to make to them. "So" is capital garnishing: but viewed as a staple of conversation, I find it a trifle vapid, not to say monotonous.

I set out on my wanderings, therefore, to go round the world on my own account and my own Manitou, which last I grew to love in time with a love passing the love of Mr. Cyrus Hitchcock. I carried the strict necessary before me in a small waterproof bicycling valise; but I sent on the portmanteau containing my whole estate, real or personal, to some point in advance which I hoped to reach from time to time in a day or two. My first day's journey was along a pleasant road from Frankfort to Heidelberg, some fifty-four miles in all, skirting the mountains the greater part of the way; the Manitou took the ups and downs so easily that I diverged at intervals, to choose side-paths over the wooded hills. I arrived at Heidelberg as fresh as a daisy, my mount not having turned a hair meanwhile—a favourite expression of cyclists which carries all the more conviction to an impartial mind because of the machine being obviously hairless. Thence I journeyed on by easy stages to Karlsruhe, Baden, Appenweier, and Offenburg; where I set my front wheel resolutely for the Black Forest. It is the prettiest and most picturesque route to Switzerland; and, being also the hilliest, it would afford me, I thought, the best opportunity for showing off the Manitou's paces, and trying my prentice hand as an amateur cycle-agent.

From the quaint little Black Eagle at Offenburg, however, before I dashed into the Forest, I sent off a letter to Elsie Petheridge, setting forth my lovely scheme for her summer holidays. She was delicate, poor child, and the London winters sorely tried her; I was now a millionaire, with the better part of fifty pounds in pocket, so I felt I could afford to be royal in my hospitality. As I was leaving Frankfort, I had called at a tourist agency and bought a second-class circular ticket from London to Lucerne and back— I made it second-class because I am opposed on principle to excessive luxury, and also because it was three guineas cheaper. Even fifty pounds will not last for ever, though I could scarce believe it. (You see, I am not wholly free, after all, from the besetting British vice of prudence.) It was a mighty joy to me to be able to send this ticket to Elsie, at her lodgings in Bayswater, pointing out to her that now the whole mischief was done, and that if she would not come out as soon as her summer vacation began—'twas a point of honour with Elsie to say *vacation*, instead of *holidays*—to join me at Lucerne, and stop with me as my guest at a mountain *pension*, the ticket would be wasted. I love burning my boats; 'tis the only safe way for securing prompt action.

Then I turned my flying wheels up into the Black Forest, growing weary of my loneliness—for it is not all jam to ride by oneself in Germany—and longing for Elsie to come out and join me. I loved to think how her dear pale cheeks would gain colour and tone on the hills about the Brünig, where, for business reasons (so I said to myself with the conscious pride of the commission agent), I proposed to pass the greater part of the summer.

From Offenburg to Hornberg the road makes a good stiff climb of twenty-seven miles, and some 1200 English feet in altitude, with a fair number of minor undulations on the way to diversify it. I will not describe the route, though it is one of the most beautiful I have ever travelled—rocky hills, ruined castles, huge, straight-stemmed pines that clamber up green slopes, or halt in sombre line against steeps of broken crag; the reality surpasses my poor powers of description. And the people I passed on the road were almost as quaint and picturesque in their way as the hills and the villages—the men in red-lined jackets; the women in black petticoats, short-waisted green bodices, and broad-brimmed straw hats with black-and-crimson pompons. But on the steepest gradient, just before reaching Hornberg, I got my first nibble—strange to say, from two German students; they wore Heidelberg caps, and were toiling up the incline with short, broken wind; I put on a spurt with the Manitou, and passed them easily. I did it just at first in pure wantonness of health and strength; but the moment I was clear of them, it occurred to the business half of me that here was a good chance of taking an order. Filled with this bright idea, I dismounted near the summit, and pretended to be engaged in lubricating my bearings; though as a matter of fact the Manitou runs in a bath of oil, self-feeding, and needs no looking after. Presently, my two Heidelbergers straggled up—hot, dusty, panting. Woman-like, I pretended to take no notice. One of them drew near and cast an eye on the Manitou.

"That's a new machine, Fräulein," he said, at last, with more politeness than I expected.

"It is," I answered, casually; "the latest model. Climbs hills like no other." And I feigned to mount and glide off towards Hornberg.

"Stop a moment, pray, Fräulein," my prospective buyer called out. "Here, Heinrich, I wish you this new so excellent mountain-climbing machine, without chain propelled, more fully to investigate."

"I am going on to Hornberg," I said, with mixed feminine guile and commercial strategy; "still, if your friend wishes to look—"

They both jostled round it, with *achs* innumerable, and, after minute inspection, pronounced its principle *wunderschön*. "Might I essay it?" Heinrich asked.

"Oh, by all means," I answered. He paced it down hill a few yards; then skimmed up again.

"It is a bird!" he cried to his friend, with many guttural interjections. "Like the eagle's flight, so soars it. Come, try the thing, Ludwig!"

"You permit, Fräulein?"

I nodded. They both mounted it several times. It behaved like a beauty. Then one of them asked, "And where can man of this new so remarkable machine nearest by purchase himself make possessor?"

"I am the Sole Agent," I burst out, with swelling dignity. "If you will give me your orders, with cash in hand for the amount, I will send the cycle, carriage paid, to any address you desire in Germany."

"You!" they exclaimed, incredulously. "The Fräulein is pleased to be humorous!"

"Oh, very well," I answered, vaulting into the saddle; "If you choose to doubt my word—" I waved one careless hand and coasted off. "Good-morning, meine Herren."

They lumbered after me on their ramshackled traction-engines. "Pardon, Fräulein! Do not thus go away! Oblige us at least with the name and address of the maker."

I perpended—like the Herr Over-Superintendent at Frankfort. "Look here," I said at last, telling the truth with frankness, "I get 25 per cent on all bicycles I sell. I am, as I say, the maker's Sole Agent. If you order through me, I touch my profit; if otherwise, I do not. Still, since you seem to be gentlemen," they bowed and swelled visibly, "I will give you the address of the firm, trusting to your honour to mention my name"—I handed them a card—"if you

decide on ordering. The price of the palfrey is 400 marks. It is
worth every pfennig of it." And before they could say more, I had
spurred my steed and swept off at full speed round a curve of the
highway.

I pencilled a note to my American that night from Hornberg,
detailing the circumstance; but I am sorry to say, for the discredit
of humanity, that when those two students wrote the same evening
from their inn in the village to order Manitous, they did *not* mention my name, doubtless under the misconception that by suppress-
ing it they would save my commission. However, it gives me pleasure to add *per contra* (as we say in business) that when I arrived
at Lucerne a week or so later I found a letter, *poste restante*, from
Mr. Cyrus Hitchcock, inclosing an English ten-pound note. He
wrote that he had received two orders for Manitous from Hornberg;
and "feeling considerable confidence that these must necessarily
originate" from my German students, he had the pleasure of for-
warding me what he hoped would be the first of many similar com-
missions.

I will not describe my further adventures on the still steeper
mountain road from Hornberg to Triberg and St. Georgen—how I
got bites on the way from an English curate, an Austrian hussar,
and two unprotected American ladies; nor how I angled for them
all by riding my machine up impossible hills, and then reclining
gracefully to eat my lunch (three times in one day) on mossy banks
at the summit. I felt a perfect little hypocrite. But Mr. Hitchcock
had remarked that business is business; and I will only add (in
confirmation of his view) that by the time I reached Lucerne, I had
sown the good seed in fifteen separate human souls, no less than
four of which brought forth fruit in orders for Manitous before the
end of the season.

I had now so little fear what the morrow might bring forth that
I settled down in a comfortable hotel at Lucerne till Elsie's holidays began; and amused myself meanwhile by picking out the hilliest roads I could find in the neighbourhood, in order to display my
steel steed's possibilities to the best advantage.

By the end of July, Elsie joined me. She was half-angry at first that I should have forced the ticket and my hospitality upon her.

"Nonsense, dear," I said, smoothing her hair, for her pale face quite frightened me. "What is the good of a friend if she will not allow you to do her little favours?"

"But, Brownie, you said you wouldn't stop and be dependent upon *me* one day longer than was necessary in London."

"That was different," I cried. "That was Me! This is You! I am a great, strong, healthy thing, fit to fight the battle of life and take care of myself; you, Elsie, are one of those fragile little flowers which 'tis everybody's duty to protect and to care for."

She would have protested more; but I stifled her mouth with kisses. Indeed, for nothing did I rejoice in my prosperity so much as for the chance it gave me of helping poor dear overworked, overwrought Elsie.

We took up our quarters thenceforth at a high-perched little guest-house near the top of the Brünig. It was bracing for Elsie; and it lay close to a tourist track where I could spread my snares and exhibit the Manitou in its true colours to many passing visitors. Elsie tried it, and found she could ride on it with ease. She wished she had one of her own. A bright idea struck me. In fear and trembling, I wrote, suggesting to Mr. Hitchcock that I had a girl friend from England stopping with me in Switzerland, and that two Manitous would surely be better than one as an advertizement. I confess I stood aghast at my own cheek; but my hand, I fear, was rapidly growing "subdued to that it worked in." Anyhow I sent the letter off, and waited developments.

By return of post came an answer from my American.

"Dear Miss—By rail herewith please receive one lady's No. 4 automatic quadruple-geared self-feeding Manitou, as per your esteemed favour of July 27th, for which I desire to thank you. The more I see of your way of doing business, the more I do admire at you. This is an elegant poster! Two high-toned

English ladies, mounted on Manitous, careering up
the Alps, represent to both of us quite a mint of
money. The mutual benefit, to me, to you, and to the
other lady, ought to be simply incalculable. I shall
be pleased at any time to hear of any further developments of your very remarkable advertising skill,
and I am obliged to you for this brilliant suggestion
you have been good enough to make to me.—Respectfully,

"Cyrus W. Hitchcock."

"What? Am I to have it for nothing, Brownie?" Elsie exclaimed,
bewildered, when I read the letter to her.

I assumed the airs of a woman of the world. "Why, certainly,
my dear," I answered, as if I always expected to find bicycles show-
ered upon me. "It's a mutual arrangement. Benefits him; benefits
you. Reciprocity is the groundwork of business. *He* gets the advertisement; *you* get the amusement. It's a form of handbill. Like the
ladies who exhibit their back hair, don't you know, in that window
in Regent Street."

Thus inexpensively mounted, we scoured the country together,
up the steepest hills between Stanzstadt and Meiringen. We had
lots of nibbles. One lady in particular often stopped to look on and
admire the Manitou. She was a nice-looking widow of forty-five,
very fresh and round-faced; a Mrs. Evelegh, we soon found out,
who owned a charming *chalet* on the hills above Lungern. She spoke
to us more than once: "What a perfect dear of a machine!" she cried.
"I wonder if I dare try it!"

"Can you cycle?" I asked.

"I could once," she answered. "I was awfully fond of it. But Dr.
Fortescue-Langley won't let me any longer."

"Try it!" I said dismounting. She got up and rode. "Oh, isn't it
just lovely!" she cried ecstatically.

"Buy one!" I put in. "They're as smooth as silk; they cost only
twenty pounds; and, on every machine I sell, I get five pounds commission."

"I should love to," she answered; "but Dr. Fortescue-Langley—"

"Who is he?" I asked. "I don't believe in drug-drenchers."

She looked quite shocked. "Oh, he's not that kind, you know," she put in, breathlessly. "He's the celebrated esoteric faith-healer. He won't let me move far away from Lungern, though I'm longing to be off to England again for the summer. My boy's at Portsmouth."

"Then, why don't you disobey him?"

Her face was a study. "I daren't," she answered in an awe-struck voice. "He comes here every summer; and he does me *so* much good, you know. He diagnoses my inner self. He treats me psychically. When my inner self goes wrong, my bangle turns dusky." She held up her right hand with an Indian silver bangle on it; and sure enough, it was tarnished with a very thin black deposit. "My soul is ailing now," she said in a comically serious voice. "But it is seldom so in Switzerland. The moment I land in England the bangle turns black and remains black till I get back to Lucerne again."

When she had gone, I said to Elsie, "That *is* odd about the bangle. State of health might affect it, I suppose. Though it looks to me like a surface deposit of sulphide." I knew nothing of chemistry, I admit; but I had sometimes messed about in the laboratory at college with some of the other girls; and I remembered now that sulphide of silver was a blackish-looking body, like the film on the bangle.

However, at the time I thought no more about it.

By dint of stopping and talking, we soon got quite intimate with Mrs. Evelegh. As always happens, I found out I had known some of her cousins in Edinburgh, where I always spent my holidays while I was at Girton. She took an interest in what she was kind enough to call my originality; and before a fortnight was out, our hotel being uncomfortably crowded, she had invited Elsie and myself to stop with her at the *chalet*. We went, and found it a delightful little home. Mrs. Evelegh was charming; but we could see at every turn that Dr. Fortescue-Langley had acquired a firm hold over her. "He's so clever, you know," she said; "and so spiritual! He exercises such strong odylic force. He binds my being together. If he misses a visit, I feel my inner self goes all to pieces."

"Does he come often?" I asked, growing interested.

"Oh, dear, no," she answered. "I wish he did: it would be ever so good for me. But he's so much run after; I am but one among many. He lives at Château d'Oex, and comes across to see patients in this district once a fortnight. It is a privilege to be attended by an intuitive seer like Dr. Fortescue-Langley."

Mrs. Evelegh was rich—"left comfortably," as the phrase goes, but with a clause which prevented her marrying again without losing her fortune; and I could gather from various hints that Dr. Fortescue-Langley, whoever he might be, was bleeding her to some tune, using her soul and her inner self as his financial lancet. I also noticed that what she said about the bangle was strictly true; generally bright as a new pin, on certain mornings it was completely blackened. I had been at the *chalet* ten days, however, before I began to suspect the real reason. Then it dawned upon me one morning in a flash of inspiration. The evening before had been cold, for at the height where we were perched, even in August, we often found the temperature chilly in the night, and I heard Mrs. Evelegh tell Cécile, her maid, to fill the hot-water bottle. It was a small point, but it somehow went home to me. Next day the bangle was black, and Mrs. Evelegh lamented that her inner self must be suffering from an attack of evil vapours.

I held my peace at the time, but I asked Cécile a little later to bring me that hot-water-bottle. As I more than half suspected, it was made of india-rubber, wrapped carefully up in the usual red flannel bag. "Lend me your brooch, Elsie," I said. "I want to try a little experiment."

"Won't a franc do as well?" Elsie asked, tendering one. "That's equally silver."

"I think not," I answered. "A franc is most likely too hard; it has base metal to alloy it. But I will vary the experiment by trying both together. Your brooch is Indian and therefore soft silver. The native jewellers never use alloy. Hand it over; it will clean with a little plate-powder, if necessary. I'm going to see what blackens Mrs. Evelegh's bangle."

I laid the franc and the brooch on the bottle, filled with hot water, and placed them for warmth in the fold of a blanket. After *déjeûner*, we inspected them. As I anticipated, the brooch had grown black on the surface with a thin iridescent layer of silver sulphide, while the franc had hardly suffered at all from the exposure.

I called in Mrs. Evelegh, and explained what I had done. She was astonished and half incredulous. "How could you ever think of it?" she cried, admiringly.

"Why, I was reading an article yesterday about india-rubber in one of your magazines," I answered; "and the person who wrote it said the raw gum was hardened for vulcanising by mixing it with sulphur. When I heard you ask Cécile for the hot-water-bottle, I thought at once: 'The sulphur and the heat account for the tarnishing of Mrs. Evelegh's bangle.'"

"And the franc doesn't tarnish! Then that must be why my other silver bracelet, which is English make, and harder, never changes colour! And Dr. Fortescue-Langley assured me it was because the soft one was of Indian metal, and had mystic symbols on it—symbols that answered to the cardinal moods of my sub-conscious self, and that darkened in sympathy."

I jumped at a clue. "He talked about your sub-conscious self?" I broke in.

"Yes," she answered. "He always does. It's the key-note of his system. He heals by that alone. But, my dear, after this, how can I ever believe in him?"

"Does he know about the hot-water-bottle?" I asked.

"Oh, yes; he ordered me to use it on certain nights; and when I go to England he says I must never be without one. I see now that was why my inner self invariably went wrong in England. It was all just the sulphur blackening the bangles."

I reflected. "A middle-aged man?" I asked. "Stout, diplomatic-looking, with wrinkles round his eyes, and a distinguished grey moustache, twirled up oddly at the corners?"

"That's the man, my dear! His very picture. Where on earth have you seen him?"

"And he talks of sub-conscious selves?" I went on.

"He practises on that basis. He says it's no use prescribing for the outer man; to do that is to treat mere symptoms: the sub-conscious self is the inner seat of diseases."

"How long has he been in Switzerland?"

"Oh, he comes here every year. He arrived this season late in May, I fancy."

"When will he visit you again, Mrs. Evelegh?"

"To-morrow morning."

I made up my mind at once. "Then I must see him, without being seen," I said. "I think I know him. He is our Count, I believe." For I had told Mrs. Evelegh and Elsie the queer story of my journey from London.

"Impossible, my dear! Im-possible! I have implicit faith in him!"

"Wait and see, Mrs. Evelegh. You acknowledge he duped you over the affair of the bangle."

There are two kinds of dupe: one kind, the commonest, goes on believing in its deceiver, no matter what happens; the other, far rarer, has the sense to know it has been deceived if you make the deception as clear as day to it. Mrs. Evelegh was, fortunately, of the rarer class. Next morning, Dr. Fortescue-Langley arrived, by appointment. As he walked up the path, I glanced at him from my window. It was the Count, not a doubt of it. On his way to gull his dupes in Switzerland, he had tried to throw in an incidental trifle of a diamond robbery.

I telegraphed the facts at once to Lady Georgina, at Schlangenbad. She answered, "I am coming. Ask the man to meet his friend on Wednesday."

Mrs. Evelegh, now almost convinced, invited him. On Wednesday morning, with a bounce, Lady Georgina burst in upon us. "My dear, such a journey!—alone, at my age—but there, I haven't known a happy day since you left me! Oh, yes, I got my Gretchen—unsophisticated?—well—h'm—that's not the word for it: I declare to you, Lois, there isn't a trick of the trade, in Paris or London—not a perquisite or a tip that that girl isn't up to. Comes straight from the remotest recesses of the Black Forest, and hadn't been with me a week, I assure you, honour bright, before she was bandolining her yellow hair, and rouging her cheeks, and wearing my brooches, and wagering gloves with the hotel waiters upon the Baden races. *And* her language: *and* her manners! Why weren't you born in that station of life, I wonder, child, so that I might offer you five hundred a year, and all found, to come and live with me for ever? But this Gretchen—her fringe, her shoes, her ribbons—upon my soul, my dear, I don't know what girls are coming to nowadays."

"Ask Mrs. Lynn-Linton," I suggested, as she paused. "She is a recognised authority on the subject."

The Cantankerous Old Lady stared at me. "And this Count?" she went on. "So you have really tracked him? You're a wonderful girl, my dear. I wish you were a lady's maid. You'd be worth me any money."

I explained how I had come to hear of Dr. Fortescue-Langley.

Lady Georgina waxed warm. "Dr. Fortescue-Langley!" she exclaimed. "The wicked wretch! But he didn't get my diamonds! I've carried them here in my hands, all the way from Wiesbaden: I wasn't going to leave them for a single day to the tender mercies of that unspeakable Gretchen. The fool would lose them. Well, we'll catch him this time, Lois: and we'll give him ten years for it!"

"Ten years!" Mrs. Evelegh cried, clasping her hands in horror. "Oh, Lady Georgina!"

We waited in Mrs. Evelegh's dining-room, the old lady and I, behind the folding doors. At three precisely Dr. Fortescue-Langley walked in. I had difficulty in restraining Lady Georgina from falling upon him prematurely. He talked a lot of high-flown nonsense to Mrs. Evelegh and Elsie about the influences of the planets, and the seventy-five emanations, and the eternal wisdom of the East, and the medical efficacy of sub-conscious suggestion. Excellent patter, all of it—quite as good in its way as the diplomatic patter he had poured forth in the train to Lady Georgina. It was rich in spheres, in elements, in cosmic forces. At last, as he was discussing the reciprocal action of the inner self upon the exhalations of the lungs, we pushed back the door and walked calmly in upon him.

His breath came and went. The exhalations of the lungs showed visible perturbation. He rose and stared at us. For a second he lost his composure. Then, as bold as brass, he turned, with a cunning smile, to Mrs. Evelegh. "Where on earth did you pick up such acquaintances?" he inquired, in a well-simulated tone of surprise.

"Yes, Lady Georgina, I have met you before, I admit; but—it can hardly be agreeable to you to reflect under what circumstances."

Lady Georgina was beside herself. "You dare?" she cried, confronting him. "You dare to brazen it out? You miserable sneak! But you can't bluff me now. I have the police outside." Which I regret to confess was a light-hearted fiction.

"The police?" he echoed, drawing back. I could see he was frightened.

I had an inspiration again. "Take off that moustache!" I said, calmly, in my most commanding voice.

He clapped his hand to it in horror. In his agitation, he managed to pull it a little bit awry. It looked so absurd, hanging there, all crooked, that I thought it kinder to him to remove it altogether. The thing peeled off with difficulty; for it was a work of art, very firmly and gracefully fastened with sticking-plaster. But it peeled off at last—and with it the whole of the Count's and Dr. Fortescue-Langley's distinction. The man stood revealed, a very palpable man-servant.

Lady Georgina stared hard at him. "Where have I seen you before?" she murmured, slowly. "That face is familiar to me. Why, yes; you went once to Italy as Mr. Marmaduke Ashurst's courier! I know you now. Your name is Higginson."

It was a come-down for the Comte de Laroche-sur-Loiret, but he swallowed it like a man at a single gulp.

"Yes, my lady," he said, fingering his hat nervously, now all was up. "You are quite right, my lady. But what would you have me do? Times are hard on us couriers. Nobody wants us now. I must take to what I can." He assumed once more the tone of the Vienna diplomat. "*Que voulez-vous*, madame? These are revolutionary days. A man of intelligence must move with the Zeitgeist!"

Lady Georgina burst into a loud laugh. "And to think," she cried, "that I talked to this lackey from London to Malines without ever suspecting him! Higginson, you're a fraud—but you're a precious clever one."

He bowed. "I am happy to have merited Lady Georgina Fawley's commendation," he answered, with his palm on his heart, in his grandiose manner.

"But I shall hand you over to the police all the same! You are a thief and a swindler!"

He assumed a comic expression. "Unhappily, not a thief," he objected. "This young lady prevented me from appropriating your diamonds. *Convey*, the wise call it. I wanted to take your jewel-case—and she put me off with a sandwich-tin. I wanted to make an honest penny out of Mrs. Evelegh; and—she confronts me with your ladyship, and tears my moustache off."

Lady Georgina regarded him with a hesitating expression. "But I shall call the police," she said, wavering visibly.

"*De grace*, my lady, *de grace*! Is it worth while, *pour si peu de chose*? Consider, I have really effected nothing. Will you charge me with having taken—in error—a small tin sandwich-case—value, elevenpence? An affair of a week's imprisonment. That is positively all you can bring up against me. And," brightening up visibly, "I have the case still; I will return it to-morrow with pleasure to your ladyship!"

"But the india-rubber water-bottle?" I put in. "You have been deceiving Mrs. Evelegh. It blackens silver. And you told her lies in order to extort money under false pretences."

He shrugged his shoulders. "You are too clever for me, young lady," he broke out. "I have nothing to say to you. But Lady Georgina, Mrs. Evelegh—you are human—let me go! Reflect; I have things I could tell that would make both of you look ridiculous. That journey to Malines, Lady Georgina! Those Indian charms, Mrs. Evelegh! Besides, you have spoiled my game. Let that suffice you! I can practise in Switzerland no longer. Allow me to go in peace, and I will try once more to be indifferent honest!"

He backed slowly towards the door, with his eyes fixed on them. I stood by and waited. Inch by inch he retreated. Lady Georgina looked down abstractedly at the carpet. Mrs. Evelegh looked up abstractedly at the ceiling. Neither spoke another word. The rogue backed out by degrees. Then he sprang downstairs, and before they could decide was well out into the open.

Lady Georgina was the first to break the silence. "After all, my dear," she murmured, turning to me, "there was a deal of sound English common-sense about Dogberry!"

I remembered then his charge to the watch to apprehend a rogue. "How if 'a will not stand?"

"Why, then, take no note of him, but let him go; and presently call the rest of the watch together, and thank God you are rid of a knave." When I remembered how Lady Georgina had hob-nobbed with the Count from Ostend to Malines, I agreed to a great extent both with her and with Dogberry.

THE ADVENTURE OF THE
IMPROMPTU MOUNTAINEER

The explosion and evaporation of Dr. Fortescue-Langley (with whom were amalgamated the Comte de Laroche-sur-Loiret, Mr. Higginson the courier, and whatever else that versatile gentleman chose to call himself) entailed many results of varying magnitudes.

In the first place, Mrs. Evelegh ordered a Great Manitou. That, however, mattered little to "the firm," as I loved to call us (because it shocked dear Elsie so); for, of course, after all her kindness we couldn't accept our commission on her purchase, so that she got her machine cheap for £15 from the maker. But, in the second place—I declare I am beginning to write like a woman of business—she decided to run over to England for the summer to see her boy at Portsmouth, being certain now that the discoloration of her bangle depended more on the presence of sulphur in the india-rubber bottle than on the passing state of her astral body. 'Tis an abrupt descent from the inner self to a hot-water bottle, I admit; but Mrs. Evelegh took the plunge with grace, like a sensible woman. Dr. Fortescue-Langley had been annihilated for her at one blow: she returned forthwith to common-sense and England.

"What will you do with the *chalet* while you're away?" Lady Georgina asked, when she announced her intention. "You can't shut it up to take care of itself. Every blessed thing in the place will go to rack and ruin. Shutting up a house means spoiling it for ever. Why, I've got a cottage of my own that I let for the summer in the best part of Surrey—a pretty little place, now vacant, for which, by

the way, I want a tenant, if you happen to know of one: and when
it's left empty for a month or two—"

"Perhaps it would do for me?" Mrs. Evelegh suggested, jumping at it. "I'm looking out for a furnished house for the summer,
within easy reach of Portsmouth and London, for myself and
Oliver."

Lady Georgina seized her arm, with a face of blank horror. "My
dear," she cried. "For you! I wouldn't dream of letting it to you. A
nasty, damp, cold, unwholesome house, on stiff clay soil, with de-
testable drains, in the deadliest part of the Weald of Surrey,—why,
you and your boy would catch your deaths of rheumatism."

"Is it the one I saw advertised in the *Times* this morning, I
wonder?" Mrs. Evelegh inquired in a placid voice. "'Charming furnished house on Holmesdale Common; six bedrooms, four recep-
tion-rooms; splendid views; pure air; picturesque surroundings;
exceptionally situated.' I thought of writing about it."

"That's it!" Lady Georgina exclaimed, with a demonstrative
wave of her hand. "I drew up the advertisement myself. Exceptionally situated! I should just think it was! Why, my dear, I wouldn't
let you rent the place for worlds; a horrid, poky little hole, stuck
down in the bottom of a boggy hollow, as damp as Devonshire, with
the paper peeling off the walls, so that I had to take my choice
between giving it up myself ten years ago, or removing to the cemetery; and I've let it ever since to City men with large families.
Nothing would induce me to allow you and your boy to expose yourself to such risks." For Lady Georgina had taken quite a fancy to
Mrs. Evelegh. "But what I was just going to say was this: you can't
shut your house up; it'll all go mouldy. Houses always go mouldy,
shut up in summer. And you can't leave it to your servants; *I* know
the baggages; no conscience—no conscience; they'll ask their entire families to come and stop with them *en bloc*, and turn your
place into a perfect piggery. Why, when I went away from my house
in town one autumn, didn't I leave a policeman and his wife in
charge—a most respectable man—only he happened to be an
Irishman. And what was the consequence? My dear, I assure you,
I came back unexpectedly from poor dear Kynaston's one day—at

a moment's notice—having quarrelled with him over Home Rule or Education or something—poor dear Kynaston's what they call a Liberal, I believe—got at by that man Rosebery—and there didn't I find all the O'Flanagans, and O'Flahertys, and O'Flynns in the neighbourhood camping out in my drawing-room; with a strong detachment of O'Donohues, and O'Dohertys, and O'Driscolls lying around loose in possession of the library? Never leave a house to the servants, my dear! It's positively suicidal. Put in a responsible caretaker of whom you know something—like Lois here, for instance."

"Lois!" Mrs. Evelegh echoed. "Dear me, that's just the very thing. What a capital idea! I never thought of Lois! She and Elsie might stop on here, with Ursula and the gardener."

I protested that if we did it was our clear duty to pay a small rent; but Mrs. Evelegh brushed that aside. "You've robbed yourselves over the bicycle," she insisted, "and I'm delighted to let you have it. It's I who ought to pay, for you'll keep the house dry for me."

I remembered Mr. Hitchcock—"Mutual advantage: benefits you, benefits me"—and made no bones about it. So in the end Mrs. Evelegh set off for England with Cécile, leaving Elsie and me in charge of Ursula, the gardener, and the *chalet*.

As for Lady Georgina, having by this time completed her "cure" at Schlangenbad (complexion as usual; no guinea yellower), she telegraphed for Gretchen—"I can't do without the idiot"—and hung round Lucerne, apparently for no other purpose but to send people up the Brünig on the hunt for our wonderful new machines, and so put money in our pockets. She was much amused when I told her that Aunt Susan (who lived, you will remember, in respectable indigence at Blackheath) had written to expostulate with me on my "unladylike" conduct in becoming a bicycle commission agent. "Unladylike!"—the Cantankerous Old Lady exclaimed, with warmth. "What does the woman mean? Has she got no gumption? It's 'ladylike,' I suppose, to be a companion, or a governess, or a music-teacher, or something else in the black-thread-glove way, in London; but not to sell bicycles for a good round commission. My dear, between you and me, I don't see it. If you had a brother,

now, *he* might sell cycles, or corner wheat, or rig the share market,
or do anything else he pleased, in these days, and nobody'd think
the worse of him—as long as he made money; and it's my opinion
that what is sauce for the goose can't be far out for the gander—
and *vice-versâ*. Besides which, what's the use of *trying* to be ladylike? You *are* a lady, child, and you couldn't help being one; why
trouble to be *like* what nature made you? Tell Aunt Susan from me
to put *that* in her pipe and smoke it!"

I *did* tell Aunt Susan by letter, giving Lady Georgina's authority for the statement; and I really believe it had a consoling effect
upon her; for Aunt Susan is one of those innocent-minded people
who cherish a profound respect for the opinions and ideas of a Lady
of Title. Especially where questions of delicacy are concerned. It
calmed her to think that though I, an officer's daughter, had declined upon trade, I was mixing at least with the Best People!

We had a lovely time at the *chalet*—two girls alone, messing
just as we pleased in the kitchen, and learning from Ursula how to
concoct *pot-au-feu* in the most approved Swiss fashion. We
pottered, as we women love to potter, half the day long; the other
half we spent in riding our cycles about the eternal hills, and en-
snaring the flies whom Lady Georgina dutifully sent up to us. She
was our decoy duck: and, in virtue of her handle, she decoyed to a
marvel. Indeed, I sold so many Manitous that I began to entertain
a deep respect for my own commercial faculties. As for Mr. Cyrus
W. Hitchcock, he wrote to me from Frankfort: "The world contin-
ues to revolve on its axis, the Manitou, and the machine is boom-
ing. Orders romp in daily. When you ventilated the suggestion of
an agency at Limburg, I concluded at a glance you had the material of a first-class business woman about you; but I reckon I did
not know what a traveller meant till you started on the road. I am
now enlarging and altering this factory, to meet increased demands. Branch offices at Berlin, Hamburg, Crefeld, and Düsseldorf.
Inspect our stock before dealing elsewhere. A liberal discount allowed to the trade. Two hundred agents wanted in all towns of
Germany. If they were every one of them like *you*, miss—well, I
guess I would hire the town of Frankfort for my business premises."

One morning, after we had spent about a week at the *chalet* by ourselves, I was surprised to see a young man with a knapsack on his back walking up the garden path towards our cottage. "Quick, quick, Elsie!" I cried, being in a mischievous mood. "Come here with the opera-glass! There's a Man in the offing!"

"A *what*?" Elsie exclaimed, shocked as usual at my levity.

"A Man," I answered, squeezing her arm. "A Man! A real live Man! A specimen of the masculine gender in the human being! Man, ahoy! He has come at last—the lodestar of our existence!"

Next minute, I was sorry I spoke; for as the man drew nearer, I perceived that he was endowed with very long legs and a languidly poetical bearing. That supercilious smile—that enticing moustache! Could it be?—yes, it was—not a doubt of it—Harold Tillington!

I grew grave at once; Harold Tillington and the situation were serious. "What can he want here?" I exclaimed, drawing back.

"Who is it?" Elsie asked; for, being a woman, she read at once in my altered demeanour the fact that the Man was not unknown to me.

"Lady Georgina's nephew," I answered, with a tell-tale cheek, I fear. "You remember I mentioned to you that I had met him at Schlangenbad. But this is really too bad of that wicked old Lady Georgina. She has told him where we lived and sent him up to see us."

"Perhaps," Elsie put in, "he wants to charter a bicycle."

I glanced at Elsie sideways. I had an uncomfortable suspicion that she said it slyly, like one who knew he wanted nothing of the sort. But at any rate, I brushed the suggestion aside frankly. "Nonsense," I answered. "He wants *me*, not a bicycle."

He came up to us, waving his hat. He *did* look handsome! "Well, Miss Cayley," he cried from afar, "I have tracked you to your lair! I have found out where you abide! What a beautiful spot! And how well you're looking!"

"This is an unexpected—" I paused. He thought I was going to say, "pleasure," but I finished it, "intrusion." His face fell. "How did you know we were at Lungern, Mr. Tillington?"

"My respected relative," he answered, laughing. "She mentioned—casually—" his eyes met mine—"that you were stopping in

a *chalet*. And as I was on my way back to the diplomatic mill, I
thought I might just as well walk over the Grimsel and the Furca,
and then on to the Gotthard. The Court is at Monza. So it occurred
to me . . . that in passing . . . I might venture to drop in and say
how-do-you-do to you."

"Thank you," I answered, severely—but my heart spoke otherwise—"I do very well. And you, Mr. Tillington?"

"Badly," he echoed. "Badly, since *you* went away from Schlangenbad."

I gazed at his dusty feet. "You are tramping," I said, cruelly. "I
suppose you will get forward for lunch to Meiringen?"

"I— I did not contemplate it."

"Indeed?"

He grew bolder. "No; to say the truth, I half hoped I might stop
and spend the day here with you."

"Elsie," I remarked firmly, "if Mr. Tillington persists in plant-
ing himself upon us like this, one of us must go and investigate the
kitchen department."

Elsie rose like a lamb. I have an impression that she gathered
we wanted to be left alone.

He turned to me imploringly. "Lois," he cried, stretching out
his arms, with an appealing air, "I *may* stay, mayn't I?"

I tried to be stern; but I fear 'twas a feeble pretence. "We are
two girls, alone in a house," I answered. "Lady Georgina, as a matron of experience, ought to have protected us. Merely to give you
lunch is almost irregular. (Good diplomatic word, irregular.) Still,
in these days, I suppose you *may* stay, if you leave early in the
afternoon. That's the utmost I can do for you."

"You are not gracious," he cried, gazing at me with a wistful look.

I did not dare to be gracious. "Uninvited guests must not quarrel with their welcome," I answered severely. Then the woman in
me broke forth. "But indeed, Mr. Tillington, I am glad to see you."

He leaned forward eagerly. "So you are not angry with me, Lois?
I may call you *Lois*?"

I trembled and hesitated. "I am not angry with you. I— I like
you too much to be ever angry with you. And I am glad you came—

just this once—to see me. . . . Yes,—when we are alone—you may
call me Lois."

He tried to seize my hand. I withdrew it. "Then I may perhaps
hope," he began, "that some day—"

I shook my head. "No, no," I said, regretfully. "You misunderstand me. I like you very much; and I like to see you. But as long as
you are rich and have prospects like yours, I could never marry
you. My pride wouldn't let me. Take that as final."

I looked away. He bent forward again. "But if I were poor?" he
put in, eagerly.

I hesitated. Then my heart rose, and I gave way. "If ever you
are poor," I faltered,—"penniless, hunted, friendless—come to me,
Harold, and I will help and comfort you. But not till then. Not till
then, I implore you."

He leant back and clasped his hands. "You have given me something to live for, dear Lois," he murmured. "I will try to be poor—
penniless, hunted, friendless. To win you I will try. And when that
day arrives, I shall come to claim you."

We sat for an hour and had a delicious talk—about nothing.
But we understood each other. Only that artificial barrier divided
us. At the end of the hour, I heard Elsie coming back by judiciously
slow stages from the kitchen to the living-room, through six feet
of passage, discoursing audibly to Ursula all the way, with a tardi-
ness that did honour to her heart and her understanding. Dear,
kind little Elsie! I believe she had never a tiny romance of her own;
yet her sympathy for others was sweet to look upon.

We lunched at a small deal table in the veranda. Around us rose
the pinnacles. The scent of pines and moist moss was in the air.
Elsie had arranged the flowers, and got ready the omelette, and
cooked the chicken cutlets, and prepared the junket. "I never
thought I could do it alone without you, Brownie; but I tried, and
it all came right by magic, somehow." We laughed and talked incessantly. Harold was in excellent cue; and Elsie took to him. A
livelier or merrier table there wasn't in the twenty-two Cantons
that day than ours, under the sapphire sky, looking out on the sun-
smitten snows of the Jungfrau.

After lunch, Harold begged hard to be allowed to stop for tea. I had misgivings, but I gave way—he *was* such good company. One may as well be hanged for a sheep as a lamb, says the wisdom of our ancestors: and, after all, Mrs. Grundy was only represented here by Elsie, the gentlest and least censorious of her daughters. So he stopped and chatted till four; when I made tea and insisted on dismissing him. He meant to take the rough mountain path over the screes from Lungern to Meiringen, which ran right behind the *chalet*. I feared lest he might be belated, and urged him to hurry.

"Thanks, I'm happier here," he answered.

I was sternness itself. "You *promised* me!" I said, in a reproachful voice.

He rose instantly, and bowed. "Your will is law—even when it pronounces sentence of exile."

Would we walk a little way with him? No, I faltered; we would not. We would follow him with the opera-glasses and wave him farewell when he reached the Kulm. He shook our hands unwillingly, and turned up the little path, looking handsomer than ever. It led ascending through a fir-wood to the rock-strewn hillside.

Once, a quarter of an hour later, we caught a glimpse of him near a sharp turn in the road; after that we waited in vain, with our eyes fixed on the Kulm; not a sign could we discern of him. At last I grew anxious. "He ought to be there," I cried, fuming.

"He ought," Elsie answered.

I swept the slopes with the opera-glasses. Anxiety and interest in him quickened my senses, I suppose. "Look here, Elsie," I burst out at last. "Just take this glass and have a glance at those birds, down the crag below the Kulm. Don't they seem to be circling and behaving most oddly?"

Elsie gazed where I bid her. "They're wheeling round and round," she answered, after a minute; "and they certainly *do* look as if they were screaming."

"They seem to be frightened," I suggested.

"It looks like it, Brownie,"

"Then he's fallen over a precipice!" I cried, rising up; "and he's lying there on a ledge by their nest. Elsie, we must go to him!"

She clasped her hands and looked terrified. "Oh, Brownie, how dreadful!" she exclaimed. Her face was deadly white. Mine burned like fire.

"Not a moment to lose!" I said, holding my breath. "Get out the rope and let us run to him!"

"Don't you think," Elsie suggested, "we had better hurry down on our cycles to Lungern and call some men from the village to help us? We are two girls, and alone. What can we do to aid him?"

"No," I answered, promptly, "that won't do. It would only lose time—and time may be precious. You and I must go; I'll send Ursula off to bring up guides from the village."

Fortunately, we had a good long coil of new rope in the house, which Mrs. Evelegh had provided in case of accident. I slipped it on my arm, and set out on foot; for the path was by far too rough for cycles. I was sorry afterwards that I had not taken Ursula, and sent Elsie to Lungern to rouse the men; for she found the climbing hard, and I had difficulty at times in dragging her up the steep and stony pathway, almost a watercourse. However, we persisted in the direction of the Kulm, tracking Harold by his footprints; for he wore mountain boots with sharp-headed nails, which made dints in the moist soil, and scratched the smooth surface of the rock where he trod on it.

We followed him thus for a mile or two, along the regular path; then of a sudden, in an open part, the trail failed us. I turned back, a few yards, and looked close, with my eyes fixed on the spongy soil, as keen as a hound that sniffs his way after his quarry. "He went off *here*, Elsie!" I said at last, pulling up short by a spindle bush on the hillside.

"How do you know, Brownie?"

"Why, see, there are the marks of his stick; he had a thick one, you remember, with a square iron spike. These are its dints; I have been watching them all the way along from the *chalet*!"

"But there are so many such marks!"

"Yes, I know; I can tell his from the older ones made by the spikes of alpenstocks because Harold's are fresher and sharper on the edge. They look so much newer. See, here, he slipped on the rock; you can know that scratch is recent by the clean way it's traced, and the little glistening crystals still left behind in it. Those other marks have been wind-swept and washed by the rain. There are no broken particles."

"How on earth did you find that out, Brownie?"

How on earth did I find it out! I wondered myself. But the emergency seemed somehow to teach me something of the instinctive lore of hunters and savages. I did not trouble to answer her. "At this bush, the tracks fail," I went on; "and, look, he must have clutched at that branch and crushed the broken leaves as the twigs slipped through his fingers. He left the path here, then, and struck off on a short cut of his own along the hillside, lower down. Elsie, we must follow him."

She shrank from it; but I held her hand. It was a more difficult task to track him now; for we had no longer the path to guide us. However, I explored the ground on my hands and knees, and soon found marks of footsteps on the boggy patches, with scratches on the rock where he had leapt from point to point, or planted his stick to steady himself. I tried to help Elsie along among the littered boulders and the dwarf growth of wind-swept daphne: but, poor child, it was too much for her: she sat down after a few minutes upon the flat juniper scrub and began to cry. What was I to do? My anxiety was breathless. I couldn't leave her there alone, and I couldn't forsake Harold. Yet I felt every minute might now be critical. We were making among wet whortleberry thicket and torn rock towards the spot where I had seen the birds wheel and circle, screaming. The only way left was to encourage Elsie and make her feel the necessity for instant action. "He is alive still," I exclaimed, looking up; "the birds are crying! If he were dead, they would return to their nest— Elsie, we *must* get to him!"

She rose, bewildered, and followed me. I held her hand tight, and coaxed her to scramble over the rocks where the scratches showed the way, or to clamber at times over fallen trunks of huge fir-trees. Yet it was hard work climbing; even Harold's sure feet had slipped often on the wet and slimy boulders, though, like most of Queen Margherita's set, he was an expert mountaineer. Then, at times, I lost the faint track, so that I had to diverge and look close to find it. These delays fretted me. "See, a stone loosed from its bed—he must have passed by here. . . . That twig is newly snapped; no doubt he caught at it. . . . Ha, the moss there has been crushed; a foot has gone by. And the ants on that ant-hill, with their eggs in their mouths—a man's tread has frightened them." So, by some instinctive sense, as if the spirit of my savage ancestors revived within me, I managed to recover the spoor again and again by a miracle, till at last, round a corner by a defiant cliff— with a terrible foreboding, my heart stood still within me.

We had come to an end. A great projecting buttress of crag rose sheer in front. Above lay loose boulders. Below was a shrub-hung precipice. The birds we had seen from home were still circling and screaming.

They were a pair of peregrine hawks. Their nest seemed to lie far below the broken scar, some sixty or seventy feet beneath us.

"He is not dead!" I cried once more, with my heart in my mouth. "If he were, they would have returned. He has fallen, and is lying, alive, below there!"

Elsie shrank back against the wall of rock. I advanced on my hands and knees to the edge of the precipice. It was not quite sheer, but it dropped like a sea-cliff, with broken ledges.

I could see where Harold had slipped. He had tried to climb round the crag that blocked the road, and the ground at the edge of the precipice had given way with him; it showed a recent founder of a few inches. Then he clutched at a branch of broom as he fell; but it slipped through his fingers, cutting them; for there was blood on the wiry stem. I knelt by the side of the cliff and craned my head over. I scarcely dared to look. In spite of the birds, my heart misgave me.

There, on a ledge deep below, he lay in a mass, half raised on one arm. But not dead, I believed. "Harold!" I cried. "Harold!"

He turned his face up and saw me; his eyes lighted with joy. He shouted back something, but I could not hear it.

I turned to Elsie. "I must go down to him!"

Her tears rose again. "Oh, Brownie!"

I unwound the coil of rope. The first thing was to fasten it. I could not trust Elsie to hold it; she was too weak and too frightened to bear my weight: even if I wound it round her body, I feared my mere mass might drag her over. I peered about at the surroundings. No tree grew near; no rock had a pinnacle sufficiently safe to depend upon. But I found a plan soon. In the crag behind me was a cleft, narrowing wedge-shape as it descended. I tied the end of the rope round a stone, a good big water-worn stone, rudely girdled with a groove near the middle, which prevented it from slipping; then I dropped it down the fissure till it jammed; after which, I tried it to see if it would bear. It was firm as the rock itself. I let the rope down by it, and waited a moment to discover whether Harold could climb. He shook his head, and took a notebook with evident pain from his pocket. Then he scribbled a few words, and pinned them to the rope. I hauled it up. "Can't move. Either severely bruised and sprained, or else legs broken."

There was no help for it, then. I must go to him.

My first idea was merely to glide down the rope with my gloved hands, for I chanced to have my dog-skin bicycling gloves in my pocket. Fortunately, however, I did not carry out this crude idea too hastily; for next instant it occurred to me that I could not swarm up again. I have had no practice in rope-climbing. Here was a problem. But the moment suggested its own solution. I began making knots, or rather nooses or loops, in the rope, at intervals of about eighteen inches. "What are they for?" Elsie asked, looking on in wonder.

"Footholds, to climb up by."

"But the ones above will pull out with your weight."

"I don't think so. Still, to make sure, I shall tie them with this string. I *must* get down to him."

I threaded a sufficient number of loops, trying the length over the edge. Then I said to Elsie, who sat cowering, propped against the crag, "You must come and look over, and do as I wave to you. Mind, dear, you *must*! Two lives depend upon it."

"Brownie, I daren't? I shall turn giddy and fall over!"

I smoothed her golden hair. "Elsie, dear," I said gently, gazing into her blue eyes, "you are a woman. A woman can always be brave, where those she loves are concerned; and I believe you love me." I led her, coaxingly, to the edge. "Sit there," I said, in my quietest voice, so as not to alarm her. "You can lie at full length, if you like, and only just peep over. But when I wave my hand, remember, you must pull the rope up."

She obeyed me like a child. I knew she loved me.

I gripped the rope and let myself down, not using the loops to descend, but just sliding with hands and knees, and allowing the knots to slacken my pace. Half-way down, I will confess, the eerie feeling of physical suspense was horrible. One hung so in mid-air! The hawks flapped their wings. But Harold was below; and a woman can always be brave where those she loves—well, just that moment, catching my breath, I knew I loved Harold.

I glided down swiftly. The air whizzed. At last, on a narrow shelf of rock, I leant over him. He seized my hand. "I knew you would come!" he cried. "I felt sure you would find out. Though, *how* you found out, Heaven only knows, you clever, brave little woman!"

"Are you terribly hurt?" I asked, bending close. His clothes were torn.

"I hardly know. I can't move. It may only be bruises."

"Can you climb by these nooses with my help?"

He shook his head. "Oh, no. I couldn't climb at all. I must be lifted, somehow. You had better go back to Lungern and bring men to help you."

"And leave you here alone! Never, Harold; never!"

"Then what can we do?"

I reflected a moment. "Lend me your pencil," I said. He pulled it out—his arms were almost unhurt, fortunately. I scribbled a line to Elsie. "Tie my plaid to the rope and let it down." Then I waved to her to pull up again.

I was half surprised to find she obeyed the signal, for she crouched there, white-faced and open-mouthed, watching; but I have often observed that women are almost always brave in the great emergencies. She pinned on the plaid and let it down with commendable quickness. I doubled it, and tied firm knots in the four corners, so as to make it into a sort of basket; then I fastened it at each corner with a piece of the rope, crossed in the middle, till it looked like one of the cages they use in mills for letting down sacks with. As soon as it was finished, I said, "Now, just try to crawl into it."

He raised himself on his arms and crawled in with difficulty. His legs dragged after him. I could see he was in great pain. But still, he managed it.

I planted my foot in the first noose. "You must sit still," I said, breathless. "I am going back to haul you up."

"Are you strong enough, Lois?"

"With Elsie to help me, yes. I often stroked a four at Girton."

"I can trust you," he answered. It thrilled me that he said so.

I began my hazardous journey; I mounted the rope by the nooses—one, two, three, four, counting them as I mounted. I did not dare to look up or down as I did so, lest I should grow giddy and fall, but kept my eyes fixed firmly always on the one noose in front of me. My brain swam: the rope swayed and creaked. Twenty, thirty, forty! Foot after foot, I slipped them in mechanically, taking up with me the longer coil whose ends were attached to the cage and Harold. My hands trembled; it was ghastly, swinging there between earth and heaven. Forty-five, forty-six, forty-seven— I knew there were forty-eight of them. At last, after some weeks, as it seemed, I reached the summit. Tremulous and half dead, I prised myself over the edge with my hands, and knelt once more on the hill beside Elsie.

She was white, but attentive. "What next, Brownie?" Her voice quivered.

I looked about me. I was too faint and shaky after my perilous ascent to be fit for work, but there was no help for it. What could I use as a pulley? Not a tree grew near; but the stone jammed in the fissure might once more serve my purpose. I tried it again. It had borne my weight; was it strong enough to bear the precious weight of Harold? I tugged at it, and thought so. I passed the rope round it like a pulley, and then tied it about my own waist. I had a happy thought: I could use myself as a windlass. I turned on my feet for a pivot. Elsie helped me to pull. "Up you go!" I cried, cheerily. We wound slowly, for fear of shaking him. Bit by bit, I could feel the cage rise gradually from the ground; its weight, taken so, with living capstan and stone axle, was less than I should have expected. But the pulley helped us, and Elsie, spurred by need, put forth more reserve of nervous strength than I could easily have believed lay in that tiny body. I twisted myself round and round, close to the edge, so as to look over from time to time, but not at all quickly, for fear of dizziness. The rope strained and gave. It was a deadly ten minutes of suspense and anxiety. Twice or thrice as I looked down I saw a spasm of pain break over Harold's face; but when I paused and glanced inquiringly, he motioned me to go on with my venturesome task. There was no turning back now. We had almost got him up when the rope at the edge began to creak ominously.

It was straining at the point where it grated against the brink of the precipice. My heart gave a leap. If the rope broke, all was over.

With a sudden dart forward, I seized it with my hands, below the part that gave; then—one fierce little run back—and I brought him level with the edge. He clutched at Elsie's hand. I turned thrice round, to wind the slack about my body. The taut rope cut deep into my flesh; but nothing mattered now, except to save him. "Catch the cloak, Elsie!" I cried; "catch it: pull him gently in!" Elsie caught it and pulled him in, with wonderful pluck and calmness. We hauled him over the edge. He lay safe on the bank. Then we all three broke down and cried like children together. I took his hand in mine and held it in silence.

When we found words again I drew a deep breath, and said, simply, "How did you manage to do it?"

"I tried to clamber past the wall that barred the way there by sheer force of stride—you know, my legs are long—and I somehow overbalanced myself. But I didn't exactly fall—if I had fallen, I must have been killed; I rolled and slid down, clutching at the weeds in the crannies as I slipped, and stumbling over the projections, without quite losing my foothold on the ledges, till I found myself brought up short with a bump at the end of it."

"And you think no bones are broken?"

"I can't feel sure. It hurts me horribly to move. I fancy just at first I must have fainted. But I'm inclined to guess I'm only sprained and bruised and sore all over. Why, you're as bad as me, I believe. See, your dear hands are all torn and bleeding!"

"How are we ever to get him back again, Brownie?" Elsie put in. She was paler than ever now, and prostrate with the after-effects of her unwonted effort.

"You are a practical woman, Elsie," I answered. "Stop with him here a minute or two. I'll climb up the hillside and halloo for Ursula and the men from Lungern."

I climbed and hallooed. In a few minutes, worn out as I was, I had reached the path above and attracted their attention. They hurried down to where Harold lay, and, using my cage for a litter, slung on a young fir-trunk, carried him back between them across their shoulders to the village. He pleaded hard to be allowed to remain at the *chalet*, and Elsie joined her prayers to his; but, there, I was adamant. It was not so much what people might say that I minded, but a deeper difficulty. For if once I nursed him through this trouble, how could I or any woman in my place any longer refuse him? So I passed him ruthlessly on to Lungern (though my heart ached for it), and telegraphed at once to his nearest relative, Lady Georgina, to come up and take care of him.

He recovered rapidly. Though sore and shaken, his worst hurts, it turned out, were sprains; and in three or four days he was ready to go on again. I called to see him before he left. I dreaded the interview; for one's own heart is a hard enemy to fight so long: but how could I let him go without one word of farewell to him?

"After this, Lois," he said, taking my hand in his—and I was weak enough, for a moment, to let it lie there—"you *cannot* say No to me!"

Oh, how I longed to fling myself upon him and cry out, "No, Harold, I cannot! I love you too dearly!" But his future and

Marmaduke Ashurst's half million restrained me: for his sake and for my own I held myself in courageously. Though, indeed, it needed some courage and self-control. I withdrew my hand slowly. "Do you remember," I said, "you asked me that first day at Schlangenbad"—it was an epoch to me now, that first day—"whether I was mediæval or modern? And I answered, 'Modern, I hope.' And you said, 'That's well!'— You see, I don't forget the least things you say to me. Well, because I am modern—" my lips trembled and belied me—"I can answer you No. I can even now refuse you. The old-fashioned girl, the mediæval girl, would have held that because she saved your life (if I *did* save your life, which is a matter of opinion) she was bound to marry you. But *I* am modern, and I see things differently. If there were reasons at Schlangenbad which made it impracticable for me to accept you—though my heart pleaded hard—I do not deny it—those reasons cannot have disappeared merely because you have chosen to fall over a precipice, and I have pulled you up again. My decision was founded, you see, not on passing accidents of situation, but on permanent considerations. Nothing has happened in the last three days to affect those considerations. We are still ourselves: you, rich; I, a penniless adventuress. I could not accept you when you asked me at Schlangenbad. On just the same grounds, I cannot accept you now. I do not see how the unessential fact that I made myself into a winch to pull you up the cliff, and that I am still smarting for it—"

He looked me all over comically. "How severe we are!" he cried, in a bantering tone. "And how extremely Girtony! A System of Logic, Ratiocinative and Inductive, by Lois Cayley! What a pity we didn't take a professor's chair. My child that isn't *you*! It's not yourself at all! It's an attempt to be unnaturally and unfemininely reasonable."

Logic fled. I broke down utterly. "Harold," I cried, rising, "I love you! I admit I love you! But I will never marry you—while you have those thousands."

"I haven't got them yet!"

"Or the chance of inheriting them."

He smothered my hand with kisses—for I withdrew my face. "If you admit you love me," he cried, quite joyously, "then all is well. When once a woman admits that, the rest is but a matter of time—and, Lois, I can wait a thousand years for you."

"Not in my case," I answered through my tears. "Not in my case, Harold! I am a modern woman, and what I say I mean. I will renew my promise. If ever you are poor and friendless, come to me; I am yours. Till then, don't harrow me by asking me the impossible!"

I tore myself away. At the hall door, Lady Georgina intercepted me. She glanced at my red eyes. "Then you have taken him?" she cried, seizing my hand.

I shook my head firmly. I could hardly speak. "No, Lady Georgina," I answered, in a choking voice. "I have refused him again. I will not stand in his way. I will not ruin his prospects."

She drew back and let her chin drop. "Well, of all the hard-hearted, cruel, obdurate young women I ever saw in my born days, if you're not the very hardest—"

I half ran from the house. I hurried home to the *chalet*. There, I dashed into my own room, locked the door behind me, flung myself wildly on my bed, and, burying my face in my hands, had a good, long, hard-hearted, cruel, obdurate cry—exactly like any other mediæval woman. It's all very well being modern; but my experience is that, when it comes to a man one loves—well, the Middle Ages are still horribly strong within us.

THE ADVENTURE OF THE
URBANE OLD GENTLEMAN

When Elsie's holidays—I beg pardon, vacation—came to an end, she proposed to return to her High School in London. Zeal for the higher mathematics devoured her. But she still looked so frail, and coughed so often—a perfect *Campo Santo* of a cough—in spite of her summer of open-air exercise, that I positively worried her into consulting a doctor—not one of the Fortescue-Langley order. The report he gave was mildly unfavourable. He spoke disrespectfully of the apex of her right lung. It was not exactly tubercular, he remarked, but he "feared tuberculosis"—excuse the long words; the phrase was his, not mine; I repeat *verbatim*. He vetoed her exposing herself to a winter in London in her present unstable condition. Davos? Well, no. *Not* Davos: with deliberative thumb and finger on close-shaven chin. He judged her too delicate for such drastic remedies. Those high mountain stations suited best the robust invalid, who had dropped by accident into casual phthisis. For Miss Petheridge's case—looking wise—he would not recommend the Riviera, either: too stimulating, too exciting. What this young lady needed most was rest: rest in some agreeable southern town, some city of the soul—say Rome or Florence—where she might find much to interest her, and might forget the apex of her right lung in the new world of art that opened around her.

"Very well," I said, promptly; "that's settled, Elsie. The apex and you shall winter in Florence."

"But, Brownie, can we afford it?"

"Afford it?" I echoed. "Goodness gracious, my dear child, what a bourgeois sentiment! Your medical attendant says to you, 'Go to Florence': and to Florence you must go; there's no getting out of it. Why, even the swallows fly south when their medical attendant tells them England is turning a trifle too cold for them."

"But what will Miss Latimer say? She depends upon me to come back at the beginning of term. She *must* have *somebody* to under-take the higher mathematics."

"And she will get somebody, dear," I answered, calmly. "Don't trouble your sweet little head about that. An eminent statistician has calculated that five hundred and thirty duly qualified young women are now standing four-square in a solid phalanx in the streets of London, all agog to teach the higher mathematics to any-one who wants them at a moment's notice. Let Miss Latimer take her pick of the five hundred and thirty. I'll wire to her at once: 'Elsie Petheridge unable through ill health to resume her duties. Ordered to Florence. Resigns post. Engage substitute.' *That's* the way to do it."

Elsie clasped her small white hands in the despair of the woman who considers herself indispensable—as if we were any of us indis-pensable! "But, dearest, the girls! They'll be *so* disappointed!"

"They'll get over it," I answered, grimly. "There are worse dis-appointments in store for them in life— Which is a fine old crusted platitude worthy of Aunt Susan. Anyhow, I've decided. Look here, Elsie: I stand to you *in loco parentis*." I have already remarked, I think, that she was three years my senior; but I was so pleased with this phrase that I repeated it lovingly. "I stand to you, dear, *in loco parentis*. Now, I can't let you endanger your precious health by returning to town and Miss Latimer this winter. Let us be cat-egorical. I go to Florence; you go with me."

"What shall we live upon?" Elsie suggested, piteously.

"Our fellow-creatures, as usual," I answered, with prompt cal-lousness. "I object to these base utilitarian considerations being imported into the discussion of a serious question. Florence is the city of art; as a woman of culture, it behooves you to revel in it. Your medical attendant sends you there; as a patient and an invalid, you can revel with a clear conscience. Money? Well, money is a secondary matter. All philosophies and all religions agree that money is mere dross, filthy lucre. Rise superior to it. We have a fair sum in hand to the credit of the firm; we can pick up some more, I suppose, in Florence."

"How?"

I reflected. "Elsie," I said, "you are deficient in Faith—which is one of the leading Christian graces. My mission in life is to correct that want in your spiritual nature. Now, observe how beautifully all these events work in together! The winter comes, when no man can bicycle, especially in Switzerland. Therefore, what is the use of my stopping on here after October? Again, in pursuance of my general plan of going round the world, I must get forward to Italy. Your medical attendant considerately orders you at the same time to Florence. In Florence we shall still have chances of selling Manitous, though possibly, I admit, in diminished numbers. I confess at once that people come to Switzerland to tour, and are therefore liable to need our machines; while they go to Florence to look at pictures, and a bicycle would doubtless prove inconvenient in the Uffizi or the Pitti. Still, we *may* sell a few. But I descry another opening. You write shorthand, don't you?"

"A little, dear; only ninety words a minute."

"*That's* not business. Advertise yourself, *à la* Cyrus Hitchcock! Say boldly, 'I write shorthand.' Leave the world to ask, 'How fast?' It will ask it quick enough without your suggesting it. Well, my idea is this. Florence is a town teeming with English tourists of the cultivated classes—men of letters, painters, antiquaries, art-critics. I suppose even art-critics may be classed as cultivated. Such people are sure to need literary aid. We exist, to supply it. We will set up the Florentine School of Stenography and Typewriting. We'll buy a couple of typewriters."

"How can we pay for them, Brownie?"

I gazed at her in despair. "Elsie," I cried, clapping my hand to my head, "you are not practical. Did I ever suggest we should pay for them? I said merely, buy them. Base is the slave that pays. That's Shakespeare. And we all know Shakespeare is the mirror of nature. Argal, it would be unnatural to pay for a typewriter. We will hire a room in Florence (on tick, of course), and begin operations. Clients will flock in; and we tide over the winter. *There's enterprise for you!*" And I struck an attitude.

Elsie's face looked her doubts. I walked across to Mrs. Evelegh's desk, and began writing a letter. It occurred to me that Mr. Hitchcock, who was a man of business, might be able to help a woman of business in this delicate matter. I put the point to him fairly and squarely, without circumlocution; we were going to start an English typewriting office in Florence; what was the ordinary way for people to become possessed of a typewriting machine, without the odious and mercenary preliminary of paying for it? The answer came back with commendable promptitude.

> Dear Miss,—Your spirit of enterprise is really remarkable! I have forwarded your letter to my friends of the Spread Eagle Typewriting and Phonograph Company, Limited, of New York City, informing them of your desire to open an agency for the sale of their machines in Florence, Italy, and giving them my estimate of your business capacities. I have advised their London house to present you with two complimentary machines for your own use and your partner's, and also to supply a number of others for disposal in the city of Florence. If you would further like to undertake an agency for the development of the trade in salt codfish (large quantities of which are, of course, consumed in Catholic Europe), I could put you into communication with my respected friends, Messrs. Abel Woodward and Co., exporters of preserved provisions, St John, Newfoundland. But, perhaps in this suggestion I am not sufficiently high-toned.—Respectfully, Cyrus W. Hitchcock.

The moment had arrived for Elsie to be firm. "I have no prejudice against trade, Brownie," she observed emphatically; "but I do draw the line at salt fish."

"So do I, dear," I answered.

She sighed her relief. I really believe she half expected to find me trotting about Florence with miscellaneous samples of Messrs. Abel Woodward's esteemed productions protruding from my pocket.

So to Florence we went. My first idea was to travel by the Brenner route through the Tyrol; but a queer little episode which met us at the outset on the Austrian frontier put a check to this plan. We cycled to the border, sending our trunks on by rail. When we went to claim them at the Austrian Custom-house, we were told they were detained "for political reasons."

"Political reasons?" I exclaimed, nonplussed.

"Even so, Fräulein. Your boxes contain revolutionary literature."

"Some mistake!" I cried, warmly. I am but a drawing-room Socialist.

"Not at all; look here." And he drew a small book out of Elsie's portmanteau.

What? Elsie a conspirator? Elsie in league with Nihilists? So mild and so meek! I could never have believed it. I took the book in my hands and read the title, "Revolution of the Heavenly Bodies."

"But this is astronomy," I burst out. "Don't you see? Sun-and-star circling. The revolution of the planets."

"It matters not, Fräulein. Our instructions are strict. We have orders to intercept *all* revolutionary literature without distinction."

"Come, Elsie," I said, firmly, "this is *too* ridiculous. Let us give them a clear berth, these Kaiserly-Kingly blockheads!" So we registered our luggage right back to Lucerne, and cycled over the Gotthard.

When at last, by leisurely stages, we arrived at Florence, I felt there was no use in doing things by halves. If you are going to start the Florentine School of Stenography and Typewriting, you may as well start it on a proper basis. So I took sunny rooms at a nice hotel for myself and Elsie, and hired a ground floor in a convenient house, close under the shadow of the great marble Campanile. (Considerations of space compel me to curtail the usual gush about Arnolfo and Giotto.) This was our office. When I had got a Tuscan painter to plant our flag in the shape of a sign-board, I

sailed forth into the street and inspected it from outside with a
swelling heart. It is true, the Tuscan painter's unaccountable pre-
dilection for the rare spellings "Scool" without an *h* and "Steno-
grafy" with an *f*, somewhat damped my exuberant pride for the
moment; but I made him take the board back and correct his
Italianate English. As soon as all was fitted up with desk and tables
we reposed upon our laurels, and waited only for customers in
shoals to pour in upon us. *I* called them "customers"; Elsie maintained that we ought rather to say "clients." Being by temperament
averse to sectarianism, I did not dispute the point with her.

We reposed on our laurels—in vain. Neither customers nor clients seemed in any particular hurry to disturb our leisure.

I confess I took this ill. It was a rude awakening. I had begun
to regard myself as the special favourite of a fairy godmother; it
surprised me to find that any undertaking of mine did not succeed
immediately. However, reflecting that my fairy godmother's name
was really Enterprise, I recalled Mr. Cyrus W. Hitchcock's advice,
and advertised.

"There's one good thing about Florence, Elsie," I said, just to
keep up her courage. "When the customers *do* come, they'll be interesting people, and it will be interesting work. Artistic work, don't
you know—Fra Angelico, and Della Robbia, and all that sort of
thing; or else fresh light on Dante and Petrarch!"

"When they *do* come, no doubt," Elsie answered, dubiously.
"But do you know, Brownie, it strikes me there isn't quite that literary stir and ferment one might expect in Florence. Dante and
Petrarch appear to be dead. The distinguished authors fail to
stream in upon us as one imagined with manuscripts to copy."

I affected an air of confidence—for I had sunk capital in the
concern (that's business-like—sunk capital!). "Oh, we're a new
firm," I assented, carelessly. "Our enterprise is yet young. When
cultivated Florence learns we're here, cultivated Florence will in-
vade us in its thousands."

But we sat in our office and bit our thumbs all day; the thousands stopped at home. We had ample opportunities for making
studies of the decorative detail on the Campanile, till we knew every

square inch of it better than Mr. Ruskin. Elsie's notebook contains, I believe, eleven hundred separate sketches of the Campanile, from the right end, the left end, and the middle of our window, with eight hundred and five distinct distortions of the individual statues that adorn its niches on the side turned towards us.

At last, after we had sat, and bitten our thumbs, and sketched the Four Greater Prophets for a fortnight on end, an immense excitement occurred. An old gentleman was distinctly seen to approach and to look up at the sign-board which decorated our office.

I instantly slipped in a sheet of foolscap, and began to typewrite with alarming speed—click, click, click; while Elsie, rising to the occasion, set to work to transcribe imaginary shorthand as if her life depended upon it.

The old gentleman, after a moment's hesitation, lifted the latch of the door somewhat nervously. I affected to take no notice of him, so breathless was the haste with which our immense business connection compelled me to finger the keyboard: but, looking up at him under my eyelashes, I could just make out he was a peculiarly bland and urbane old person, dressed with the greatest care, and some attention to fashion. His face was smooth; it tended towards portliness.

He made up his mind, and entered the office. I continued to click till I had reached the close of a sentence—"Or to take arms against a sea of troubles, and by opposing, end them." Then I looked up sharply. "Can I do anything for you?" I inquired, in the smartest tone of business. (I observe that politeness is not professional.)

The Urbane Old Gentleman came forward with his hat in his hand. He looked as if he had just landed from the Eighteenth Century. His figure was that of Mr. Edward Gibbon. "Yes, madam," he said, in a markedly deferential tone, fussing about with the rim of his hat as he spoke, and adjusting his *pince-nez*. "I was recommended to your—ur—your establishment for shorthand and typewriting. I have some work which I wish done, if it falls within your province. But I am *rather* particular. I require a quick worker. Excuse my asking it, but how many words can you do a minute?"

"Shorthand?" I asked, sharply, for I wished to imitate official habits.

The Urbane Old Gentleman bowed. "Yes, shorthand. Certainly."

I waved my hand with careless grace towards Elsie—as if these things happened to us daily. "Miss Petheridge undertakes the short-hand department," I said, with decision. "I am the typewriting from dictation. Miss Petheridge, forward!"

Elsie rose to it like an angel. "A hundred," she answered, con-fronting him.

The old gentleman bowed again. "And your terms?" he inquired, in a honey-tongued voice. "If I may venture to ask them."

We handed him our printed tariff. He seemed satisfied.

"Could you spare me an hour this morning?" he asked, still fin-gering his hat nervously with his puffy hand. "But perhaps you are engaged. I fear I intrude upon you."

"Not at all," I answered, consulting an imaginary engagement list. "This work can wait. Let me see: 11.30. Elsie, I think you have nothing to do before one, that cannot be put off? Quite so!—very well, then; yes, we are both at your service."

The Urbane Old Gentleman looked about him for a seat. I pushed him our one easy chair. He withdrew his gloves with great deliberation, and sat down in it with an apologetic glance. I could gather from his dress and his diamond pin that he was wealthy. Indeed, I half guessed who he was already. There was a fussiness about his manner which seemed strangely familiar to me.

He sat down by slow degrees, edging himself about till he was thoroughly comfortable. I could see he was of the kind that will have comfort. He took out his notes and a packet of letters, which he sorted slowly. Then he looked hard at me and at Elsie. He seemed to be making his choice between us. After a time he spoke. "I *think*," he said, in a most leisurely voice, "I will not trouble your friend to write shorthand for me, after all. Or should I say your assistant? Excuse my change of plan. I will content myself with dictation. You can follow on the machine?"

"As fast as you choose to dictate to me."

He glanced at his notes and began a letter. It was a curious communication. It seemed to be all about buying Bertha and selling Clara—a cold-blooded proceeding which almost suggested slave-dealing. I gathered he was giving instructions to his agent: could he have business relations with Cuba, I wondered. But there were also hints of mysterious middies—brave British tars to the rescue, possibly! Perhaps my bewilderment showed itself upon my face, for at last he looked queerly at me. "You don't quite like this, I'm afraid," he said, breaking off short.

I was the soul of business. "Not at all," I answered. "I am an automaton—nothing more. It is a typewriter's function to transcribe the words a client dictates as if they were absolutely meaningless to her."

"Quite right," he answered, approvingly. "Quite right. I see you understand. A very proper spirit!"

Then the Woman within me got the better of the Typewriter. "Though I confess," I continued, "I *do* feel it is a little unkind to sell Clara at once for whatever she will fetch. It seems to me—well—unchivalrous."

He smiled, but held his peace.

"Still—the middies," I went on: "they will perhaps take care that these poor girls are not ill-treated."

He leaned back, clasped his hands, and regarded me fixedly. "Bertha," he said, after a pause, "is Brighton A's—to be strictly correct, London, Brighton, and South Coast First Preference Debentures. Clara is Glasgow and South-Western Deferred Stock. Middies are Midland Ordinary. But I respect your feeling. You are a young lady of principle." And he fidgeted more than ever.

He went on dictating for just an hour. His subject-matter bewildered me. It was all about India Bills, and telegraphic transfers, and selling cotton short, and holding tight to Egyptian Unified. Markets, it seemed, were glutted. Hungarians were only to be dealt in if they hardened—hardened sinners I know, but what are hardened Hungarians? And fears were not unnaturally expressed that Turks might be "irregular," Consols, it appeared, were certain

to give way for political reasons; but the downward tendency of
Australians, I was relieved to learn, for the honour of so great a
group of colonies, could only be temporary. Greeks were growing
decidedly worse, though I had always understood Greeks were bad
enough already; and Argentine Central were likely to be weak; but
Provincials must soon become commendably firm, and if Uruguays
went flat, something good ought to be made out of them. Scotch
rails might shortly be quiet— I always understood they were based
upon sleepers; but if South-Eastern stiffened, advantage should
certainly be taken of their stiffening. He would telegraph particulars on Monday morning. And so on till my brain reeled. Oh, artistic Florence! was *this* the Filippo Lippi, the Michael Angelo I
dreamed of?

At the end of the hour, the Urbane Old Gentleman rose ur-
banely. He drew on his gloves again with the greatest deliberation, and hunted for his stick as if his life depended upon it. "Let
me see; I had a pencil; oh, thanks; yes, that is it. This cover pro-
tects the point. My hat? Ah, certainly. And my notes; much obliged;
notes *always* get mislaid. People are so careless. Then I will come
again to-morrow; the same hour, if you will kindly keep yourself
disengaged. Though, excuse me, you had better make an entry of
it at once upon your agenda."

"I shall remember it," I answered, smiling.

"No; will you? But you haven't my name."

"I know it," I answered. "At least, I think so. You are Mr.
Marmaduke Ashurst. Lady Georgina Fawley sent you here."

He laid down his hat and gloves again, so as to regard me more
undistracted. "You are a most remarkable young lady," he said, in a
very slow voice. "I impressed upon Georgina that she must not mention to you that I was coming. How on earth did you recognise me?"

"Intuition, most likely."

He stared at me with a sort of suspicion. "*Please* don't tell me
you think me like my sister," he went on. "For though, of course,
every right-minded man feels—ur—a natural respect and affection
for the members his family—bows, if I may so say, to the inscrutable decrees of Providence—which has mysteriously burdened him

with them—still, there *are* points about Lady Georgina which I cannot conscientiously assert I approve of."

I remembered "Marmy's a fool," and held my tongue judiciously.

"I do not resemble her, I hope," he persisted, with a look which I could almost describe as wistful.

"A family likeness, perhaps," I put in. "Family likenesses exist, you know—often with complete divergence of tastes and character."

He looked relieved. "That is true. Oh, how true! But the likeness in my case, I must admit, escapes me."

I temporised. "Strangers see these things most," I said, airing the stock platitudes. "It may be superficial. And, of course, one knows that profound differences of intellect and moral feeling often occur within the limits of a single family."

"You are quite right," he said, with decision. "Georgina's principles are not mine. Excuse my remarking it, but you seem to be a young lady of unusual penetration."

I saw he took my remark as a compliment. What I really meant to say was that a commonplace man might easily be brother to so clever a woman as Lady Georgina.

He gathered up his hat, his stick, his gloves, his notes, and his typewritten letters, one by one, and backed out politely. He was a punctilious millionaire. He had risen by urbanity to his brother directors, like a model guinea-pig. He bowed to us each separately as if we had been duchesses.

As soon as he was gone, Elsie turned to me. "Brownie, how on earth did you guess it? They're so awfully different!"

"Not at all," I answered. "A few surface unlikenesses only just mask an underlying identity. Their features are the same; but his are plump; hers, shrunken. Lady Georgina's expression is sharp and worldly; Mr. Ashurst's is smooth, and bland, and financial. And then their manner! Both are fussy; but Lady Georgina's is honest, open, ill-tempered fussiness; Mr. Ashurst's is concealed under an artificial mask of obsequious politeness. One's cantankerous; the other's only pernicketty. It's one tune, after all, in two different keys."

From that day forth, the Urbane Old Gentleman was a daily
visitor. He took an hour at a time at first; but after a few days, the
hour lengthened out (apologetically) to an entire morning. He "pre-
sumed to ask" my Christian name the second day, and remembered
my father—"a man of excellent principles." But he didn't care for
Elsie to work for him. Fortunately for her, other work dropped in,
once we had found a client, or else, poor girl, she would have felt
sadly slighted. I was glad she had something to do; the sense of
dependence weighed heavily upon her.

The Urbane Old Gentleman did not confine himself entirely,
after the first few days, to Stock Exchange literature. He was engaged on a Work—he spoke of it always with bated breath, and a
capital letter was implied in his intonation; the Work was one on
the Interpretation of Prophecy. Unlike Lady Georgina, who was
tart and crisp, Mr. Marmaduke Ashurst was devout and decorous;
where she said "pack of fools," he talked with unction of "the mental deficiencies of our poorer brethren." But his religious opinions
and his stockbroking had got strangely mixed up at the wash somehow. He was convinced that the British nation represented the Lost
Ten Tribes of Israel—and in particular Ephraim—a matter on
which, as a mere lay-woman, I would not presume either to agree
with him or to differ from him. "That being so, Miss Cayley, we
can easily understand that the existing commercial prosperity of
England depends upon the promises made to Abraham."

I assented, without committing myself. "It would seem to follow."

Mr. Ashurst, encouraged by so much assent, went on to unfold
his System of Interpretation, which was of a strictly commercial
or company-promoting character. It ran like a prospectus. "We
have inherited the gold of Australia and the diamonds of the Cape,"
he said, growing didactic, and lifting one fat forefinger; "we are
now inheriting Klondike and the Rand, for it is morally certain that
we shall annex the Transvaal. Again, 'the chief things of the ancient mountains, and the precious things of the everlasting hills.'
What does that mean? The ancient mountains are clearly the
Rockies; can the everlasting hills be anything but the Himalayas?
'For they shall suck of the abundance of the seas'—that refers, of

course, to our world-wide commerce, due mainly to imports—'and of the treasures hid in the sand.' Which sand? Undoubtedly, I say, the desert of Mount Sinai. What then is our obvious destiny? A lady of your intelligence must gather at once that it is—?" He paused and gazed at me.

"To drive the Sultan out of Syria," I suggested tentatively, "and to annex Palestine to our practical province of Egypt?"

He leaned back in his chair and folded his fat hands in undisguised satisfaction. "Now, you are a thinker of exceptional penetration," he broke out. "Do you know, Miss Cayley, I have tried to make that point clear to the War Office, and the Prime Minister, and many leading financiers in the City of London, and I *can't* get them to see it. They have no heads, those people. But *you* catch at it at a glance. Why, I endeavoured to interest Rothschild and induce him to join me in my Palestine Development Syndicate, and, will you believe it, the man refused point blank. Though if he had only looked at Nahum iii. 17—"

"Mere financiers," I said, smiling, "will not consider these questions from a historical and prophetic point of view. They see nothing above percentages."

"That's it," he replied, lighting up. "They have no higher feelings. Though, mind you, there will be dividends too; mark my words, there will be dividends. This syndicate, besides fulfilling the prophecies, will pay forty per cent on every penny embarked in it."

"Only forty per cent for Ephraim!" I murmured, half below my breath. "Why, Judah is said to batten upon sixty."

He caught at it eagerly, without perceiving my gentle sarcasm.

"In that case, we might even expect seventy," he put in with a gasp of anticipation. "Though I approached Rothschild first with my scheme on purpose, so that Israel and Judah might once more unite in sharing the promises."

"Your combined generosity and commercial instinct does you credit," I answered. "It is rare to find so much love for an abstract study side by side with such conspicuous financial ability."

His guilelessness was beyond words. He swallowed it like an infant. "So I think," he answered. "I am glad to observe that you understand my character. Mere City men don't. They have no soul above shekels. Though, as I show them, there are shekels in it, too. Dividends, dividends, di-vidends. But *you* are a lady of understanding and comprehension. You have been to Girton, haven't you? Perhaps you read Greek, then?"

"Enough to get on with."

"Could you look things up in Herodotus?"

"Certainly?"

"In the original?"

"Oh, dear, yes."

He regarded me once more with the same astonished glance. His own classics, I soon learnt, were limited to the amount which a public school succeeds in dinning, during the intervals of cricket and football, into an English gentleman. Then he informed me that he wished me to hunt up certain facts in Herodotus "and elsewhere" confirmatory of his view that the English were the descendants of the Ten Tribes. I promised to do so, swallowing even that comprehensive "elsewhere." It was none of my business to believe or disbelieve: I was paid to get up a case, and I got one up to the best of my ability. I imagine it was at least as good as most other cases in similar matters: at any rate, it pleased the old gentleman vastly.

By dint of listening, I began to like him. But Elsie couldn't bear him. She hated the fat crease at the back of his neck, she told me.

After a week or two devoted to the Interpretation of Prophecy on a strictly commercial basis of Founders' Shares, with interludes of mining engineers' reports upon the rubies of Mount Sinai and the supposed auriferous quartzites of Palestine, the Urbane Old Gentleman trotted down to the office one day, carrying a packet of notes of most voluminous magnitude. "Can we work in a room alone this morning, Miss Cayley?" he asked, with mystery in his voice: he was always mysterious. "I want to intrust you with a piece of work of an exceptionally private and confidential character. It concerns Property. In point of fact," he dropped his voice to a whisper. "I want you to draw up my will for me."

"Certainly," I said, opening the door into the back office. But I trembled in my shoes. Could this mean that he was going to draw up a will, disinheriting Harold Tillington?

And, suppose he did, what then? My heart was in a tumult. If Harold were rich—well and good, I could never marry him. But, if Harold were poor— I must keep my promise. Could I wish him to be rich? Could I wish him to be poor? My heart stood divided two ways within me.

The Urbane Old Gentleman began with immense deliberation, as befits a man of principle when Property is at stake. "You will kindly take down notes from my dictation," he said, fussing with his papers; "and afterwards, I will ask you to be so good as to copy it all out fair on your typewriter for signature."

"Is a typewritten form legal?" I ventured to inquire.

"A most perspicacious young lady!" he interjected, well pleased. "I have investigated that point, and find it perfectly regular. Only, if I may venture to say so, there should be no erasures."

"There shall be none," I answered.

The Urbane Old Gentleman leant back in his easy chair, and began dictating from his notes with tantalising deliberateness. This was the last will and testament of him, Marmaduke Courtney Ashurst. Its verbiage wearied me. I was eager for him to come to the point about Harold. Instead of that, he did what it seems is usual in such cases—set out with a number of unimportant legacies to old family servants and other hangers-on among "our poorer brethren." I fumed and fretted inwardly. Next came a series of quaint bequests of a quite novel character. "I give and bequeath to James Walsh and Sons, of 720 High Holborn, London, the sum of Five Hundred Pounds, in consideration of the benefit they have conferred upon humanity by the invention of a sugar-spoon or silver sugar-sifter, by means of which it is possible to dust sugar upon a tart or pudding without letting the whole or the greater part of the material run through the apertures uselessly in transit. You must have observed, Miss Cayley—with your usual perspicacity— that most sugar-sifters allow the sugar to fall through them on to the table prematurely."

"I have noticed it," I answered, trembling with anxiety.

"James Walsh and Sons, acting on a hint from me, have succeeded in inventing a form of spoon which does not possess that regrettable drawback. 'Run through the apertures uselessly

in transit,' I think I said last. Yes, thank you. Very good. We will
now continue. And I give and bequeath the like sum of Five Hundred Pounds—did I say, free of legacy duty? No? Then please add
it to James Walsh's clause. Five Hundred Pounds, free of legacy
duty, to Thomas Webster Jones, of Wheeler Street, Soho, for his
admirable invention of a pair of braces which will not slip down
on the wearer's shoulders after half an hour's use. Most braces,
you must have observed, Miss Cayley—"

"My acquaintance with braces is limited, not to say abstract," I
interposed, smiling.

He gazed at me, and twirled his fat thumbs.

"*Of* course," he murmured. "*Of* course. But most braces, you
may not be aware, slip down unpleasantly on the shoulder-blade,
and so lead to an awkward habit of hitching them up by the sleeve-
hole of the waistcoat at frequent intervals. Such a habit must be
felt to be ungraceful. Thomas Webster Jones, to whom I pointed
out this error of manufacture, has invented a brace the two halves
of which diverge at a higher angle than usual, and fasten further
towards the centre of the body in front—pardon these details—so
as to obviate that difficulty. He has given me satisfaction, and he
deserves to be rewarded."

I heard through it all the voice of Lady Georgina observing,
tartly, "Why the idiots can't make braces to fit one at first passes
my comprehension. But, there, my dear; the people who manufacture them are a set of born fools, and what can you expect from an
imbecile?" Mr. Ashurst was Lady Georgina, veneered with a thin
layer of ingratiating urbanity. Lady Georgina was clever, and therefore acrimonious. Mr. Ashurst was astute, and therefore obsequious.

He went on with legacies to the inventor of a sauce-bottle which
did not let the last drop dribble down so as to spot the table-cloth;
of a shoe-horn the handle of which did not come undone; and of a
pair of sleeve-links which you could put off and on without injury
to the temper. "A real benefactor, Miss Cayley; a real benefactor
to the link-wearing classes; for he has sensibly diminished the average annual output of profane swearing."

When he left Five Hundred Pounds to his faithful servant Frederic Higginson, courier, I was tempted to interpose; but I refrained in time, and I was glad of it afterwards.

At last, after many divagations, my Urbane Old Gentleman arrived at the central point—"and I give and bequeath to my nephew, Harold Ashurst Tillington, Younger of Gledcliffe, Dumfriesshire, attaché to Her Majesty's Embassy at Rome—"

I waited, breathless.

He was annoyingly dilatory. "My house and estate of Ashurst Court, in the County of Gloucester, and my town house at 24 Park Lane North, in London, together with the residue of all my estate, real or personal—" and so forth.

I breathed again. At least, I had not been called upon to disinherit Harold.

"Provided always—" he went on, in the same voice.

I wondered what was coming.

"Provided always that the said Harold Ashurst Tillington does not marry—leave a blank there, Miss Cayley. I will find out the name of the young person I desire to exclude, and fill it in afterward. I don't recollect it at this moment, but Higginson, no doubt, will be able to supply the deficiency. In fact, I don't think I ever heard it; though Higginson has told me all about the woman."

"Higginson?" I inquired. "Is he here?"

"Oh, dear, yes. You heard of him, I suppose, from Georgina. Georgina is prejudiced. He has come back to me, I am glad to say. An excellent servant, Higginson, though a trifle too omniscient. All men are equal in the eyes of their Maker, of course; but we must have due subordination. A courier ought not to be better informed than his master—or ought at least to conceal the fact dexterously. Well, Higginson knows this young person's name; my sister wrote to me about her disgraceful conduct when she first went to Schlangenbad. An adventuress, it seems; an adventuress; quite a shocking creature. Foisted herself upon Lady Georgina in Kensington Gardens—unintroduced, if you can believe such a thing—with the most astonishing effrontery; and Georgina, who will forgive anything on earth, for the sake of what she calls originality—another name for impudence, as I am sure you must know—took the young woman with her as her maid to Germany. There, this minx tried to set her cap at my nephew Harold, who can be caught at once by a pretty face; and Harold was bowled over—almost got engaged to her. Georgina took a fancy to the girl later, having a taste for dubious people (I cannot say I approve of Georgina's friends), and wrote again to say her first suspicions were unfounded: the young woman was in reality a paragon of virtue. But *I* know better than that. Georgina has no judgment. I regret to be obliged to confess it, but cleverness, I fear, is the only thing in the world my excellent sister cares for. The hussy, it seems, was certainly clever. Higginson has told me about her. He says her bare appearance would suffice to condemn her—a bold, fast, shameless, brazen-faced creature. But you will forgive me, I am sure, my dear young lady: I ought not to discuss such painted Jezebels before you. We will leave this person's name blank. I will not sully your pen—I mean, your typewriter—by asking you to transcribe it."

I made up my mind at once. "Mr. Ashurst," I said, looking up from my keyboard, "*I* can give you this girl's name; and then you can insert the proviso immediately."

"*You* can? My dear young lady, what a wonderful person you are! You seem to know everybody, and everything. But perhaps she was at Schlangenbad with Lady Georgina, and you were there also?"

"She was," I answered, deliberately. "The name you want is—Lois Cayley!"

He let his notes drop in his astonishment.

I went on with my typewriting, unmoved. "Provided always that the said Harold Ashurst Tillington does not marry Lois Cayley; in which case I will and desire that the said estate shall pass to—whom shall I put in, Mr. Ashurst?"

He leant forward with his fat hands on his ample knees. "It was really *you*?" he inquired, open-mouthed.

I nodded. "There is no use in denying the truth. Mr. Tillington did ask me to be his wife, and I refused him."

"But, my dear Miss Cayley—"

"The difference in station?" I said; "the difference, still greater, in this world's goods? Yes, I know. I admit all that. So I declined his offer. I did not wish to ruin his prospects."

The Urbane Old Gentleman eyed me with a sudden tenderness in his glance. "Young men are lucky," he said, slowly, after a short pause; "—and—Higginson is an idiot. I say it deliberately—an idiot! How could one dream of trusting the judgment of a flunkey about a lady? My dear, excuse the familiarity from one who may consider himself in a certain sense a contingent uncle—suppose we amend the last clause by the omission of the word *not*. It strikes me as superfluous. 'Provided always the said Harold Ashurst Tillington consents to marry'—I think that sounds better!"

He looked at me with such fatherly regard that it pricked my heart ever to have poked fun at his Interpretation of Prophecy on Stock Exchange principles. I think I flushed crimson. "No, no," I answered, firmly. "That will not do either, please. That's worse than the other way. You must not put it, Mr. Ashurst. I could not consent to be willed away to anybody."

He leant forward, with real earnestness. "My dear," he said, "that's not the point. Pardon my reminding you that you are here in your capacity as my amanuensis. I am drawing up my will, and if you will allow me to say so, I cannot admit that anyone has a claim to influence me in the disposition of my Property."

"*Please!*" I cried, pleadingly.

He looked at me and paused. "Well," he went on at last, after a long interval; "since *you* insist upon it, I will leave the bequest to stand without condition."

"Thank you," I murmured, bending low over my machine.

"If I did as I like, though," he went on, "I should say, Unless he marries Miss Lois Cayley (who is a deal too good for him) the estate shall revert to Kynaston's eldest son, a confounded jackass. I do not usually indulge in intemperate language; but I desire to assure you, with the utmost calmness, that Kynaston's eldest son, Lord Southminster, is a con-founded jackass."

I rose and took his hand in my own spontaneously. "Mr. Ashurst," I said, "you may interpret prophecy as long as ever you like, but you are a dear kind old gentleman. I am truly grateful to you for your good opinion."

"And you will marry Harold?"

"Never," I answered; "while he is rich. I have said as much to him."

"That's hard," he went on, slowly. "For . . . I should like to be your uncle."

I trembled all over. Elsie saved the situation by bursting in abruptly.

I will only add that when Mr. Ashurst left, I copied the will out neatly, without erasures. The rough original I threw (somewhat carelessly) into the waste-paper basket.

That afternoon, somebody called to fetch the fair copy for Mr. Ashurst. I went out into the front office to see him. To my surprise, it was Higginson—in his guise as courier.

He was as astonished as myself. "What, *you* here!" he cried. "You dog me!"

"I was thinking the same thing of you, M. le Comte," I answered, curtsying.

He made no attempt at an excuse. "Well, I have been sent for the will," he broke out, curtly.

"And you were sent for the jewel-case," I retorted. "No, no, Dr. Fortescue-Langley; *I* am in charge of the will, and I will take it myself to Mr. Ashurst."

"I will be even with you yet," he snapped out. "I have gone back to my old trade, and am trying to lead an honest life; but *you* won't let me."

"On the contrary," I answered, smiling a polite smile. "I rejoice to hear it. If you say nothing more against me to your employer, I will not disclose to him what I know about you. But if you slander me, I will. So now we understand one another."

And I kept the will till I could give it myself into Mr. Ashurst's own hands in his rooms that evening.

THE ADVENTURE OF
THE UNOBTRUSIVE OASIS

I will not attempt to describe to you the minor episodes of our next twelve months—the manuscripts we type-wrote and the Manitous we sold. 'Tis one of my aims in a world so rich in bores to avoid being tedious. I will merely say, therefore, that we spent the greater part of the year in Florence, where we were building up a connection, but rode back for the summer months to Switzerland, as being a livelier place for the trade in bicycles. The net result was not only that we covered our expenses, but that, as chancellor of the exchequer, I found myself with a surplus in hand at the end of the season.

When we returned to Florence for the winter, however, I confess I began to chafe. "This is slow work, Elsie!" I said. "I started out to go round the world; it has taken me eighteen months to travel no further than Italy! At this rate, I shall reach New York a gray-haired old lady, in a nice lace cap, and totter back into London a venerable crone on the verge of ninety."

However, those invaluable doctors came to my rescue unexpectedly. I do love doctors; they are always sending you off at a moment's notice to delightful places you never dreamt of. Elsie was better, but still far from strong. I took it upon me to consult our medical attendant; and his verdict was decisive. He did just what a doctor ought to do. "She is getting on very well in Florence," he said; "but if you want to restore her health completely, I should advise you to take her for a winter to Egypt. After six months of the dry, warm desert air, I don't doubt she might return to her work in London."

That last point I used as a lever with Elsie. She positively revels in teaching mathematics. At first, to be sure, she objected that we had only just money enough to pay our way to Cairo, and that when we got there we might starve—her favourite programme. I have not this extraordinary taste for starving; *my* idea is, to go where you like, and find something decent to eat when you get there. However, to humour her, I began to cast about me for a source of income. There is no absolute harm in seeing your way clear before you for a twelvemonth, though of course it deprives you of the plot-interest of poverty.

"Elsie," I said, in my best didactic style—I excel in didactics— "you do not learn from the lessons that life sets before you. Look at the stage, for example; the stage is universally acknowledged at the present day to be a great teacher of morals. Does not Irving say so?—and he ought to know. There is that splendid model for imitation, for instance, the Clown in the pantomime. How does Clown regulate his life? Does he take heed for the morrow? Not a bit of it! 'I wish I had a goose,' he says, at some critical juncture; and just as he says it—pat—a super strolls upon the stage with a property goose on a wooden tray; and Clown cries, 'Oh, look here, Joey; *here's* a goose!' and proceeds to appropriate it. Then he puts his fingers in his mouth and observes, 'I wish I had a few apples to make the sauce with'; and as the words escape him—pat again—a small boy with a very squeaky voice runs on, carrying a basket of apples. Clown trips him up, and bolts with the basket. *There's* a model for imitation! The stage sets these great moral lessons before you regularly every Christmas; yet you fail to profit by them. Govern your life on the principles exemplified by Clown; expect to find that whatever you want will turn up with punctuality and dispatch at the proper moment. Be adventurous and you will be happy. Take that as a new maxim to put in your copy-book!"

"I wish I could think so, dear," Elsie answered. "But your confidence staggers me."

That evening at our *table-d'hôte*, however, it was amply justified. A smooth-faced young man of ample girth and most prosperous exterior happened to sit next us. He had his wife with him, so I judged it safe to launch on conversation. We soon found out he was the millionaire editor-proprietor of a great London daily, with many more strings to his journalistic bow; his honoured name was Elworthy. I mentioned casually that we thought of going for the winter to Egypt. He pricked his ears up. But at the time he said nothing. After dinner, we adjourned to the cosy *salon*. I talked to him and his wife; and somehow, that evening, the devil entered into me. I am subject to devils. I hasten to add, they are mild ones. I had one of my reckless moods just then, however, and I reeled off rattling stories of our various adventures. Mr. Elworthy believed in youth and audacity; I could see I interested him. The more he was amused, the more reckless I became. "That's bright," he said at last, when I told him the tale of our amateur exploits in the sale of Manitous. "That would make a good article!"

"Yes," I answered, with bravado, determined to strike while the iron was hot. "What the *Daily Telephone* lacks is just one enlivening touch of feminine brightness."

He smiled. "What is your forte?" he inquired.

"My forte," I answered, "is—to go where I choose, and write what I like about it."

He smiled again. "And a very good new departure in journalism, too! A roving commission! Have you ever tried your hand at writing?"

Had I ever tried! It was the ambition of my life to see myself in print; though, hitherto, it had been ineffectual. "I have written a few sketches," I answered, with becoming modesty. As a matter of fact, our office bulged with my unpublished manuscripts.

"Could you let me see them?" he asked.

I assented, with inner joy, but outer reluctance. "If you wish it," I murmured; "but—you must be *very* lenient!"

Though I had not told Elsie, the truth of the matter was, I had just then conceived an idea for a novel—my *magnum opus*—the setting of which compelled Egyptian local colour; and I was therefore dying to get to Egypt, if chance so willed it. I submitted a few of my picked manuscripts accordingly to Mr. Elworthy, in fear and trembling. He read them, cruel man, before my very eyes; I sat and waited, twiddling my thumbs, demure but apprehensive.

When he had finished, he laid them down.

"Racy!" he said. "Racy! You're quite right, Miss Cayley. That's just what we want on the *Daily Telephone*. I should like to print these three," selecting them out, "at our usual rate of pay per thousand."

"You are very kind." But the room reeled with me.

"Not at all. I am a man of business. And these are good copy. Now, about this Egypt. I will put the matter in the shape of a business proposition. Will you undertake, if I pay your passage, and your friend's, with all travelling expenses, to let me have three descriptive articles a week, on Cairo, the Nile, Syria, and India, running to about two thousand words apiece, at three guineas a thousand?"

My breath came and went. It was positive opulence. The super with the goose couldn't approach it for patness. My editor had brought me the apple sauce as well, without even giving me the trouble of cooking it.

The very next day everything was arranged. Elsie tried to protest, on the foolish ground that she had no money: but the faculty had ordered the apex of her right lung to go to Egypt, and I couldn't let her fly in the face of the faculty. We secured our berths in a P. and O. steamer from Brindisi; and within a week we were tossing upon the bosom of the blue Mediterranean.

People who haven't crossed the blue Mediterranean cherish an absurd idea that it is always calm and warm and sunny. I am sorry to take away any sea's character; but I speak of it as I find it (to borrow a phrase from my old gyp at Girton); and I am bound to admit that the Mediterranean did not treat me as a lady expects to be treated. It behaved disgracefully. People may rhapsodize as long as they choose about a life on the ocean wave; for my own part, I wouldn't give a pin for sea-sickness. We glided down the Adriatic from Brindisi to Corfu with a reckless profusion of lateral motion which suggested the idea that the ship must have been drinking.

I tried to rouse Elsie when we came abreast of the Ionian Islands, and to remind her that "Here was the home of Nausicaa in the Odyssey." Elsie failed to respond; she was otherwise occupied.

At last, I succumbed and gave it up. I remember nothing further till a day and a half later, when we got under lee of Crete, and the ship showed a tendency to resume the perpendicular. Then I began once more to take a languid interest in the dinner question.

I may add parenthetically that the Mediterranean is a mere bit of a sea, when you look at it on the map—a pocket sea, to be regarded with mingled contempt and affection; but you learn to respect it when you find that it takes four clear days and nights of abject misery merely to run across its eastern basin from Brindisi to Alexandria. I respected the Mediterranean immensely while we lay off the Peloponnesus in the trough of the waves with a north wind blowing; I only began to temper my respect with a distant liking when we passed under the welcome shelter of Crete on a calm, star-lit evening.

It was deadly cold. We had not counted upon such weather in the sunny south. I recollected now that the Greeks were wont to represent Boreas as a chilly deity, and spoke of the Thracian breeze with the same deferentially deprecating adjectives which we ourselves apply to the east wind of our fatherland; but that apt classical memory somehow failed to console or warm me. A good-natured male passenger, however, volunteered to ask us, "Will I get ye a rug, ladies?" The form of his courteous question suggested the probability of his Irish origin.

"You are very kind," I answered. "If you don't want it for yourself, I'm sure my friend would be glad to have the use of it."

"Is it meself? Sure I've got me big ulsther, and I'm as warrum as a toast in it. But ye're not provided for this weather. Ye've thrusted too much to those rascals the po-uts. 'Where breaks the blue Sicilian say,' the rogues write. *I'd* like to set them down in it, wid a nor'-easter blowing!"

He fetched up his rug. It was ample and soft, a smooth brown camel-hair. He wrapped us both up in it. We sat late on deck that night, as warm as a toast ourselves, thanks to our genial Irishman.

We asked his name. "'Tis Dr. Macloghlen," he answered. "I'm from County Clare, ye see; and I'm on me way to Egypt for thravel and exploration. Me fader whisht me to see the worruld a bit before I'd

settle down to practise me profession at Liscannor. Have ye ever
been in County Clare? Sure, 'tis the pick of Oireland."

"We have that pleasure still in store," I answered, smiling. "It
spreads gold-leaf over the future, as George Meredith puts it."

"Is it Meredith? Ah, there's the foine writer! 'Tis jaynius the
man has: I can't undtherstand a word of him. But he's half Oirish,
ye know. What proof have I got of it? An' would he write like that
if there wasn't a dhrop of the blood of the Celt in him?"

Next day and next night, Mr. Macloghlen was our devoted slave.
I had won his heart by admitting frankly that his countrywomen
had the finest and liveliest eyes in Europe—eyes with a deep
twinkle, half fun, half passion. He took to us at once, and talked to
us incessantly. He was a red-haired, raw-boned Munster-man, but
a real good fellow. We forgot the aggressive inequalities of the
Mediterranean while he talked to us of "the pizzantry." Late the
second evening he propounded a confidence. It was a lovely night;
Orion overhead, and the plashing phosphorescence on the water
below conspired with the hour to make him specially confidential.
"Now, Miss Cayley," he said, leaning forward on his deck chair,
and gazing earnestly into my eyes, "there's wan question I'd like
to ask ye. The ambition of me life is to get into Parlimint. And I
want to know from ye, as a frind—if I accomplish me heart's wish—
is there annything, in me apparence, ar in me voice, ar in me accent, ar in me manner, that would lade annybody to suppose I was
an Oirishman?"

I succeeded, by good luck, in avoiding Elsie's eye. What on earth
could I answer? Then a happy thought struck me. "Dr. Macloghlen,"
I said, "it would not be the slightest use your trying to conceal it;
for even if nobody ever detected a faint Irish intonation in your
words or phrases—how could your eloquence fail to betray you for
a countryman of Sheridan and Burke and Grattan?"

He seized my hand with such warmth that I thought it best to
hurry down to my state-room at once, under cover of my compliment.

At Alexandria and Cairo we found him invaluable. He looked
after our luggage, which he gallantly rescued from the lean hands
of fifteen Arab porters, all eagerly struggling to gain possession of

our effects; he saw us safe into the train; and he never quitted us till he had safely ensconced us in our rooms at Shepheard's. For himself, he said, with subdued melancholy, 'twas to some cheaper hotel he must go; Shepheard's wasn't for the likes of him; though if land in County Clare was wort' what it ought to be, there wasn't a finer estate in all Oireland than his fader's.

Our Mr. Elworthy was a modern proprietor, who knew how to do things on the lordly scale. Having commissioned me to write this series of articles, he intended them to be written in the first style of art, and he had instructed me accordingly to hire one of Cook's little steam dahabeeahs, where I could work at leisure. Dr. Macloghlen was in his element arranging for the trip. "Sure the only thing I mind," he said, "is—that I'll not be going wid ye." I think he was half inclined to invite himself; but there again I drew a line. I will not sell salt fish; and I will not go up the Nile, unchaperoned, with a casual man acquaintance.

He did the next best thing, however: he took a place in a sailing dahabeeah; and as we steamed up slowly, stopping often on the way, to give me time to write my articles, he managed to arrive almost always at every town or ruin exactly when we did.

I will not describe the voyage. The Nile is the Nile. Just at first, before we got used to it, we conscientiously looked up the name of every village we passed on the bank in our Murray and our Baedeker. After a couple of days' Niling, however, we found that formality quite unnecessary. They were all the same village, under a number of aliases. They did not even take the trouble to disguise themselves anew, like Dr. Fortescue-Langley, on each fresh appearance. They had every one of them a small whitewashed mosque, with a couple of tall minarets; and around it spread a number of mud-built cottages, looking more like bee-hives than human habitations. They had also every one of them a group of date-palms, overhanging a cluster of mean bare houses; and they all alike had a picturesque and even imposing air from a distance, but faded away into indescribable squalor as one got abreast of them. Our progress was monotonous. At twelve, noon, we would pass Aboo-Teeg, with its mosque, its palms, its mud-huts, and its camels; then

for a couple of hours we would go on through the midst of a green
field on either side, studded by more mud-huts, and backed up by
a range of gray desert mountains; only to come at 2 p.m., twenty
miles higher up, upon Aboo-Teeg once more, with the same
mosque, the same mud-huts, and the same haughty camels, placidly chewing the same aristocratic cud, but under the alias of Koos-
kam. After a wild hubbub at the quay, we would leave Koos-kam
behind, with its camels still serenely munching day-before-
yesterday's dinner; and twenty miles further on, again, having
passed through the same green plain, backed by the same gray
mountains, we would stop once more at the identical Koos-kam,
which this time absurdly described itself as Tahtah. But whether it
was Aboo-Teeg or Koos-kam or Tahtah or anything else, only the
name differed: it was always the same town, and had always the
same camels at precisely the same stage of the digestive process.
It seemed to us immaterial whether you saw all the Nile or only
five miles of it. It was just like wall-paper. A sample sufficed; the
whole was the sample infinitely repeated.

However, I had my letters to write, and I wrote them valiantly.
I described the various episodes of the complicated digestive process in the camel in the minutest detail. I gloated over the date-
palms, which I knew in three days as if I had been brought up upon
dates. I gave word-pictures of every individual child, veiled woman,
Arab sheikh, and Coptic priest whom we encountered on the voyage. And I am open to reprint those conscientious studies of mud-
huts and minarets with any enterprising publisher who will make
me an offer.

Another disillusion weighed upon my soul. Before I went up
the Nile, I had a fancy of my own that the bank was studded with
endless ruined temples, whose vast red colonnades were reflected
in the water at every turn. I think Macaulay's Lays were primarily
answerable for that particular misapprehension. As a matter of fact,
it surprised me to find that we often went for two whole days' hard
steaming without ever a temple breaking the monotony of those
eternal date-palms, those calm and superciliously irresponsive
camels. In my humble opinion, Egypt is a fraud; there is too much

Nile—very dirty Nile at that—and not nearly enough temple. Besides, the temples, when you *do* come up with them, are just like the villages; they are the same temple over again, under a different name each time, and they have the same gods, the same kings, the same wearisome bas-reliefs, except that the gentleman in a chariot, ten feet high, who is mowing down enemies a quarter his own size, with unsportsmanslike recklessness, is called Rameses in this place, and Sethi in that, and Amen-hotep in the other. With this trifling variation, when you have seen one temple, one obelisk, one hieroglyphic table, you have seen the whole of Ancient Egypt.

At last, after many days' voyage through the same scenery daily—rising in the morning off a village with a mosque, ten palms, and two minarets, and retiring late at night off the same village once more, with mosque, palms, and minarets, as before, *da capo*— we arrived one evening at a place called Geergeh. In itself, I believe, Geergeh did not differ materially from all the other places we had passed on our voyage: it had its mosque, its ten palms, and its two minarets as usual. But I remember its name, because something mysterious went wrong there with our machinery; and the engineer informed us we must wait at least three days to mend it. Dr. Macloghlen's dahabeeah happened opportunely to arrive at the same spot on the same day; and he declared with fervour he would "see us through our throubles." But what on earth were we to do with ourselves through three long days and nights at Geergeh? There were the ruins of Abydus close at hand, to be sure; though I defy anybody not a professed Egyptologist to give more than one day to the ruins of Abydus. In this emergency, Dr. Macloghlen came gallantly to our aid. He discovered by inquiring from an English-speaking guide that there was an unobtrusive oasis, never visited by Europeans, one long day's journey off, across the desert. As a rule, it takes at least three days to get camels and guides together for such an expedition: for Egypt is not a land to hurry in. But the indefatigable Doctor further unearthed the fact that a sheikh had just come in, who (for a consideration) would lend us camels for a two days' trip; and we seized the chance to do our duty by Mr.

Elworthy and the world-wide circulation. An unvisited oasis—and
two Christian ladies to be the first to explore it: there's journalistic enterprise for you! If we happened to be killed, so much the
better for the *Daily Telephone*. I pictured the excitement at
Piccadilly Circus. "Extra Special, Our Own Correspondent brutally
murdered!" I rejoiced at the opportunity.

I cannot honestly say that Elsie rejoiced with me. She cher-
ished a prejudice against camels, massacres, and the new journalism. She didn't like being murdered: though this was premature,
for she had never tried it. She objected that the fanatical Mohammedans of the Senoosi sect, who were said to inhabit the oasis in
question, might cut our throats for dogs of infidels. I pointed out
to her at some length that it was just that chance which added zest
to our expedition as a journalistic venture: fancy the glory of being
the first lady journalists martyred in the cause! But she failed to
grasp this aspect of the question. However, if I went, she would go
too, she said, like a dear girl that she is: she would not desert me
when I was getting my throat cut.

Dr. Macloghlen made the bargain for us, and insisted on accompanying us across the desert. He told us his method of negotiation
with the Arabs with extreme gusto. "'Is it pay in advance ye want?'
says I to the dirty beggars: 'divvil a penny will ye get till ye bring
these ladies safe back to Geergeh. And remimber, Mr. Sheikh,' says
I, fingering me pistol, so, by way of emphasis, 'we take no money
wid us; so if yer friends at Wadi Bou choose to cut our throats, 'tis
for the pleasure of it they'll be cutting them, not for anything they'll
gain by it.' 'Provisions, effendi?' says he, salaaming. 'Provisions,
is it?' says I. 'Take everything ye'll want wid you; I suppose ye can
buy food fit for a Crischun in the bazaar in Geergeh; and never
wan penny do ye touch for it all till ye've landed us on the bank
again, as safe as ye took us. So if the religious sintiments of the
faithful at Wadi Bou should lade them to hack us to pieces,' says I,
just waving me revolver, 'thin 'tis yerself that will be out of pocket
by it.' And the ould divvil cringed as if he took me for the Prince of
Wales. Faix, 'tis the purse that's the best argumint to catch these
haythen Arabs upon."

When we set out for the desert in the early dawn next day, it looked as if we were starting for a few months' voyage. We had a company of camels that might have befitted a caravan. We had two large tents, one for ourselves, and one for Dr. Macloghlen, with a third to dine in. We had bedding, and cushions, and drinking water tied up in swollen pig-skins, which were really goat-skins, looking far from tempting. We had bread and meat, and a supply of presents to soften the hearts and weaken the religious scruples of the sheikhs at Wadi Bou. "We thravel *en prince*," said the Doctor. When all was ready we got under way solemnly, our camels rising and sniffing the breeze with a superior air, as who should say, "I happen to be going where you happen to be going; but don't for a moment suppose I do it to please you. It is mere coincidence. You are bound for Wadi Bou: I have business of my own which chances to take me there."

Over the incidents of the journey I draw a veil. Riding a camel, I find, does not greatly differ from sea-sickness. They are the same phenomenon under altered circumstances. We had been assured beforehand on excellent authority that "much of the comfort on a desert journey depends upon having a good camel." On this matter, I am no authority. I do not set up as a judge of camel-flesh. But I did not notice *any* of the comfort; so I venture to believe my camel must have been an exceptionally bad one.

We expected trouble from the fanatical natives; I am bound to admit, we had most trouble with Elsie. She was not insubordinate, but she did not care for camel-riding. And her beast took advantage of her youth and innocence. A well-behaved camel should go almost as fast as a child can walk, and should not sit down plump on the burning sand without due reason. Elsie's brute crawled, and called halts for prayer at frequent intervals; it tried to kneel like a good Mussulman many times a day; and it showed an intolerant disposition to crush the infidel by rolling over on top of Elsie. Dr. Macloghlen admonished it with Irish eloquence, not always in language intended for publication; but it only turned up its supercilious lip and inquired in its own unspoken tongue what *he* knew about the desert.

"I feel like a wurrum before the baste," the Doctor said, non-plussed.

If the Nile was monotonous, the road to Wadi Bou was nothing short of dreary. We crossed a great ridge of bare, gray rock, and followed a rolling valley of sand, scored by dry ravines, and baking in the sun. It was ghastly to look upon. All day long, save at the mid-day rest by some brackish wells, we rode on and on, the brutes stepping forward with slow, outstretched legs; though sometimes we walked by the camels' sides to vary the monotony; but ever through that dreary upland plain, sand in the centre, rocky moun-tain at the edge, and not a thing to look at. We were relieved to-wards evening to stumble against stunted tamarisks, half buried in sand, and to feel we were approaching the edge of the oasis.

When at last our arrogant beasts condescended to stop, in their patronising way, we saw by the dim light of the moon a sort of uneven basin or hollow, studded with date-palms, and in the midst of the depression a crumbling walled town, with a whitewashed mosque, two minarets by its side, and a crowd of mud-houses. It was strangely familiar. We had come all this way just to see Aboo-Teeg or Koos-kam over again!

We camped outside the fortified town that night. Next morn-ing we essayed to make our entry.

At first, the servants of the Prophet on watch at the gate raised serious objections. No infidel might enter. But we had a pass from Cairo, exhorting the faithful in the name of the Khedive to give us food and shelter; and after much examination and many loud dis-cussions, the gatemen passed us. We entered the town, and stood alone, three Christian Europeans, in the midst of three thousand fanatical Mohammedans.

I confess it was weird. Elsie shrank by my side. "Suppose they were to attack us, Brownie?"

"Thin the sheikh here would never get paid," Dr. Macloghlen put in with true Irish recklessness. "Faix, he'll whistle for his money on the whistle I gave him." That touch of humour saved us. We laughed; and the people about saw we could laugh. They left off scowling, and pressed around trying to sell us pottery and native brooches. In the intervals of fanaticism, the Arab has an eye to business.

We passed up the chief street of the bazaar. The inhabitants told us in pantomime the chief of the town was away at Asioot, whither he had gone two days ago on business. If he were here, our interpreter gave us to understand, things might have been different; for the chief had determined that, whatever came, no infidel dog should settle in *his* oasis.

The women with their veiled faces attracted us strangely. They were wilder than on the river. They ran when one looked at them. Suddenly, as we passed one, we saw her give a little start. She was veiled like the rest, but her agitation was evident even through her thick covering.

"She is afraid of Christians," Elsie cried, nestling towards me.

The woman passed close to us. She never looked in our direction, but in a very low voice she murmured, as she passed, "Then you are English!"

I had presence of mind enough to conceal my surprise at this unexpected utterance. "Don't seem to notice her, Elsie," I said, looking away. "Yes, we are English."

She stopped and pretended to examine some jewellery on a stall. "So am I," she went on, in the same suppressed low voice. "For Heaven's sake, help me!"

"What are you doing here?"

"I live here—married. I was with Gordon's force at Khartoum. They carried me off. A mere girl then. Now I am thirty."

"And you have been here ever since?"

She turned away and walked off, but kept whispering behind her veil. We followed, unobtrusively. "Yes; I was sold to a man at Dongola. He passed me on again to the chief of this oasis. I don't know where it is; but I have been here ever since. I hate this life. Is there any chance of a rescue?"

"Anny chance of a rescue, is it?" the Doctor broke in, a trifle too ostensibly. "If it costs us a whole British Army, me dear lady, we'll fetch you away and save you."

"But now—to-day? You won't go away and leave me? You are the first Europeans I have seen since Khartoum fell. They may sell me again. You will not desert me?"

"No," I said. "We will not." Then I reflected a moment.

What on earth could we do? This was a painful dilemma. If we once lost sight of her, we might not see her again. Yet if we walked with her openly, and talked like friends, we would betray ourselves, and her, to those fanatical Senoosis.

I made my mind up promptly. I may not have much of a mind; but, such as it is, I flatter myself I can make it up at a moment's notice.

"Can you come to us outside the gate at sunset?" I asked, as if speaking to Elsie.

The woman hesitated. "I think so."

"Then keep us in sight all day, and when evening comes, stroll out behind us."

She turned over some embroidered slippers on a booth, and seemed to be inspecting them. "But my children?" she murmured anxiously.

The Doctor interposed. "Is it childern she has?" he asked. "Thin they'll be the Mohammedan gintleman's. We mustn't interfere wid *them*. We can take away the lady—she's English, and detained against her will: but we can't deprive anny man of his own childern'."

I was firm, and categorical. "Yes, we can," I said, stoutly; "if he has forced a woman to bear them to him whether she would or not. That's common justice. I have no respect for the Mohammedan gentleman's rights. Let her bring them with her. How many are there?"

"Two—a boy and girl; not very old; the eldest is seven." She spoke wistfully. A mother is a mother.

"Then say no more now, but keep us always in sight, and we will keep *you*. Come to us at the gate about sundown. We will carry you off with us."

She clasped her hands and moved off with the peculiar gliding air of the veiled Mohammedan woman. Our eyes followed her. We walked on through the bazaar, thinking of nothing else now. It was strange how this episode made us forget our selfish fears for our own safety. Even dear timid Elsie remembered only that an Englishwoman's life and liberty were at stake. We kept her more or less in view all day. She glided in and out among the people in the alleys. When we went back to the camels at lunch-time, she followed us unobtrusively through the open gate, and sat watching us from a little way off, among a crowd of gazers; for all Wadi Bou was of course agog at this unwonted invasion.

We discussed the circumstance loudly, so that she might hear our plans. Dr. Macloghlen advised that we should tell our sheikh we meant to return part of the way to Geergeh that evening by moonlight. I quite agreed with him. It was the only way out. Besides, I didn't like the looks of the people. They eyed us askance. This was getting exciting now. I felt a professional journalistic interest. Whether we escaped or got killed, what splendid business for the *Daily Telephone*!

The sheikh, of course, declared it was impossible to start that evening. The men wouldn't move—the camels needed rest. But Dr. Macloghlen was inexorable. "Very well, thin, Mr. Sheikh," he answered, philosophically. "Ye'll plaze yerself about whether ye come on wid us or whether ye shtop. That's yer own business. But *we* set out at sundown; and whin ye return by yerself on foot to Geergeh, ye can ask for yer camels at the British Consulate."

All through that anxious afternoon we sat in our tents, under the shade of the mud-wall, wondering whether we could carry out our plan or not. About an hour before sunset the veiled woman strolled out of the gate with her two children. She joined the crowd of sight-seers once more, for never through the day were we left alone for a second. The excitement grew intense. Elsie and I moved up carelessly towards the group, talking as if to one another. I looked hard at Elsie: then I said, as though I were speaking about one of the children, "Go straight along the road to Geergeh till you are past the big clump of palms at the edge of the oasis. Just beyond it comes a sharp ridge of rock. Wait behind the ridge where no one can see you. When we get there," I patted the little girl's head, "don't say a word, but jump on my camel. My two friends will each take one of the children. If you understand and consent, stroke your boy's curls. We will accept that for a signal."

She stroked the child's head at once without the least hesitation. Even through her veil and behind her dress, I could somehow feel and see her trembling nerves, her beating heart. But she gave no overt token. She merely turned and muttered something carelessly in Arabic to a woman beside her.

We waited once more, in long-drawn suspense. Would she manage to escape them? Would they suspect her motives?

After ten minutes, when we had returned to our crouching-place under the shadow of the wall, the woman detached herself slowly from the group, and began strolling with almost overdone nonchalance along the road to Geergeh. We could see the little girl was frightened and seemed to expostulate with her mother: fortunately, the Arabs about were too much occupied in watching the suspicious strangers to notice this episode of their own people. Presently, our new friend disappeared; and, with beating hearts, we awaited the sunset.

Then came the usual scene of hubbub with the sheikh, the camels, the porters, and the drivers. It was eagerness against apathy. With difficulty we made them understand we meant to get under way at all hazards. I stormed in bad Arabic. The Doctor inveighed in very choice Irish. At last they yielded, and set out. One by one the camels rose, bent their slow knees, and began to stalk in their lordly way with outstretched necks along the road to the river. We moved through the palm groves, a crowd of boys following us and shouting for backsheesh. We began to be afraid they would accompany us too far and discover our fugitive; but fortunately they all turned back with one accord at a little whitewashed shrine near the edge of the oasis. We reached the clump of palms; we turned the corner of the ridge. Had we missed one another? No! There, crouching by the rocks, with her children by her side, sat our mysterious stranger.

The Doctor was equal to the emergency. "Make those bastes kneel!" he cried authoritatively to the sheikh.

The sheikh was taken aback. This was a new exploit burst upon him. He flung his arms up, gesticulating wildly. The Doctor, unmoved, made the drivers understand by some strange pantomime what he wanted. They nodded, half terrified. In a second, the stranger was by my side, Elsie had taken the girl, the Doctor the boy, and the camels were passively beginning to rise again. That is the best of your camel. Once set him on his road, and he goes mechanically.

The sheikh broke out with several loud remarks in Arabic, which we did not understand, but whose hostile character could not easily escape us. He was beside himself with anger. Then I was suddenly aware of the splendid advantage of having an Irishman on our side. Dr. Macloghlen drew his revolver, like one well used to such episodes, and pointed it full at the angry Arab. "Look here, Mr. Sheikh," he said, calmly, yet with a fine touch of bravado; "do ye see this revolver? Well, unless ye make yer camels thravel sthraight to Geergeh widout wan other wurrud, 'tis yer own brains will be spattered, sor, on the sand of this desert! And if ye touch wan hair of our heads, ye'll answer for it wid yer life to the British Government."

I do not feel sure that the sheikh comprehended the exact nature of each word in this comprehensive threat, but I am certain he took in its general meaning, punctuated as it was with some flourishes of the revolver. He turned to the drivers and made a gesture of despair. It meant, apparently, that this infidel was too much for him. Then he called out a few sharp directions in Arabic. Next minute, our camels' legs were stepping out briskly along the road to Geergeh with a promptitude which I'm sure must have astonished their owners. We rode on and on through the gloom in a fever of suspense. Had any of the Senoosis noticed our presence? Would they miss the chief's wife before long, and follow us under arms? Would our own sheikh betray us? I am no coward, as women go, but I confess, if it had not been for our fiery Irishman, I should have felt my heart sink. We were grateful to him for the reckless and good-humoured courage of the untamed Celt. It kept us from giving way. "Ye'll take notice, Mr. Sheikh," he said, as we threaded

our way among the moon-lit rocks, "that I have twinty-wan cartridges in me case for me revolver; and that if there's throuble to-
night, 'tis twinty of them there'll be for your frinds the Senoosis,
and wan for yerself; but for fear of disappointing a gintleman, 'tis
yer own special bullet I'll disthribute first, if it comes to fighting."

The sheikh's English was a vanishing quantity, but to judge by
the way he nodded and salaamed at this playful remark, I am convinced he understood the Doctor's Irish quite as well as I did.

We spoke little by the way; we were all far too frightened, except the Doctor, who kept our hearts up by a running fire of wild
Celtic humour. But I found time meanwhile to learn by a few questions from our veiled friend something of her captivity. She had
seen her father massacred before her eyes at Khartoum, and had
then been sold away to a merchant, who conveyed her by degrees
and by various exchanges across the desert through lonely spots
to the Senoosi oasis. There she had lived all those years with the
chief to whom her last purchaser had trafficked her. She did not
even know that her husband's village was an integral part of the
Khedive's territory; far less that the English were now in practical
occupation of Egypt. She had heard nothing and learnt nothing
since that fateful day; she had waited in vain for the off-chance of
a deliverer.

"But did you never try to run away to the Nile?" I cried, astonished.

"Run away? How could I? I did not even know which way the
river lay; and was it possible for me to cross the desert on foot, or
find the chance of a camel? The Senoosis would have killed me.
Even with you to help me, see what dangers surround me; alone, I
should have perished, like Hagar in the wilderness, with no angel
to save me."

"An' ye've got the angel now," Dr. Macloghlen exclaimed, glancing at me. "Steady, there, Mr. Sheikh. What's this that's coming?"

It was another caravan, going the opposite way, on its road to
the oasis! A voice halloaed from it.

Our new friend clung tight to me. "My husband!" she whispered,
gasping.

They were still far off on the desert, and the moon shone bright. A few hurried words to the Doctor, and with a wild resolve we faced the emergency. He made the camels halt, and all of us, springing off, crouched down behind their shadows in such a way that the coming caravan must pass on the far side of us. At the same moment the Doctor turned resolutely to the sheikh. "Look here, Mr. Arab," he said in a quiet voice, with one more appeal to the simple Volapuk of the pointed revolver; "I cover ye wid this. Let these frinds of yours go by. If there's anny unnecessary talking betwixt ye, or anny throuble of anny kind, remimber, the first bullet goes sthraight as an arrow t'rough that haythen head of yours!"

The sheikh salaamed more submissively than ever.

The caravan drew abreast of us. We could hear them cry aloud on either side the customary salutes: "In Allah's name, peace!" answered by "Allah is great; there is no god but Allah."

Would anything more happen? Would our sheikh play us false? It was a moment of breathlessness. We crouched and cowered in the shade, holding our hearts with fear, while the Arab drivers pretended to be unsaddling the camels. A minute or two of anxious suspense; then, peering over our beasts' backs, we saw their long line filing off towards the oasis. We watched their turbaned heads, silhouetted against the sky, disappear slowly. One by one they faded away. The danger was past. With beating hearts we rose up again.

The Doctor sprang into his place and seated himself on his camel. "Now ride on, Mr. Sheikh," he said, "wid all yer men, as if grim death was afther ye. Camels or no camels, ye've got to march all night, for ye'll never draw rein till we're safe back at Geergeh!"

And sure enough we never halted, under the persuasive influence of that loaded revolver, till we dismounted once more in the early dawn upon the Nile bank, under British protection.

Then Elsie and I and our rescued country-woman broke down together in an orgy of relief. We hugged one another and cried like so many children.

THE ADVENTURE OF
THE PEA-GREEN PATRICIAN

Away to India! A life on the ocean wave once more; and—may it prove less wavy!

In plain prose, my arrangement with "my proprietor," Mr. Elworthy (thus we speak in the newspaper trade), included a trip to Bombay for myself and Elsie. So, as soon as we had drained Upper Egypt journalistically dry, we returned to Cairo on our road to Suez. I am glad to say, my letters to the *Daily Telephone* gave satisfaction. My employer wrote, "You are a born journalist." I confess this surprised me; for I have always considered myself a truthful person. Still, as he evidently meant it for praise, I took the doubtful compliment in good part, and offered no remonstrance.

I have a mercurial temperament. My spirits rise and fall as if they were Consols. Monotonous Egypt depressed me, as it depressed the Israelites; but the passage of the Red Sea set me sounding my timbrel. I love fresh air; I love the sea, if the sea will but behave itself; and I positively revelled in the change from Egypt.

Unfortunately, we had taken our passages by a P. and O. steamer from Suez to Bombay many weeks beforehand, so as to secure good berths; and still more unfortunately, in a letter to Lady Georgina, I had chanced to mention the name of our ship and the date of the voyage. I kept up a spasmodic correspondence with Lady Georgina nowadays—tuppence-ha'penny a fortnight; the dear, cantankerous, racy old lady had been the foundation of my fortunes, and I was genuinely grateful to her; or, rather, I ought to say, she had been their second foundress, for I will do myself the justice to admit that the first was my own initiative and enterprise. I flatter myself I have the knack of taking the tide on the turn, and I am justly proud of it. But, being a grateful animal, I wrote once a fortnight to report progress to Lady Georgina. Besides—let me whisper—strictly between ourselves—'twas an indirect way of hearing about Harold.

This time, however, as events turned out, I recognised that I had made a grave mistake in confiding my movements to my shrewd old lady. She did not betray me on purpose, of course; but I gathered later that casually in conversation she must have mentioned the fact and date of my sailing before somebody who ought to have had no concern in it; and the somebody, I found, had governed himself accordingly. All this, however, I only discovered afterwards. So, without anticipating, I will narrate the facts exactly as they occurred to me.

When we mounted the gangway of the *Jumna* at Suez, and began the process of frizzling down the Red Sea, I noted on deck almost at once an odd-looking young man of twenty-two or thereabouts, with a curious faint pea-green complexion. He was the wishy-washiest young man I ever beheld in my life; an achromatic study: in spite of the delicate pea-greenness of his skin, all the colouring matter of the body seemed somehow to have faded out of him. Perhaps he had been bleached. As he leant over the taffrail, gazing down with open mouth and vacant stare at the water, I took a good long look at him. He interested me much—because he was so exceptionally uninteresting; a pallid, anæmic, indefinite hobbledehoy, with a high, narrow forehead, and sketchy features. He had watery, restless eyes of an insipid light blue; thin, yellow hair, almost white in its paleness; and twitching hands that played nervously all the time with a shadowy moustache. This shadowy moustache seemed to absorb as a rule the best part of his attention; it was so sparse and so blanched that he felt it continually—to assure himself, no doubt, of the reality of its existence. I need hardly add that he wore an eye-glass.

He was an aristocrat, I felt sure; Eton and Christ Church: no ordinary person could have been quite so flavourless. Imbecility like his is only to be attained as the result of long and judicious selection.

He went on gazing in a vacant way at the water below, an ineffectual patrician smile playing feebly round the corners of his mouth meanwhile. Then he turned and stared at me as I lay back in my deck-chair. For a minute he looked me over as if I were a horse for sale. When he had finished inspecting me, he beckoned to somebody at the far end of the quarter-deck.

The somebody sidled up with a deferential air which confirmed my belief in the pea-green young man's aristocratic origin. It was such deference as the British flunkey pays only to blue blood; for he has gradations of flunkeydom. He is respectful to wealth; polite to acquired rank; but servile only to hereditary nobility. Indeed, you can make a rough guess at the social status of the person he addresses by observing which one of his twenty-seven nicely graduated manners he adopts in addressing him.

The pea-green young man glanced over in my direction, and murmured something to the satellite, whose back was turned towards me. I felt sure, from his attitude, he was asking whether I was the person he suspected me to be. The satellite nodded assent, whereat the pea-green young man, screwing up his face to fix his eye-glass, stared harder than ever. He must be heir to a peerage, I felt convinced; nobody short of that rank would consider himself entitled to stare with such frank unconcern at an unknown lady.

Presently it further occurred to me that the satellite's back seemed strangely familiar. "I have seen that man somewhere, Elsie," I whispered, putting aside the wisps of hair that blew about my face.

"So have I, dear," Elsie answered, with a slight shudder. And I was instinctively aware that I too disliked him.

As Elsie spoke, the man turned, and strolled slowly past us, with that ineffable insolence which is the other side of the flunkey's insufferable self-abasement. He cast a glance at us as he went by, a withering glance of brazen effrontery. We knew him now, of course: it was that variable star, our old acquaintance, Mr. Higginson the courier.

He was here as himself this time; no longer the count or the mysterious faith-healer. The diplomat hid his rays under the garb of the man-servant.

"Depend upon it, Elsie," I cried, clutching her arm with a vague sense of fear, "this man means mischief. There is danger ahead. When a creature of Higginson's sort, who has risen to be a count and a fashionable physician, descends again to be a courier, you may rest assured it is because he has something to gain by it. He has some deep scheme afloat. And *we* are part of it."

"His master looks weak enough and silly enough for anything," Elsie answered, eyeing the suspected lordling. "I should think he is just the sort of man such a wily rogue would naturally fasten upon."

"When a wily rogue gets hold of a weak fool, who is also dishonest," I said, "the two together may make a formidable combination. But never mind. We're forewarned. I think I shall be even with him."

That evening, at dinner in the saloon, the pea-green young man strolled in with a jaunty air and took his seat next to us. The Red Sea, by the way, was kinder than the Mediterranean: it allowed us to dine from the very first evening. Cards had been laid on the plates to mark our places. I glanced at my neighbour's. It bore the inscription, "Viscount Southminster."

That was the name of Lord Kynaston's eldest son—Lady Georgina's nephew; Harold Tillington's cousin! So *this* was the man who might possibly inherit Mr. Marmaduke Ashurst's money! I remembered now how often and how fervently Lady Georgina had said, "Kynaston's sons are all fools." If the rest came up to sample, I was inclined to agree with her.

It also flashed across me that Lord Southminster might have heard through Higginson of our meeting with Mr. Marmaduke Ashurst at Florence, and of my acquaintance with Harold Tillington at Schlangenbad and Lungern. With a woman's instinct, I jumped at the fact that the pea-green young man had taken passage by this boat, on purpose to baffle both me and Harold.

Thinking it over, it seemed to me, too, that he might have various possible points of view on the matter. He might desire, for example,

that Harold should marry me, under the impression that his marriage with a penniless outsider would annoy his uncle; for the pea-
green young man doubtless thought that I was still to Mr. Ashurst
just that dreadful adventuress. If so, his obvious cue would be to
promote a good understanding between Harold and myself, in order to make us marry, so that the urbane old gentlemen might then
disinherit his favourite nephew, and make a new will in Lord Southminster's interest. Or again, the pea-green young man might, on
the contrary, be aware that Mr. Ashurst and I had got on admirably together when we met at Florence; in which case his aim would
naturally be to find out something that might set the rich uncle
against me. Yet once more, he might merely have heard that I had
drawn up Uncle Marmaduke's will at the office, and he might desire to worm the contents of it out of me. Whichever was his design, I resolved to be upon my guard in every word I said to him,
and leave no door open to any trickery either way. For of one thing
I felt sure, that the colourless young man had torn himself away
from the mud-honey of Piccadilly for this voyage to India only because he had heard there was a chance of meeting me.

That was a politic move, whoever planned it—himself or Higginson; for a week on board ship with a person or persons is the very
best chance of getting thrown in with them; whether they like it or
lump it, they can't easily avoid you.

It was while I was pondering these things in my mind, and re-
solving with myself not to give myself away, that the young man
with the pea-green face lounged in and dropped into the next seat
to me. He was dressed (amongst other things) in a dinner jacket
and a white tie; for myself, I detest such fopperies on board ship;
they seem to me out of place; they conflict with the infinite possibilities of the situation. One stands too near the realities of things.
Evening dress and *mal-de-mer* sort ill together.

As my neighbour sat down, he turned to me with an inane smile
which occupied all his face. "Good evening," he said, in a baronial
drawl. "Miss Cayley, I gathah? I asked the skippah's leave to set
next yah. We ought to be friends—rathah. I think yah know my
poor deah old aunt, Lady Georgina Fawley."

I bowed a somewhat, freezing bow. "Lady Georgina is one of my dearest friends," I answered.

"No, really? Poor deah old Georgey! Got somebody to stick up for her at last, has she? Now that's what I call chivalrous of yah. Magnanimous, isn't it? I like to see people stick up for their friends. And it must be a novelty for Georgey. For between you and me, a moah cantankerous spiteful acidulated old cough-drop than the poor deah soul it 'ud be difficult to hit upon."

"Lady Georgina has brains," I answered; "and they enable her to recognise a fool when she sees him. I will admit that she does not suffer fools gladly."

He turned to me with a sudden sharp look in the depths of the lack-lustre eyes. Already it began to strike me that, though the pea-green young man was inane, he had his due proportion of a certain insidious practical cunning. "That's true," he answered, measuring me. "And according to her, almost everybody's a fool—especially her relations. There's a fine knack of sweeping generalisation about deah skinny old Georgey. The few people she reahlly likes are all archangels; the rest are blithering idiots; there's no middle course with her."

I held my peace frigidly.

"She thinks me a very special and peculiah fool," he went on, crumbling his bread.

"Lady Georgina," I answered, "is a person of exceptional discrimination. I would almost always accept her judgment on anyone as practically final."

He laid down his soup-spoon, fondled the imperceptible moustache with his tapering fingers, and then broke once more into a cheerful expanse of smile which reminded me of nothing so much as of the village idiot. It spread over his face as the splash from a stone spreads over a mill-pond. "Now that's a nice cheerful sort of thing to say to a fellah," he ejaculated, fixing his eye-glass in his eye, with a few fierce contortions of his facial muscles. "That's encouraging, don't yah know, as the foundation of an acquaintance. Makes a good cornah-stone. Calculated to place things at once upon what yah call a friendly basis. Georgey said you had a pretty wit; I see now why she admiahed it. Birds of a feathah: very wise old proverb."

I reflected that, after all, this young man had nothing overt against him, beyond a fishy blue eye and an inane expression; so, feeling that I had perhaps gone a little too far, I continued after a minute, "And your uncle, how is he?"

"Marmy?" he inquired, with another elephantine smile; and then I perceived it was a form of humour with him (or rather, a cheap substitute) to speak of his elder relations by their abbreviated Christian names, without any prefix. "Marmy's doing very well, thank yah; as well as could be expected. In fact, bettah. Habakkuk on the brain: it's carrying him off at last. He has Bright's disease very bad—drank port, don't yah know—and won't trouble this wicked world much longah with his presence. It will be a happy release—especially for his nephews."

I was really grieved, for I had grown to like the urbane old gentleman, as I had grown to like the cantankerous old lady. In spite of his fussiness and his Stock Exchange views on the interpretation of Scripture, his genuine kindliness and his real liking for me had softened my heart to him; and my face must have shown my distress, for the pea-green young man added quickly with an afterthought: "But *you* needn't be afraid, yah know. It's all right for Harold Tillington. You ought to know that as well as anyone—and bettah: for it was you who drew up his will for him at Florence."

I flushed crimson, I believe. Then he knew all about me! "I was not asking on Mr. Tillington's account," I answered. "I asked because I have a personal feeling of friendship for your uncle, Mr. Ashurst."

His hand strayed up to the straggling yellow hairs on his upper lip once more, and he smiled again, this time with a curious undercurrent of foolish craftiness. "That's a good one," he answered. "Georgey told me you were original. Marmy's a millionaire, and many people love millionaires for their money. But to love Marmy for himself— I do call that originality! Why, weight for age, he's acknowledged to be the most portentous old boah in London society!"

"I like Mr. Ashurst because he has a kind heart and some genuine instincts," I answered. "He has not allowed all human feeling to be replaced by a cheap mask of Pall Mall cynicism."

"Oh, I say; how's that for preaching? Don't you manage to give it hot to a fellah, neithah! And at sight, too, without the usual three days of grace. Have some of my champagne? I'm a forgiving creachah."

"No, thank you. I prefer this hock."

"Your friend, then?" And he motioned the steward to pass the bottle.

To my great disgust, Elsie held out her glass. I was annoyed at that. It showed she had missed the drift of our conversation, and was therefore lacking in feminine intuition. I should be sorry if I had allowed the higher mathematics to kill out in me the most distinctively womanly faculty.

From that first day forth, however, in spite of this beginning, Lord Southminster almost persecuted me with his persistent attentions. He did all a fellah could possibly do to please me. I could not make out precisely what he was driving at; but I saw he had some artful game of his own to play, and that he was playing it subtly. I also saw that, vapid as he was, his vapidity did not prevent him from being worldly wise with the wisdom of the self-seeking man of the world, who utterly distrusts and disbelieves in all the higher emotions of humanity. He harped so often on this string that on our second day out, as we lolled on deck in the heat, I had to rebuke him sharply. He had been sneering for some hours. "There are two kinds of silly simplicity, Lord Southminster," I said, at last. "One kind is the silly simplicity of the rustic who trusts everybody; the other kind is the silly simplicity of the Pall Mall clubman who trusts nobody. It is just as foolish and just as one-sided to overlook the good as to overlook the evil in humanity. If you trust everyone, you are likely to be taken in; but if you trust no one, you put yourself at a serious practical disadvantage, besides losing half the joy of living."

"Then you think me a fool, like Georgey?" he broke out.

"I should never be rude enough to say so," I answered, fanning myself.

"Well, you're what I call a first-rate companion for a voyage down the Red Sea," he put in, gazing abstractedly at the awnings. "Such a lovely freezing mixture! A fellah doesn't need ices when *you're* on tap. I recommend you as a refrigeratah."

"I am glad," I answered demurely, "if I have secured your approbation in that humble capacity. I'm sure I have tried hard for it."

Yet nothing that I could say seemed to put the man down. In spite of rebuffs, he was assiduous in running down the companion-ladder for my parasol or my smelling-bottle; he fetched me chairs; he stayed me with cushions; he offered to lend me books; he pestered me to drink his wine; and he kept Elsie in champagne, which she annoyed me by accepting. Poor dear Elsie clearly failed to understand the creature. "He's so kind and polite, Brownie, isn't he?" she would observe in her simple fashion. "Do you know, I think he's taken quite a fancy to you! And he'll be an earl by-and-by. I call it romantic. How lovely it would seem, dear, to see you a countess."

"Elsie," I said severely, with one hand on her arm, "you are a dear little soul, and I am very fond of you; but if you think I could sell myself for a coronet to a pasty-faced young man with a pea-green complexion and glassy blue eyes—I can only say, my child, you have misread my character. He isn't a man: he's a lump of putty!"

I think Elsie was quite shocked that I should apply these terms to a courtesy lord, the eldest son of a peer. Nature had endowed her with the profound British belief that peers should be spoken of in choice and peculiar language. "If a peer's a fool," Lady Georgina said once to me, "people think you should say his temperament does not fit him for the conduct of affairs: if he's a roué or a drunkard, they think you should say he has unfortunate weaknesses."

What most of all convinced me, however, that the wishy-washy young man with the pea-green complexion must be playing some stealthy game, was the demeanour and mental attitude of Mr. Higginson, his courier. After the first day, Higginson appeared to be politeness and deference itself to us. He behaved to us both, *almost* as if we belonged to the titled classes. He treated us with the second best of his twenty-seven graduated manners. He fetched and carried for us with a courtly grace which recalled that distinguished diplomat, the Comte de Laroche-sur-Loiret, at the station at Malines with Lady Georgina. It is true, at his politest moments,

I often caught the undercurrent of a wicked twinkle in his eye, and felt sure he was doing it all with some profound motive. But his external demeanour was everything that one could desire from a well-trained man-servant; I could hardly believe it was the same man who had growled to me at Florence, "I shall be even with you yet," as he left our office.

"Do you know, Brownie," Elsie mused once, "I really begin to think we must have misjudged Higginson. He's so extremely polite. Perhaps, after all, he is really a count, who has been exiled and impoverished for his political opinions."

I smiled and held my tongue. Silence costs nothing. But Mr. Higginson's political opinions, I felt sure, were of that simple communistic sort which the law in its blunt way calls fraudulent. They consisted in a belief that all was his which he could lay his hands on.

"Higginson's a splendid fellah for his place, yah know, Miss Cayley," Lord Southminster said to me one evening as we were approaching Aden. "What I like about him is, he's so doosid intelligent."

"Extremely so," I answered. Then the devil entered into me again. "He had the doosid intelligence even to take in Lady Georgina."

"Yaas; that's just it, don't you know. Georgey told me that story. Screamingly funny, wasn't it? And I said to myself at once, 'Higginson's the man for me. I want a courier with jolly lots of brains and no blooming scruples. I'll entice this chap away from Marmy.' And I did. I outbid Marmy. Oh, yaas, he's a first-rate fellah, Higginson. What *I* want is a man who will do what he's told, and ask no beastly unpleasant questions. Higginson's that man. He's as sharp as a ferret."

"And as dishonest as they make them."

He opened his hands with a gesture of unconcern. "All the bettah for my purpose. See how frank I am, Miss Cayley. I tell the truth. The truth is very rare. You ought to respect me for it."

"It depends somewhat upon the *kind* of truth," I answered, with a random shot. "I don't respect a man, for instance, for confessing to a forgery."

He winced. Not for months after did I know how a stone thrown at a venture had chanced to hit the spot, and had vastly enhanced his opinion of my cleverness.

"You have heard about Dr. Fortescue-Langley too, I suppose?" I went on.

"Oh, yaas. Wasn't it real jam? He did the doctor-trick on a lady in Switzerland. And the way he has come it ovah deah simple old Marmy! He played Marmy with Ezekiel! Not so dusty, was it? He's too lovely for anything!"

"He's an edged tool," I said.

"Yaas; that's why I use him."

"And edged tools may cut the user's fingers."

"Not mine," he answered, taking out a cigarette. "Oh deah no. He can't turn against *me*. He wouldn't dare to. Yah see, I have the fellah entirely in my powah. I know all his little games, and I can expose him any day. But it suits me to keep him. I don't mind telling yah, since I respect your intellect, that he and I are engaged in pulling off a big *coup* togethah. If it were not for that, I wouldn't be heah. Yah don't catch me going away so fah from Newmarket and the Empire for nothing."

"I judged as much," I answered. And then I was silent.

But I wondered to myself why the neutral-tinted young man should be so communicative to an obviously hostile stranger.

For the next few days it amused me to see how hard our lordling tried to suit his conversation to myself and Elsie. He was absurdly anxious to humour us. Just at first, it is true, he had discussed the subjects that lay nearest to his own heart. He was an ardent votary of the noble quadruped; and he loved the turf—whose sward, we judged, he trod mainly at Tattersall's. He spoke to us with erudition on "two-year-old form," and gave us several "safe things" for the spring handicaps. The Oaks he considered "a moral" for Clorinda. He also retailed certain choice anecdotes about ladies whose Christian names were chiefly Tottie and Flo, and whose honoured surnames have escaped my memory. Most of them flourished, I recollect, at the Frivolity Music Hall. But when he learned that our interest in the noble quadruped was scarcely more than tepid, and that we had never even visited "the Friv.," as he affectionately called it, he did his best in turn to acquire our subjects. He had heard us talk about Florence, for example, and he gathered from our talk that we loved its art treasures. So he set himself to work to be studiously artistic. It was a beautiful study in human ineptitude. "Ah, yaas," he, murmured, turning up the pale blue eyes ecstatically towards the mast-head. "Chawming place, Florence! I dote on the pickchahs. I know them all by heart. I assuah yah, I've spent houahs and houahs feeding my soul in the galleries."

"And what particular painter does your soul most feed upon?" I asked bluntly, with a smile.

The question staggered him. I could see him hunting through the vacant chambers of his brain for a Florentine painter. Then a faint light gleamed in the leaden eyes, and he fingered the straw-coloured moustache with that nervous hand till he almost put a visible point upon it. "Ah, Raphael?" he said, tentatively, with an inquiring air, yet beaming at his success. "Don't you think so? Splendid artist, Raphael!"

"And a very safe guess," I answered, leading him on. "You can't go far wrong in mentioning Raphael, can you? But after him?"

He dived into the recesses of his memory again, peered about him for a minute or two, and brought back nothing. "I can't remembah the othah fellahs' names," he went on; "they're all so much alike: all in *elli*, don't yah know; but I recollect at the time they impressed me awfully."

"No doubt," I answered.

He tried to look through me, and failed. Then he plunged, like a noble sportsman that he was, on a second fetch of memory. "Ah—and Michael Angelo," he went on, quite proud of his treasure-trove. "Sweet things, Michael Angelo's!"

"Very sweet," I admitted. "So simple; so touching; so tender; so domestic!"

I thought Elsie would explode; but she kept her countenance. The pea-green young man gazed at me uneasily. He had half an idea by this time that I was making game of him.

However, he fished up a name once more, and clutched at it. "Savonarola, too," he adventured. "I adore Savonarola. His pickchahs are beautiful."

"And so rare!" Elsie murmured.

"Then there is Fra Diavolo?" I suggested, going one better. "How do you like Fra Diavolo?"

He seemed to have heard the name before, but still he hesitated. "Ah—what did he paint?" he asked, with growing caution.

I stuffed him valiantly. "Those charming angels, you know," I answered. "With the roses and the glories!"

"Oh, yaas; I recollect. All askew, aren't they; like this! I remembah them very well. But—" a doubt flitted across his brain, "wasn't his name Fra Angelico?"

"His brother," I replied, casting truth to the winds. "They worked together, you must have heard. One did the saints; the other did the opposite. Division of labour, don't you see; Fra Angelico, Fra Diavolo."

He fingered his cigarette with a dubious hand, and wriggled his eye-glass tighter. "Yaas, beautiful; beautiful! But—" growing suspicious apace, "wasn't Fra Diavolo also a composah?"

"Of course," I assented. "In his off time, he composed. Those early Italians—so versatile, you see; so versatile!"

He had his doubts, but he suppressed them.

"And Torricelli," I went on, with a side glance at Elsie, who was choking by this time. "And Chianti, and Frittura, and Cinquevalli, and Giulio Romano."

His distrust increased. "Now you're trying to make me commit myself," he drawled out. "I remembah Torricelli—he's the fellah who used to paint all his women crooked. But Chianti's a wine; I've often drunk it; and Romano's—well, every fellah knows Romano's is a restaurant near the Gaiety Theatre."

"Besides," I continued, in a drawl like his own, "there are Risotto, and Gnocchi, and Vermicelli, and Anchovy—all famous paintahs, and all of whom I don't doubt you admiah."

Elsie exploded at last. But he took no offence. He smiled inanely, as if he rather enjoyed it. "Look heah, you know," he said, with his crafty smile; "that's one too much. I'm not taking any. You think yourselves very clevah for kidding me with paintahs who are really macaroni and cheese and claret; yet if I were to tell you the Lejah was run at Ascot, or the Cesarewitch at Doncastah, why, you'd be no wisah. When it comes to art, I don't have a look in; but I could tell you a thing or two about starting prices."

And I was forced to admit that there he had reason.

Still, I think he realised that he had better avoid the subject of art in future, as we avoided the noble quadruped. He saw his limitations.

Not till the last evening before we reached Bombay did I really understand the nature of my neighbour's project. That evening, as it chanced, Elsie had a headache and went below early. I stopped with her till she dozed off; then I slipped up on deck once more for a breath of fresh air, before retiring for the night to the hot and stuffy cabin. It was an exquisite evening. The moon rode in the pale green sky of the tropics. A strange light still lingered on the western horizon. The stifling heat of the Red Sea had given way long since to the refreshing coolness of the Indian Ocean. I strolled a while on the quarter-deck, and sat down at last near the stern. Next moment, I was aware of somebody creeping up to me.

"Look heah, Miss Cayley," a voice broke in; "I'm in luck at last! I've been waiting, oh, evah so long, for this opportunity."

I turned and faced him. "Have you, indeed?" I answered. "Well, I have *not*, Lord Southminster."

I tried to rise, but he motioned me back to my chair. There were ladies on deck, and to avoid being noticed I sank into my seat again.

"I want to speak to you," he went on, in a voice that (for him) was almost impressive. "Half a mo, Miss Cayley. I want to say—this last night—you misunderstand me."

"On the contrary," I answered, "the trouble is—that I understand you perfectly."

"No, yah don't. Look heah." He bent forward quite romantically. "I'm going to be perfectly frank. Of course yah know that when I came on board this ship I came—to checkmate yah."

"Of course," I replied. "Why else should you and Higginson have bothered to come here?"

He rubbed his hands together. "That's just it. You're always clevah. You hit it first shot. But there's wheah the point comes in.

At first, I only thought of how we could circumvent yah. I treated yah as the enemy. Now, it's all the othah way. Miss Cayley, you're the cleverest woman I evah met in this world; you extort my admiration."

I could not repress a smile. I didn't know how it was, but I could see I possessed some mysterious attraction for the Ashurst family. I was fatal to Ashursts. Lady Georgina, Harold Tillington, the Honourable Marmaduke, Lord Southminster—different types as they were, all succumbed without one blow to me.

"You flatter me," I answered, coldly.

"No, I don't," he cried, flashing his cuffs and gazing affectionately at his sleeve-links. "'Pon my soul, I assuah yah, I mean it. I can't tell you how much I admiah yah. I admiah your intellect. Every day I have seen yah, I feel it moah and moah. Why, you're the only person who has evah out-flanked my fellah, Higginson. As a rule I don't think much of women. I've been through several London seasons, and lots of 'em have tried their level best to catch me; the cleverest mammas have been aftah me for their Ethels. But I wasn't so easily caught: I dodged the Ethels. With you, it's different. I feel"—he paused—"you're a woman a fellah might be really proud of."

"You are too kind," I answered, in my refrigerator voice.

"Well, will you take me?" he asked, trying to seize my hand. "Miss Cayley, if you will, you will make me unspeakably happy."

It was a great effort—for him—and I was sorry to crush it. "I regret," I said, "that I am compelled to deny you unspeakable happiness."

"Oh, but you don't catch on. You mistake. Let me explain. You're backing the othah man. Now, I happen to know about that: and I assuah you, it's an error. Take my word for it, you're staking your money on the wrong fellah."

"I do not understand you," I replied, drawing away from his approach. "And what is more, I may add, you could never understand me."

"Yaas, but I do. I understand perfectly. I can see where you go wrong. You drew up Marmy's will; and you think Marmy has left all he's worth to Harold Tillington; so you're putting every penny you've got on Harold. Well, that's mere moonshine. Harold may think it's all right; but it's not all right. There's many a slip 'twixt the cup and the Probate Court. Listen heah, Miss Cayley: Higginson and I are a jolly sight sharpah than your friend Harold. Harold's what they call a clevah fellah in society, and I'm what they call a fool; but I know bettah than Harold which side of my bread's buttahed."

"I don't doubt it," I answered.

"Well, I have managed this business. I don't mind telling you now, I had a telegram from Marmy's valet when we touched at Aden; and poor old Marmy's sinking. Habakkuk's been too much for him. Sixteen stone going under. Why am I not with him? yah may ask. Because, when a man of Marmy's temperament is dying, it's safah to be away from him. There's plenty of time for Marmy to altah his will yet—and there are othah contingencies. Still, Harold's quite out of it. You take my word for it; if you back Harold, you back a man who's not going to get anything; while if you back me, you back the winnah, with a coronet into the bargain." And he smiled fatuously.

I looked at him with a look that would have made a wiser man wince. But it fell flat on Lord Southminster. "Do you know why I do not rise and go down to my cabin at once?" I said, slowly. "Because, if I did, somebody as I passed might see my burning cheeks—cheeks flushed with shame at your insulting proposal—and might guess that you had asked me, and that I had refused you. And I should shrink from the disgrace of anyone's knowing that you had put such a humiliation upon me. You have been frank with me—after your kind, Lord Southminster; frank with the frankness of a low and purely commercial nature. I will be frank with you in turn. You are right in supposing that I love Harold Tillington—a man whose name I hate to mention in your presence. But you are wrong in supposing that the disposition of Mr. Marmaduke Ashurst's money has or can have anything to do with the feelings I entertain towards him. I would marry him all the sooner if he were poor and penniless. You cannot *understand* that state of mind, of course:

but you must be content to *accept* it. And I would not marry *you* if
there were no other man left in the world to marry. I should as
soon think of marrying a lump of dough." I faced him all crimson.
"Is *that* plain enough? Do you see now that I really mean it?"

He gazed at me with a curious look, and twirled what he considered his moustache once more, quite airily. The man was imperturbable—a pachydermatous imbecile. "You're all wrong, yah
know," he said, after a long pause, during which he had regarded
me through his eye-glass as if I were a specimen of some rare new
species. "You're all wrong, and yah won't believe me. But I tell yah,
I know what I'm talking about. You think it's quite safe about
Marmy's money—that he's left it to Harold, because you drew the
will up. I assuah you that will's not worth the paper it's written on.
You fancy Harold's a hot favourite: he's a rank outsidah. I give you
a chance, and you won't take it. I want yah because you're a remarkable woman. Most of the Ethels cry when they're trying to
make a fellah propose to 'em; and I don't like 'em damp: but *you*
have some go about yah. You insist upon backing the wrong man.
But you'll find your mistake out yet." A bright idea struck him. "I
say—why don't you hedge? Leave it open till Marmy's gone, and
then marry the winnah?"

It was hopeless trying to make this clod understand. His brain
was not built with the right cells for understanding me. "Lord
Southminster," I said, turning upon him and clasping my hands,
"I will not go away while you stop here. But you have some spark
enough of a gentleman in your composition, I hope, not to inflict
your company any longer upon a woman who does not desire it. I
ask you to leave me here alone. When you have gone, and I have
had time to recover from your degrading offer, I may perhaps feel
able to go down to my cabin."

He stared at me with open blue eyes—those watery blue eyes.
"Oh, just as you like," he answered. "I wanted to do you a good
turn, because you're the only woman I evah really admiahed—to
say admiah, don't you know; not trotted round like the Ethels: but
you won't allow me. I'll go if you wish it; though I tell you again,
you're backing the wrong man, and soonah or latah you'll discover

it. I don't mind laying you six to four against him. Howevah, I'll do one thing for yah: I'll leave this offah always open. I'm not likely to marry any othah woman—not good enough, is it?—and if evah you find out you're mistaken about Harold Tillington, remembah, honour bright, I shall be ready at any time to renew my offah."

By this time I was at boiling-point. I could not find words to answer him. I waved him away angrily with one hand. He raised his hat with quite a jaunty air and strolled off forward, puffing his cigarette. I don't think he even knew the disgust with which he inspired me.

I sat some hours with the cool air playing about my burning cheeks before I mustered up courage to rise and go down below again.

THE ADVENTURES OF THE
MAGNIFICENT MAHARAJAH

Our arrival at Bombay was a triumphal entry. We were received like royalty. Indeed, to tell you the truth, Elsie and I were beginning to get just a little bit spoiled. It struck us now that our casual connection with the Ashurst family in its various branches had succeeded in saddling us, like the Lady of Burleigh, "with the burden of an honour unto which we were not born." We were everywhere treated as persons of importance; and, oh dear, by dint of such treatment we began to feel at last almost as if we had been raised in the purple. I felt that when we got back to England we should turn up our noses at plain bread and butter.

Yes, life has been kind to me. Have your researches into English literature ever chanced to lead you into reading Horace Walpole, I wonder? That polite trifler is fond of a word which he coined himself—"Serendipity." It derives from the name of a certain happy Indian Prince Serendip, whom he unearthed (or invented) in some obscure Oriental story; a prince for whom the fairies or the genii always managed to make everything pleasant. It implies the faculty, which a few of us possess, of finding whatever we want turn up accidentally at the exact right moment. Well, I believe I must have been born with serendipity in my mouth, in place of the proverbial silver spoon, for wherever I go, all things seem to come out exactly right for me.

The *Jumna*, for example, had hardly heaved to in Bombay Harbour when we noticed on the quay a very distinguished-looking Oriental potentate, in a large, white turban with a particularly big diamond stuck ostentatiously in its front. He stalked on board with a martial air, as soon as we stopped, and made inquiries from our captain after someone he expected. The captain received him with that odd mixture of respect for rank and wealth, combined with true British contempt for the inferior black man, which is universal among his class in their dealings with native Indian nobility. The Oriental potentate, however, who was accompanied by a gorgeous suite like that of the Wise Men in Italian pictures, seemed satisfied with his information, and moved over with his stately glide in our direction. Elsie and I were standing near the gangway among our rugs and bundles, in the hopeless helplessness of disembarkation. He approached us respectfully, and, bowing with extended hands and a deferential air, asked, in excellent English, "May I venture to inquire which of you two ladies is Miss Lois Cayley?"

"*I* am," I replied, my breath taken away by this unexpected greeting. "May I venture to inquire in return how you came to know I was arriving by this steamer?"

He held out his hand, with a courteous inclination. "I am the Maharajah of Moozuffernuggar," he answered in an impressive tone, as if everybody knew of the Maharajah of Moozuffernuggar as familiarly as they knew of the Duke of Cambridge. "Moozuffernuggar in Rajputana—*not* the one in the Doab. You must have heard my name from Mr. Harold Tillington."

I had not; but I dissembled, so as to salve his pride. "Mr. Tillington's friends are *our* friends," I answered, sententiously.

"And Mr. Tillington's friends are *my* friends," the Maharajah retorted, with a low bow to Elsie. "This is no doubt, Miss Petheridge. I have heard of your expected arrival, as you will guess, from Tillington. He and I were at Oxford together; I am a Merton man. It was Tillington who first taught me all I know of cricket. He took me to stop at his father's place in Dumfriesshire. I owe much to his friendship; and when he wrote me that friends of his were arriving by the *Jumna*, why, I made haste to run down to Bombay to greet them."

The episode was one of those topsy-turvy mixtures of all places and ages which only this jumbled century of ours has witnessed; it impressed me deeply. Here was this Indian prince, a feudal Rajput chief, living practically among his vassals in the Middle Ages when at home in India; yet he said "I am a Merton man," as Harold himself might have said it; and he talked about cricket as naturally as Lord Southminster talked about the noble quadruped. The oddest part of it all was, we alone felt the incongruity; to the Maharajah, the change from Moozuffernuggar to Oxford and from Oxford back again to Moozuffernuggar seemed perfectly natural. They were but two alternative phases in a modern Indian gentleman's education and experience.

Still, what were we to do with him? If Harold had presented me with a white elephant I could hardly have been more embarrassed than I was at the apparition of this urbane and magnificent Hindoo prince. He was young; he was handsome; he was slim, for a rajah; he wore European costume, save for the huge white turban with its obtrusive diamond; and he spoke English much better than a great many Englishmen. Yet what place could he fill in my life and Elsie's? For once, I felt almost angry with Harold. Why couldn't he have allowed us to go quietly through India, two simple unofficial journalistic pilgrims, in our native obscurity?

His Highness of Moozuffernuggar, however, had his own views on this question. With a courteous wave of one dusky hand, he motioned us gracefully into somebody else's deck chairs, and then sat down on another beside us, while the gorgeous suite stood by in respectful silence—unctuous gentlemen in pink-and-gold brocade—forming a court all round us. Elsie and I, unaccustomed to be so observed, grew conscious of our hands, our skirts, our postures. But the Maharajah posed himself with perfect unconcern, like one well used to the fierce light of royalty. "I have come," he said, with simple dignity, "to superintend the preparations for your reception."

"Gracious heavens!" I exclaimed. "Our reception, Maharajah? I think you misunderstand. We are two ordinary English ladies of the proletariat, accustomed to the level plain of professional society. We expect no reception."

He bowed again, with stately Eastern deference. "Friends of Tillington's," he said, shortly, "are persons of distinction. Besides, I have heard of you from Lady Georgina Fawley."

"Lady Georgina is too good," I answered, though inwardly I raged against her. Why couldn't she leave us alone, to feed in peace on dak-bungalow chicken, instead of sending this regal-mannered heathen to bother us?

"So I have come down to Bombay to make sure that you are met in the style that befits your importance in society," he went on, waving his suite away with one careless hand, for he saw it fussed us. "I mentioned you to His Honour the Acting-Governor, who had not heard you were coming. His Honour's aide-de-camp will follow shortly with an invitation to Government House while you remain in Bombay—which will not be many days, I don't doubt, for there is nothing in this city of plague to stop for. Later on, during your progress up country, I do myself the honour to hope that you will stay as my guests for as long as you choose at Moozuffernuggar."

My first impulse was to answer: "Impossible, Maharajah; we couldn't dream of accepting your kind invitation." But on second thoughts, I remembered my duty to my proprietor. Journalism first: inclination afterwards! My letter from Egypt on the rescue of the Englishwoman who escaped from Khartoum had brought me great *éclat* as a special correspondent, and the *Daily Telephone* now billed my name in big letters on its placards, so Mr. Elworthy wrote me. Here was another noble chance; must I not strive to rise to it? Two English ladies at a native court in Rajputana! that ought to afford scope for some rattling journalism!

"It is extremely kind of you," I said, hesitating, "and it would give us great pleasure, were it feasible, to accept your friendly offer. But—English ideas, you know, prince! Two unprotected women! I hardly see how we could come alone to Moozuffernuggar, unchaperoned."

The Maharajah's face lighted up; he was evidently flattered that we should even thus dubiously entertain his proposal. "Oh, I've thought about that, too," he answered, growing more colloquial in tone. "I've been some days in Bombay, making inquiries and preparations. You see, you had not informed the authorities of your intended visit, so that you were travelling *incognito*—or should it be *incognita?*—and if Tillington hadn't written to let me know your movements, you might have arrived at this port without anybody's knowing it, and have been compelled to take refuge in an hotel on landing." He spoke as if we had been accustomed all our lives long to be received with red cloth by the Mayor and Corporation, and presented with illuminated addresses and the freedom of the city in a gold snuff-box. "But I have seen to all that. The Acting-Governor's aide-de-camp will be down before long, and I have arranged that if you consent a little later to honour my humble roof in Rajputana with your august presence, Major Balmossie and his wife will accompany you and chaperon you. I have lived in England: of course I understand that two English ladies of your rank and position cannot travel alone—as if you were Americans. But Mrs. Balmossie is a nice little soul, of unblemished character"—that sweet touch charmed me—"received at Government House"—he had learned the respect due to Mrs. Grundy—"so that if you will accept my invitation, you may rest assured that everything will be done with the utmost regard to the—the unaccountable prejudices of Europeans."

His thoughtfulness took me aback. I thanked him warmly. He unbent at my thanks. "And I am obliged to you in return," he said. "It gives me real pleasure to be able, through you, to repay Harold Tillington part of the debt I owe him. He was so good to me at Oxford. Miss Cayley, you are new to India, and therefore—as yet— no doubt unprejudiced. You treat a native gentleman, I see, like a human being. I hope you will not stop long enough in our country to get over that stage—as happens to most of your countrymen and countrywomen. In England, a man like myself is an Indian prince; in India, to ninety-nine out of a hundred Europeans, he is just 'a damned nigger.'"

I smiled sympathetically. "I think," I said, venturing under these circumstances on a harmless little swear-word—of course, in quotation marks—"you may trust me never to reach 'damn-nigger' point."

"So I believe," he answered, "if you are a friend of Harold Till-ington's. Ebony or ivory, he never forgot we were two men together."

Five minutes later, when the Maharajah had gone to inquire about our luggage, Lord Southminster strolled up. "Oh, I say, Miss Cayley," he burst out, "I'm off now; ta-ta: but remembah, that offah's always open. By the way, who's your black friend? I couldn't help laughing at the airs the fellah gave himself. To see a niggah sitting theah, with his suite all round him, waving his hands and sunning his rings, and behaving for all the world as if he were a gentleman; it's reahly too ridiculous. Harold Tillington picked up with a fellah like that at Oxford—doosid good cricketer too; wondah if this is the same one?"

"Good-bye, Lord Southminster," I said, quietly, with a stiff little bow. "Remember, on your side, that your 'offer' was rejected once for all last night. Yes, the Indian prince *is* Harold Tillington's friend, the Maharajah of Moozuffernuggar—whose ancestors were princes while ours were dressed in woad and oak-leaves. But you were right about one thing; *he* behaves—like a gentleman."

"Oh, I say," the pea-green young man ejaculated, drawing back; "that's anothah in the eye for me. You're a good 'un at facers. You gave me one for a welcome, and you give me one now for a parting shot. Nevah mind though, I can wait; you're backing the wrong fellah—but you're not the Ethels, and you're well worth waiting for." He waved his hand. "So-long! See yah again in London."

And he retired, with that fatuous smile still absorbing his features.

Our three days in Bombay were uneventful; we merely waited to get rid of the roll of the ship, which continued to haunt us for hours after we landed—the floor of our bedrooms having acquired an ugly trick of rising in long undulations, as if Bombay were suf-fering from chronic earthquake. We made the acquaintance of His Honour the Acting Governor, and His Honour's consort. We were also introduced to Mrs. Balmossie, the lady who was to chaperon us to Moozuffernuggar. Her husband was a soldierly Scotchman from Forfarshire, but she herself was English—a flighty little body with a perpetual giggle. She giggled so much over the idea of the Maharajah's inviting us to his palace that I wondered why on earth she accepted his invitation. At this she seemed surprised. "Why, it's one of the jolliest places in Rajputana," she answered, with a bland Simla smile; "*so* picturesque—he, he, he—and *so* delightful. Simpkin flows like water—Simpkin's baboo English for champagne, you know—he, he, he; and though of course the Maharajah's only a native like the rest of them—he, he, he—still, he's been educated at Oxford, and has mixed with Europeans, and he knows how to make one—he, he, he—well, thoroughly comfortable."

"But what shall we eat?" I asked. "Rice, ghee, and chupatties?"

"Oh dear no—he, he, he—Europe food, every bit of it. Foie gras, and York ham, and wine *ad lib*. His hospitality's massive. If it weren't for that, of course, one wouldn't dream of going there. But Archie hopes some day to be made Resident, don't you know; and it will do him no harm—he, he, he—with the Foreign Office, to have cultivated friendly relations beforehand with His Highness of Moozuffernuggar. These natives—he, he, he—so absurdly sensitive!"

For myself, the Maharajah interested me, and I rather liked him. Besides, he was Harold's friend, and that was in itself suffi-cient recommendation. So I determined to push straight into the heart of native India first, and only afterwards to do the regula-tion tourist round of Agra and Delhi, the Taj and the mosques, Benares and Allahabad, leaving the English and Calcutta for the tail-end of my journey. It was better journalism; as I thought that thought, I began to fear that Mr. Elworthy was right after all, and that I was a born journalist.

On the day fixed for our leaving Bombay, whom should I meet but Lord Southminster—with the Maharajah—at the railway station!

He lounged up to me with that eternal smile still vaguely per-vading his empty features. "Well, we shall have a jolly party, I gathah," he said. "They tell me this niggah is famous for his tigahs."

I gazed at him, positively taken aback. "You don't mean to tell me," I cried, "you actually propose to accept the Maharajah's hos-pitality?"

His smile absorbed him. "Yaas," he answered twirling his yellow moustache, and gazing across at the unconscious prince, who was engaged in overlooking the arrangements for our saloon carriage. "The black fellah discovahed I was a cousin of Harold's, so he came to call upon me at the club, of which some Johnnies heah made me an honorary membah. He's offahed me the run of his place while I'm in Indiah, and, of course, I've accepted. Eccentric sort of chap; can't make him out myself: says anyone connected with Harold Tillington is always deah to him. Rum start, isn't it?"

"He is a mere Oriental," I answered, "unused to the ways of civilised life. He cherishes the superannuated virtue of gratitude."

"Yaas; no doubt—so I'm coming along with you."

I drew back, horrified. "Now? While I am there? After what I told you last week on the steamer?"

"Oh, that's all right. I bear yah no malice. If I want any fun, of course I must go while *you're* at Moozuffernuggar."

"Why so?"

"Yah see, this black boundah means to get up some big things at his place in your honah; and one naturally goes to stop with anyone who has big things to offah. Hang it all, what does it mattah who a fellah is if he can give yah good shooting? It's shooting, don't yah know, that keeps society in England togethah!"

"And therefore you propose to stop in the same house with me!" I exclaimed, "in spite of what I have told you! Well, Lord Southminster, I should have thought there were limits which even *your* taste—"

He cut me short with an inane grin. "There you make your blooming little erraw," he answered, airily. "I told yah, I keep my offah still open; and, hang it all, I don't mean to lose sight of yah in a hurry. Some other fellah might come along and pick you up when I wasn't looking; and I don't want to miss yah. In point of fact, I don't mind telling yah, I back myself still for a couple of thou' soonah or latah to marry yah. It's dogged as does it; faint heart, they say, nevah won fair lady!"

If it had not been that I could not bear to disappoint my Indian prince, I think, when I heard this, I should have turned back then and there at the station.

The journey up country was uneventful, but dusty. The Mofussil appears to consist mainly of dust; indeed, I can now recall nothing of it but one pervading white cloud, which has blotted from my memory all its other components. The dust clung to my hair after many washings, and was never really beaten out of my travelling clothes; I believe part of it thus went round the world with me to England. When at last we reached Moozuffernuggar, after two days' and a night's hard travelling, we were met by a crowd of local grandees, who looked as if they had spent the greater part of their lives in brushing back their whiskers, and we drove up at once, in European carriages, to the Maharajah's palace. The look of it astonished me. It was a strange and rambling old Hindoo hill-fort, high perched on a scarped crag, like Edinburgh Castle, and accessible only on one side, up a gigantic staircase, guarded on either hand by huge sculptured elephants cut in the living sandstone. Below clustered the town, an intricate mass of tangled alleys. I had never seen anything so picturesque or so dirty in my life; as for Elsie, she was divided between admiration for its beauty and terror at the big-whiskered and white-turbaned attendants.

"What sort of rooms shall we have?" I whispered to our moral guarantee, Mrs. Balmossie.

"Oh, beautiful, dear," the little lady smirked back. "Furnished throughout—he, he, he—by Liberty. The Maharajah wants to do honour to his European guests—he, he, he—he fancies, poor man, he's quite European. That's what comes of sending these creatures to Oxford! So he's had suites of rooms furnished for any white visitors who may chance to come his way. Ridiculous, isn't it? *And* champagne—oh, gallons of it! He's quite proud of his rooms, he, he, he—he's always asking people to come and occupy them; he thinks he's done them up in the best style of decoration."

He had reason, for they were as tasteful as they were dainty and comfortable. And I could not for the life of me make out why his hospitable inclination should be voted "ridiculous." But Mrs. Balmossie appeared to find all natives alike a huge joke together. She never even spoke of them without a condescending smile of distant compassion. Indeed, most Anglo-Indians seem first to do their best to Anglicise the Hindoo, and then to laugh at him for aping the Englishman.

After we had been three days at the palace and had spent hours in the wonderful temples and ruins, the Maharajah announced with considerable pride at breakfast one morning that he had got up a tiger-hunt in our special honour.

Lord Southminster rubbed his hands.

"Ha, that's right, Maharaj," he said, briskly. "I do love big game. To tell yah the truth, old man, that's just what I came heah for."

"You do me too much honour," the Hindoo answered, with quiet sarcasm. "My town and palace may have little to offer that is worth your attention; but I am glad that my big game, at least, has been lucky enough to attract you."

The remark was thrown away on the pea-green young man. He had described his host to me as "a black boundah." Out of his own mouth I condemned him—he supplied the very word—he was himself nothing more than a born bounder.

During the next few days, the preparations for the tiger-hunt occupied all the Maharajah's energies. "You know, Miss Cayley," he said to me, as we stood upon the big stairs, looking down on the Hindoo city, "a tiger-hunt is not a thing to be got up lightly. Our people themselves don't like killing a tiger. They reverence it too much. They're afraid its spirit might haunt them afterwards and bring them bad luck. That's one of our superstitions."

"You do not share it yourself, then?" I asked.

He drew himself up and opened his palms, with a twinkling of pendant emeralds. "I am royal," he answered, with naïve dignity, "and the tiger is a royal beast. Kings know the ways of kings. If a king kills what is kingly, it owes him no grudge for it. But if a common man or a low caste man were to kill a tiger—who can say what might happen?"

I saw he was not himself quite free from the superstition.

"Our peasants," he went on, fixing me with his great black eyes, "won't even mention the tiger by name, for fear of offending him: they believe him to be the dwelling-place of a powerful spirit. If they wish to speak of him, they say, 'the great beast,' or 'my lord, the striped one.' Some think the spirit is immortal except at the hands of a king. But they have no objection to see him destroyed by others. They will even point out his whereabouts, and rejoice over his death; for it relieves the village of a serious enemy, and they believe the spirit will only haunt the huts of those who actually kill him."

"Then you know where each tiger lives?" I asked.

"As well as your gamekeepers in England know which covert may be drawn for foxes. Yes; 'tis a royal sport, and we keep it for Maharajahs. I myself never hunt a tiger till some European visitor of distinction comes to Moozuffernuggar, that I may show him good sport. This tiger we shall hunt to-morrow, for example, he is a bad old hand. He has carried off the buffaloes of my villagers over yonder for years and years, and of late he has also become a man-eater. He once ate a whole family at a meal—a man, his wife, and his three children. The people at Janwargurh have been pestering me for weeks to come and shoot him; and each week he has eaten somebody—a child or a woman; the last was yesterday—but I waited till you came, because I thought it would be something to show you that you would not be likely to see elsewhere."

"And you let the poor people go on being eaten, that we might enjoy this sport!" I cried.

He shrugged his shoulders, and opened his palms. "They were villagers, you know—ryots: mere tillers of the soil—poor naked peasants. I have thousands of them to spare. If a tiger eats ten of them, they only say, 'It was written upon their foreheads.' One woman more or less—who would notice her at Moozuffernuggar?"

Then I perceived that the Maharajah was a gentleman, but still a barbarian.

The eventful morning arrived at last, and we started, all agog, for the jungle where the tiger was known to live. Elsie excused herself. She remarked to me the night before, as I brushed her back hair for her, that she had "half a mind" not to go. "My dear," I answered, giving the brush a good dash, "for a higher mathematician, that phrase lacks accuracy. If you were to say 'seven-eighths of a mind' it would be nearer the mark. In point of fact, if you ask my opinion, your inclination to go is a vanishing quantity."

She admitted the impeachment with an accusing blush. "You're quite right, Brownie; to tell you the truth, I'm afraid of it."

"So am I, dear; horribly afraid. Between ourselves, I'm in a deadly funk of it. But 'the brave man is not he that feels no fear'; and I believe the same principle applies almost equally to the brave woman. I mean 'that fear to subdue' as far as I am able. The Maharajah says I shall be the first girl who has ever gone tiger-hunting. I'm frightened out of my life. I never held a gun in my born days before. But, Elsie, recollect, this is *splendid* journalism! I intend to go through with it."

"You offer yourself on the altar, Brownie."

"I do, dear; I propose to die in the cause. I expect my proprietor to carve on my tomb, 'Sacred to the memory of the martyr of journalism. She was killed, in the act of taking shorthand notes, by a Bengal tiger.'"

We started at early dawn, a motley mixture. My short bicycling skirt did beautifully for tiger-hunting. There was a vast company of native swells, nawabs and ranas, in gorgeous costumes, whose precise names and titles I do not pretend to remember; there were also Major Balmossie, Lord Southminster, the Maharajah, and myself—all mounted on gaily-caparisoned elephants. We had likewise, on foot, a miserable crowd of wretched beaters, with dirty white loin-cloths. We were all very brave, of course—demonstratively brave—and we talked a great deal at the start about the exhilaration given by "the spice of danger." But it somehow struck me that the poor beaters on foot had the majority of the danger and extremely little of the exhilaration. Each of us great folk was mounted on his own elephant, which carried a light basket-work howdah in two compartments: the front one intended for the noble sportsman, the back one for a servant with extra guns and ammunition. I pretended to like it, but I fear I trembled visibly. Our mahouts sat on the elephants' necks, each armed with a pointed goad, to whose admonition the huge beasts answered like clock-work. A born journalist always pretends to know everything before hand, so I speak carelessly of the "mahout," as if he were a familiar acquaintance. But I don't mind telling you aside, in confidence, that I had only just learnt the word that morning.

The Maharajah protested at first against my taking part in the actual hunt, but I think his protest was merely formal. In his heart of hearts I believe he was proud that the first lady tiger-hunter should have joined his party.

Dusty and shadeless, the road from Moozuffernuggar fares straight across the plain towards the crumbling mountains. Behind, in the heat mist, the castle and palace on their steeply-scarped crag, with the squalid town that clustered at their feet, reminded me once more most strangely of Edinburgh, where I used to spend my vacations from Girton. But the pitiless sun differed greatly from the gray haar of the northern metropolis. It warmed into intense white the little temples of the wayside, and beat on our heads with tropical garishness.

I am bound to admit also that tiger-hunting is not quite all it is cracked up to be. In my fancy I had pictured the gallant and bloodthirsty beast rushing out upon us full pelt from some grass-grown nullah at the first sniff of our presence, and fiercely attacking both men and elephants. Instead of that, I will confess the whole truth: frightened as at least one of us was of the tiger, the tiger was still more desperately frightened of his human assailants. I could see clearly that, so far from rushing out of his own accord to attack us, his one desire was to be let alone. He was horribly afraid; he skulked in the jungle like a wary old fox in a trusty spinney. There was no nullah (whatever a nullah may be), there was only a waste of dusty cane-brake. We encircled the tall grass patch where he lurked, forming a big round with a ring-fence of elephants. The beaters on foot, advancing, half naked, with a caution with which I could fully sympathise, endeavoured by loud shouts and gesticulations to rouse the royal beast to a sense of his position. Not a bit of it: the royal beast declined to be drawn; he preferred retirement. The Maharajah, whose elephant was stationed next to mine, even apologised for the resolute cowardice with which he clung to his ignoble lurking-place.

The beaters drew in: the elephants, raising their trunks in air and sniffing suspicion, moved slowly inward. We had girt him round now with a perfect ring, through which he could not possibly break without attacking somebody. The Maharajah kept a fixed eye on my personal safety. But still the royal animal crouched and skulked, and still the black beaters shrieked, howled, and gesticulated. At last, among the tall perpendicular lights and shadows of the big grasses and bamboos, I seemed to see something move—something striped like the stems, yet passing slowly, slowly, slowly between them. It moved in a stealthy undulating line. No one could believe till he saw it how the bright flame-coloured bands of vivid orange-yellow on the monster's flanks, and the interspersed black stripes, could fade away and harmonise, in their native surroundings, with the lights and shades of the upright jungle. It was a marvel of mimicry. "Look there!" I cried to the Maharajah, pointing one eager hand. "What is that thing there, moving?"

He stared where I pointed. "By Jove," he cried, raising his rifle with a sportsman's quickness, "you have spotted him first! The tiger!"

The terrified beast stole slowly and cautiously through the tall grasses, his lithe, silken side gliding in and out snakewise, and only his fierce eyes burning bright with gleaming flashes between the gloom of the jungle. Once I had seen him, I could follow with ease his sinuous path among the tangled bamboos, a waving line of beauty in perpetual motion. The Maharajah followed him too, with his keen eyes, and pointed his rifle hastily. But, quick as he was, Lord Southminster was before him. I had half expected to find the pea-green young man turn coward at the last moment; but in that I was mistaken: I will do him the justice to say, whatever else he was, he was a born sportsman. The gleam of joy in his leaden eye when he caught sight of the tiger, the flush of excitement on his pasty face, the eagerness of his alert attitude, were things to see and remember. That moment almost ennobled him. In sight of danger, the best instincts of the savage seemed to revive within him. In civilised life he was a poor creature; face to face with a wild beast he became a mighty shikari. Perhaps that was why he was so fond of big-game shooting. He may have felt it raised him in the scale of being.

He lifted his rifle and fired. He was a cool shot, and he wounded the beast upon its left shoulder. I could see the great crimson stream gush out all at once across the shapely sides, staining the flame-coloured stripes and reddening the black shadows. The tiger drew back, gave a low, fierce growl, and then crouched among the jungle. I saw he was going to leap; he bent his huge backbone into a strong downward curve, took in a deep breath, and stood at bay, glaring at us. Which elephant would he attack? That was what he was now debating. Next moment, with a frightful R'-r'-r'-r', he had straightened out his muscles, and, like a bolt from a bow, had launched his huge bulk forward.

I never saw his charge. I never knew he had leapt upon me. I only felt my elephant rock from side to side like a ship in a storm. He was trumpeting, shaking, roaring with rage and pain, for the tiger was on his flanks, its claws buried deep in the skin of his forehead. I could not keep my seat; I felt myself tossed about in the frail howdah like a pill in a pill-box. The elephant, in a death grapple, was trying to shake off his ghastly enemy. For a minute or two, I was conscious of nothing save this swinging movement. Then, opening my eyes for a second, I saw the tiger, in all his terrible beauty, clinging to the elephant's head by the claws of his fore paws, and struggling for a foothold on its trunk with his mighty hind legs, in a wounded agony of despair and vengeance. He would sell his life dear; he would have one or other of us.

Lord Southminster raised his rifle again; but the Maharajah shouted aloud in an angry voice: "Don't fire! Don't fire! You will kill the lady! You can't aim at him like that. The beast is rocking so that no one can say where a shot will take effect. Down with your gun, sir, instantly!"

My mahout, unable to keep his seat with the rocking, now dropped off his cushion among the scrub below. He could speak a few words of English. "Shoot, Mem Sahib, shoot!" he cried, flinging his hands up. But I was tossed to and fro, from side to side, with my rifle under my arm. It was impossible to aim. Yet in sheer terror I tried to draw the trigger. I failed; but somehow I caught my rifle against the side of my cage. Something snapped in it somewhere. It went off unexpectedly, without my aiming or firing. I shut my eyes. When I opened them again, I saw a swimming picture of the great sullen beast, loosing his hold on the elephant. I saw his brindled face; I saw his white tusks. But his gleaming pupils burned bright no longer. His jaw was full towards me: I had shot him between the eyes. He fell, slowly, with blood streaming from his nostrils, and his tongue lolling out. His muscles relaxed; his huge limbs grew limp. In a minute, he lay stretched at full length on the ground, with his head on one side, a grand, terrible picture.

My mahout flung up his hands in wonder and amazement. "My father!" he cried aloud. "Truly, the Mem Sahib is a great shikari!"

The Maharajah stretched across to me. "That was a wonderful shot!" he exclaimed. "I could never have believed a woman could show such nerve and coolness."

Nerve and coolness, indeed! I was trembling all over like an Italian greyhound, every limb a jelly; and I had not even fired: the rifle went off of itself without me. I am innocent of having ever endangered the life of a haycock. But once more I dissembled. "Yes, it *was* a difficult shot," I said jauntily, as if I rather liked tiger-hunting. "I didn't think I'd hit him." Still the effect of my speech was somewhat marred, I fear, by the tears that in spite of me rolled down my cheek silently.

"'Pon honah, I nevah saw a finah piece of shooting in my life," Lord Southminster drawled out. Then he added aside, in an undertone, "Makes a fellow moah determined to annex her than evah!"

I sat in my howdah, half dazed. I hardly heard what they were saying. My heart danced like the elephant. Then it stood still within me. I was only aware of a feeling of faintness. Luckily for my reputation as a mighty sportswoman, however, I just managed to keep up, and did not actually faint, as I was more than half inclined to do.

Next followed the native pæan. The beaters crowded round the fallen beast in a chorus of congratulation. Many of the villagers also ran out, with prayers and ejaculations, to swell our triumph. It was all like a dream. They hustled round me and salaamed to me. A woman had shot him! Wonderful! A babel of voices resounded in my ears. I was aware that pure accident had elevated me into a heroine.

"Put the beast on a pad elephant," the Maharajah called out.

The beaters tied ropes round his body and raised him with difficulty.

The Maharajah's face grew stern. "Where are the whiskers?" he asked, fiercely, in his own tongue, which Major Balmossie interpreted for me.

The beaters and the villagers, bowing low and expanding their hands, made profuse expressions of ignorance and innocence. But the fact was patent—the grand face had been mangled. While they had crowded in a dense group round the fallen carcass, somebody had cut off the lips and whiskers and secreted them.

"They have ruined the skin!" the Maharajah cried out in angry tones. "I intended it for the lady. I shall have them all searched, and the man who has done this thing—"

He broke off, and looked around him. His silence was more terrible by far than the fiercest threat. I saw him now the Oriental despot. All the natives drew back, awe-struck.

"The voice of a king is the voice of a great god," my mahout murmured, in a solemn whisper. Then nobody else said anything.

"Why do they want the whiskers?" I asked, just to set things straight again. "They seem to have been in a precious hurry to take them!"

The Maharajah's brow cleared. He turned to me once more with his European manner. "A tiger's body has wonderful power after his death," he answered. "His fangs and his claws are very potent charms. His heart gives courage. Whoever eats of it will never know fear. His liver preserves against death and pestilence. But the highest virtue of all exists in his whiskers. They are mighty talismans. Chopped up in food, they act as a slow poison, which no doctor can detect, no antidote guard against. They are also a sovereign remedy against magic or the evil eye. And administered to women, they make an irresistible philtre, a puissant love-potion. They secure you the heart of whoever drinks them."

"I'd give a couple of monkeys for those whiskahs," Lord Southminster murmured, half unnoticed.

We began to move again. "We'll go on to where we know there is another tiger," the Maharajah said, lightly, as if tigers were partridges. "Miss Cayley, you will come with us?"

I rested on my laurels. (I was quivering still from head to foot.) "No, thank you, Maharajah," as unconcernedly as I could; "I've had quite enough sport for my first day's tiger-hunting. I think I'll go back now, and write a newspaper account of this little adventure."

"You have had luck," he put in. "Not everyone kills a tiger his first day out. This will make good reading."

"I wouldn't have missed it for a hundred pounds," I answered.

"Then try another."

"I wouldn't try another for a thousand," I cried, fervently. That evening, at the palace, I was the heroine of the day. They toasted me in a bumper of Heidsieck's dry monopole. The men made speeches. Everybody talked gushingly of my splendid courage and my steadiness of hand. It was a brilliant shot, under such difficult circumstances. For myself, I said nothing. I pretended to look modest. I dared not confess the truth—that I never fired at all. And from that day to this I have never confessed it, till I write it down now in these confiding memoirs.

One episode cast a gloom over my ill-deserved triumph. In the course of the evening, a telegram arrived for the pea-green young man by a white-turbaned messenger. He read it, and crumpled it up carelessly in his hand. I looked inquiry. "Yaas," he answered, nodding. "You're quite right. It's that! Pooah old Marmy has gone, aftah all! Ezekiel and Habakkuk have carried off his sixteen stone at last! And I don't mind telling yah now—though it was a neah thing—it's *I* who am the winnah!"

THE ADVENTURE OF
THE CROSS-EYED Q.C.

The "cold weather," as it is humorously called, was now drawing to a close, and the young ladies in sailor hats and cambric
blouses, who flock to India each autumn for the annual marriage-
market, were beginning to resign themselves to a return to England—unless, of course, they had succeeded in "catching." So I
realised that I must hurry on to Delhi and Agra, if I was not to be
intercepted by the intolerable summer.

When we started from Moozuffernuggar for Delhi and the East,
Lord Southminster was starting for Bombay and Europe. This surprised me not a little, for he had confided to my unsympathetic
ear a few nights earlier, in the Maharajah's billiard-room, that he
was "stony broke," and must wait at Moozuffernuggar for lack of
funds "till the oof-bird laid" at his banker's in England. His conversation enlarged my vocabulary, at any rate.

"So you've managed to get away?" I exclaimed, as he dawdled
up to me at the hot and dusty station.

"Yaas," he drawled, fixing his eye-glass, and lighting a cigarette.
"I've—p'f—managed to get away. Maharaj seems to have thought—p'f—
it would be cheepah in the end to pay me out than to keep me."

"You don't mean to say he offered to lend you money?" I cried.

"No; not exactly that: *I* offahed to borrow it."

"From the man you call a nigger?"

His smile spread broader over his face than ever. "Well, we
borrow from the Jews, yah know," he said pleasantly, "so why the
jooce shouldn't we borrow from the heathen also? Spoiling the

Egyptians, don't yah see?—the same as we used to read about in the Scripchah when we were innocent kiddies. Like marriage, quite. You borrow in haste—and repay at leisure."

He strolled off and took his seat. I was glad to get rid of him at the main line junction.

In accordance with my usual merciful custom, I spare you the details of our visit to Agra, Muttra, Benares. At Calcutta, Elsie left me. Her health was now quite restored, dear little soul— I felt I had done that one good thing in life if no other—and she could no longer withstand the higher mathematics, which were beckoning her to London with invisible fingers. For myself, having so far accomplished my original design of going round the world with twopence in my pocket, I could not bear to draw back at half the circuit; and Mr. Elworthy having willingly consented to my return by Singapore and Yokohama, I set out alone on my homeward journey.

Harold wrote me from London that all was going well. He had found the will which I drew up at Florence in his uncle's escritoire, and everything was left to him; but he trusted, in spite of this untoward circumstance, long absence might have altered my determination. "Dear Lois," he wrote, "I *expect* you to come back to England and marry me!"

I was brief, but categorical. Nothing, meanwhile, had altered my resolve. I did not wish to be considered mercenary. While he was rich and honoured, I could never take him. If, some day, fortune frowned—but, there—let us not forestall the feet of calamity: let us await contingencies.

Still, I was heavy in heart. If only it had been otherwise! To say the truth, I should be thrown away on a millionaire; but just think what a splendid managing wife a girl like me would have made for a penniless pauper!

At Yokohama, however, while I dawdled in curiosity shops, a telegram from Harold startled me into seriousness. My chance at last! I knew what it meant; that villain Higginson!

"Come home at once. I want your evidence to clear my character. Southminster opposes the will as a forgery. He has a strong case; the experts are with him."

Forgery! That was clever. I never thought of that. I suspected them of trying to forge a will of their own; but to upset the real one—to throw the burden of suspicion on Harold's shoulders—how much subtler and craftier!

I saw at a glance it gave them every advantage. In the first place, it put Harold virtually in the place of the accused, and compelled him to defend instead of attacking—an attitude which prejudices people against one from the outset. Then, again, it implied positive criminality on his part, and so allowed Lord Southminster to assume the air of injured innocence. The eldest son of the eldest brother, unjustly set aside by the scheming machinations of an unscrupulous cousin! Primogeniture, the ingrained English love for keeping up the dignity of a noble family, the prejudice in favour of the direct male line as against the female—all were astutely utilised in Lord Southminster's interest. But worst of all, it was *I* who had typewritten the will—I, a friend of Harold's, a woman whom Lord Southminster would doubtless try to exhibit as his *fiancée*. I saw at once how much like conspiracy it looked: Harold and I had agreed together to concoct a false document, and Harold had forged his uncle's signature to it. Could a British jury doubt when a Lord declared it?

Fortunately, I was just in time to catch the Canadian steamer from Japan to Vancouver. But, oh, the endless breadth of that broad Pacific! How time seemed to lag, as each day one rose in the morning, in the midst of space; blue sky overhead; behind one, the hard horizon; in front of one, the hard horizon; and nothing else visible: then steamed on all day, to arrive at night, where?—why, in the midst of space; starry sky overhead; behind one, the dim horizon; in front of one, the dim horizon; and nothing else visible. The Nile was child's play to it.

Day after day we steamed, and night after night were still where we began—in the centre of the sea, no farther from our starting-point, no nearer to our goal, yet forever steaming. It was endlessly wearisome; who could say what might be happening meanwhile in England?

At last, after months, as it seemed, of this slow torture, we reached Vancouver. There, in the raw new town, a telegram awaited me. "Glad to hear you are coming. Make all haste. You may be just in time to arrive for the trial."

Just in time! I would not waste a moment. I caught the first train on the Canadian Pacific, and travelled straight through, day and night, to Montreal and Quebec, without one hour's interval.

I cannot describe to you that journey across a continent I had never before seen. It was endless and hopeless. I only know that we crawled up the Rocky Mountains and the Selkirk Range, over spider-like viaducts, with interminable effort, and that the prairies were just the broad Pacific over again. They rolled on forever. But we did reach Quebec—in time we reached it; and we caught by an hour the first liner to Liverpool.

At Prince's Landing-stage another telegram awaited me. "Come on at once. Case now proceeding. Harold is in court. We need your evidence.—Georgina Fawley."

I might still be in time to vindicate Harold's character.

At Euston, to my surprise, I was met not only by my dear cantankerous old lady, but also by my friend, the magnificent Maharajah, dressed this time in a frock-coat and silk hat of Bond Street glossiness.

"What has brought you to England?" I asked, astonished. "The Jubilee?"

He smiled, and showed his two fine rows of white teeth. "That, nominally. In reality, the cricket season (I play for Berks). But most of all, to see dear Tillington safe through this trouble."

"He's a brick!" Lady Georgina cried with enthusiasm. "A regular brick, my dear Lois! His carriage is waiting outside to take you up to my house. He has stood by Harold—well, like a Christian!"

"Or a Hindu," the Maharajah corrected, smiling.

"And how have you been all this time, dear Lady Georgina?" I asked, hardly daring to inquire about what was nearest to my soul—Harold.

The cantankerous old lady knitted her brows in a familiar fashion. "Oh, my dear, don't ask: I haven't known a happy hour since you left me in Switzerland. Lois, I shall never be happy again without you! It would pay me to give you a retaining fee of a thousand a year—honour bright, it would, I assure you. What I've suffered

from the Gretchens since you've been in the East has only been
equalled by what I've suffered from the Mary Annes and the
Célestines. Not a hair left on my scalp; not one hair, I declare to
you. They've made my head into a *tabula rasa* for the various re-
storers. George R. Sims and Mrs. S. A. Allen are going to fight it
out between them. My dear, I wish *you* could take my maid's place;
I've always said—"

I finished the speech for her. "A lady can do better whatever
she turns her hand to than any of these hussies."

She nodded. "And why? Because her hands *are* hands; while as
for the Gretchens and the Mary Annes, 'paws' is the only word one
can honestly apply to them. Then, on top of it all comes this trouble
about Harold. So distressing, isn't it? You see, at the point which
the matter has reached, it's simply impossible to save Harold's
reputation without wrecking Southminster's. Pretty position that
for a respectable family! The Ashursts hitherto have been *quite*
respectable: a co-respondent or two, perhaps, but never anything
serious. Now, either Southminster sends Harold to prison, or
Harold sends Southminster. There's a nice sort of dilemma! I always knew Kynaston's boys were born fools; but to find they're
born knaves, too, is hard on an old woman in her hairless dotage.
However, *you've* come, my child, and *you'll* soon set things right.
You're the one person on earth I can trust in this matter."

Harold go to prison! My head reeled at the thought. I staggered
out into the open air, and took my seat mechanically in the
Maharajah's carriage. All London swam before me. After so many
months' absence, the polychromatic decorations of our English
streets, looming up through the smoke, seemed both strange and
familiar. I drove through the first half mile with a vague consciousness that Lipton's tea is the perfection of cocoa and matchless for
the complexion, but that it dyes all colours, and won't wash clothes.

After a while, however, I woke up to the full terror of the situation. "Where are you taking me?" I inquired.

"To my house, dear," Lady Georgina answered, looking anxiously at me; for my face was bloodless.

"No, that won't do," I answered. "My cue must be now to keep
myself as aloof as possible from Harold and Harold's backers. I

must put up at an hotel. It will sound so much better in cross-examination."

"She's quite right," the Maharajah broke in, with sudden conviction. "One must block every ball with these nasty swift bowlers."

"Where's Harold?" I asked, after another pause. "Why didn't he come to meet me?"

"My dear, how could he? He's under examination. A cross-eyed Q.C. with an odious leer. Southminster's chosen the biggest bully at the Bar to support his contention."

"Drive to some hotel in the Jermyn Street district," I cried to the Maharajah's coachman. "That will be handy for the law courts."

He touched his hat and turned. In a sort of dickey behind sat two gorgeous-turbaned Rajput servants.

That evening Harold came round to visit me at my rooms. I could see he was much agitated. Things had gone very badly. Lady Georgina was there; she had stopped to dine with me, dear old thing, lest I should feel lonely and give way; so had Elsie Petheridge. Mr. Elworthy sent a telegram of welcome from Devonshire. I knew at least that my friends were rallying round me in this hour of trial. The kind Maharajah himself would have come too, if I had allowed him, but I thought it inexpedient. They explained everything to me. Harold had propounded Mr. Ashurst's will—the one I drew up at Florence—and had asked for probate. Lord Southminster intervened and opposed the grant of probate on the ground that the signatures were forgeries. He propounded instead another will, drawn some twenty years earlier, when they were both children, duly executed at the time, and undoubtedly genuine; in it, testator left everything without reserve to the eldest son of his eldest brother, Lord Kynaston.

"Marmy didn't know in those days that Kynaston's sons would all grow up fools," Lady Georgina said tartly. "Besides which, that was before the poor dear soul took to plunging on the Stock Exchange and made his money. IIe had nothing to leave then but his best silk hat and a few paltry hundreds. Afterwards, when he'd feathered his nest in soap and cocoa, he discovered that Bertie— that's Lord Southminster—was a first-class idiot. Marmy never liked Southminster, nor Southminster Marmy. For after all, with all his faults, Marmy *was* a gentleman; while Bertie—well, my dear, we needn't put a name to it. So he altered his will, as you know, when he saw the sort of man Southminster turned out, and left practically everything he possessed to Harold."

"Who are the witnesses to the will?" I asked.

"There's the trouble. Who do you think? Why, Higginson's sister, who was Marmy's *masseuse*, and a waiter—Franz Markheim—at the hotel at Florence, who's dead they say—or, at least, not forthcoming."

"And Higginson's sister forswears her signature," Harold added gloomily; "while the experts are, most of them, dead against the genuineness of my uncle's."

"That's clever," I said, leaning back, and taking it in slowly. "Higginson's sister! How well they've worked it. They couldn't prevent Mr. Ashurst from making this will, but they managed to supply their own tainted witnesses! If it had been Higginson himself now, he'd have had to be cross-examined; and in cross-examination, of course, we could have shaken his credit, by bringing up the episodes of the Count de Laroche-sur-Loiret and Dr. Fortescue-Langley. But his sister! What's she like? Have you anything against her?"

"My dear," Lady Georgina cried, "there the rogue has bested us. Isn't it just like him? What do you suppose he has done? Why, provided himself with a sister of tried respectability and blameless character."

"And she denies that it is her handwriting?" I asked.

"Declares on her Bible oath she never signed the document."

I was fairly puzzled. It was a stupendously clever dodge. Higginson must have trained up his sister for forty years in the ways of wickedness, yet held her in reserve for this supreme moment.

"And where is Higginson?" I asked.

Lady Georgina broke into a hysterical laugh. "Where is he, my dear? That's the question. With consummate strategy, the wretch has disappeared into space at the last moment."

"That's artful again," I said. "His presence could only damage their case. I can see, of course, Lord Southminster has no need of him."

"Southminster's the wiliest fool that ever lived," Harold broke out bitterly. "Under that mask of imbecility, he's a fox for trickiness."

I bit my lip. "Well, if you succeed in evading him," I said, "you will have cleared your character. And if you don't—then, Harold, our time will have come: you will have your longed-for chance of trying me."

"That won't do me much good," he answered, "if I have to wait fourteen years for you—at Portland."

Next morning, in court, I heard Harold's cross-examination. He described exactly where he had found the contested will in his uncle's escritoire. The cross-eyed Q.C, a heavy man with bloated features and a bulbous nose, begged him, with one fat uplifted forefinger, to be very careful. How did he know where to look for it?

"Because I knew the house well: I knew where my uncle was likely to keep his valuables."

"Oh, indeed; *not* because you had put it there?"

The court rang with laughter. My face grew crimson.

After an hour or two of fencing, Harold was dismissed. He stood down, baffled. Counsel recalled Lord Southminster.

The pea-green young man, stepping briskly up, gazed about him, open-mouthed, with a vacant stare. The look of cunning on his face was carefully suppressed. He wore, on the contrary, an air of injured innocence combined with an eye-glass.

"*You* did not put this will in the drawer where Mr. Tillington found it, did you?" counsel asked.

The pea-green young man laughed. "No, I certainly didn't put it theah. My cousin Harold was man in possession. He took jolly good care *I* didn't come neah the premises."

"Do you think you could forge a will if you tried?"

Lord Southminster laughed. "No, I don't," he answered, with a well-assumed *naïveté*. "That's just the difference between us, don't yah know. *I'm* what they call a fool, and my cousin Harold's a precious clevah fellah."

There was another loud laugh.

"That's not evidence," the judge observed, severely.

It was not. But it told far more than much that was. It told strongly against Harold.

"Besides," Lord Southminster continued, with engaging frankness, "if I forged a will at all, I'd take jolly good care to forge it in my own favah."

My turn came next. Our counsel handed me the incriminated will. "Did you draw up this document?" he asked.

I looked at it closely. The paper bore our Florentine water-mark, and was written with a Spread-Eagle. "I type-wrote it," I answered, gazing at it with care to make sure I recognised it.

Our counsel's business was to uphold the will, not to cast aspersions upon it. He was evidently annoyed at my close examination. "You have no doubts about it?" he said, trying to prompt me.

I hesitated. "No, no doubts," I answered, turning over the sheet and inspecting it still closer. "I type-wrote it at Florence."

"Do you recognise that signature as Mr. Marmaduke Ashurst's?" he went on.

I stared at it. Was it his? It was like it, certainly. Yet that *k*? and those *s*'s? I almost wondered.

Counsel was obviously annoyed at my hesitation. He thought I was playing into the enemy's hands. "Is it his, or is it not?" he inquired again, testily.

"It is his," I answered. Yet I own I was troubled.

He asked many questions about the circumstances of the interview when I took down the will. I answered them all. But I vaguely felt he and I were at cross-purposes. I grew almost as uncomfortable under his gaze as if he had been examining me in the interest of the other side. He managed to fluster me. As a witness for Harold, I was a grotesque failure.

Then the cross-eyed Q.C., rising and shaking his huge bulk, began to cross-examine me. "Where did you type-write this thing, do you say?" he said, pointing to it contemptuously.

"In my office at Florence."

"Yes, I understand; you had an office in Florence—after you gave up retailing bicycles on the public roads; and you had a partner,

I think—a Miss Petherick, or Petherton, or Pennyfarthing, or something?"

"Miss Petheridge," I corrected, while the Court tittered.

"Ah, Petheridge, you call it! Well, now answer this question carefully. Did your Miss Petheridge hear Mr. Ashurst dictate the terms of his last will and testament?"

"No," I answered. "The interview was of a strictly confidential character. Mr. Ashurst took me aside into the back room at our office."

"Oh, he took you aside? Confidential? Well, now we're getting at it. And did anybody but yourself see or hear any part whatsoever of this precious document?"

"Certainly not," I replied. "It was a private matter."

"Private! oh, very! Nobody else saw it. Did Mr. Ashurst take it away from the office in person?"

"No; he sent his courier for it."

"His courier? The man Higginson?"

"Yes; but I refused to give it to Higginson. I took it myself that night to the hotel where Mr. Ashurst was stopping."

"Ah! You took it yourself. So the only other person who knows anything at first hand about the existence of the alleged will is this person Higginson?"

"Miss Petheridge knows," I said, flushing. "At the time, I told her of it."

"Oh, *you* told her. Well, that doesn't help us much. If what you are swearing isn't true—remember, you are on your oath—what you told Miss Petherick or Petheridge or Pennyfarthing, 'at the time,' can hardly be regarded as corroborative evidence. Your word then and your word now are just equally valuable—or equally worthless. The only person who knows besides yourself is Higginson. Now, I ask you, *where* is Higginson? *Are* you going to produce him?"

The wicked cunning of it struck me dumb. They were keeping him away, and then using his absence to cast doubts on my veracity. "Stop," I cried, taken aback, "Higginson is well known to be a rogue, and he is keeping away lest he may damage your side. I know nothing of Higginson."

"Yes, I'm coming to that in good time. Don't be afraid that we're going to pass over Higginson. You admit this man is a man of bad character. Now, what do you know of him?"

I told the stories of the Count and of Dr. Fortescue-Langley.

The cross-eyed cross-examiner leant across towards me and leered. "And this is the man," he exclaimed, with a triumphant air, "whose sister you pretended you had got to sign this precious document of yours?"

"Whom Mr. Ashurst got to sign it," I answered, red-hot. "It is not *my* document."

"And you have heard that she swears it is not her signature at all?"

"So they tell me. She is Higginson's sister. For all I know, she may be prepared to swear, or to forswear, anything."

"Don't cast doubt upon our witnesses without cause! Miss Higginson is an eminently respectable woman. You gave this document to Mr. Ashurst, you say. There your knowledge of it ends. A signature is placed on it which is not his, as our experts testify. It purports to be witnessed by a Swiss waiter, who is not forthcoming, and who is asserted to be dead, as well as by a nurse who denies her signature. And the only other person who knows of its existence before Mr. Tillington 'discovers' it in his uncle's desk is—the missing man Higginson. Is that, or is it not, the truth of the matter?"

"I suppose so," I said, baffled.

"Well, now, as to this man Higginson. He first appears upon the scene, so far as you are concerned, on the day when you travelled from London to Schlangenbad?"

"That is so," I answered.

"And he nearly succeeded then in stealing Lady Georgina Fawley's jewel-case?"

"He nearly took it, but I saved it." And I explained the circumstance.

The cross-eyed Q.C. held his fat sides with his hands, looking incredulously at me, and smiled. His vast width of waistcoat shook with silent merriment. "You are a very clever young lady," he murmured. "You can explain away anything. But don't you think it just as likely that it was a plot between you two, and that owing to some mistake the plot came off unsuccessful?"

"I do not," I cried, crimson. "I never saw the Count before that morning."

He tried another tack. "Still, wherever you went, this man Higginson—the only other person, you admit, who knows about the previous existence of the will—turned up simultaneously. He was always turning up—at the same place as you did. He turned up at Lucerne, as a faith-healer, didn't he?"

"If you will allow me to explain," I cried, biting my lip.

He bowed, all blandness. "Oh, certainly," he murmured. "Explain away everything!"

I explained, but of course he had discounted and damaged my explanation.

He made no comment. "And then," he went on, with his hands on his hips, and his obtrusive rotundity, "he turned up at Florence, as courier to Mr. Ashurst, at the very date when this so-called will was being concocted?"

"He was at Florence when Mr. Ashurst dictated it to me," I answered, growing desperate.

"You admit he was in Florence. Good! Once more he turned up in India with my client, Lord Southminster, upon whose youth and inexperience he had managed to impose himself. And he carried him off, did he not, by one of these strange coincidences to which *you* are peculiarly liable, on the very same steamer on which *you* happened to be travelling?"

"Lord Southminster told me he took Higginson with him because a rogue suited his book," I answered, warmly.

"Will you swear his lordship didn't say 'the rogue suited his book'—which is quite another thing?" the Q.C. asked blandly.

"I will swear he did not," I replied. "I have correctly reported him."

"Then I congratulate you, young lady, on your excellent memory. My lud, will you allow me later to recall Lord Southminster to testify on this point?"

The judge nodded.

"Now, once more, as to your relations with the various members of the Ashurst family. You introduced yourself to Lady

Georgina Fawley, I believe, quite casually, on a seat in Kensington Gardens?"

"That is true," I answered.

"You had never seen her before?"

"Never."

"And you promptly offered to go with her as her lady's maid to Schlangenbad in Germany?"

"In place of her lady's maid, for one week," I answered.

"Ah; a delicate distinction! 'In place of her lady's maid.' You are a lady, I believe; an officer's daughter, you told us; educated at Girton?"

"So I have said already," I replied, crimson.

"And you stick to it? By all means. Tell—the truth—and stick to it. It's always safest. Now, don't you think it was rather an odd thing for an officer's daughter to do—to run about Germany as maid to a lady of title?"

I tried to explain once more; but the jury smiled. You can't justify originality to a British jury. Why, they would send you to prison at once for that alone, if they made the laws as well as dispensing them.

He passed on after a while to another topic. "I think you have boasted more than once in society that when you first met Lady Georgina Fawley you had twopence in your pocket to go round the world with?"

"I had," I answered—"and I went round the world with it."

"Exactly. I'm getting there in time. With it—and other things. A few months later, more or less, you were touring up the Nile in your steam dahabeeah, and in the lap of luxury; you were taking saloon-carriages on Indian railways, weren't you?"

I explained again. "The dahabeeah was in the service of the *Daily Telephone*," I answered. "I became a journalist."

He cross-questioned me about that. "Then I am to understand," he said at last, leaning forward with all his waistcoat, "that you sprang yourself upon Mr. Elworthy at sight, pretty much as you sprang yourself upon Lady Georgina Fawley?"

"We arranged matters quickly," I admitted. The dexterous wretch was making my strongest points all tell against me.

"H'm! Well, he was a man: and you will admit, I suppose," fingering his smooth fat chin, "that you are a lady of—what is the stock phrase the reporters use?—considerable personal attractions?"

"My Lord," I said, turning to the Bench, "I appeal to you. Has he the right to compel me to answer that question?"

The judge bowed slightly. "The question requires no answer," he said, with a quiet emphasis. I burned bright scarlet.

"Well, my lud, I defer to your ruling," the cross-eyed cross-examiner continued, radiant. "I go on to another point. When in India, I believe, you stopped for some time as a guest in the house of a native Maharajah."

"Is that matter relevant?" the judge asked, sharply.

"My lud," the Q.C. said, in his blandest voice, "I am striving to suggest to the jury that this lady—the only person who ever beheld this so-called will till Mr. Harold Tillington—described in its terms as 'Younger of Gledcliffe,' whatever that may be—produced it out of his uncle's desk—I am striving to suggest that this lady is—my duty to my client compels me to say—an adventuress."

He had uttered the word. I felt my character had not a leg left to stand upon before a British jury.

"I went there with my friend, Miss Petheridge—" I began.

"Oh, Miss Petheridge once more—you hunt in couples?"

"Accompanied and chaperoned by a married lady, the wife of a Major Balmossie, on the Bombay Staff Corps."

"That was certainly prudent. One ought to be chaperoned. Can you produce the lady?"

"How is it possible?" I cried. "Mrs. Balmossie is in India."

"Yes; but the Maharajah, I understand, is in London?"

"That is true," I answered.

"And he came to meet you on your arrival yesterday."

"With Lady Georgina Fawley," I cried, taken off my guard.

"Do you not consider it curious," he asked, "that these Higginsons and these Maharajahs should happen to follow you so closely round the world?—should happen to turn up wherever you do?"

"He came to be present at this trial," I exclaimed.

"And so did you. I believe he met you at Euston last night, and drove you to your hotel in his private carriage."

"With Lady Georgina Fawley," I answered, once more.

"And Lady Georgina is on Mr. Tillington's side, I fancy? Ah, yes, I thought so. And Mr. Tillington also called to see you; and likewise Miss Petherick—I beg your pardon, Petheridge. We must be strictly accurate—where Miss Petheridge is concerned. And, in fact, you had quite a little family party."

"My friends were glad to see me back again," I murmured.

He sprang a fresh innuendo. "But Mr. Tillington did not resent your visit to this gallant Maharajah?"

"Certainly not," I cried, bridling. "Why should he?"

"Oh, we're getting to that too. Now answer me this carefully. We want to find out what interest you might have, supposing a will were forged, on either side, in arranging its terms. We want to find out just who would benefit by it. Please reply to this question, yes or no, without prevarication. Are you or are you not conditionally engaged to Mr. Harold Tillington?"

"If I might explain—" I began, quivering.

He sneered. "You have a genius for explaining, we are aware. Answer me first, yes or no; we will qualify afterward."

I glanced appealingly at the judge. He was adamant. "Answer as counsel directs you, witness," he said, sternly.

"Yes, I am," I faltered. "But—"

"Excuse me one moment. You promised to marry him conditionally upon the result of Mr. Ashurst's testamentary dispositions?"

"I did," I answered; "but—"

My explanation was drowned in roars of laughter, in which the judge joined, in spite of himself. When the mirth in court had subsided a little, I went on: "I told Mr. Tillington I would only marry him in case he was poor and without expectations. If he inherited Mr. Marmaduke Ashurst's money, I could never be his wife," I said it proudly.

The cross-eyed Q.C. drew himself up and let his rotundity take care of itself. "Do you take me," he inquired, "for one of Her Majesty's horse-marines?"

There was another roar of laughter—feebly suppressed by a judicial frown—and I slank away, annihilated.

"You can go," my persecutor said. "I think we have got—well, everything we wanted from you. You promised to marry him, if all went ill! That is a delicate feminine way of putting it. Women like these equivocations. They relieve one from the onus of speaking frankly."

I stood down from the box, feeling, for the first time in my life, conscious of having scored an ignominious failure.

Our counsel did not care to re-examine me; I recognised that it would be useless. The hateful Q.C. had put all my history in such an odious light that explanation could only make matters worse—it must savour of apology. The jury could never understand my point of view. It could never be made to see that there are adventuresses and adventuresses.

Then came the final speeches on either side. Harold's advocate said the best he could in favour of the will our party propounded; but his best was bad; and what galled me most was this— I could see he himself did not believe in its genuineness. His speech amounted to little more than a perfunctory attempt to put the most favourable face on a probable forgery.

As for the cross-eyed Q.C., he rose to reply with humorous confidence. Swaying his big body to and fro, he crumpled our will and our case in his fat fingers like so much flimsy tissue-paper. Mr. Ashurst had made a disposition of his property twenty years ago—the right disposition, the natural disposition; he had left the bulk of it as childless English gentlemen have ever been wont to leave their wealth—to the eldest son of the eldest son of his family. The Honourable Marmaduke Courtney Ashurst, the testator, was the scion of a great house, which recent agricultural changes, he regretted to say, had relatively impoverished; he had come to the succour of that great house, as such a scion should, with his property acquired by honest industry elsewhere. It was fitting and reasonable that Mr. Ashurst should wish to see the Kynaston peerage regain, in the person of the amiable and accomplished young nobleman whom he had the honour to represent, some portion of its ancient dignity and splendour.

But jealousy and greed intervened. (Here he frowned at Harold.) Mr. Harold Tillington, the son of one of Mr. Ashurst's married sisters, cast longing eyes, as he had tried to suggest to them, on his cousin Lord Southminster's natural heritage. The result, he feared, was an unnatural intrigue. Mr. Harold Tillington formed the acquaintance of a young lady—should we say young lady?—(he withered me with his glance)—well, yes, a lady, indeed, by birth and education, but an adventuress by choice—a lady who, brought up in a respectable, though not (he must admit) a distinguished sphere, had lowered herself by accepting the position of a lady's maid, and had trafficked in patent American cycles on the public high-roads of Germany and Switzerland. This clever and designing woman (he would grant her ability—he would grant her good looks) had fascinated Mr. Tillington—that was the theory he ventured to lay before the jury to-day; and the jury would see for themselves that whatever else the young lady might be, she had distinctly a certain outer gift of fascination. It was for them to decide whether Miss Lois Cayley had or had not suggested to Mr. Harold Tillington the design of substituting a forged will for Mr. Marmaduke Ashurst's undeniable testament. He would point out to them her singular connection with the missing man Higginson, whom the young lady herself described as a rogue, and from whom she had done her very best to dissociate herself in this court—but ineffectually. Wherever Miss Cayley went, the man Higginson went independently. Such frequent recurrences, such apt juxtapositions could hardly be set down to mere accidental coincidence.

He went on to insinuate that Higginson and I had concocted the disputed will between us; that we had passed it on to our fellow-conspirator, Harold; and that Harold had forged his uncle's signature to it, and had appended those of the two supposed witnesses. But who, now, were these witnesses? One, Franz Markheim, was dead or missing; dead men tell no tales: the other was obviously suggested by Higginson. It was his own sister. Perhaps he forged her name to the document. Doubtless he thought that family feeling would induce her, when it came to the pinch, to accept and endorse her brother's lie; nay, he might even have been foolish enough to suppose that this cock-and-bull will would not be disputed. If so, he and his master had reckoned without Lord Southminster, a gentleman who concealed beneath the careless exterior of a man of fashion the solid intelligence of a man of affairs, and the hard head of a man not to be lightly cheated in matters of business.

The alleged will had thus not a leg to stand upon. It was "typewritten" (save the mark!) "from dictation" at Florence, by whom? By the lady who had most to gain from its success—the lady who was to be transformed from a shady adventuress, tossed about between Irish doctors and Hindu Maharajahs, into the lawful wife of a wealthy diplomatist of noble family, on one condition only—if this pretended will could be satisfactorily established. The signatures were forgeries, as shown by the expert evidence, and also by the oath of the one surviving witness.

The will left all the estate—practically—to Mr. Harold Tillington, and five hundred pounds to whom?—why, to the accomplice Higginson. The minor bequests the Q.C. regarded as ingenious inventions, pure play of fancy, "intended to give artistic verisimilitude," as Pooh-Bah says in the opera, "to an otherwise bald and unconvincing narrative." The fads, it was true, were known fads of Mr. Ashurst's: but what sort of fads? Bimetallism? Anglo-Israel? No, braces and shoe-horns—clearly the kind that would best be known to a courier like Higginson, the sole begetter, he believed, of this nefarious conspiracy.

The cross-eyed Q.C., lifting his fat right hand in solemn adjuration, called upon the jury confidently to set aside this ridiculous fabrication, and declare for a will of undoubted genuineness, a will drawn up in London by a firm of eminent solicitors, and preserved ever since by the testator's bankers. It would then be for his lordship to decide whether in the public interest he should recommend the Crown to prosecute on a charge of forgery the clumsy fabricator of this preposterous document.

The judge summed up—strongly in favour of Lord Southminster's will. If the jury believed the experts and Miss Higginson, one verdict alone was possible. The jury retired for three minutes only. It was a foregone conclusion. They found for Lord Southminster. The judge, looking grave, concurred in their finding. A most proper verdict. And he considered it would be the duty of the Public Prosecutor to pursue Mr. Harold Tillington on the charge of forgery.

I reeled where I sat. Then I looked round for Harold.

He had slipped from the court, unseen, during counsel's address, some minutes earlier!

That distressed me more than anything else on that dreadful day. I wished he had stood up in his place like a man to face this vile and cruel conspiracy.

I walked out slowly, supported by Lady Georgina, who was as white as a ghost herself, but very straight and scornful. "I always knew Southminster was a fool," she said aloud; "I always knew he was a sneak; but I did not know till now he was also a particularly bad type of criminal."

On the steps of the court, the pea-green young man met us. His air was jaunty. "Well, I was right, yah see," he said, smiling and withdrawing his cigarette. "You backed the wrong fellah! I told you I'd win. I won't say moah now; this is not the time or place to recur to that subject; but, by-and-by, you'll come round; you'll think bettah of it still; you'll back the winnah!"

I wished I were a man, that I might have the pleasure of kicking him.

We drove back to my hotel and waited for Harold. To my horror and alarm, he never came near us. I might almost have doubted him—if he had not been Harold.

I waited and waited. He did not come at all. He sent no word, no message. And all that evening we heard the newsboys shouting at the top of their voice in the street, "Extra Speshul! the Ashurst Will Kise; Sensational Developments" "Mysterious Disappearance of Mr. 'Arold Tillington."

THE ADVENTURE OF
THE ORIENTAL ATTENDANT

I did not sleep that night. Next morning, I rose very early from a restless bed with a dry, hot mouth, and a general feeling that the solid earth had failed beneath me.

Still no news from Harold! It was cruel, I thought. My faith almost flagged. He was a man and should be brave. How could he run away and hide himself at such a time? Even if I set my own anxiety aside, just think to what serious misapprehension it laid him open!

I sent out for the morning papers. They were full of Harold. Rumours, rumours, rumours! Mr. Tillington had deliberately chosen to put himself in the wrong by disappearing mysteriously at the last moment. He had only himself to blame if the worst interpretation were put upon his action. But the police were on his track; Scotland Yard had "a clue": it was confidently expected an arrest would be made before evening at latest. As to details, authorities differed. The officials of the Great Western Railway at Paddington were convinced that Mr. Tillington had started, alone and undisguised, by the night express for Exeter. The South-Eastern inspectors at Charing Cross, on the other hand, were equally certain that he had slipped away with a false beard, in company with his "accomplice" Higginson, by the 8.15 p.m. to Paris. Everybody took it for granted, however, that he had left London.

Conjecture played with various ultimate destinations—Spain, Morocco, Sicily, the Argentine. In Italy, said the *Chronicle*, he

might lurk for a while—he spoke Italian fluently, and could manage to put up at tiny *osterie* in out-of-the-way places seldom visited by Englishmen. He might try Albania, said the *Morning Post*,
airing its exclusive "society" information: he had often hunted
there, and might in turn be hunted. He would probably attempt to
slink away to some remote spot in the Carpathians or the Balkans,
said the *Daily News*, quite proud of its geography. Still, wherever
he went, leaden-footed justice in this age, said the *Times*, must
surely overtake him. The day of universal extradition had dawned;
we had no more Alsatias: even the Argentine itself gives up its
rogues—at last; not an asylum for crime remains in Europe, not a
refuge in Asia, Africa, America, Australia, or the Pacific Islands.

I noted with a shudder of horror that all the papers alike took
his guilt as certain. In spite of a few decent pretences at not pre-
judging an untried cause, they treated him already as the detected
criminal, the fugitive from justice. I sat in my little sitting-room at
the hotel in Jermyn Street, a limp rag, looking idly out of the window with swimming eyes, and waiting for Lady Georgina. It was
early, too early, but—oh, why didn't she come! Unless *somebody*
soon sympathised with me, my heart would break under this load
of loneliness!

Presently, as I looked out on the sloppy morning street, I was
vaguely aware through the mist that floated before my dry eyes
(for tears were denied me) of a very grand carriage driving up to
the doorway—the porch with the four wooden Ionic pillars. I took
no heed of it. I was too heart-sick for observation. My life was
wrecked, and Harold's with it. Yet, dimly through the mist, I became conscious after a while that the carriage was that of an Indian
prince; I could see the black faces, the white turbans, the gold bro-
cades of the attendants in the dickey. Then it came home to me
with a pang that this was the Maharajah.

It was kindly meant; yet after all that had been insinuated in
court the day before, I was by no means over-pleased that his dusky
Highness should come to call upon me. Walls have eyes and ears.
Reporters were hanging about all over London, eager to distinguish
themselves by successful eavesdropping. They would note, with

brisk innuendoes after their kind, how "the Maharajah of Moozuf-fernuggar called early in the day on Miss Lois Cayley, with whom he remained for at least half an hour in close consultation." I had half a mind to send down a message that I could not see him. My face still burned with the undeserved shame of the cross-eyed Q.C.'s unspeakable suggestions.

Before I could make my mind up, however, I saw to my surprise that the Maharajah did not propose to come in himself. He leaned back in his place with his lordly Eastern air, and waited, looking down on the gapers in the street, while one of the two gorgeous attendants in the dickey descended obsequiously to receive his orders. The man was dressed as usual in rich Oriental stuffs, and wore his full white turban swathed in folds round his head. I could not see his features. He bent forward respectfully with Oriental suppleness to take his Highness's orders. Then, receiving a card and bowing low, he entered the porch with the wooden Ionic pillars, and disappeared within, while the Maharajah folded his hands and seemed to resign himself to a temporary Nirvana.

A minute later, a knock sounded on my door. "Come in!" I said, faintly; and the messenger entered.

I turned and faced him. The blood rushed to my cheek. "Harold!" I cried, darting forward. My joy overcame me. He folded me in his arms. I allowed him, unreproved. For the first time he kissed me. I did not shrink from it.

Then I stood away a little and gazed at him. Even at that crucial moment of doubt and fear, I could not help noticing how admirably he made up as a handsome young Rajput. Three years earlier, at Schlangenbad, I remembered he had struck me as strangely Oriental-looking: he had the features of a high-born Indian gentleman, without the complexion. His large, poetical eyes, his regular, oval face, his even teeth, his mouth and moustache, all vaguely recalled the highest type of the Eastern temperament. Now, he had blackened his face and hands with some permanent stain—Indian ink, I learned later—and the resemblance to a Rajput chief was positively startling. In his gold brocade and ample white turban, no passer-by, I felt sure, would ever have dreamt of doubting him.

"Then you knew me at once?" he said, holding my face between his hands. "That's bad, darling! I flattered myself I had transformed my face into the complete Indian."

"Love has sharp eyes," I answered. "It can see through brick walls. But the disguise is perfect. No one else would detect you."

"Love is blind, I thought."

"Not where it ought to see. There, it pierces everything. I knew you instantly, Harold. But all London, I am sure, would pass you by, unknown. You are absolute Orient."

"That's well; for all London is looking for me," he answered, bitterly. "The streets bristle with detectives. Southminster's knaveries have won the day. So I have tried this disguise. Otherwise, I should have been arrested the moment the jury brought in their verdict."

"And why were you not?" I asked, drawing back. "Oh, Harold, I trust you; but why did you disappear and make all the world believe you admitted yourself guilty?"

He opened his arms. "Can't you guess?" he cried, holding them out to me.

I nestled in them once more; but I answered through my tears— I had found tears now—"No Harold; it baffles me."

"You remember what you promised me?" he murmured, leaning over me and clasping me. "If ever I were poor, friendless, hunted—you would marry me. Now the opportunity has come when we can both prove ourselves. To-day, except you and dear Georgey, I haven't a friend in the world. Everyone else has turned against me. Southminster holds the field. I am a suspected forger; in a very few days I shall doubtless be a convicted felon. Unjustly, as you know; yet still—we must face it—a convicted felon. So I have come to claim you. I have come to ask you now, in this moment of despair, will you keep your promise?"

I lifted my face to his. He bent over it trembling. I whispered the words in his ear. "Yes, Harold, I will keep it. I have always loved you. And now I will marry you."

"I knew you would!" he cried, and pressed me to his bosom.

We sat for some minutes, holding each other's hands, and saying nothing; we were too full of thought for words. Then suddenly,

Harold roused himself. "We must make haste, darling," he cried. "We are keeping Partab outside, and every minute is precious, every minute's delay dangerous. We ought to go down at once. Partab's carriage is waiting at the door for us."

"Go down?" I exclaimed, clinging to him. "How? Why? I don't understand. What is your programme?"

"Ah, I forgot I hadn't explained to you! Listen here, dearest— quick; I can waste no words over it. I said just now I had no friends in the world but you and Georgey. That's not true, for dear old Partab has stuck to me nobly. When all my English friends fell away, the Rajput was true to me. He arranged all this; it was his own idea; he foresaw what was coming. He urged me yesterday, just before the verdict (when he saw my acquaintances beginning to look askance), to slip quietly out of court, and make my way by unobtrusive roads to his house in Curzon Street. There, he darkened my face like his, and converted me to Hinduism. I don't suppose the disguise will serve me for more than a day or two; but it will last long enough for us to get safely away to Scotland."

"Scotland?" I murmured. "Then you mean to try a Scotch marriage?"

"It is the only thing possible. We must be married to-day, and in England, of course, we cannot do it. We would have to be called in church, or else to procure a license, either of which would involve disclosure of my identity. Besides, even the license would keep us waiting about for a day or two. In Scotland, on the other hand, we can be married at once. Partab's carriage is below, to take you to King's Cross. He is staunch as steel, dear fellow. Do you consent to go with me?"

My faculty for promptly making up such mind as I possess stood me once more in good stead. "Implicitly," I answered. "Dear Harold, this calamity has its happy side—for without it, much as I love you, I could never have brought myself to marry you!"

"One moment," he cried. "Before you go, recollect, this step is irrevocable. You will marry a man who may be torn from you this evening, and from whom fourteen years of prison may separate you."

"I know it," I cried, through my tears. "But— I shall be showing my confidence in you, my love for you."

He kissed me once more, fervently. "This makes amends for all," he cried. "Lois, to have won such a woman as you, I would go through it all a thousand times over. It was for this, and for this alone, that I hid myself last night. I wanted to give you the chance of showing me how much, how truly you loved me."

"And after we are married?" I asked, trembling.

"I shall give myself up at once to the police in Edinburgh."

I clung to him wistfully. My heart half urged me to urge him to escape. But I knew that was wrong. "Give yourself up, then," I said, sobbing. "It is a brave man's place. You must stand your trial; and, come what will, I will strive to bear it with you."

"I knew you would," he cried. "I was not mistaken in you."

We embraced again, just once. It was little enough after those years of waiting.

"Now, come!" he cried. "Let us go."

I drew back. "Not with you, dearest," I whispered. "Not in the Maharajah's carriage. You must start by yourself. I will follow you at once, to King's Cross, in a hansom."

He saw I was right. It would avoid suspicion, and it would prevent more scandal. He withdrew without a word. "We meet," I said, "at ten, at King's Cross Station."

I did not even wait to wash the tears from my eyes. All red as they were, I put on my hat and my little brown travelling jacket. I don't think I so much as glanced once at the glass. The seconds were precious. I saw the Maharajah drive away, with Harold in the dickey, arms crossed, imperturbable, Orientally silent. He looked the very counterpart of the Rajput by his side. Then I descended the stairs and walked out boldly. As I passed through the hall, the servants and the visitors stared at me and whispered. They spoke with nods and liftings of the eyebrows. I was aware that that morning I had achieved notoriety.

At Piccadilly Circus, I jumped of a sudden into a passing hansom. "King's Cross!" I cried, as I mounted the step. "Drive quick! I have no time to spare." And, as the man drove off, I saw, by a convulsive dart of someone across the road, that I had given the slip to a disappointed reporter.

At the station I took a first-class ticket for Edinburgh. On the platform, the Maharajah and his attendants were waiting. He lifted his hat to me, though otherwise he took no overt notice. But I saw his keen eyes follow me down the train. Harold, in his Oriental dress, pretended not to observe me. One or two porters, and a few curious travellers, cast inquiring eyes on the Eastern prince, and made remarks about him to one another. "That's the chap as was up yesterday in the Ashurst will kise!" said one lounger to his neighbour. But nobody seemed to look at Harold; his subordinate position secured him from curiosity. The Maharajah had always two Eastern servants, gorgeously dressed, in attendance; he had been a well-known figure in London society, and at Lord's and the Oval, for two or three seasons.

"Bloomin' fine cricketer!" one porter observed to his mate as he passed.

"Yuss; not so dusty for a nigger," the other man replied. "Fust-rite bowler; but, Lord, he can't 'old a candle to good old Ranji."

As for myself, nobody seemed to recognise me. I set this fact down to the fortunate circumstance that the evening papers had published rough wood-cuts which professed to be my portrait, and which naturally led the public to look out for a brazen-faced, raw-boned, hard-featured termagant.

I took my seat in a ladies' compartment by myself. As the train was about to start, Harold strolled up as if casually for a moment. "You think it better so?" he queried, without moving his lips or seeming to look at me.

"Decidedly," I answered. "Go back to Partab. Don't come near me again till we get to Edinburgh. It is dangerous still. The police may at any moment hear we have started and stop us half-way; and now that we have once committed ourselves to this plan it would be fatal to be interrupted before we have got married."

"You are right," he cried; "Lois, you are always right, somehow."

I wished I could think so myself; but 'twas with serious misgivings that I felt the train roll out of the station.

Oh, that long journey north, alone, in a ladies' compartment—with the feeling that Harold was so near, yet so unapproachable: it was an endless agony. *He* had the Maharajah, who loved and admired him, to keep him from brooding; but I, left alone, and confined with my own fears, conjured up before my eyes every possible misfortune that Heaven could send us. I saw clearly now that if we failed in our purpose this journey would be taken by everyone for a flight, and would deepen the suspicion under which we both laboured. It would make me still more obviously a conspirator with Harold.

Whatever happened, we must strain every nerve to reach Scotland in safety, and then to get married, in order that Harold might immediately surrender himself.

At York, I noticed with a thrill of terror that a man in plain clothes, with the obtrusively unobtrusive air of a detective, looked carefully though casually into every carriage. I felt sure he was a spy, because of his marked outer jauntiness of demeanour, which hardly masked an underlying hang-dog expression of scrutiny. When he reached my place, he took a long, careless stare at me—a seemingly careless stare, which was yet brim-full of the keenest observation. Then he paced slowly along the line of carriages, with a glance at each, till he arrived just opposite the Maharajah's compartment. There he stared hard once more. The Maharajah descended; so did Harold and the Hindu attendant, who was dressed just like him. The man I took for a detective indulged in a frank, long gaze at the unconscious Indian prince, but cast only a hasty eye on the two apparent followers. That touch of revelation relieved my mind a little. I felt convinced the police were watching the Maharajah and myself, as suspicious persons connected with the case; but they had not yet guessed that Harold had disguised himself as one of the two invariable Rajput servants.

We steamed on northward. At Newcastle, the same detective strolled, with his hands in his pockets, along the train once more, and puffed a cigar with the nonchalant air of a sporting gentleman. But I was certain now, from the studious unconcern he was anxious to exhibit, that he must be a spy upon us. He overdid his mood of careless observation. It was too obvious an assumption. Precisely the same thing happened again when we pulled up at

Berwick. I knew now that we were watched. It would be impossible for us to get married at Edinburgh if we were thus closely pursued. There was but one chance open; we must leave the train abruptly at the first Scotch stopping station.

The detective knew we were booked through for Edinburgh. So much I could tell, because I saw him make inquiries of the ticket examiner at York, and again at Berwick, and because the ticket-examiner thereupon entered a mental note of the fact as he punched my ticket each time: "Oh, Edinburgh, miss? All right"; and then stared at me suspiciously. I could tell he had heard of the Ashurst will case. He also lingered long about the Maharajah's compartment, and then went back to confer with the detective. Thus, putting two and two together, as a woman will, I came to the conclusion that the spy did not expect us to leave the train before we reached Edinburgh. That told in our favour. Most men trust much to just such vague expectations. They form a theory, and then neglect the adverse chances. You can only get the better of a skilled detective by taking him thus, psychologically and humanly.

By this time, I confess, I felt almost like a criminal. Never in my life had danger loomed so near—not even when we returned with the Arabs from the oasis. For then we feared for our lives alone; now, we feared for our honour.

I drew a card from my case before we left Berwick station, and scribbled a few hasty words on it in German. "We are watched. A detective! If we run through to Edinburgh, we shall doubtless be arrested or at least impeded. This train will stop at Dunbar for one minute. Just before it leaves again, get out as quietly as you can—at the last moment. I will also get out and join you. Let Partab go on; it will excite less attention. The scheme I suggest is the only safe plan. If you agree, as soon as we have well started from Berwick, shake your handkerchief unobtrusively out of your carriage window."

I beckoned a porter noiselessly without one word. The detective was now strolling along the fore-part of the train, with his back turned towards me, peering as he went into all the windows. I gave the porter a shilling. "Take this to a black gentleman in the next carriage but one," I said, in a confidential whisper. The porter touched his hat, nodded, smiled, and took it.

Would Harold see the necessity for acting on my advice?— I wondered. I gazed out along the train as soon as we had got well clear of Berwick. A minute—two minutes—three minutes passed; and still no handkerchief. I began to despair. He was debating, no doubt. If he refused, all was lost, and we were disgraced for ever.

At last, after long waiting, as I stared still along the whizzing line, with the smoke in my eyes, and the dust half blinding me, I saw, to my intense relief, a handkerchief flutter. It fluttered once, not markedly, then a black hand withdrew it. Only just in time, for even as it disappeared, the detective's head thrust itself out of a farther window. He was not looking for anything in particular, as far as I could tell—just observing the signals. But it gave me a strange thrill to think even now we were so nearly defeated.

My next trouble was—would the train draw up at Dunbar? The 10 A.M. from King's Cross is not set down to stop there in Brad-shaw, for no passengers are booked to or from the station by the day express; but I remembered from of old when I lived at Edin-burgh, that it used always to wait about a minute for some engine-driver's purpose. This doubt filled me with fresh fear; did it draw up there still?—they have accelerated the service so much of late years, and abolished so many old accustomed stoppages. I counted the familiar stations with my breath held back. They seemed so much farther apart than usual. Reston—Grant's House—Cock-burnspath—Innerwick.

The next was Dunbar. If we rolled past *that*, then all was lost. We could never get married. I trembled and hugged myself.

The engine screamed. Did that mean she was running through? Oh, how I wished I had learned the interpretation of the signals!

Then gradually, gently, we began to slow. Were we slowing to pass the station only? No; with a jolt she drew up. My heart gave a bound as I read the word "Dunbar" on the station notice-board.

I rose and waited, with my fingers on the door. Happily it had one of those new-fashioned slip-latches which open from inside. No need to betray myself prematurely to the detective by a hand displayed on the outer handle. I glanced out at him cautiously. His head was thrust through his window, and his sloping shoulders revealed the spy, but he was looking the other way—observing the signals, doubtless, to discover why we stopped at a place not mentioned in Bradshaw.

Harold's face just showed from another window close by. Too soon or too late might either of them be fatal. He glanced inquiry at me. I nodded back, "Now!" The train gave its first jerk, a faint backward jerk, indicative of the nascent intention of starting. As it braced itself to go on, I jumped out; so did Harold. We faced one another on the platform without a word. "Stand away there:" the station-master cried, in an angry voice. The guard waved his green flag. The detective, still absorbed on the signals, never once looked back. One second later, we were safe at Dunbar, and he was speeding away by the express for Edinburgh.

It gave us a breathing space of about an hour.

For half a minute I could not speak. My heart was in my mouth. I hardly even dared to look at Harold. Then the station-master stalked up to us with a threatening manner. "You can't get out here," he said, crustily, in a gruff Scotch voice. "This train is not timed to set down before Edinburgh."

"We *have* got out," I answered, taking it upon me to speak for my fellow-culprit, the Hindu—as he was to all seeming. "The logic of facts is with us. We were booked through to Edinburgh, but we wanted to stop at Dunbar; and as the train happened to pull up, we thought we needn't waste time by going on all that way and then coming back again."

"Ye should have changed at Berwick," the station-master said, still gruffly, "and come on by the slow train." I could see his careful Scotch soul was vexed (incidentally) at our extravagance in paying the extra fare to Edinburgh and back again.

In spite of agitation, I managed to summon up one of my sweetest smiles—a smile that ere now had melted the hearts of rickshaw coolies and of French *douaniers*. He thawed before it visibly. "Time was important to us," I said—oh, he guessed not how important; "and besides, you know, it is so good for the company!"

"That's true," he answered, mollified. He could not tilt against the interests of the North British shareholders. "But how about yer luggage? It'll have gone on to Edinburgh, I'm thinking."

"We *have* no luggage," I answered boldly.

He stared at us both, puckered his brow a moment, and then burst out laughing. "Oh, ay, I see," he answered, with a comic air of amusement. "Well, well, it's none of my business, no doubt, and I will not interfere with ye; though why a lady like you—" He glanced curiously at Harold.

I saw he had guessed right, and thought it best to throw myself unreservedly on his mercy. Time was indeed important. I glanced at the station clock. It was not very far from the stroke of six, and we must manage to get married before the detective could miss us at Edinburgh, where he was due at 6.30.

So I smiled once more, that heart-softening smile. "We have each our own fancies," I said blushing—and, indeed (such is the pride of race among women), I felt myself blush in earnest at the bare idea that I was marrying a black man, in spite of our good Maharajah's kindness. "He is a gentleman, and a man of education and culture." I thought that recommendation ought to tell with a Scotchman. "We are in sore straits now, but our case is a just one. Can you tell me who in this place is most likely to sympathise—most likely to marry us?"

He looked at me—and surrendered at discretion. "I should think anybody would marry ye who saw yer pretty face and heard yer sweet voice," he answered. "But, perhaps, ye'd better present yerself to Mr. Schoolcraft, the U.P. minister at Little Kirkton. He was aye soft-hearted."

"How far from here?" I asked.

"About two miles," he answered.

"Can we get a trap?"

"Oh ay, there's machines always waiting at the station."

We interviewed a "machine," and drove out to Little Kirkton. There, we told our tale in the fewest words possible to the obliging and good-natured U.P. minister. He looked, as the station-master had said, "soft-hearted"; but he dashed our hopes to the ground at once by telling us candidly that unless we had had our residence in Scotland for twenty-one days immediately preceding the marriage, it would not be legal. "If you were Scotch," he added, "I could go through the ceremony at once, of course; and then you could apply to the sheriff to-night for leave to register the marriage in proper form afterward: but as one of you is English, and the other I judge"—he smiled and glanced towards Harold—"an Indian-born subject of Her Majesty, it would be impossible for me to do it: the ceremony would be invalid, under Lord Brougham's Act, without previous residence."

This was a terrible blow. I looked away appealingly. "Harold," I cried in despair, "do you think we could manage to hide ourselves safely anywhere in Scotland for twenty-one days?"

His face fell. "How could I escape notice? All the world is hunting for me. And then the scandal! No matter where you stopped—however far from me—no, Lois darling, I could never expose you to it."

The minister glanced from one to the other of us, puzzled. "Harold?" he said, turning over the word on his tongue. "Harold? That doesn't sound like an Indian name, does it? And—" he hesitated, "you speak wonderful English!"

I saw the safest plan was to make a clean breast of it. He looked the sort of man one could trust on an emergency. "You have heard of the Ashurst will case?" I said, blurting it out suddenly.

"I have seen something about it in the newspapers; yes. But it did not interest me: I have not followed it."

I told him the whole truth; the case against us—the facts as we knew them. Then I added, slowly, "This is Mr. Harold Tillington, whom they accuse of forgery. Does he look like a forger? I want to marry him before he is tried. It is the only way by which I can prove my implicit trust in him. As soon as we are married, he will give himself up at once to the police—if you wish it, before your eyes. But married we must be. *Can't* you manage it somehow?"

My pleading voice touched him. "Harold Tillington?" he murmured. "I know of his forebears. Lady Guinevere Tillington's son, is it not? Then you must be 'Younger of Gledcliffe.' For Scotland is a village: everyone in it seems to have heard of every other."

"What does he mean?" I asked. "Younger of Gledcliffe?" I remembered now that the phrase had occurred in Mr. Ashurst's will, though I never understood it.

"A Scotch fashion," Harold answered. "The heir to a laird is called Younger of so-and-so. My father has a small estate of that name in Dumfriesshire; a *very* small estate: I was born and brought up there."

"Then you are a Scotchman?" the minister asked.

"Yes," Harold answered frankly: "by remote descent. We are trebly of the female line at Gledcliffe; still, I am no doubt more or less Scotch by domicile."

"Younger of Gledcliffe! Oh, yes, that ought certainly to be quite sufficient for our purpose. Do you live there?"

"I have been living there lately. I always live there when I'm in Britain. It is my only home. I belong to the diplomatic service."

"But then—the lady?"

"She is unmitigatedly English," Harold admitted, in a gloomy voice.

"Not quite," I answered. "I lived four years in Edinburgh. And I spent my holidays there while I was at Girton. I keep my boxes still at my old rooms in Maitland Street."

"Oh, that will do," the minister answered, quite relieved; for it was clear that our anxiety and the touch of romance in our tale had enlisted him in our favour. "Indeed, now I come to think of it, it suffices for the Act if one only of the parties is domiciled in Scotland. And as Mr. Tillington lives habitually at Gledcliffe, that settles the question. Still, I can do nothing save marry you now by religious service in the presence of my servants—which constitutes what we call an ecclesiastical marriage—it becomes legal if afterwards registered; and then you must apply to the sheriff for a warrant to register it. But I will do what I can; later on, if you like, you can be re-married by the rites of your own Church in England."

"Are you quite sure our Scotch domicile is good enough in law?" Harold asked, still doubtful.

"I can turn it up, if you wish. I have a legal handbook. Before Lord Brougham's Act, no formalities were necessary. But the Act was passed to prevent Gretna Green marriages. The usual phrase is that such a marriage does not hold good unless one or other of the parties either has had his or her usual residence in Scotland, or else has lived there for twenty-one days immediately preceding the date of the marriage. If you like, I will wait to consult the authorities."

"No, thank you," I cried. "There is no time to lose. Marry us first, and look it up afterwards. 'One or other' will do, it seems. Mr. Tillington is Scotch enough, I am sure; he has no address in Britain but Gledcliffe: we will rest our claim upon that. Even if the marriage turns out invalid, we only remain where we were. This is a preliminary ceremony to prove good faith, and to bind us to one another. We can satisfy the law, if need be, when we return to England."

The minister called in his wife and servants, and explained to them briefly. He exhorted us and prayed. We gave our solemn consent in legal form before two witnesses. Then he pronounced us duly married. In a quarter of an hour more, we had made declaration to that effect before the sheriff, the witnesses accompanying us, and were formally affirmed to be man and wife before the law of Great Britain. I asked if it would hold in England as well.

"You couldn't be firmer married," the sheriff said, with decision, "by the Archbishop of Canterbury in Westminster Abbey."

Harold turned to the minister. "Will you send for the police?" he said, calmly. "I wish to inform them that I am the man for whom they are looking in the Ashurst will case."

Our own cabman went to fetch them. It was a terrible moment. But Harold sat in the sheriff's study and waited, as if nothing unusual were happening. He talked freely but quietly. Never in my life had I felt so proud of him.

At last the police came, much inflated with the dignity of so great a capture, and took down our statement. "Do you give yourself in charge on a confession of forgery?" the superintendent asked, as Harold ended.

"Certainly not," Harold answered. "I have not committed forgery. But I do not wish to skulk or hide myself. I understand a warrant is out against me in London. I have come to Scotland, hurriedly, for the sake of getting married, not to escape apprehension.

I am here, openly, under my own name. I tell you the facts; 'tis for you to decide; if you choose, you can arrest me."

The superintendent conferred for some time in another room with the sheriff. Then he returned to the study. "Very well, sir," he said, in a respectful tone, "I arrest you."

So that was the beginning of our married life. More than ever, I felt sure I could trust in Harold.

The police decided, after hearing by telegram from London, that we must go up at once by the night express, which they stopped for the purpose. They were forced to divide us. I took the sleeping-car; Harold travelled with two constables in a ordinary carriage. Strange to say, notwithstanding all this, so great was our relief from the tension of our flight, that we both slept soundly.

Next morning we arrived in London, Harold guarded. The police had arranged that the case should come up at Bow Street that afternoon. It was not an ideal honeymoon, and yet, I was somehow happy.

At King's Cross, they took him away from me. Still, I hardly cried. All the way up in the train, whenever I was awake, an idea had been haunting me—a possible clue to this trickery of Lord Southminster's. Petty details cropped up and fell into their places. I began to unravel it all now. I had an inkling of a plan to set Harold right again.

The will we had proved——but I must not anticipate.

When we parted, Harold kissed me on the forehead, and murmured rather sadly, "Now, I suppose it's all up. Lois, I must go. These rogues have been too much for us."

"Not a bit of it," I answered, new hope growing stronger and stronger within me. "I see a way out. I have found a clue. I believe, dear Harold, the right will still be vindicated."

And red-eyed as I was, I jumped into a hansom, and called to the cabman to drive at once to Lady Georgina's.

THE ADVENTURE OF THE
UNPROFESSIONAL DETECTIVE

"Is Lady Georgina at home?" The discreet man-servant in sober black clothes eyed me suspiciously. "No, miss," he answered. "That is to say—no, ma'am. Her ladyship is still at Mr. Marmaduke Ashurst's—the late Mr. Marmaduke Ashurst, I mean—in Park Lane North. You know the number, ma'am?"

"Yes, I know it," I replied, with a gasp; for this was indeed a triumph. My one fear had been lest Lord Southminster should already have taken possession—why, you will see hereafter; and it relieved me to learn that Lady Georgina was still at hand to guard my husband's interests. She had been living at the house, practically, since her brother's death. I drove round with all speed, and flung myself into my dear old lady's arms.

"Kiss me," I cried, flushed. "I am your niece!" But she knew it already, for our movements had been fully reported by this time (with picturesque additions) in the morning papers. Imagination, ill-developed in the English race, seems to concentrate itself in the lower order of journalists.

She kissed me on both cheeks with unwonted tenderness. "Lois," she cried, with tears in her eyes, "you're a brick!" It was not exactly poetical at such a moment, but from her it meant more than much gushing phraseology.

"And you're here in possession!" I murmured.

The Cantankerous Old Lady nodded. She was in her element, I must admit. She dearly loved a row—above all, a family row; but to be in the thick of a family row, and to feel herself in the right, with the law against her—that was joy such as Lady Georgina had seldom before experienced. "Yes, dear," she burst out volubly, "I'm in possession, thank Heaven. And what's more, they won't oust me without a legal process. I've been here, off and on, you know, ever since poor dear Marmy died, looking after things for Harold; and I shall look after them still, till Bertie Southminster succeeds in ejecting me, which won't be easy. Oh, I've held the fort by main force, I can tell you; held it like a Trojan. Bertie's in a precious great hurry to move in, I can see; but I won't allow him. He's been down here this morning, fatuously blustering, and trying to carry the post by storm, with a couple of policemen."

"Policemen!" I cried. "To turn you out?"

"Yes, my dear, policemen: but (the Lord be praised) I was too much for him. There are legal formalities to fulfil yet; and I won't budge an inch, Lois, not one inch, my dear, till he's fulfilled every one of them. Mark my words, child, that boy's up to some devilry."

"He is," I answered.

"Yes, he wouldn't be in such a rampaging hurry to get in—being as lazy as he's empty-headed—takes after Gwendoline in that—if he hadn't some excellent reason for wishing to take possession: and depend upon it, the reason is that he wants to get hold of something or other that's Harold's. But he sha'n't if I can help it; and, thank my stars, I'm a dour woman to reckon with. If he comes, he comes over my old bones, child. I've been overhauling everything of Marmy's, I can tell you, to checkmate the boy if I can; but I've found nothing yet, and till I've satisfied myself on that point, I'll hold the fort still, if I have to barricade that pasty-faced scoundrel of a nephew of mine out by piling the furniture against the front door— I will, as sure as my name's Georgina Fawley!"

"I know you will, dear," I assented, kissing her, "and so I shall venture to leave you, while I go out to institute another little enquiry."

"What enquiry?"

I shook my head. "It's only a surmise," I said, hesitating. "I'll tell you about it later. I've had time to think while I've been coming back in the train, and I've thought of many things. Mount guard till I return, and mind you don't let Lord Southminster have access to anything."

"I'll shoot him first, dear." And I believe she meant it.

I drove on in the same cab to Harold's solicitor. There I laid my fresh doubts at once before him. He rubbed his bony hands. "You've hit it!" he cried, charmed. "My dear madam, you've hit it! I never did like that will. I never did like the signatures, the witnesses, the look of it. But what could I do? Mr. Tillington propounded it. Of course it wasn't my business to go dead against my own client."

"Then you doubted Harold's honour, Mr. Hayes?" I cried, flushing.

"Never!" he answered. "Never! I felt sure there must be some mistake somewhere, but not any trickery on—your husband's part. Now, *you* supply the right clue. We must look into this, immediately."

He hurried round with me at once in the same cab to the court. The incriminated will had been "impounded," as they call it; but, under certain restrictions, and subject to the closest surveillance, I was allowed to examine it with my husband's solicitor, before the eyes of the authorities. I looked at it long with the naked eye and also with a small pocket lens. The paper, as I had noted before, was the same kind of foolscap as that which I had been in the habit of using at my office in Florence; and the typewriting—was it mine? The longer I looked at it, the more I doubted it.

After a careful examination I turned round to our solicitor. "Mr. Hayes," I said, firmly, having arrived at my conclusion, "this is *not* the document I type-wrote at Florence."

"How do you know?" he asked. "A different machine? Some small peculiarity in the shape of the letters?"

"No, the rogue who typed this will was too cunning for that. He didn't allow himself to be foiled by such a scholar's mate. It is written with a Spread Eagle, the same sort of machine precisely as my own. I know the type perfectly. But—" I hesitated.

"But what?"

"Well, it is difficult to explain. There is character in typewriting, just as there is in handwriting, only, of course, not quite so much of it. Every operator is liable to his own peculiar tricks and blunders. If I had some of my own typewritten manuscript here to show you, I could soon make that evident."

"I can easily believe it. Individuality runs through all we do, however seemingly mechanical. But are the points of a sort that you could make clear in court to the satisfaction of a jury?"

"I think so. Look here, for example. Certain letters get habitually mixed up in typewriting; *c* and *v* stand next one another on the keyboard of the machine, and the person who typed this draft sometimes strikes a *c* instead of a *v*, or *vice versâ*. I never do that. The letters I tend to confuse are *s* and *w*, or else *e* and *r*, which also come very near one another in the arbitrary arrangement. Besides, when I type-wrote the original of this will, I made no errors at all; I took such very great pains about it."

"And this person did make errors?"

"Yes; struck the wrong letter first, and then corrected it often by striking another rather hard on top of it. See, this was a *v* to begin with, and he turned it into a *c*. Besides, the hand that wrote this will is heavier than mine: it comes down *thump, thump, thump*, while mine glides lightly. And the hyphens are used with a space between them, and the character of the punctuation is not exactly as I make it."

"Still," Mr. Hayes objected, "we have nothing but your word. I'm afraid, in such a case, we could never induce a jury to accept your unsupported evidence."

"I don't want them to accept it," I answered. "I am looking this up for my own satisfaction. I want to know, first, who wrote this will. And of one thing I am quite clear: it is *not* the document I drew up for Mr. Ashurst. Just look at that *x*. The *x* alone is conclusive. My typewriter had the upper right-hand stroke of the small *x* badly formed, or broken, while this one is perfect. I remember it well, because I used always to improve all my lower-case *x*'s with a pen when I re-read and corrected. I see their dodge clearly now. It is a most diabolical conspiracy. Instead of forging a will in Lord Southminster's favour, they have substituted a forgery for the real will, and then managed to make my poor Harold prove it."

"In that case, no doubt, they have destroyed the real one, the original," Mr. Hayes put in.

"I don't think so," I answered, after a moment's deliberation. "From what I know of Mr. Ashurst, I don't believe it is likely he would have left his will about carelessly anywhere. He was a secretive man, fond of mysteries and mystifications. He would be sure to conceal it. Besides, Lady Georgina and Harold have been taking care of everything in the house ever since he died."

"But," Mr. Hayes objected, "the forger of this document, supposing it to be forged, must have had access to the original, since you say the terms of the two are identical; only the signatures are forgeries. And if he saw and copied it, why might he not also have destroyed it?"

A light flashed across me all at once. "The forger *did* see the original," I cried, "but not the fair copy. I have it all now! I detect their trick! It comes back to me vividly! When I had finished typing the copy at Florence from my first rough draft, which I had taken down on the machine before Mr. Ashurst's eyes, I remember now that I threw the original into the waste-paper basket. It must have been there that evening when Higginson called and asked for the will to take it back to Mr. Ashurst. He called for it, no doubt, hoping to open the packet before he delivered it and make a copy of the document for this very purpose. But I refused to let him have it. Before he saw me, however, he had been left by himself for ten minutes in the office; for I remember coming out to him and finding him there alone: and during that ten minutes, being what he is, you may be sure he fished out the rough draft and appropriated it!"

"That is more than likely," my solicitor nodded. "You are tracking him to his lair. We shall have him in our power."

I grew more and more excited as the whole cunning plot unravelled itself mentally step by step before me. "He must then have gone to Lord Southminster," I went on, "and told him of the legacy he expected from Mr. Ashurst. It was five hundred pounds—a mere trifle to Higginson, who plays for thousands. So he must have offered to arrange matters for Lord Southminster if Southminster would consent to make good that sum and a great deal more to him. That odious little cad told me himself on the *Jumna* they were engaged in pulling off 'a big *coup*' between them. He thought then I would marry him, and that he would so secure my connivance in his plans; but who would marry such a piece of moist clay? Besides, I could never have taken anyone but Harold." Then another clue came home to me. "Mr. Hayes," I cried, jumping at it, "Higginson, who forged this will, never saw the real document itself at all; he saw only the draft: for Mr. Ashurst altered one word *viva voce* in the original at the last moment, and I made a pencil note of it on my cuff at the time: and see, it isn't here, though I inserted it in the final clean copy of the will—the word 'especially.' It grows upon me more and more each minute that the real instrument is hidden somewhere in Mr. Ashurst's house—Harold's house—our house; and that *because* it is there Lord Southminster is so indecently anxious to oust his aunt and take instant possession."

"In that case," Mr. Hayes remarked, "we had better go back to Lady Georgina without one minute's delay, and, while she still holds the house, institute a thorough search for it."

No sooner said than done. We jumped again into our cab and started. As we drove back, Mr. Hayes asked me where I thought we were most likely to find it.

"In a secret drawer in Mr. Ashurst's desk," I answered, by a flash of instinct, without a second's hesitation.

"How do you know there's a secret drawer?"

"I don't know it. I infer it from my general knowledge of Mr. Ashurst's character. He loved secret drawers, ciphers, cryptograms, mystery-mongering."

"But it was in that desk that your husband found the forged document," the lawyer objected.

Once more I had a flash of inspiration or intuition. "Because White, Mr. Ashurst's valet, had it in readiness in his possession," I answered, "and hid it there, in the most obvious and unconcealed place he could find, as soon as the breath was out of his master's body. I remember now Lord Southminster gave himself away to some extent in that matter. The hateful little creature isn't really clever enough, for all his cunning,—and with Higginson to back him,—to mix himself up in such tricks as forgery. He told me at Aden he had had a telegram from 'Marmy's valet,' to report pro-gress; and he received another, the night Mr. Ashurst died, at Moozuffernuggar. Depend upon it, White was more or less in this plot; Higginson left him the forged will when they started for India; and, as soon as Mr. Ashurst died, White hid it where Harold was bound to find it."

"If so," Mr. Hayes answered, "that's well; we have something to go upon. The more of them, the better. There is safety in num-bers—for the honest folk. I never knew three rogues hold long to-gether, especially when threatened with a criminal prosecution. Their confederacy breaks down before the chance of punishment. Each tries to screen himself by betraying the others."

"Higginson was the soul of this plot," I went on. "Of that you may be sure. He's a wily old fox, but we'll run him to earth yet. The more I think of it, the more I feel sure, from what I know of Mr. Ashurst's character, he would never have put that will in so ex-posed a place as the one where Harold says he found it."

We drew up at the door of the disputed house just in time for the siege. Mr. Hayes and I walked in. We found Lady Georgina face to face with Lord Southminster. The opposing forces were still at the stage of preliminaries of warfare.

"Look heah," the pea-green young man was observing, in his drawling voice, as we entered; "it's no use your talking, deah Geor-gey. This house is mine, and I won't have you meddling with it."

"This house is not yours, you odious little scamp," his aunt re-torted, raising her shrill voice some notes higher than usual; "and while I can hold a stick you shall not come inside it."

"Very well, then; you drive me to hostilities, don't yah know. I'm sorry to show disrespect to your gray hairs—if any—but I shall be obliged to call in the police to eject yah."

"Call them in if you like," I answered, interposing between them. "Go out and get them! Mr. Hayes, while he's gone, send for a carpenter to break open the back of Mr. Ashurst's escritoire."

"A carpentah?" he cried, turning several degrees whiter than his pasty wont. "What for? A carpentah?"

I spoke distinctly. "Because we have reason to believe Mr. Ashurst's real will is concealed in this house in a secret drawer, and because the keys were in the possession of White, whom we believe to be your accomplice in this shallow conspiracy."

He gasped and looked alarmed. "No, you don't," he cried, stepping briskly forward. "You don't, I tell yah! Break open Marmy's desk! Why, hang it all, it's my property."

"We shall see about that after we've broken it open," I answered grimly. "Here, this screw-driver will do. The back's not strong. Now, your help, Mr. Hayes—one, two, three; we can prise it apart between us."

Lord Southminster rushed up and tried to prevent us. But Lady Georgina, seizing both wrists, held him tight as in a vice with her dear skinny old hands. He writhed and struggled all in vain: he could not escape her. "I've often spanked you, Bertie," she cried, "and if you attempt to interfere, I'll spank you again; that's the long and the short of it!"

He broke from her and rushed out, to call the police, I believe, and prevent our desecration of pooah Marmy's property.

Inside the first shell were several locked drawers, and two or three open ones, out of one of which Harold had fished the false will. Instinct taught me somehow that the central drawer on the left-hand side was the compartment behind which lay the secret receptacle. I prised it apart and peered about inside it. Presently I saw a slip-panel, which I touched with one finger. The pigeon-hole flew open and disclosed a narrow slit I clutched at something—the will! Ho, victory! the will! I raised it aloft with a wild shout. Not a doubt of it! The real, the genuine document!

We turned it over and read it. It was my own fair copy, written at Florence, and bearing all the small marks of authenticity about it which I had pointed out to Mr. Hayes as wanting to the forged and impounded document. Fortunately, Lady Georgina and four of the servants had stood by throughout this scene, and had watched our demeanour, as well as Lord Southminster's.

We turned next to the signatures. The principal one was clearly Mr. Ashurst's—I knew it at once—his legible fat hand, "Marmaduke

Courtney Ashurst." And then the witnesses? They fairly took our breath away.

"Why, Higginson's sister isn't one of them at all," Mr. Hayes cried, astonished.

A flush of remorse came over me. I saw it all now. I had misjudged that poor woman! She had the misfortune to be a rogue's sister, but, as Harold had said, was herself a most respectable and blameless person. Higginson must have forged her name to the document; that was all; and she had naturally sworn that she never signed it. He knew her honesty. It was a master-stroke of rascality.

"The other one isn't here, either," I exclaimed, growing more puzzled. "The waiter at the hotel! Why, that's another forgery! Higginson must have waited till the man was safely dead, and then used him similarly. It was all very clever. Now, who are these people who really witnessed it?"

"The first one," Mr. Hayes said, examining the handwriting, "is Sir Roger Bland, the Dorsetshire baronet: he's dead, poor fellow; but he was at Florence at the time, and I can answer for his signature. He was a client of mine, and died at Mentone. The second is Captain Richards, of the Mounted Police: he's living still, but he's away in South Africa."

"Then they risked his turning up?"

"If they knew who the real witnesses were at all—which is doubtful. You see, as you say, they may have seen the rough draft only."

"Higginson would know," I answered. "He was with Mr. Ashurst at Florence at the time, and he would take good care to keep a watch upon his movements. In my belief, it was he who suggested this whole plot to Lord Southminster."

"Of course it was," Lady Georgina put in. "That's absolutely certain. Bertie's a rogue as well as a fool: but he's too great a fool to invent a clever roguery, and too great a knave not to join in it foolishly when anybody else takes the pains to invent it."

"And it *was* a clever roguery," Mr. Hayes interposed. "An ordinary rascal would have forged a later will in Lord Southminster's favour and run the risk of detection; Higginson had the acuteness to forge a will exactly like the real one, and to let your husband bear the burden of the forgery. It was as sagacious as it was ruthless."

"The next point," I said, "will be for us to prove it."

At that moment the bell rang, and one of the house-servants—all puzzled by this conflict of interests—came in with a telegram, which he handed me on a salver. I broke it open, without glancing at the envelope. Its contents baffled me: "My address is Hotel Bristol, Paris; name as usual. Send me a thousand pounds on account at once. I can't afford to wait. No shillyshallying."

The message was unsigned. For a moment, I couldn't imagine who sent it, or what it was driving at.

Then I took up the envelope. "Viscount Southminster, 24 Park Lane North, London."

My heart gave a jump. I saw in a second that chance, or Providence, had delivered the conspirators into my hands that day. The telegram was from Higginson! I had opened it by accident.

It was obvious what had happened. Lord Southminster must have written to him on the result of the trial, and told him he meant to take possession of his uncle's house immediately. Higginson had acted on that hint, and addressed his telegram where he thought it likely Lord Southminster would receive it earliest. I had opened it in error, and that, too, was fortunate, for even in dealing with such a pack of scoundrels, it would never have occurred to me to violate somebody else's correspondence had I not thought it was addressed to me. But having arrived at the truth thus unintentionally, I had, of course, no scruples about making full use of my information.

I showed the despatch at once to Lady Georgina and Mr. Hayes. They recognised its importance. "What next?" I inquired. "Time presses. At half-past three Harold comes up for examination at Bow Street."

Mr. Hayes was ready with an apt expedient. "Ring the bell for Mr. Ashurst's valet," he said, quietly. "The moment has now arrived when we can begin to set these conspirators by the ears. As soon as they learn that we know all, they will be eager to inform upon one another."

I rang the bell. "Send up White," I said. "We wish to speak to him."

The valet stole up, self-accused, a timid, servile creature, rubbing his hands nervously, and suspecting mischief. He was a rat in trouble. He had thin brown hair, neatly brushed and plastered down, so as to make it look still thinner, and his face was the average narrow cunning face of the dishonest man-servant. It had an ounce of wile in it to a pound or two of servility. He seemed just the sort of rogue meanly to join in an underhand conspiracy, and then meanly to back out of it. You could read at a glance that his principle in life was to save his own bacon.

He advanced, fumbling his hands all the time, and smiling and fawning. "You wished to see me, sir?" he murmured, in a deprecatory voice, looking sideways at Lady Georgina and me, but addressing the lawyer.

"Yes, White, I wished to see you. I have a question to ask you. *Who* put the forged will in Mr. Ashurst's desk? Was it you, or some other person?"

The question terrified him. He changed colour and gasped. But he rubbed his hands harder than ever and affected a sickly smile. "Oh, sir, how should *I* know, sir? *I* had nothing to do with it. I suppose—it was Mr. Tillington."

Our lawyer pounced upon him like a hawk on a titmouse. "Don't prevaricate with me, sir," he said, sternly. "If you do, it may be worse for you. This case has assumed quite another aspect. It is you and your associates who will be placed in the dock, not Mr. Tillington. You had better speak the truth; it is your one chance, I warn you. Lie to me, and instead of calling you as a witness for our case, I shall include you in the indictment."

White looked down uneasily at his shoes, and cowered. "Oh, sir, I don't understand you."

"Yes you do. You understand me, and you know I mean it. Wriggling is useless; we intend to prosecute. We have unravelled this vile plot. We know the whole truth. Higginson and Lord Southminster forged a will between them—"

"Oh, sir, *not* Lord Southminster! His lordship, I'm sure—"

Mr. Hayes's keen eye had noted the subtle shade of distinction and admission. But he said nothing openly. "Well, then, Higginson forged, and Lord Southminster accepted, a false will, which purported to be Mr. Marmaduke Ashurst's. Now, follow me clearly. That will could not have been put into the escritoire during Mr. Ashurst's life, for there would have been risk of his discovering it. It must, therefore, have been put there afterward. The moment he was dead, you, or somebody else with your consent and connivance, slipped it into the escritoire; and you afterwards showed Mr. Tillington the place where you had set it or seen it set, leading him to believe it was Mr. Ashurst's will, and so involved him in all this trouble. Note that that was a felonious act. We accuse you of felony. Do you mean to confess, and give evidence on our behalf, or will you force me to send for a policeman to arrest you?"

The cur hesitated still. "Oh, sir," drawing back, and fumbling his hands on his breast, "you don't mean it."

Mr. Hayes was prompt. "Hesslegrave, go for a policeman."

That curt sentence brought the rogue on his marrow-bones at once. He clasped his hands and debated inwardly. "If I tell you all I know," he said, at last, looking about him with an air of abject terror, as if he thought Lord Southminster or Higginson would hear him, "will you promise not to prosecute me?" His tone became insinuating. "For a hundred pounds, I could find the real will for you. You'd better close with me. To-day is the last chance. As soon as his lordship comes in, he'll hunt it up and destroy it."

I flourished it before him, and pointed with one hand to the broken desk, which he had not yet observed in his craven agitation. "We do not need your aid," I answered. "We have found the will, ourselves. Thanks to Lady Georgina, it is safe till this minute."

"And to me," he put in, cringing, and trying after his kind, to curry favour with the winners at the last moment. "It's all *my* doing, my lady! I wouldn't destroy it. His lordship offered me a hundred pounds more to break open the back of the desk at night, while your ladyship was asleep, and burn the thing quietly. But I told him he might do his own dirty work if he wanted it done. It wasn't good enough while your ladyship was here in possession. Besides,

I wanted the right will preserved, for I thought things might turn up so; and I wouldn't stand by and see a gentleman like Mr. Tillington, as has always behaved well to me, deprived of his inheritance."

"Which is why you conspired with Lord Southminster to rob him of it, and to send him to prison for Higginson's crime," I interposed calmly.

"Then you confess you put the forged will there?" Mr. Hayes said, getting to business.

White looked about him helplessly. He missed his headpiece, the instigator of the plot. "Well, it was like this, my lady," he began, turning to Lady Georgina, and wriggling to gain time. "You see, his lordship and Mr. Higginson—" he twirled his thumbs and tried to invent something plausible.

Lady Georgina swooped. "No rigmarole!" she said, sharply. "Do you confess you put it there or do you not—reptile?" Her vehemence startled him.

"Yes, I confess I put it there," he said at last, blinking. "As soon as the breath was out of Mr. Ashurst's body I put it there." He began to whimper. "I'm a poor man with a wife and family, sir," he went on, "though in Mr. Ashurst's time I always kep' that quiet; and his lordship offered to pay me well for the job; and when you're paid well for a job yourself, sir—"

Mr. Hayes waved him off with one imperious hand. "Sit down in the corner there, man, and don't move or utter another word," he said, sternly, "until I order you. You will be in time still for me to produce at Bow Street."

Just at that moment, Lord Southminster swaggered back, accompanied by a couple of unwilling policemen. "Oh, I say," he cried, bursting in and staring around him, jubilant. "Look heah, Georgey, *are* you going quietly, or must I ask these coppahs to evict you?" He was wreathed in smiles now, and had evidently been fortifying himself with brandics and soda.

Lady Georgina rose in her wrath. "Yes, I'll go if you wish it, Bertie," she answered, with calm irony. "I'll leave the house as soon as you like—for the present—till we come back again with Harold and *his* policemen to evict you. This house is Harold's. Your game

is played, boy." She spoke slowly. "We have found the other will—
we have discovered Higginson's present address in Paris—and we
know from White how he and you arranged this little conspiracy."

She rapped out each clause in this last accusing sentence with
deliberate effect, like so many pistol-shots. Each bullet hit home.
The pea-green young man, drawing back and staring, stroked his
shadowy moustache with feeble fingers in undisguised astonishment. Then he dropped into a chair and fixed his gaze blankly on
Lady Georgina. "Well, this is a fair knock-out," he ejaculated, fatuously disconcerted. "I wish Higginson was heah. I really don't quite
know what to do without him. That fellah had squared it all up so
neatly, don't yah know, that I thought there couldn't be any sort of
hitch in the proceedings."

"You reckoned without Lois," Lady Georgina said, calmly.

"Ah, Miss Cayley—that's true. I mean, Mrs. Tillington. Yaas, yaas,
I know, she's a doosid clevah person—for a woman,—now isn't she?"

It was impossible to take this flabby creature seriously, even
as a criminal. Lady Georgina's lips relaxed. "Doosid clever," she
admitted, looking at me almost tenderly.

"But not quite so clevah, don't yah know, as Higginson!"

"There you make your blooming little erraw," Mr. Hayes burst
in, adopting one of Lord Southminster's favourite witticisms—the
sort of witticism that improves, like poetry, by frequent repetition.
"Policemen, you may go into the next room and wait: this is a family affair; we have no immediate need of you."

"Oh, certainly," Lord Southminster echoed, much relieved.
"Very propah sentiment! Most undesirable that the constables
should mix themselves up in a family mattah like this. Not the place
for inferiahs!"

"Then why introduce them?" Lady Georgina burst out, turning
on him.

He smiled his fatuous smile. "That's just what I say," he answered.
"Why the jooce introduce them? But don't snap my head off!"

The policemen withdrew respectfully, glad to be relieved of this
unpleasant business, where they could gain no credit, and might

possibly involve themselves in a charge of assault. Lord South-minster rose with a benevolent grin, and looked about him pleasantly. The brandies and soda had endowed him with irrepressible cheerfulness.

"Well?" Lady Georgina murmured.

"Well, I think I'll leave now, Georgey. You've trumped my ace, yah know. Nasty trick of White to go and round on a fellah. I don't like the turn this business is taking. Seems to me, the only way I have left to get out of it is—to turn Queen's evidence."

Lady Georgina planted herself firmly against the door. "Bertie," she cried, "no, you don't—not till we've got what we want out of you!"

He gazed at her blandly. His face broke once more into an imbecile smile. "You were always a rough 'un, Georgey. Your hand did sting! Well, what do you want now? We've each played our cards, and you needn't cut up rusty over it—especially when you're winning! Hang it all, I wish I had Higginson heah to tackle you!"

"If you go to see the Treasury people, or the Solicitor-General, or the Public Prosecutor, or whoever else it may be," Lady Georgina said, stoutly, "Mr. Hayes must go with you. We've trumped your ace, as you say, and we mean to take advantage of it. And then you must trundle yourself down to Bow Street afterwards, confess the whole truth, and set Harold at liberty."

"Oh, I say now, Georgey! The whole truth! the whole blooming truth! That's really what I call humiliating a fellah!"

"If you don't, we arrest you this minute—fourteen years' imprisonment!"

"Fourteen yeahs?" He wiped his forehead. "Oh, I say. How doosid uncomfortable. I was nevah much good at doing anything by the sweat of my brow. I ought to have lived in the Garden of Eden. Georgey, you're hard on a chap when he's down on his luck. It would be confounded cruel to send me to fourteen yeahs at Portland."

"You would have sent my husband to it," I broke in, angrily, confronting him.

"What? You too, Miss Cayley?—I mean Mrs. Tillington. Don't look at me like that. Tigahs aren't in it."

His jauntiness disarmed us. However wicked he might be, one felt it would be ridiculous to imprison this schoolboy. A sound flogging and a month's deprivation of wine and cigarettes was the obvious punishment designed for him by nature.

"You must go down to the police-court and confess this whole conspiracy," Lady Georgina went on after a pause, as sternly as she was able. "I prefer, if we can, to save the family—even you, Bertie. But I can't any longer save the family honour—I can only save Harold's. You must help me to do that; and then, you must give me your solemn promise—in writing—to leave England for ever, and go to live in South Africa."

He stroked the invisible moustache more nervously than before. That penalty came home to him. "What, leave England for evah? Newmarket—Ascot—the club—the music-halls!"

"Or fourteen years' imprisonment!"

"Georgey, you spank as hard as evah!"

"Decide at once, or we arrest you!"

He glanced about him feebly. I could see he was longing for his lost confederate. "Well, I'll go," he said at last, sobering down; "and your solicitaw can trot round with me. I'll do all that you wish, though I call it most unfriendly. Hang it all, fourteen yeahs would be so beastly unpleasant!"

We drove forthwith to the proper authorities, who, on hearing the facts, at once arranged to accept Lord Southminster and White as Queen's evidence, neither being the actual forger. We also telegraphed to Paris to have Higginson arrested, Lord Southminster giving us up his assumed name with the utmost cheerfulness, and without one moment's compunction. Mr. Hayes was quite right: each conspirator was only too ready to save himself by betraying his fellows. Then we drove on to Bow Street (Lord Southminster consoling himself with a cigarette on the way), just in time for Harold's case, which was to be taken, by special arrangement, at 3.30.

A very few minutes sufficed to turn the tables completely on the conspirators. Harold was discharged, and a warrant was issued for the arrest of Higginson, the actual forger. He had drawn up the false will and signed it with Mr. Ashurst's name, after which he had presented it for Lord Southminster's approval. The pea-green young man told his tale with engaging frankness. "Bertie's a simple Simon," Lady Georgina commented to me; "but he's also a rogue; and Higginson saw his way to make excellent capital of him in both capacities—first use him as a catspaw, and then blackmail him."

On the steps of the police-court, as we emerged triumphant, Lord Southminster met us—still radiant as ever. He seemed wholly unaware of the depths of his iniquity: a fresh dose of brandy had restored his composure. "Look heah," he said, "Harold, your wife has bested me! Jolly good thing for you that you managed to get hold of such a clevah woman! If you hadn't, deah boy, you'd have found yourself in Queeah Street! But, I say, Lois—I call yah Lois because you're my cousin now, yah know—you were backing the wrong man aftah all, as I told yah. For if you'd backed *me*, all this wouldn't have come out; you'd have got the tin and been a countess as well, aftah the governah's dead and gone, don't yah see. You'd have landed the double event. So you'd have pulled off a bettah thing for yourself in the end, as I said, if you'd laid your bottom dollah on me for winnah!"

Higginson is now doing fourteen years at Portland; Harold and I are happy in the sweetest place in Gloucestershire; and Lord Southminster, blissfully unaware of the contempt with which the rest of the world regards him, is shooting big game among his "boys" in South Africa. Indeed, he bears so little malice that he sent us a present of a trophy of horns for our hall last winter.

HILDA WADE

A WOMAN WITH
TENACITY OF PURPOSE

PUBLISHERS' NOTE

In putting before the public the last work by Mr. Grant Allen, the publishers desire to express their deep regret at the author's unexpected and lamented death—a regret in which they are sure to be joined by the many thousand readers whom he did so much to entertain. A man of curiously varied and comprehensive knowledge, and with the most charming personality; a writer who, treating of a wide variety of subjects, touched nothing which he did not make distinctive, he filled a place which no man living can exactly occupy. The last chapter of this volume had been roughly sketched by Mr. Allen before his final illness, and his anxiety, when debarred from work, to see it finished, was relieved by the considerate kindness of his friend and neighbour, Dr. Conan Doyle, who, hearing of his trouble, talked it over with him, gathered his ideas, and finally wrote it out for him in the form in which it now appears—a beautiful and pathetic act of friendship which it is a pleasure to record.

THE EPISODE OF THE PATIENT
WHO DISAPPOINTED HER DOCTOR

Hilda Wade's gift was so unique, so extraordinary, that I must illustrate it, I think, before I attempt to describe it. But first let me say a word of explanation about the Master.

I have never met anyone who impressed me so much with a sense of *greatness* as Professor Sebastian. And this was not due to his scientific eminence alone: the man's strength and keenness struck me quite as forcibly as his vast attainments. When he first came to St. Nathaniel's Hospital, an eager, fiery-eyed physiologist, well past the prime of life, and began to preach with all the electric force of his vivid personality that the one thing on earth worth a young man's doing was to work in his laboratory, attend his lectures, study disease, and be a scientific doctor, dozens of us were infected by his contagious enthusiasm. He proclaimed the gospel of germs; and the germ of his own zeal flew abroad in the hospital: it ran through the wards as if it were typhoid fever. Within a few months, half the students were converted from lukewarm observers of medical routine into flaming apostles of the new methods.

The greatest authority in Europe on comparative anatomy, now that Huxley was taken from us, he had devoted his later days to the pursuit of medicine proper, to which he brought a mind stored with luminous analogies from the lower animals. His very appearance held one. Tall, thin, erect, with an ascetic profile not unlike Cardinal Manning's, he represented that abstract form of asceticism which consists in absolute self-sacrifice to a mental ideas, not that which consists in religious abnegation. Three years of travel in Africa had tanned his skin for life. His long white hair, straight and silvery as it fell, just curled in one wave-like inward sweep where it turned and rested on the stooping shoulders. His pale face was clean-shaven, save for a thin and wiry grizzled moustache, which cast into stronger relief the deep-set, hawk-like eyes and the acute, intense, intellectual features. In some respects, his countenance reminded me often of Dr. Martineau's: in others it recalled the knife-like edge, unturnable, of his great predecessor, Professor Owen. Wherever he went, men turned to stare at him. In Paris, they took him for the head of the English Socialists; in Russia, they declared he was a Nihilist emissary. And they were not far wrong—in essence; for Sebastian's stern, sharp face was above all things the face of a man absorbed and engrossed by one overpowering pursuit in life—the sacred thirst of knowledge, which had swallowed up his entire nature.

He *was* what he looked—the most single-minded person I have ever come across. And when I say single-minded, I mean just that, and no more. He had an End to attain—the advancement of science, and he went straight towards the End, looking neither to the right nor to the left for anyone. An American millionaire once remarked to him of some ingenious appliance he was describing: "Why, if you were to perfect that apparatus, Professor, and take out a patent for it, I reckon you'd make as much money as I have made." Sebastian withered him with a glance. "I have no time to waste," he replied, "on making money!"

So, when Hilda Wade told me, on the first day I met her, that she wished to become a nurse at Nathaniel's, "to be near Sebastian," I was not at all astonished. I took her at her word. Everybody who meant business in any branch of the medical art, however humble, desired to be close to our rare teacher—to drink in his large thought, to profit by his clear insight, his wide experience. The man of Nathaniel's was revolutionising practice; and those who wished to feel themselves abreast of the modern movement were naturally anxious to cast in their lot with him. I did not wonder, therefore, that Hilda Wade, who herself possessed in so large a measure the deepest feminine gift—intuition—should seek a place under the famous professor who represented the other side of the same endowment in its masculine embodiment—instinct of diagnosis.

Hilda Wade herself I will not formally introduce to you: you will learn to know her as I proceed with my story.

I was Sebastian's assistant, and my recommendation soon procured Hilda Wade the post she so strangely coveted. Before she had been long at Nathaniel's, however, it began to dawn upon me that her reasons for desiring to attend upon our revered Master were not wholly and solely scientific. Sebastian, it is true, recognised her value as a nurse from the first; he not only allowed that she was a good assistant, but he also admitted that her subtle knowledge of temperament sometimes enabled her closely to approach his own reasoned scientific analysis of a case and its probable development. "Most women," he said to me once, "are quick at reading *the passing emotion*. They can judge with astounding correctness from a shadow on one's face, a catch in one's breath, a movement of one's hands, how their words or deeds are affecting us. We cannot conceal our feelings from them. But underlying character they do not judge so well as fleeting expression. Not what Mrs. Jones *is* in herself, but what Mrs. Jones is now thinking and feeling—there lies their great success as psychologists. Most men, on the contrary, guide their life by definite *facts*—by signs, by symptoms, by observed data. Medicine itself is built upon a collection of such reasoned facts. But this woman, Nurse Wade, to a certain extent, stands intermediate mentally between the two sexes. She recognises *temperament*—the fixed form of character, and what it is likely to do—in a degree which I have never seen equaled elsewhere. To that extent, and within proper limits of supervision, I acknowledge her faculty as a valuable adjunct to a scientific practitioner."

Still, though Sebastian started with a predisposition in favour of Hilda Wade—a pretty girl appeals to most of us—I could see from the beginning that Hilda Wade was by no means enthusiastic for Sebastian, like the rest of the hospital:

"He is extraordinarily able," she would say, when I gushed to her about our Master; but that was the most I could ever extort from her in the way of praise. Though she admitted intellectually

Sebastian's gigantic mind, she would never commit herself to any-thing that sounded like personal admiration. To call him "the prince of physiologists" did not satisfy me on that head. I wanted her to exclaim, "I adore him! I worship him! He is glorious, won-derful!"

I was also aware from an early date that, in an unobtrusive way, Hilda Wade was watching Sebastian, watching him quietly, with those wistful, earnest eyes, as a cat watches a mouse-hole; watch-ing him with mute inquiry, as if she expected each moment to see him do something different from what the rest of us expected of him. Slowly I gathered that Hilda Wade, in the most literal sense, had come to Nathaniel's, as she herself expressed it, "to be near Sebastian."

Gentle and lovable as she was in every other aspect, towards Sebastian she seemed like a lynx-eyed detective. She had some object in view, I thought, almost as abstract as his own—some ob-ject to which, as I judged, she was devoting her life quite as single-mindedly as Sebastian himself had devoted his to the advancement of science.

"Why did she become a nurse at all?" I asked once of her friend, Mrs. Mallet. "She has plenty of money, and seems well enough off to live without working."

"Oh, dear, yes," Mrs. Mallet answered. "She is independent, quite; has a tidy little income of her own—six or seven hundred a year—and she could choose her own society. But she went in for this mission fad early; she didn't intend to marry, she said; so she would like to have some work to do in life. Girls suffer like that, nowadays. In her case, the malady took the form of nursing."

"As a rule," I ventured to interpose, "when a pretty girl says she doesn't intend to marry, her remark is premature. It only means—"

"Oh, yes, I know. Every girl says it; 'tis a stock property in the popular masque of Maiden Modesty. But with Hilda it is different. And the difference is—that Hilda means it!"

"You are right," I answered. "I believe she means it. Yet I know one man at least—" for I admired her immensely.

Mrs. Mallet shook her head and smiled. "It is no use, Dr. Cumberledge," she answered. "Hilda will never marry. Never, that is to say, till she has attained some mysterious object she seems to have in view, about which she never speaks to anyone—not even to me. But I have somehow guessed it!"

"And it is?"

"Oh, I have not guessed what it *is*: I am no Œdipus. I have merely guessed that it exists. But whatever it may be, Hilda's life is bounded by it. She became a nurse to carry it out, I feel confident. From the very beginning, I gather, a part of her scheme was to go to St. Nathaniel's. She was always bothering us to give her introductions to Dr. Sebastian; and when she met you at my brother Hugo's, it was a preconcerted arrangement; she asked to sit next you, and meant to induce you to use your influence on her behalf with the Professor. She was dying to get there."

"It is very odd," I mused. "But there!—women are inexplicable!"

"And Hilda is in that matter the very quintessence of woman. Even I, who have known her for years, don't pretend to understand her."

A few months later, Sebastian began his great researches on his new anaesthetic. It was a wonderful set of researches. It promised so well. All Nat's (as we familiarly and affectionately styled St. Nathaniel's) was in a fever of excitement over the drug for a twelvemonth.

The Professor obtained his first hint of the new body by a mere accident. His friend, the Deputy Prosector of the Zoölogical Society, had mixed a draught for a sick raccoon at the Gardens, and, by some mistake in a bottle, had mixed it wrongly. (I purposely refrain from mentioning the ingredients, as they are drugs which can be easily obtained in isolation at any chemist's, though when compounded they form one of the most dangerous and difficult to detect of organic poisons. I do not desire to play into the hands of would-be criminals.) The compound on which the Deputy Prosector had thus accidentally lighted sent the raccoon to sleep in the most extraordinary manner. Indeed, the raccoon slept for thirty-six hours on end, all attempts to awake him, by pulling his tail or tweaking his hair being quite unavailing. This was a novelty in narcotics; so Sebastian was asked to come and look at the slumbering brute. He suggested the attempt to perform an operation on the somnolent raccoon by removing, under the influence of the drug, an internal growth, which was considered the probable cause of his illness. A surgeon was called in, the growth was found and removed, and the raccoon, to everybody's surprise, continued to slumber peacefully on his straw for five hours afterwards. At the end of that time he awoke, and stretched himself as if nothing had happened; and though he was, of course, very weak from loss of blood, he immediately displayed a most royal hunger. He ate up all the maize that was offered him for breakfast, and proceeded to manifest a desire for more by most unequivocal symptoms.

Sebastian was overjoyed. He now felt sure he had discovered a drug which would supersede chloroform—a drug more lasting in its immediate effects, and yet far less harmful in its ultimate results on the balance of the system. A name being wanted for it, he christened it "lethodyne." It was the best pain-luller yet invented.

For the next few weeks, at Nat's, we heard of nothing but lethodyne. Patients recovered and patients died; but their deaths or recoveries were as dross to lethodyne, an anaesthetic that might revolutionise surgery, and even medicine! A royal road through disease, with no trouble to the doctor and no pain to the patient! Lethodyne held the field. We were all of us, for the moment, intoxicated with lethodyne.

Sebastian's observations on the new agent occupied several months. He had begun with the raccoon; he went on, of course, with those poor scapegoats of physiology, domestic rabbits. Not that in this particular case any painful experiments were in contemplation. The Professor tried the drug on a dozen or more quite healthy young animals—with the strange result that they dozed off quietly, and never woke up again. This nonplussed Sebastian. He experimented once more on another raccoon, with a smaller dose; the raccoon fell asleep, and slept like a top for fifteen hours, at the end of which time he woke up as if nothing out of the common had happened. Sebastian fell back upon rabbits again, with smaller and smaller doses. It was no good; the rabbits all died with great unanimity, until the dose was so diminished that it did not send them off to sleep at all. There was no middle course, apparently, to the rabbit kind, lethodyne was either fatal or else inoperative. So it proved to sheep. The new drug killed, or did nothing.

I will not trouble you with all the details of Sebastian's further researches; the curious will find them discussed at length in Volume 237 of the *Philosophical Transactions*. (See also *Comptes Rendus de l'Académie de Médecine*: tome 49, pp. 72 and sequel.) I will restrict myself here to that part of the inquiry which immediately refers to Hilda Wade's history.

"If I were you," she said to the Professor one morning, when he was most astonished at his contradictory results, "I would test it on a hawk. If I dare venture on a suggestion, I believe you will find that hawks recover."

"The deuce they do!" Sebastian cried. However, he had such confidence in Nurse Wade's judgment that he bought a couple of hawks and tried the treatment on them. Both birds took considerable doses, and, after a period of insensibility extending to several hours, woke up in the end quite bright and lively.

"I see your principle," the Professor broke out. "It depends upon diet. Carnivores and birds of prey can take lethodyne with impunity; herbivores and fruit-eaters cannot recover, and die of it. Man, therefore, being partly carnivorous, will doubtless be able more or less to stand it."

Hilda Wade smiled her sphinx-like smile. "Not quite that, I fancy," she answered. "It will kill cats, I feel sure; at least, most domesticated ones. But it will *not* kill weasels. Yet both are carnivores."

"That young woman knows too much!" Sebastian muttered to me, looking after her as she glided noiselessly with her gentle tread down the long white corridor. "We shall have to suppress her, Cumberledge. . . . But I'll wager my life she's right, for all that. I wonder, now, how the dickens she guessed it!"

"Intuition," I answered.

He pouted his under lip above the upper one, with a dubious acquiescence. "Inference, I call it," he retorted. "All woman's so-called intuition is, in fact, just rapid and half-unconscious inference."

He was so full of the subject, however, and so utterly carried away by his scientific ardour, that I regret to say he gave a strong dose of lethodyne at once to each of the matron's petted and pampered Persian cats, which lounged about her room and were the delight of the convalescents. They were two peculiarly lazy sultanas of cats—mere jewels of the harem—Oriental beauties that loved to bask in the sun or curl themselves up on the rug before the fire and dawdle away their lives in congenial idleness. Strange to say, Hilda's prophecy came true. Zuleika settled herself down comfortably in the Professor's easy chair and fell into a sound sleep from which there was no awaking; while Roxana met fate on the tiger-skin she loved, coiled up in a circle, and passed from this life of dreams, without knowing it, into one where dreaming is not. Sebastian noted the facts with a quiet gleam of satisfaction in his watchful eye, and explained afterwards, with curt glibness to the angry matron, that her favourites had been "canonised in the roll of science, as painless martyrs to the advancement of physiology."

The weasels, on the other hand, with an equal dose, woke up after six hours as lively as crickets. It was clear that carnivorous tastes were not the whole solution, for Roxana was famed as a notable mouser.

"Your principle?" Sebastian asked our sibyl, in his brief, quick way.

Hilda's cheek wore a glow of pardonable triumph. The great teacher had deigned to ask her assistance. "I judged by the analogy of Indian hemp," she answered. "This is clearly a similar, but much stronger, narcotic. Now, whenever I have given Indian hemp by your direction to people of sluggish, or even of merely bustling temperament, I have noticed that small doses produce serious effects, and that the after-results are most undesirable. But when you have prescribed the hemp for nervous, overstrung, imaginative people, I have observed that they can stand large amounts of the tincture without evil results, and that the after-effects pass off rapidly. I who am mercurial in temperament, for example, can take any amount of Indian hemp without being made ill by it; while ten drops will send some slow and torpid rustics mad drunk with excitement—drive them into homicidal mania."

Sebastian nodded his head. He needed no more explanation. "You have hit it," he said. "I see it at a glance. The old antithesis! All men and all animals fall, roughly speaking, into two great divisions of type: the impassioned and the unimpassioned; the vivid and the phlegmatic. I catch your drift now. Lethodyne is poison to phlegmatic patients, who have not active power enough to wake up from it unhurt; it is relatively harmless to the vivid and impassioned, who can be put asleep by it, indeed, for a few hours more or less, but are alive enough to live on through the coma and reassert their vitality after it."

I recognised as he spoke that this explanation was correct. The dull rabbits, the sleepy Persian cats, and the silly sheep had died outright of lethodyne; the cunning, inquisitive raccoon, the quick hawk, and the active, intense-natured weasels, all most eager, wary, and alert animals, full of keenness and passion, had recovered quickly.

"Dare we try it on a human subject?" I asked, tentatively.

Hilda Wade answered at once, with that unerring rapidity of hers: "Yes, certainly; on a few—the right persons. *I*, for one, am not afraid to try it."

"You?" I cried, feeling suddenly aware how much I thought of her. "Oh, not *you*, please, Nurse Wade. Some other life, less valuable!"

Sebastian stared at me coldly. "Nurse Wade volunteers," he said. "It is in the cause of science. Who dares dissuade her? That tooth of yours? Ah, yes. Quite sufficient excuse. You wanted it out, Nurse Wade. Wells-Dinton shall operate."

Without a moment's hesitation, Hilda Wade sat down in an easy chair and took a measured dose of the new anaesthetic, proportioned to the average difference in weight between raccoons and humanity. My face displayed my anxiety, I suppose, for she turned to me, smiling with quiet confidence. "I know my own constitution," she said, with a reassuring glance that went straight to my heart. "I do not in the least fear."

As for Sebastian, he administered the drug to her as unconcernedly as if she were a rabbit. Sebastian's scientific coolness and calmness have long been the admiration of younger practitioners.

Wells-Dinton gave one wrench. The tooth came out as though the patient were a block of marble. There was not a cry or a movement, such as one notes when nitrous oxide is administered. Hilda Wade was to all appearance a mass of lifeless flesh. We stood round and watched. I was trembling with terror. Even on Sebastian's pale face, usually so unmoved, save by the watchful eagerness of scientific curiosity, I saw signs of anxiety.

After four hours of profound slumber—breath hovering, as it seemed, between life and death—she began to come to again. In half an hour more she was wide awake; she opened her eyes and asked for a glass of hock, with beef essence or oysters.

That evening, by six o'clock, she was quite well and able to go about her duties as usual.

"Sebastian is a wonderful man," I said to her, as I entered her ward on my rounds at night. "His coolness astonishes me. Do you know, he watched you all the time you were lying asleep there as if nothing were the matter."

"Coolness?" she inquired, in a quiet voice. "Or cruelty?"

"Cruelty?" I echoed, aghast. "Sebastian cruel! Oh, Nurse Wade, what an idea! Why, he has spent his whole life in striving against all odds to alleviate pain. He is the apostle of philanthropy!"

"Of philanthropy, or of science? To alleviate pain, or to learn the whole truth about the human body?"

"Come, come, now," I cried. "You analyse too far. I will not let even *you* put me out of conceit with Sebastian." (Her face flushed at that "even you"; I almost fancied she began to like me.) "He is the enthusiasm of my life; just consider how much he has done for humanity!"

She looked me through searchingly. "I will not destroy your illusion," she answered, after a pause. "It is a noble and generous one. But is it not largely based on an ascetic face, long white hair, and a moustache that hides the cruel corners of the mouth? For the corners *are* cruel. Some day, I will show you them. Cut off the long hair, shave the grizzled moustache—and what then will remain?" She drew a profile hastily. "Just that," and she showed it me. 'Twas a face like Robespierre's, grown harder and older and lined with observation. I recognised that it was in fact the essence of Sebastian.

Next day, as it turned out, the Professor himself insisted upon testing lethodyne in his own person. All Nat's strove to dissuade him. "Your life is so precious, sir—the advancement of science!" But the Professor was adamantine.

"Science can only be advanced if men of science will take their lives in their hands," he answered, sternly. "Besides, Nurse Wade has tried. Am I to lag behind a woman in my devotion to the cause of physiological knowledge?"

"Let him try," Hilda Wade murmured to me. "He is quite right. It will not hurt him. I have told him already he has just the proper temperament to stand the drug. Such people are rare: *he* is one of them."

We administered the dose, trembling. Sebastian took it like a man, and dropped off instantly, for lethodyne is at least as instantaneous in its operation as nitrous oxide.

He lay long asleep. Hilda and I watched him.

After he had lain for some minutes senseless, like a log, on the couch where we had placed him, Hilda stooped over him quietly and lifted up the ends of the grizzled moustache. Then she pointed one accusing finger at his lips. "I told you so," she murmured, with a note of demonstration.

"There is certainly something rather stern, or even ruthless, about the set of the face and the firm ending of the lips," I admitted, reluctantly.

"That is why God gave men moustaches," she mused, in a low voice; "to hide the cruel corners of their mouths."

"Not *always* cruel," I cried.

"Sometimes cruel, sometimes cunning, sometimes sensuous; but nine times out of ten best masked by moustaches."

"You have a bad opinion of our sex!" I exclaimed.

"Providence knew best," she answered. "*It* gave you moustaches. That was in order that we women might be spared from always seeing you as you are. Besides, I said 'Nine times out of ten.' There are exceptions—*such* exceptions!"

On second thought, I did not feel sure that I could quarrel with her estimate.

The experiment was that time once more successful. Sebastian woke up from the comatose state after eight hours, not quite as fresh as Hilda Wade, perhaps, but still tolerably alive; less alert, however, and complaining of dull headache. He was not hungry. Hilda Wade shook her head at that. "It will be of use only in a very few cases," she said to me, regretfully; "and those few will need to be carefully picked by an acute observer. I see resistance to the coma is, even more than I thought, a matter of temperament. Why, so impassioned a man as the Professor himself cannot entirely recover. With more sluggish temperaments, we shall have deeper difficulty."

"Would you call him impassioned?" I asked. "Most people think him so cold and stern."

She shook her head. "He is a snow-capped volcano!" she answered. "The fires of his life burn bright below. The exterior alone is cold and placid."

However, starting from that time, Sebastian began a course of experiments on patients, giving infinitesimal doses at first, and venturing slowly on somewhat larger quantities. But only in his own case and Hilda's could the result be called quite satisfactory. One dull and heavy, drink-sodden navvy, to whom he administered no more than one-tenth of a grain, was drowsy for a week, and listless long after; while a fat washerwoman from West Ham, who took only two-tenths, fell so fast asleep, and snored so stertorously, that we feared she was going to doze off into eternity, after the fashion of the rabbits. Mothers of large families, we noted, stood the drug very ill; on pale young girls of the consumptive tendency its effect was not marked; but only a patient here and there, of exceptionally imaginative and vivid temperament, seemed able to endure it. Sebastian was discouraged. He saw the anaesthetic was not destined to fulfil his first enthusiastic humanitarian expectations. One day, while the investigation was just at this stage, a case was admitted into the observation-cots in which Hilda Wade took a particular interest. The patient was a young girl named Isabel Huntley—tall, dark, and slender, a markedly quick and imaginative type, with large black eyes which clearly bespoke a passionate nature. Though distinctly hysterical, she was pretty and pleasing. Her rich dark hair was as copious as it was beautiful. She held herself erect and had a finely poised head. From the first moment she arrived, I could see Nurse Wade was strongly drawn towards her. Their souls sympathised. Number Fourteen—that is our impersonal way of describing *cases*—was constantly on Hilda's lips. "I like the girl," she said once. "She is a lady in fibre."

"And a tobacco-trimmer by trade," Sebastian added, sarcastically.

As usual, Hilda's was the truer description. It went deeper.

Number Fourteen's ailment was a rare and peculiar one, into which I need not enter here with professional precision. (I have described the case fully for my brother practitioners in my paper in the fourth volume of Sebastian's *Medical Miscellanies*.) It will be enough for my present purpose to say, in brief, that the lesion consisted of an internal growth which is always dangerous and most often fatal, but which nevertheless is of such a character that, if it be once happily eradicated by supremely good surgery, it never tends to recur, and leaves the patient as strong and well as ever. Sebastian was, of course, delighted with the splendid opportunity thus afforded him. "It is a beautiful case!" he cried, with professional enthusiasm. "Beautiful! Beautiful! I never saw one so deadly or so malignant before. We are indeed in luck's way. Only a miracle can save her life. Cumberledge, we must proceed to perform the miracle."

Sebastian loved such cases. They formed his ideal. He did not greatly admire the artificial prolongation of diseased and unwholesome lives, which could never be of much use to their owners or anyone else; but when a chance occurred for restoring to perfect health a valuable existence which might otherwise, be extinguished before its time, he positively revelled in his beneficent calling.

"What nobler object can a man propose to himself," he used to say, "than to raise good men and true from the dead, as it were, and return them whole and sound to the family that depends upon them? Why, I had fifty times rather cure an honest coal-heaver of a wound in his leg than give ten years more lease of life to a gouty lord, diseased from top to toe, who expects to find a month of Carlsbad or Homburg once every year make up for eleven months of over-eating, over-drinking, vulgar debauchery, and under-thinking." He had no sympathy with men who lived the lives of swine: his heart was with the workers.

Of course, Hilda Wade soon suggested that, as an operation was absolutely necessary, Number Fourteen would be a splendid subject on whom to test once more the effects of lethodyne. Sebastian, with his head on one side, surveying the patient, promptly coincided. "Nervous diathesis," he observed. "Very vivid fancy. Twitches her hands the right way. Quick pulse, rapid perceptions, no meaningless unrest, but deep vitality. I don't doubt she'll stand it."

We explained to Number Fourteen the gravity of the case, and also the tentative character of the operation under lethodyne. At first, she shrank from taking it. "No, no!" she said; "let me die quietly." But Hilda, like the Angel of Mercy that she was, whispered in the girl's ear: "*If* it succeeds, you will get quite well, and—you can marry Arthur."

The patient's dark face flushed crimson.

"Ah! Arthur," she cried. "Dear Arthur! I can bear anything you choose to do to me—for Arthur!"

"How soon you find these things out!" I cried to Hilda, a few minutes later. "A mere man would never have thought of that. And who is Arthur?"

"A sailor—on a ship that trades with the South Seas. I hope he is worthy of her. Fretting over Arthur's absence has aggravated the case. He is homeward-bound now. She is worrying herself to death for fear she should not live to say good-bye to him."

"She *will* live to marry him," I answered, with confidence like her own, "if *you* say she can stand it."

"The lethodyne—oh, yes; *that's* all right. But the operation itself is so extremely dangerous; though Dr. Sebastian says he has called in the best surgeon in London for all such cases. They are rare, he tells me—and Nielsen has performed on six, three of them successfully."

We gave the girl the drug. She took it, trembling, and went off at once, holding Hilda's hand, with a pale smile on her face, which persisted there somewhat weirdly all through the operation. The work of removing the growth was long and ghastly, even for us who were well seasoned to such sights; but at the end Nielsen expressed himself as perfectly satisfied. "A very neat piece of work!" Sebastian exclaimed, looking on. "I congratulate you, Nielsen. I never saw anything done cleaner or better."

"A successful operation, certainly!" the great surgeon admitted, with just pride in the Master's commendation.

"*And* the patient?" Hilda asked, wavering.

"Oh, the patient? The patient will die," Nielsen replied, in an unconcerned voice, wiping his spotless instruments.

"That is not *my* idea of the medical art," I cried, shocked at his callousness. "An operation is only successful if—"

He regarded me with lofty scorn. "A certain percentage of losses," he interrupted, calmly, "is inevitable, of course, in all surgical operations. We are obliged to average it. How could I preserve my precision and accuracy of hand if I were always bothered by sentimental considerations of the patient's safety?"

Hilda Wade looked up at me with a sympathetic glance. "We will pull her through yet," she murmured, in her soft voice, "if care and skill can do it,—*my* care and *your* skill. This is now *our* patient, Dr. Cumberledge."

It needed care and skill. We watched her for hours, and she showed no sign or gleam of recovery. Her sleep was deeper than either Sebastian's or Hilda's had been. She had taken a big dose, so as to secure immobility. The question now was, would she recover at all from it? Hour after hour we waited and watched; and not a sign of movement! Only the same deep, slow, hampered breathing, the same feeble, jerky pulse, the same deathly pallor on the dark cheeks, the same corpse-like rigidity of limb and muscle.

At last our patient stirred faintly, as in a dream; her breath faltered. We bent over her. Was it death, or was she beginning to recover?

Very slowly, a faint trace of colour came back to her cheeks. Her heavy eyes half opened. They stared first with a white stare. Her arms dropped by her side. Her mouth relaxed its ghastly smile. . . . We held our breath. . . . She was coming to again!

But her coming to was slow—very, very slow. Her pulse was still weak. Her heart pumped feebly. We feared she might sink from inanition at any moment. Hilda Wade knelt on the floor by the girl's side and held a spoonful of beef essence coaxingly to her lips. Number Fourteen gasped, drew a long, slow breath, then gulped and swallowed it. After that she lay back with her mouth open, looking like a corpse. Hilda pressed another spoonful of the soft jelly upon her; but the girl waved it away with one trembling hand. "Let me die," she cried. "Let me die! I feel dead already."

Hilda held her face close. "Isabel," she whispered—and I recognised in her tone the vast moral difference between "Isabel" and "Number Fourteen,"—"Is-a-bel, you must take it. For Arthur's sake, I say, you *must* take it."

The girl's hand quivered as it lay on the white coverlet. "For Arthur's sake!" she murmured, lifting her eyelids dreamily. "For Arthur's sake! Yes, nurse, dear!"

"Call me Hilda, please! Hilda!"

The girl's face lighted up again. "Yes, Hilda, dear," she answered, in an unearthly voice, like one raised from the dead. "I will call you what you will. Angel of light, you have been so good to me."

She opened her lips with an effort and slowly swallowed another spoonful. Then she fell back, exhausted. But her pulse improved within twenty minutes. I mentioned the matter, with enthusiasm, to Sebastian later. "It is very nice in its way," he answered; "but . . . it is not nursing."

I thought to myself that that was just what it *was*; but I did not say so. Sebastian was a man who thought meanly of women. "A doctor, like a priest," he used to declare, "should keep himself unmarried. His bride is medicine." And he disliked to see what he called *philandering* going on in his hospital. It may have been on that account that I avoided speaking much of Hilda Wade thenceforth before him.

He looked in casually next day to see the patient. "She will die," he said, with perfect assurance, as we passed down the ward together. "Operation has taken too much out of her."

"Still, she has great recuperative powers," Hilda answered. "They all have in her family, Professor. You may, perhaps, remember Joseph Huntley, who occupied Number Sixty-seven in the Accident Ward, some nine months since—compound fracture of the arm—a dark, nervous engineer's assistant—very hard to restrain—well, *he* was her brother; he caught typhoid fever in the hospital, and you commented at the time on his strange vitality. Then there was her cousin, again, Ellen Stubbs. We had *her* for stubborn chronic laryngitis—a very bad case—anyone else would have died—yielded at once to your treatment; and made, I recollect, a splendid convalescence."

"What a memory you have!" Sebastian cried, admiring against his will. "It is simply marvellous! I never saw anyone like you in my life . . . except once. *He* was a man, a doctor, a colleague of mine—dead long ago. . . . Why—" he mused, and gazed hard at her. Hilda shrank before his gaze. "This is curious," he went on slowly, at last; "very curious. You—why, you resemble him!"

"Do I?" Hilda replied, with forced calm, raising her eyes to his. Their glances met. That moment, I saw each had recognised something; and from that day forth I was instinctively aware that a duel was being waged between Sebastian and Hilda,—a duel between the two ablest and most singular personalities I had ever met; a duel of life and death—though I did not fully understand its purport till much, much later.

Every day after that, the poor, wasted girl in Number Fourteen grew feebler and fainter. Her temperature rose; her heart throbbed weakly. She seemed to be fading away. Sebastian shook his head. "Lethodyne is a failure," he said, with a mournful regret. "One cannot trust it. The case might have recovered from the operation, or recovered from the drug; but she could not recover from both together. Yet the operation would have been impossible without the drug, and the drug is useless except for the operation."

It was a great disappointment to him. He hid himself in his room, as was his wont when disappointed, and went on with his old work at his beloved microbes.

"I have one hope still," Hilda murmured to me by the bedside, when our patient was at her worst. "If one contingency occurs, I believe we may save her."

"What is that?" I asked.

She shook her head waywardly. "You must wait and see," she answered. "If it comes off, I will tell you. If not, let it swell the limbo of lost inspirations."

Next morning early, however, she came up to me with a radiant face, holding a newspaper in her hand. "Well, it *has* happened!" she cried, rejoicing. "We shall save poor Isabel Number Fourteen, I mean; our way is clear, Dr. Cumberledge."

I followed her blindly to the bedside, little guessing what she could mean. She knelt down at the head of the cot. The girl's eyes were closed. I touched her cheek; she was in a high fever. "Temperature?" I asked.

"A hundred and three."

I shook my head. Every symptom of fatal relapse. I could not imagine what card Hilda held in reserve. But I stood there, waiting.

She whispered in the girl's ear: "Arthur's ship is sighted off the Lizard."

The patient opened her eyes slowly, and rolled them for a moment as if she did not understand.

"Too late!" I cried. "Too late! She is delirious—insensible!"

Hilda repeated the words slowly, but very distinctly. "Do you hear, dear? Arthur's ship . . . it is sighted. . . . Arthur's ship . . . at the Lizard."

The girl's lips moved. "Arthur! Arthur! . . . Arthur's ship!" A deep sigh. She clenched her hands. "He is coming?" Hilda nodded and smiled, holding her breath with suspense.

"Up the Channel now. He will be at Southampton tonight. Arthur . . . at Southampton. It is here, in the papers; I have telegraphed to him to hurry on at once to see you."

She struggled up for a second. A smile flitted across the worn face. Then she fell back wearily.

I thought all was over. Her eyes stared white. But ten minutes later she opened her lids again. "Arthur is coming," she murmured. "Arthur . . . coming."

"Yes, dear. Now sleep. He is coming."

All through that day and the next night she was restless and agitated; but still her pulse improved a little. Next morning she was again a trifle better. Temperature falling—a hundred and one, point three. At ten o'clock Hilda came in to her, radiant.

"Well, Isabel, dear," she cried, bending down and touching her cheek (kissing is forbidden by the rules of the house), "Arthur has come. He is here . . . down below . . . I have seen him."

"Seen him!" the girl gasped.

"Yes, seen him. Talked with him. Such a nice, manly fellow; and such an honest, good face! He is longing for you to get well. He says he has come home this time to marry you."

The wan lips quivered. "He will *never* marry me!"

"Yes, yes, he *will*—if you will take this jelly. Look here—he wrote these words to you before my very eyes: 'Dear love to my Isa!' . . . If you are good, and will sleep, he may see you—to-morrow."

The girl opened her lips and ate the jelly greedily. She ate as much as she was desired. In three minutes more her head had fallen like a child's upon her pillow and she was sleeping peacefully.

I went up to Sebastian's room, quite excited with the news. He was busy among his bacilli. They were his hobby, his pets. "Well, what do you think, Professor?" I cried. "That patient of Nurse Wade's—"

He gazed up at me abstractedly, his brow contracting. "Yes, yes; I know," he interrupted. "The girl in Fourteen. I have discounted her case long ago. She has ceased to interest me. . . . Dead, of course! Nothing else was possible."

I laughed a quick little laugh of triumph. "No, sir; *not* dead. Recovering! She has fallen just now into a normal sleep; her breathing is natural."

He wheeled his revolving chair away from the germs and fixed me with his keen eyes. "Recovering?" he echoed. "Impossible! Rallying, you mean. A mere flicker. I know my trade. She *must* die this evening."

"Forgive my persistence," I replied; "but—her temperature has gone down to ninety-nine and a trifle."

He pushed away the bacilli in the nearest watch-glass quite angrily. "To ninety-nine!" he exclaimed, knitting his brows. "Cumberledge, this is disgraceful! A most disappointing case! A most provoking patient!"

"But surely, sir—" I cried.

"Don't talk to *me*, boy! Don't attempt to apologise for her. Such conduct is unpardonable. She *ought* to have died. It was her clear duty. *I said* she would die, and she should have known better than to fly in the face of the faculty. Her recovery is an insult to medical science. What is the staff about? Nurse Wade should have prevented it."

"Still, sir," I exclaimed, trying to touch him on a tender spot, "the anaesthetic, you know! Such a triumph for lethodyne! This case shows clearly that on certain constitutions it may be used with advantage under certain conditions."

He snapped his fingers. "Lethodyne! pooh! I have lost interest in it. Impracticable! It is not fitted for the human species."

"Why so? Number Fourteen proves—"

He interrupted me with an impatient wave of his hand; then he rose and paced up and down the room testily. After a pause, he spoke again. "The weak point of lethodyne is this: nobody can be trusted to say *when* it may be used—except Nurse Wade,—which is *not* science."

For the first time in my life, I had a glimmering idea that I distrusted Sebastian. Hilda Wade was right—the man was cruel. But I had never observed his cruelty before—because his devotion to science had blinded me to it.

THE EPISODE OF THE GENTLEMAN
WHO HAD FAILED FOR EVERYTHING

One day, about those times, I went round to call on my aunt, Lady Tepping. And lest you accuse me of the vulgar desire to flaunt my fine relations in your face, I hasten to add that my poor dear old aunt is a very ordinary specimen of the common Army widow. Her husband, Sir Malcolm, a crusty old gentleman of the ancient school, was knighted in Burma, or thereabouts, for a successful raid upon naked natives, on something that is called the Shan frontier. When he had grown grey in the service of his Queen and country, besides earning himself incidentally a very decent pension, he acquired gout and went to his long rest in Kensal Green Cemetery. He left his wife with one daughter, and the only pretence to a title in our otherwise blameless family.

My cousin Daphne is a very pretty girl, with those quiet, sedate manners which often develop later in life into genuine self-respect and real depth of character. Fools do not admire her; they accuse her of being "heavy." But she can do without fools; she has a fine, strongly built figure, an upright carriage, a large and broad forehead, a firm chin, and features which, though well-marked and well-moulded, are yet delicate in outline and sensitive in expression. Very young men seldom take to Daphne: she lacks the desired inanity. But she has mind, repose, and womanly tenderness. Indeed, if she had not been my cousin, I almost think I might once have been tempted to fall in love with her.

When I reached Gloucester Terrace, on this particular afternoon, I found Hilda Wade there before me. She had lunched at my

aunt's, in fact. It was her "day out" at St. Nathaniel's, and she had
come round to spend it with Daphne Tepping. I had introduced
her to the house some time before, and she and my cousin had
struck up a close acquaintance immediately. Their temperaments
were sympathetic; Daphne admired Hilda's depth and reserve,
while Hilda admired Daphne's grave grace and self-control, her
perfect freedom from current affectations. She neither giggled nor
aped Ibsenism.

A third person stood back in the room when I entered—a tall
and somewhat jerry-built young man, with a rather long and solemn face, like an early stage in the evolution of a Don Quixote. I
took a good look at him. There was something about his air that
impressed me as both lugubrious and humorous; and in this I was
right, for I learned later that he was one of those rare people who
can sing a comic song with immense success while preserving a
sour countenance, like a Puritan preacher's. His eyes were a little
sunken, his fingers long and nervous; but I fancied he looked a
good fellow at heart, for all that, though foolishly impulsive. He
was a punctilious gentleman, I felt sure; his face and manner grew
upon one rapidly.

Daphne rose as I entered, and waved the stranger forward with
an imperious little wave. I imagined, indeed, that I detected in the
gesture a faint touch of half-unconscious proprietorship. "Good-
morning, Hubert," she said, taking my hand, but turning towards
the tall young man. "I don't think you know Mr. Cecil Holsworthy."

"I have heard you speak of him," I answered, drinking him in
with my glance. I added internally, "Not half good enough for you."

Hilda's eyes met mine and read my thought. They flashed back
word, in the language of eyes, "I do not agree with you."

Daphne, meanwhile, was watching me closely. I could see she
was anxious to discover what impression her friend Mr. Holsworthy
was making on me. Till then, I had no idea she was fond of anyone
in particular; but the way her glance wandered from him to me
and from me to Hilda showed clearly that she thought much of
this gawky visitor.

We sat and talked together, we four, for some time. I found the
young man with the lugubrious countenance improved immensely

on closer acquaintance. His talk was clever. He turned out to be the son of a politician high in office in the Canadian Government, and he had been educated at Oxford. The father, I gathered, was rich, but he himself was making an income of nothing a year just then as a briefless barrister, and he was hesitating whether to accept a post of secretary that had been offered him in the colony, or to continue his negative career at the Inner Temple, for the honour and glory of it.

"Now, which would *you* advise me, Miss Tepping?" he inquired, after we had discussed the matter some minutes.

Daphne's face flushed up. "It is so hard to decide," she answered. "To decide to *your* best advantage, I mean, of course. For naturally all your English friends would wish to keep you as long as possible in England."

"No, do you think so?" the gawky young man jerked out with evident pleasure. "Now, that's awfully kind of you. Do you know, if *you* tell me I ought to stay in England, I've half a mind . . . I'll cable over this very day and refuse the appointment."

Daphne flushed once more. "Oh, please don't!" she exclaimed, looking frightened. "I shall be quite distressed if a stray word of mine should debar you from accepting a good offer of a secretaryship."

"Why, your least wish—" the young man began—then checked himself hastily—"must be always important," he went on, in a different voice, "to everyone of your acquaintance."

Daphne rose hurriedly. "Look here, Hilda," she said, a little tremulously, biting her lip, "I have to go out into Westbourne Grove to get those gloves for to-night, and a spray for my hair; will you excuse me for half an hour?"

Holsworthy rose too. "Mayn't I go with you?" he asked, eagerly.

"Oh, if you like. How very kind of you!" Daphne answered, her cheek a blush rose. "Hubert, will you come too? and you, Hilda?"

It was one of those invitations which are given to be refused. I did not need Hilda's warning glance to tell me that my company would be quite superfluous. I felt those two were best left together.

"It's no use, though, Dr. Cumberledge!" Hilda put in, as soon as they were gone. "He *won't* propose, though he has had every encouragement. I don't know what's the matter; but I've been watching them both for weeks, and somehow things seem never to get any forwarder."

"You think he's in love with her?" I asked.

"In love with her! Well, you have eyes in your head, I know; where could they have been looking? He's madly in love—a very good kind of love, too. He genuinely admires and respects and appreciates all Daphne's sweet and charming qualities."

"Then what do you suppose is the matter?"

"I have an inkling of the truth: I imagine Mr. Cecil must have let himself in for a prior attachment."

"If so, why does he hang about Daphne?"

"Because—he can't help himself. He's a good fellow and a chivalrous fellow. He admires your cousin; but he must have got himself into some foolish entanglement elsewhere which he is too honourable to break off; while at the same time he's far too much impressed by Daphne's fine qualities to be able to keep away from her. It's the ordinary case of love *versus* duty."

"Is he well off? Could he afford to marry Daphne?"

"Oh, his father's very rich: he has plenty of money; a Canadian millionaire, they say. That makes it all the likelier that some undesirable young woman somewhere may have managed to get hold of him. Just the sort of romantic, impressionable hobbledehoy such women angle for."

I drummed my fingers on the table. Presently Hilda spoke again. "Why don't you try to get to know him, and find out precisely what's the matter?"

"I *know* what's the matter—now you've told me," I answered. "It's as clear as day. Daphne is very much smitten with him, too. I'm sorry for Daphne! Well, I'll take your advice; I'll try to have some talk with him."

"Do, please; I feel sure I have hit upon it. He has got himself engaged in a hurry to some girl he doesn't really care about, and he is far too much of a gentleman to break it off, though he's in love quite another way with Daphne."

Just at that moment the door opened and my aunt entered.

"Why, where's Daphne?" she cried, looking about her and arranging her black lace shawl.

"She has just run out into Westbourne Grove to get some gloves and a flower for the *fête* this evening," Hilda answered. Then she added, significantly, "Mr. Holsworthy has gone with her."

"What? That boy's been here again?"

"Yes, Lady Tepping. He called to see Daphne."

My aunt turned to me with an aggrieved tone. It is a peculiarity of my aunt's—I have met it elsewhere—that if she is angry with Jones, and Jones is not present, she assumes a tone of injured asperity on his account towards Brown or Smith, or any other innocent person whom she happens to be addressing. "Now, this is really too bad, Hubert," she burst out, as if *I* were the culprit. "Disgraceful! Abominable! I'm sure I can't make out what the young fellow means by it. Here he comes dangling after Daphne every day and all day long—and never once says whether he means anything by it or not. In *my* young days, such conduct as that would not have been considered respectable."

I nodded and beamed benignly.

"Well, why don't you answer me?" my aunt went on, warming up. "*Do* you mean to tell me you think his behaviour respectful to a nice girl in Daphne's position?"

"My dear aunt," I answered, "you confound the persons. I am not Mr. Holsworthy. I decline responsibility for him. I meet him here, in *your* house, for the first time this morning."

"Then that shows how often you come to see your relations, Hubert!" my aunt burst out, obliquely. "The man's been here, to my certain knowledge, every day this six weeks."

"Really, Aunt Fanny," I said; "you must recollect that a professional man—"

"Oh, yes. *That's* the way! Lay it all down to your profession, do, Hubert! Though I *know* you were at the Thorntons' on Saturday—saw it in the papers—the Morning Post—'among the guests were Sir Edward and Lady Burnes, Professor Sebastian, Dr. Hubert Cumberledge,' and so forth, and so forth. *You* think you can conceal these things; but you can't. I get to know them!"

"Conceal them! My dearest aunt! Why, I danced twice with Daphne."

"Daphne! Yes, Daphne. They all run after Daphne," my aunt exclaimed, altering the venue once more. "But there's no respect for age left. *I* expect to be neglected. However, that's neither here nor there. The point is this: you're the one man now living in the family. You ought to behave like a brother to Daphne. Why don't you board this Holsworthy person and ask him his intentions?"

"Goodness gracious!" I cried; "most excellent of aunts, that epoch has gone past. The late lamented Queen Anne is now dead. It's no use asking the young man of to-day to explain his intentions. He will refer you to the works of the Scandinavian dramatists."

My aunt was speechless. She could only gurgle out the words: "Well, I can safely say that of all the monstrous behaviour—" then language failed her and she relapsed into silence.

However, when Daphne and young Holsworthy returned, I had as much talk with him as I could, and when he left the house I left also.

"Which way are you walking?" I asked, as we turned out into the street.

"Towards my rooms in the Temple."

"Oh! I'm going back to St. Nathaniel's," I continued. "If you'll allow me, I'll walk part way with you."

"How very kind of you!"

We strode side by side a little distance in silence. Then a thought seemed to strike the lugubrious young man. "What a charming girl your cousin is!" he exclaimed, abruptly.

"You seem to think so," I answered, smiling.

He flushed a little; the lantern jaw grew longer. "I admire her, of course," he answered. "Who doesn't? She is so extraordinarily handsome."

"Well, not exactly handsome," I replied, with more critical and kinsman-like deliberation. "Pretty, if you will; and decidedly pleasing and attractive in manner."

He looked me up and down, as if he found me a person singularly deficient in taste and appreciation. "Ah, but then, you are her cousin," he said at last, with a compassionate tone. "That makes a difference."

"I quite see all Daphne's strong points," I answered, still smiling, for I could perceive he was very far gone. "She is good-looking, and she is clever."

"Clever!" he echoed. "Profound! She has a most unusual intellect. She stands alone."

"Like her mother's silk dresses," I murmured, half under my breath.

He took no notice of my flippant remark, but went on with his rhapsody. "Such depth; such penetration! And then, how sympathetic! Why, even to a mere casual acquaintance like myself, she is so kind, so discerning!"

"*Are* you such a casual acquaintance?" I inquired, with a smile. (It might have shocked Aunt Fanny to hear me; but *that* is the way we ask a young man his intentions nowadays.)

He stopped short and hesitated. "Oh, quite casual," he replied, almost stammering. "Most casual, I assure you. . . . I have never ventured to do myself the honour of supposing that . . . that Miss Tepping could possibly care for me."

"There is such a thing as being *too* modest and unassuming," I answered. "It sometimes leads to unintentional cruelty."

"No, do you think so?" he cried, his face falling all at once. "I should blame myself bitterly if that were so. Dr. Cumberledge, you are her cousin. *Do* you gather that I have acted in such a way as to—to lead Miss Tepping to suppose I felt any affection for her?"

I laughed in his face. "My dear boy," I answered, laying one hand on his shoulder, "may I say the plain truth? A blind bat could see you are madly in love with her."

His mouth twitched. "That's very serious!" he answered, gravely; "very serious."

"It is," I responded, with my best paternal manner, gazing blankly in front of me.

He stopped short again. "Look here," he said, facing me. "Are you busy? No? Then come back with me to my rooms; and—I'll make a clean breast of it."

"By all means," I assented. "When one is young—and foolish—I have often noticed, as a medical man, that a drachm of clean breast is a magnificent prescription."

He walked back by my side, talking all the way of Daphne's many adorable qualities. He exhausted the dictionary for laudatory adjectives. By the time I reached his door it was not *his* fault if I had not learned that the angelic hierarchy were not in the running with my pretty cousin for graces and virtues. I felt that Faith, Hope, and Charity ought to resign at once in favour of Miss Daphne Tepping, promoted.

He took me into his comfortably furnished rooms—the luxurious rooms of a rich young bachelor, with taste as well as money—and offered me a partaga. Now, I have long observed, in the course of my practice, that a choice cigar assists a man in taking a philosophic outlook on the question under discussion; so I accepted the partaga. He sat down opposite me and pointed to a photograph in the centre of his mantlepiece. "I am engaged to that lady," he put in, shortly.

"So I anticipated," I answered, lighting up.

He started and looked surprised. "Why, what made you guess it?" he inquired.

I smiled the calm smile of superior age—I was some eight years or so his senior. "My dear fellow," I murmured, "what else could prevent you from proposing to Daphne—when you are so undeniably in love with her?"

"A great deal," he answered. "For example, the sense of my own utter unworthiness."

"One's own unworthiness," I replied, "though doubtless real— p'f, p'f—is a barrier that most of us can readily get over when our admiration for a particular lady waxes strong enough. So *this* is the prior attachment!" I took the portrait down and scanned it.

"Unfortunately, yes. What do you think of her?"

I scrutinised the features. "Seems a nice enough little thing," I answered. It was an innocent face, I admit; very frank and girlish.

He leaned forward eagerly. "That's just it. A nice enough little thing! Nothing in the world to be said against her. While Daphne— Miss Tepping, I mean—" His silence was ecstatic.

I examined the photograph still more closely. It displayed a lady of twenty or thereabouts, with a weak face, small, vacant features, a feeble chin, a good-humoured, simple mouth, and a wealth of golden hair that seemed to strike a keynote.

"In the theatrical profession?" I inquired at last, looking up.

He hesitated. "Well, not exactly," he answered.

I pursed my lips and blew a ring. "Music-hall stage?" I went on, dubiously.

He nodded. "But a girl is not necessarily any the less a lady because she sings at a music-hall," he added, with warmth, displaying an evident desire to be just to his betrothed, however much he admired Daphne.

"Certainly not," I admitted. "A lady is a lady; no occupation can in itself unladify her. . . . But on the music-hall stage, the odds, one must admit, are on the whole against her."

"Now, *there* you show prejudice!"

"One may be quite unprejudiced," I answered, "and yet allow that connection with the music-halls does not, as such, afford clear proof that a girl is a compound of all the virtues."

"I think she's a good girl," he retorted, slowly.

"Then why do you want to throw her over?" I inquired.

"I don't. That's just it. On the contrary, I mean to keep my word and marry her."

"*In order* to keep your word?" I suggested.

He nodded. "Precisely. It is a point of honour."

"That's a poor ground of marriage," I went on. "Mind, I don't want for a moment to influence you, as Daphne's cousin. I want to get at the truth of the situation. I don't even know what Daphne thinks of you. But you promised me a clean breast. Be a man and bare it."

He bared it instantly. "I thought I was in love with this girl, you see," he went on, "till I saw Miss Tepping."

"That makes a difference," I admitted.

"And I couldn't bear to break her heart."

"Heaven forbid!" I cried. "It is the one unpardonable sin. Better anything than that." Then I grew practical. "Father's consent?"

"*My* father's? *Is* it likely? He expects me to marry into some distinguished English family."

I hummed a moment. "Well, out with it!" I exclaimed, pointing my cigar at him.

He leaned back in his chair and told me the whole story. A pretty girl; golden hair; introduced to her by a friend; nice, simple little thing; mind and heart above the irregular stage on to which she had been driven by poverty alone; father dead; mother in reduced circumstances. "To keep the home together, poor Sissie decided—"

"Precisely so," I murmured, knocking off my ash. "The usual self-sacrifice! Case quite normal! Everything *en règle!*"

"You don't mean to say you doubt it?" he cried, flushing up, and evidently regarding me as a hopeless cynic. "I do assure you, Dr. Cumberledge, the poor child—though miles, of course, below Miss Tepping's level—is as innocent, and as good—"

"As a flower in May. Oh, yes; I don't doubt it. How did you come to propose to her, though?"

He reddened a little. "Well, it was almost accidental," he said, sheepishly. "I called there one evening, and her mother had a headache and went up to bed. And when we two were left alone, Sissie talked a great deal about her future and how hard her life was. And after a while she broke down and began to cry. And then—"

I cut him short with a wave of my hand. "You need say no more," I put in, with a sympathetic face. "We have all been there."

We paused a moment, while I puffed smoke at the photograph again. "Well," I said at last, "her face looks to me really simple and nice. It is a good face. Do you see her often?"

"Oh, no; she's on tour."

"In the provinces?"

"M'yes; just at present, at Scarborough."

"But she writes to you?"

"Every day."

"Would you think it an unpardonable impertinence if I made bold to ask whether it would be possible for you to show me a specimen of her letters?"

He unlocked a drawer and took out three or four. Then he read one through, carefully. "I don't think," he said, in a deliberative voice, "it would be a serious breach of confidence in me to let you look through this one. There's really nothing in it, you know—just the ordinary average every-day love-letter."

I glanced through the little note. He was right. The conventional hearts and darts epistle. It sounded nice enough: "Longing to see you again; so lonely in this place; your dear sweet letter; looking forward to the time; your ever-devoted Sissie."

"That seems straight," I answered. "However, I am not quite sure. Will you allow me to take it away, with the photograph? I know I am asking much. I want to show it to a lady in whose tact and discrimination I have the greatest confidence."

"What, Daphne?"

I smiled. "No, not Daphne," I answered. "Our friend, Miss Wade. She has extraordinary insight."

"I could trust anything to Miss Wade. She is true as steel."

"You are right," I answered. "That shows that you, too, are a judge of character."

He hesitated. "I feel a brute," he cried, "to go on writing every day to Sissie Montague—and yet calling every day to see Miss Tepping. But still—I do it."

I grasped his hand. "My dear fellow," I said, "nearly ninety per cent. of men, after all—are human!"

I took both letter and photograph back with me to Nathaniel's. When I had gone my rounds that night, I carried them into Hilda Wade's room and told her the story. Her face grew grave. "We must be just," she said at last. "Daphne is deeply in love with him; but even for Daphne's sake, we must not take anything for granted against the other lady."

I produced the photograph. "What do you make of that?" I asked. "*I* think it an honest face, myself, I may tell you."

She scrutinised it long and closely with a magnifier. Then she put her head on one side and mused very deliberately. "Madeline Shaw gave me her photograph the other day, and said to me, as she gave it, 'I do so like these modern portraits; they show one *what might have been.*'"

"You mean they are so much touched up!"

"Exactly. That, as it stands, is a sweet, innocent face—an honest girl's face—almost babyish in its transparency but . . . the innocence has all been put into it by the photographer."

"You think so?"

"I know it. Look here at those lines just visible on the cheek. They disappear, nowhere, at impossible angles. *And* the corners of that mouth. They couldn't go so, with that nose and those puckers. The thing is not real. It has been atrociously edited. Part is nature's; part, the photographer's; part, even possibly paint and powder."

"But the underlying face?"

"Is a minx's."

I handed her the letter. "This next?" I asked, fixing my eyes on her as she looked.

She read it through. For a minute or two she examined it. "The letter is right enough," she answered, after a second reading, "though its guileless simplicity is, perhaps, under the circumstances, just a leetle overdone; but the handwriting—the handwriting is duplicity itself: a cunning, serpentine hand, no openness or honesty in it. Depend upon it, that girl is playing a double game."

"You believe, then, there is character in handwriting?"

"Undoubtedly; when we know the character, we can see it in the writing. The difficulty is, to see it and read it *before* we know it; and I have practised a little at that. There is character in all we do, of course—our walk, our cough, the very wave of our hands; the only secret is, not all of us have always skill to see it. Here, however, I feel pretty sure. The curls of the g's and the tails of the y's—how full they are of wile, of low, underhand trickery!"

I looked at them as she pointed. "That is true!" I exclaimed. "I see it when you show it. Lines meant for effect. No straightness or directness in them!"

Hilda reflected a moment. "Poor Daphne!" she murmured. "I would do anything to help her. . . . I'll tell what might be a good plan." Her face brightened. "My holiday comes next week. I'll run down to Scarborough—it's as nice a place for a holiday as any—and I'll observe this young lady. It can do no harm—and good may come of it."

"How kind of you!" I cried. "But you are always all kindness."

Hilda went to Scarborough, and came back again for a week before going on to Bruges, where she proposed to spend the greater part of her holidays. She stopped a night or two in town to report progress, and, finding another nurse ill, promised to fill her place till a substitute was forthcoming.

"Well, Dr. Cumberledge," she said, when she saw me alone, "I was right! I have found out a fact or two about Daphne's rival!"

"You have seen her?" I asked.

"Seen her? I have stopped for a week in the same house. A very nice lodging-house on the Spa front, too. The girl's well enough off. The poverty plea fails. She goes about in good rooms and carries a mother with her."

"That's well," I answered. "That looks all right."

"Oh, yes, she's quite presentable: has the manners of a lady whenever she chooses. But the chief point is this: she laid her letters every day on the table in the passage outside her door for post—laid them all in a row, so that when one claimed one's own one couldn't help seeing them."

"Well, that was open and aboveboard," I continued, beginning to fear we had hastily misjudged Miss Sissie Montague.

"Very open—too much so, in fact; for I was obliged to note the fact that she wrote two letters regularly every day of her life—'to my two mashes,' she explained one afternoon to a young man who was with her as she laid them on the table. One of them was always addressed to Cecil Holsworthy, Esq."

"And the other?"

"Wasn't."

"Did you note the name?" I asked, interested.

"Yes; here it is." She handed me a slip of paper.

I read it: "Reginald Nettlecraft, Esq., 427, Staples Inn, London."

"What, Reggie Nettlecraft!" I cried, amused. "Why, he was a very little boy at Charterhouse when I was a big one; he afterwards went to Oxford, and got sent down from Christ Church for the part he took in burning a Greek bust in Tom Quad—an antique Greek bust—after a bump supper."

"Just the sort of man I should have expected," Hilda answered, with a suppressed smile. "I have a sort of inkling that Miss Montague likes *him* best; he is nearer her type; but she thinks Cecil Holsworthy the better match. Has Mr. Nettlecraft money?"

"Not a penny, I should say. An allowance from his father, perhaps, who is a Lincolnshire parson; but otherwise, nothing."

"Then, in my opinion, the young lady is playing for Mr. Holsworthy's money; failing which, she will decline upon Mr. Nettlecraft's heart."

We talked it all over. In the end I said abruptly: "Nurse Wade, you have seen Miss Montague, or whatever she calls herself. I have not. I won't condemn her unheard. I have half a mind to run down one day next week to Scarborough and have a look at her."

"Do. That will suffice. You can judge then for yourself whether or not I am mistaken."

I went; and what is more, I heard Miss Sissie sing at her hall—a pretty domestic song, most childish and charming. She impressed me not unfavourably, in spite of what Hilda said. Her peach-blossom cheek might have been art, but looked like nature. She had an open face, a baby smile and there was a frank girlishness about her dress and manner that took my fancy. "After all," I thought to myself, "even Hilda Wade is fallible."

So that evening, when her "turn" was over, I made up my mind to go round and call upon her. I had told Cecil Holsworthy my intentions beforehand, and it rather shocked him. He was too much of a gentleman to wish to spy upon the girl he had promised to marry. However, in my case, there need be no such scruples. I found the house and asked for Miss Montague. As I mounted the stairs to the drawing-room floor, I heard a sound of voices—the murmur of laughter; idiotic guffaws, suppressed giggles, the masculine and feminine varieties of tomfoolery.

"*You'd* make a splendid woman of business, *you* would!" a young man was saying. I gathered from his drawl that he belonged to that sub-species of the human race which is known as the Chappie.

"Wouldn't I just?" a girl's voice answered, tittering. I recognised it as Sissie's. "You ought to see me at it! Why, my brother set up a place once for mending bicycles; and I used to stand about at the door, as if I had just returned from a ride; and when fellows came in, with a nut loose or something, I'd begin talking with them while Bertie tightened it. Then, when *they* weren't looking, I'd dab the business end of a darning-needle, so, just plump into their tires; and of course, as soon as they went off, they were back again in a minute to get a puncture mended! I call *that* business."

A roar of laughter greeted the recital of this brilliant incident in a commercial career. As it subsided, I entered. There were two men in the room, besides Miss Montague and her mother, and a second young lady.

"Excuse this late call," I said, quietly, bowing. "But I have only one night in Scarborough, Miss Montague, and I wanted to see you. I'm a friend of Mr. Holsworthy's. I told him I'd look you up, and this is my sole opportunity."

I *felt* rather than saw that Miss Montague darted a quick glance of hidden meaning at her friends the chappies; their faces, in response, ceased to snigger and grew instantly sober.

She took my card; then, in her alternative manner as the perfect lady, she presented me to her mother. "Dr. Cumberledge, mamma," she said, in a faintly warning voice. "A friend of Mr. Holsworthy's."

The old lady half rose. "Let me see," she said, staring at me. "*Which* is Mr. Holsworthy, Siss?—is it Cecil or Reggie?"

One of the chappies burst into a fatuous laugh once more at this remark. "Now, you're giving away the whole show, Mrs. Montague!" he exclaimed, with a chuckle. A look from Miss Sissie immediately checked him.

I am bound to admit, however, that after these untoward incidents of the first minute, Miss Montague and her friends behaved throughout with distinguished propriety. Her manners were perfect—I may even say demure. She asked about "Cecil" with charming *naiveté*. She was frank and girlish. Lots of innocent fun in her, no doubt—she sang us a comic song in excellent taste, which is a severe test—but not a suspicion of double-dealing. If I had not overheard those few words as I came up the stairs, I think I should have gone away believing the poor girl an injured child of nature.

As it was, I went back to London the very next day, determined
to renew my slight acquaintance with Reggie Nettlecraft.

Fortunately, I had a good excuse for going to visit him. I had
been asked to collect among old Carthusians for one of those endless "testimonials" which pursue one through life, and are, perhaps, the worst Nemesis which follows the crime of having wasted
one's youth at a public school: a testimonial for a retiring master,
or professional cricketer, or washerwoman, or something; and in
the course of my duties as collector it was quite natural that I
should call upon all my fellow-victims. So I went to his rooms in
Staples Inn and reintroduced myself.

Reggie Nettlecraft had grown up into an unwholesome, spotty,
indeterminate young man, with a speckled necktie, and cuffs of
which he was inordinately proud, and which he insisted on "flashing" every second minute. He was also evidently self-satisfied;
which was odd, for I have seldom seen anyone who afforded less
cause for rational satisfaction. "Hullo," he said, when I told him
my name. "So it's you, is it, Cumberledge?" He glanced at my card.
"St. Nathaniel's Hospital! What rot! Why, blow me tight if you
haven't turned sawbones!"

"That is my profession," I answered, unashamed. "And you?"

"Oh, I don't have any luck, you know, old man. They turned me
out of Oxford because I had too much sense of humour for the authorities there—beastly set of old fogeys! Objected to my 'chucking'
oyster shells at the tutors' windows—good old English custom, fast
becoming obsolete. Then I crammed for the Army. But, bless your
heart, a *gentleman* has no chance for the Army nowadays; a pack
of blooming cads, with what they call 'intellect,' read up for the
exams, and don't give *us* a look-in; I call it sheer piffle. Then the
Guv'nor set me on electrical engineering—electrical engineering's
played out. I put no stock in it; besides, it's such beastly fag; and
then, you get your hands dirty. So now I'm reading for the Bar;
and if only my coach can put me up to tips enough to dodge the
examiners, I expect to be called some time next summer."

"And when you have failed for everything?" I inquired, just to
test his sense of humour.

He swallowed it like a roach. "Oh, when I've failed for everything, I shall stick up to the Guv'nor. Hang it all, a *gentleman* can't be expected to earn his own livelihood. England's going to the dogs, that's where it is; no snug little sinecures left for chaps like you and me; all this beastly competition. And no respect for the feelings of gentlemen, either! Why, would you believe it, Cumberground—we used to call you Cumberground at Charterhouse, I remember, or was it Fig Tree?—I happened to get a bit lively in the Haymarket last week, after a rattling good supper, and the chap at the police court—old cove with a squint—positively proposed to send me to prison, *without the option of a fine!*—I'll trouble you for that—send *me* to prison just—for knocking down a common brute of a bobby. There's no mistake about it; England's *not* a country now for a gentleman to live in."

"Then why not mark your sense of the fact by leaving it?" I inquired, with a smile.

He shook his head. "What? Emigrate? No, thank you! I'm not taking any. None of your colonies for *me*, *if* you please. I shall stick to the old ship. I'm too much attached to the Empire."

"And yet imperialists," I said, "generally gush over the colonies—the Empire on which the sun never sets."

"The Empire in Leicester Squire!" he responded, gazing at me with unspoken contempt. "Have a whisky-and-soda, old chap? What, no? 'Never drink between meals?' Well, you *do* surprise me! I suppose that comes of being a sawbones, don't it?"

"Possibly," I answered. "We respect our livers." Then I went on to the ostensible reason of my visit—the Charterhouse testimonial. He slapped his thighs metaphorically, by way of suggesting the depleted condition of his pockets. "Stony broke, Cumberledge," he murmured; "stony broke! Honour bright! Unless Bluebird pulls off the Prince of Wales's Stakes, I really don't know how I'm to pay the Benchers."

"It's quite unimportant," I answered. "I was asked to ask you, and I *have* asked you."

"So I twig, my dear fellow. Sorry to have to say *no*. But I'll tell you what I can do for you; I can put you upon a straight thing—"

I glanced at the mantelpiece. "I see you have a photograph of Miss Sissie Montague," I broke in casually, taking it down and examining it. "*with* an autograph, too. 'Reggie, from Sissie.' You are a friend of hers?"

"A friend of hers? I'll trouble you. She *is* a clinker, Sissie is! You should see that girl smoke. I give you my word of honour, Cumberledge, she can consume cigarettes against any fellow I know in London. Hang it all, a girl like that, you know—well, one can't help admiring her! Ever seen her?"

"Oh, yes; I know her. I called on her, in fact, night before last, at Scarborough."

He whistled a moment, then broke into an imbecile laugh. "My gum," he cried; "this *is* a start, this is! You don't mean to tell me *you* are the other Johnnie."

"What other Johnnie?" I asked, feeling we were getting near it.

He leaned back and laughed again. "Well, you know that girl Sissie, she's a clever one, she is," he went on after a minute, staring at me. "She's a regular clinker! Got two strings to her bow; that's where the trouble comes in. Me and another fellow. She likes me for love and the other fellow for money. Now, don't you come and tell me that *you* are the other fellow."

"I have certainly never aspired to the young lady's hand," I answered, cautiously. "But don't you know your rival's name, then?"

"That's Sissie's blooming cleverness. She's a caulker, Sissie is; you don't take a rise out of Sissie in a hurry. She knows that if I knew who the other bloke was, I'd blow upon her little game to him and put him off her. And I *would*, s'ep me taters; for I'm nuts on that girl. I tell you, Cumberledge, she *is* a clinker!"

"You seem to me admirably adapted for one another," I answered, truthfully. I had not the slightest compunction in handing Reggie Nettlecraft over to Sissie, nor in handing Sissie over to Reggie Nettlecraft.

"Adapted for one another? That's just it. There, you hit the right nail plump on the cocoanut, Cumberground! But Sissie's an artful one, she is. She's playing for the other Johnnie. He's got the dibs, you know; and Sissie wants the dibs even more than she wants yours truly."

"Got what?" I inquired, not quite catching the phrase.

"The dibs, old man; the chink; the oof; the ready rhino. He rolls in it, she says. I can't find out the chap's name, but I know his Guv'nor's something or other in the millionaire trade somewhere across in America."

"She writes to you, I think?"

"That's so; every blooming day; but how the dummy did you come to know it?"

"She lays letters addressed to you on the hall table at her lodgings in Scarborough."

"The dickens she does! Careless little beggar! Yes, she writes to me—pages. She's awfully gone on me, really. She'd marry me if it wasn't for the Johnnie with the dibs. She doesn't care for *him*: she wants his money. He dresses badly, don't you see; and, after all, the clothes make the man! *I'd* like to get at him. *I'd* spoil his pretty face for him." And he assumed a playfully pugilistic attitude.

"You really want to get rid of this other fellow?" I asked, seeing my chance.

"Get rid of him? Why, of course! Chuck him into the river some nice dark night if I could once get a look at him!"

"As a preliminary step, would you mind letting me see one of Miss Montague's letters?" I inquired.

He drew a long breath. "They're a bit affectionate, you know," he murmured, stroking his beardless chin in hesitation. "She's a hot 'un, Sissie is. She pitches it pretty warm on the affection-stop, I can tell you. But if you really think you can give the other Johnnie a cut on the head with her letters—well, in the interests of true love, which never *does* run smooth, I don't mind letting you have a squint, as my friend, at one of her charming billy-doos."

He took a bundle from a drawer, ran his eye over one or two with a maudlin air, and then selected a specimen not wholly unsuitable for publication. "*There's* one in the eye for C.," he said, chuckling. "What would C. say to that, I wonder? She always calls him C., you know; it's so jolly non-committing. She says, 'I only wish that beastly old bore C. were at Halifax—which is where he comes from and then I would fly at once to my own dear Reggie! But, hang it all, Reggie boy, what's the good of true love if you haven't got the dibs? I *must* have my comforts. Love in a cottage is all very well in its way; but who's to pay for the fizz, Reggie?' That's her refinement, don't you see? Sissie's awfully refined. She was brought up with the tastes and habits of a lady."

"Clearly so," I answered. "Both her literary style and her liking for champagne abundantly demonstrate it!" His acute sense of humour did not enable him to detect the irony of my observation. I doubt if it extended much beyond oyster shells. He handed me the letter. I read it through with equal amusement and gratification. If Miss Sissie had written it on purpose in order to open Cecil Holsworthy's eyes, she couldn't have managed the matter better or more effectually. It breathed ardent love, tempered by a determination to sell her charms in the best and highest matrimonial market.

"Now, I know this man, C.," I said when I had finished. "And I want to ask whether you will let me show him Miss Montague's letter. It would set him against the girl, who, as a matter of fact, is wholly unwor—I mean totally unfitted for him."

"Let you show it to him? Like a bird! Why, Sissie promised me herself that if she couldn't bring 'that solemn ass, C.,' up to the scratch by Christmas, she'd chuck him and marry me. It's here, in writing." And he handed me another gem of epistolary literature.

"You have no compunctions?" I asked again, after reading it.

"Not a blessed compunction to my name."

"Then neither have I," I answered.

I felt they both deserved it. Sissie was a minx, as Hilda rightly judged; while as for Nettlecraft—well, if a public school and an English university leave a man a cad, a cad he will be, and there is nothing more to be said about it.

I went straight off with the letters to Cecil Holsworthy. He read them through, half incredulously at first; he was too honest-natured himself to believe in the possibility of such double-dealing—that one could have innocent eyes and golden hair and yet be a trickster. He read them twice; then he compared them word for word with the simple affection and childlike tone of his own last letter received from the same lady. Her versatility of style would have done honour to a practised literary craftsman. At last he handed them back to me. "Do you think," he said, "on the evidence of these, I should be doing wrong in breaking with her?"

"Wrong in breaking with her!" I exclaimed. "You would be doing wrong if you didn't,—wrong to yourself; wrong to your family; wrong, if I may venture to say so, to Daphne; wrong even in the long run to the girl herself; for she is not fitted for you, and she *is* fitted for Reggie Nettlecraft. Now, do as I bid you. Sit down at once and write her a letter from my dictation."

He sat down and wrote, much relieved that I took the responsibility off his shoulders.

> "*Dear Miss Montague*," I began, "the inclosed letters have come into my hands without my seeking it. After reading them, I feel that I have absolutely no right to stand between you and the man of your real choice. It would not be kind or wise of me to do so. I release you at once, and consider myself released. You may therefore regard our engagement as irrevocably cancelled.
>
> > "Faithfully yours,
> > "Cecil Holsworthy."

"Nothing more than that?" he asked, looking up and biting his pen. "Not a word of regret or apology?"

"Not a word," I answered. "You are really too lenient."

I made him take it out and post it before he could invent conscientious scruples. Then he turned to me irresolutely. "What shall I do next?" he asked, with a comical air of doubt.

I smiled. "My dear fellow, that is a matter for your own consideration."

"But—do you think she will laugh at me?"

"Miss Montague?"

"No! Daphne."

"I am not in Daphne's confidence," I answered. "I don't know how she feels. But, on the face of it, I think I can venture to assure you that at least she won't laugh at you."

He grasped my hand hard. "You don't mean to say so!" he cried. "Well, that's really very, kind of her! A girl of Daphne's high type! And I, who feel myself so utterly unworthy of her!"

"We are all unworthy of a good woman's love," I answered. "But, thank Heaven, the good women don't seem to realise it."

That evening, about ten, my new friend came back in a hurry to my rooms at St. Nathaniel's. Nurse Wade was standing there, giving her report for the night when he entered. His face looked some inches shorter and broader than usual. His eyes beamed. His mouth was radiant.

"Well, you won't believe it, Dr. Cumberledge," he began; "but—"

"Yes, I *do* believe it," I answered. "I know it. I have read it already."

"Read it!" he cried. "Where?"

I waved my hand towards his face. "In a special edition of the evening papers," I answered, smiling. "Daphne has accepted you!"

He sank into an easy chair, beside himself with rapture. "Yes, yes; that angel! Thanks to *you*, she has accepted me!"

"Thanks to Miss Wade," I said, correcting him. "It is really all *her* doing. If *she* had not seen through the photograph to the face, and through the face to the woman and the base little heart of her, we might never have found her out."

He turned to Hilda with eyes all gratitude. "You have given me the dearest and best girl on earth," he cried, seizing both her hands.

"And I have given Daphne a husband who will love and appreciate her," Hilda answered, flushing.

"You see," I said, maliciously; "I told you they never find us out, Holsworthy!"

As for Reggie Nettlecraft and his wife, I should like to add that they are getting on quite as well as could be expected. Reggie has joined his Sissie on the music-hall stage; and all those who have witnessed his immensely popular performance of the Drunken

Gentleman before the Bow Street Police Court acknowledge without reserve that, after "failing for everything," he has dropped at last into his true vocation. His impersonation of the part is said to be "nature itself." I see no reason to doubt it.

THE EPISODE OF THE
WIFE WHO DID HER DUTY

To make you understand my next yarn, I must go back to the date of my introduction to Hilda.

"It is witchcraft!" I said the first time I saw her, at Le Geyt's luncheon-party.

She smiled a smile which was bewitching, indeed, but by no means witch-like,—a frank, open smile with just a touch of natural feminine triumph in it. "No, not witchcraft," she answered, helping herself with her dainty fingers to a burnt almond from the Venetian glass dish,—"not witchcraft,—memory; aided, perhaps, by some native quickness of perception. Though I say it myself, I never met anyone, I think, whose memory goes quite as far as mine does."

"You don't mean quite as far *back*," I cried, jesting; for she looked about twenty-four, and had cheeks like a ripe nectarine, just as pink and just as softly downy.

She smiled again, showing a row of semi-transparent teeth, with a gleam in the depths of them. She was certainly most attractive. She had that indefinable, incommunicable, unanalysable personal quality which we know as *charm*. "No, not as far *back*," she repeated. "Though, indeed, I often seem to remember things that happened before I was born (like Queen Elizabeth's visit to Kenilworth): I recollect so vividly all that I have heard or read about them. But as far *in extent*, I mean. I never let anything drop out of my memory. As this case shows you, I can recall even quite unimportant and casual bits of knowledge when any chance clue happens to bring them back to me."

She had certainly astonished me. The occasion for my astonishment was the fact that when I handed her my card, "Dr. Hubert Ford Cumberledge, St. Nathaniel's Hospital," she had glanced at it for a second and exclaimed, without sensible pause or break, "Oh, then, of course, you're half Welsh, as I am."

The instantaneous and apparent inconsecutiveness of her inference took me aback. "Well, m'yes: I *am* half Welsh," I replied. "My mother came from Carnarvonshire. But, why *then*, and *of course?* I fail to perceive your train of reasoning."

She laughed a sunny little laugh, like one well accustomed to receive such inquiries. "Fancy asking *a woman* to give you 'the train of reasoning' for her intuitions!" she cried, merrily. "That shows, Dr. Cumberledge, that you are a mere man—a man of science, perhaps, but *not* a psychologist. It also suggests that you are a confirmed bachelor. A married man accepts intuitions, without expecting them to be based on reasoning. . . . Well, just this once, I will stretch a point to enlighten you. If I recollect right, your mother died about three years ago?"

"You are quite correct. Then you knew my mother?"

"Oh, dear me, no! I never even met her. Why *then?*" Her look was mischievous. "But, unless I mistake, I think she came from Hendre Coed, near Bangor."

"Wales is a village!" I exclaimed, catching my breath. "Every Welsh person seems to know all about every other."

My new acquaintance smiled again. When she smiled she was irresistible: a laughing face protruding from a cloud of diaphanous drapery. "Now, shall I tell you how I came to know that?" she asked, poising a *glacé* cherry on her dessert fork in front of her. "Shall I explain my trick, like the conjurers?"

"Conjurers never explain anything," I answered. "They say: 'So, you see, *that's* how it's done!'—with a swift whisk of the hand— and leave you as much in the dark as ever. Don't explain like the conjurers, but tell me how you guessed it."

She shut her eyes and seemed to turn her glance inward.

"About three years ago," she began slowly, like one who reconstructs with an effort a half-forgotten scene, "I saw a notice in the

Times—Births, Deaths, and Marriages—'On the 27th of October'—
was it the 27th?" The keen brown eyes opened again for a second
and flashed inquiry into mine.

"Quite right," I answered, nodding.

"I thought so. 'On the 27th of October, at Brynmor, Bourne-
mouth, Emily Olwen Josephine, widow of the late Thomas
Cumberledge, sometime colonel of the 7th Bengal Regiment of
Foot, and daughter of Iolo Gwyn Ford, Esq., J.P., of Hendre Coed,
near Bangor. Am I correct?" She lifted her dark eyelashes once
more and flooded me.

"You are quite correct," I answered, surprised. "And that is really all that you knew of my mother?"

"Absolutely all. The moment I saw your card, I thought to myself, in a breath: 'Ford, Cumberledge; what do I know of those two
names? I have some link between them. Ah, yes; found Mrs. Cumberledge, wife of Colonel Thomas Cumberledge, of the 7th Bengals,
was a Miss Ford, daughter of a Mr. Ford, of Bangor.' That came to
me like a lightning-gleam. Then I said to myself again, 'Dr. Hubert
Ford Cumberledge must be their son.' So there you have 'the train
of reasoning.' Women *can* reason—sometimes. I had to think twice,
though, before I could recall the exact words of the *Times* notice."

"And can you do the same with everyone?"

"Everyone! Oh, come, now: that is expecting too much! I have
not read, marked, learned, and inwardly digested everyone's family announcements. I don't pretend to be the Peerage, the Clergy
List, and the London Directory rolled into one. I remembered *your*
family all the more vividly, no doubt, because of the pretty and
unusual old Welsh names, 'Olwen' and 'Iolo Gwyn Ford,' which
fixed themselves on my memory by their mere beauty. Everything
about Wales always attracts me; my Welsh side is uppermost. But
I have hundreds—oh, thousands—of such facts stored and pigeon-
holed in my memory. If anybody else cares to try me," she glanced
round the table, "perhaps we may be able to test my power that
way."

Two or three of the company accepted her challenge, giving the
full names of their sisters or brothers; and, in three cases out of

five, my witch was able to supply either the notice of their marriage or some other like published circumstance. In the instance of Charlie Vere, it is true, she went wrong, just at first, though only in a single small particular; it was not Charlie himself who was gazetted to a sub-lieutenancy in the Warwickshire Regiment, but his brother Walter. However, the moment she was told of this slip, she corrected herself at once, and added, like lightning, "Ah, yes: how stupid of me! I have mixed up the names. Charles Cassilis Vere got an appointment on the same day in the Rhodesian Mounted Police, didn't he?" Which was in point of fact quite accurate.

But I am forgetting that all this time I have not even now introduced my witch to you.

Hilda Wade, when I first saw her, was one of the prettiest, cheeriest, and most graceful girls I have ever met—a dusky blonde, brown-eyed, brown-haired, with a creamy, waxen whiteness of skin that was yet warm and peach-downy. And I wish to insist from the outset upon the plain fact that there was nothing uncanny about her. In spite of her singular faculty of insight, which sometimes seemed to illogical people almost weird or eerie, she was in the main a bright, well-educated, sensible, winsome, lawn-tennis-playing English girl. Her vivacious spirits rose superior to her surroundings, which were often sad enough. But she was above all things wholesome, unaffected, and sparkling—a gleam of sunshine. She laid no claim to supernatural powers; she held no dealings with familiar spirits; she was simply a girl of strong personal charm, endowed with an astounding memory and a rare measure of feminine intuition. Her memory, she told me, she shared with her father and all her father's family; they were famous for their prodigious faculty in that respect. Her impulsive temperament and quick instincts, on the other hand, descended to her, she thought, from her mother and her Welsh ancestry.

Externally, she seemed thus at first sight little more than the ordinary pretty, light-hearted English girl, with a taste for field sports (especially riding), and a native love of the country. But at times one caught in the brightened colour of her lustrous brown eyes certain curious undercurrents of depth, of reserve, and of a

GRANT ALLEN

questioning wistfulness which made you suspect the presence of profounder elements in her nature. From the earliest moment of our acquaintance, indeed, I can say with truth that Hilda Wade interested me immensely. I felt drawn. Her face had that strange quality of compelling attention for which we have as yet no English name, but which everybody recognises. You could not ignore her. She stood out. She was the sort of girl one was constrained to notice.

It was Le Geyt's first luncheon-party since his second marriage. Big-bearded, genial, he beamed round on us jubilant. He was proud of his wife and proud of his recent Q.C.-ship. The new Mrs. Le Geyt sat at the head of the table, handsome, capable, self-possessed; a vivid, vigorous woman and a model hostess. Though still quite young, she was large and commanding. Everybody was impressed by her. "Such a good mother to those poor motherless children!" all the ladies declared in a chorus of applause. And, indeed, she had the face of a splendid manager.

I said as much in an undertone over the ices to Miss Wade, who sat beside me—though I ought not to have discussed them at their own table. "Hugo Le Geyt seems to have made an excellent choice," I murmured. "Maisie and Ettie will be lucky, indeed, to be taken care of by such a competent stepmother. Don't you think so?"

My witch glanced up at her hostess with a piercing dart of the keen brown eyes, held her wine-glass half raised, and then electrified me by uttering, in the same low voice, audible to me alone, but quite clearly and unhesitatingly, these astounding words:

"I think, before twelve mouths are out, *Mr. Le Geyt will have murdered her!*"

For a minute I could not answer, so startling was the effect of this confident prediction. One does not expect to be told such things at lunch, over the port and peaches, about one's dearest friends, beside their own mahogany. And the assured air of unfaltering conviction with which Hilda Wade said it to a complete stranger took my breath away. *Why* did she think so at all? And *if* she thought so why choose *me* as the recipient of her singular confidences?

I gasped and wondered.

"What makes you fancy anything so unlikely?" I asked aside at last, behind the babel of voices. "You quite alarm me."

She rolled a mouthful of apricot ice reflectively on her tongue, and then murmured, in a similar aside, "Don't ask me now. Some other time will do. But I mean what I say. Believe me; I do not speak at random."

She was quite right, of course. To continue would have been equally rude and foolish. I had perforce to bottle up my curiosity for the moment and wait till my sibyl was in the mood for interpreting.

After lunch we adjourned to the drawing-room. Almost at once, Hilda Wade flitted up with her brisk step to the corner where I was sitting. "Oh, Dr. Cumberledge," she began, as if nothing odd had occurred before, "I *was* so glad to meet you and have a chance of talking to you, because I *do* so want to get a nurse's place at St. Nathaniel's."

"A nurse's place!" I exclaimed, a little surprised, surveying her dress of palest and softest Indian muslin; for she looked to me far too much of a butterfly for such serious work. "Do you really mean it; or are you one of the ten thousand modern young ladies who are in quest of a Mission, without understanding that Missions are unpleasant? Nursing, I can tell you, is not all crimped cap and becoming uniform."

"I know that," she answered, growing grave. "I ought to know it. I am a nurse already at St. George's Hospital."

"You are a nurse! And at St. George's! Yet you want to change to Nathaniel's? Why? St. George's is in a much nicer part of London, and the patients there come on an average from a much better class than ours in Smithfield."

"I know that too; but . . . Sebastian is at St. Nathaniel's—and I want to be near Sebastian."

"Professor Sebastian!" I cried, my face lighting up with a gleam of enthusiasm at our great teacher's name. "Ah, if it is to be under Sebastian that you, desire, I can see you mean business. I know now you are in earnest."

"In earnest?" she echoed, that strange deeper shade coming over her face as she spoke, while her tone altered. "Yes, I think I am in earnest! It is my object in life to be near Sebastian—to watch him and observe him. I mean to succeed. . . . But I have given you my confidence, perhaps too hastily, and I must implore you not to mention my wish to him."

"You may trust me implicitly," I answered.

"Oh, yes; I saw that," she put in, with a quick gesture. "Of course, I saw by your face you were a man of honour—a man one could trust or I would not have spoken to you. But—you promise me?"

"I promise you," I replied, naturally flattered. She was delicately pretty, and her quaint, oracular air, so incongruous with the dainty face and the fluffy brown hair, piqued me not a little. That special mysterious commodity of *charm* seemed to pervade all she did and said. So I added: "And I will mention to Sebastian that you wish for a nurse's place at Nathaniel's. As you have had experience, and can be recommended, I suppose, by Le Geyt's sister," with whom she had come, "no doubt you can secure an early vacancy."

"Thanks so much," she answered, with that delicious smile. It had an infantile simplicity about it which contrasted most piquantly with her prophetic manner.

"Only," I went on, assuming a confidential tone, "you really *must* tell me why you said that just now about Hugo Le Geyt. Recollect, your Delphian utterances have gravely astonished and disquieted me. Hugo is one of my oldest and dearest friends; and I want to know why you have formed this sudden bad opinion of him."

"Not of *him*, but of *her*," she answered, to my surprise, taking a small Norwegian dagger from the what-not and playing with it to distract attention.

"Come, come, now," I cried, drawing back. "You are trying to mystify me. This is deliberate seer-mongery. You are presuming on your powers. But I am not the sort of man to be caught by horoscopes. I decline to believe it."

She turned on me with a meaning glance. Those truthful eyes fixed me. "I am going from here straight to my hospital," she murmured, with a quiet air of knowledge—talking, I mean to say, like one who really knows. "This room is not the place to discuss this matter, is it? If you will walk back to St. George's with me, I think I can make you see and feel that I am speaking, not at haphazard, but from observation and experience."

Her confidence roused my most vivid curiosity. When she left I left with her. The Le Geyts lived in one of those new streets of large houses on Campden Hill, so that our way eastward lay naturally through Kensington Gardens.

It was a sunny June day, when light pierced even through the smoke of London, and the shrubberies breathed the breath of white lilacs. "Now, what did you mean by that enigmatical saying?" I asked my new Cassandra, as we strolled down the scent-laden path. "Woman's intuition is all very well in its way; but a mere man may be excused if he asks for evidence."

She stopped short as I spoke, and gazed full into my eyes. Her hand fingered her parasol handle. "I meant what I said," she answered, with emphasis. "Within one year, Mr. Le Geyt will have murdered his wife. You may take my word, for it."

"Le Geyt!" I cried. "Never! I know the man so well! A big, good-natured, kindly schoolboy! He is the gentlest and best of mortals. Le Geyt a murderer! Im—possible!"

Her eyes were far away. "Has it never occurred to you," she asked, slowly, with her pythoness air, "that there are murders and murders?—murders which depend in the main upon the murderer . . . and also murders which depend in the main upon the victim?"

"The victim? What do you mean?"

"Well, there are brutal men who commit murder out of sheer brutality—the ruffians of the slums; and there are sordid men who commit murder for sordid money—the insurers who want to forestall their policies, the poisoners who want to inherit property; but have you ever realised that there are also murderers who become so by accident, through their victims' idiosyncrasy? I thought all the time while I was watching Mrs. Le Geyt, 'That woman is of the sort predestined to be murdered.' . . . And when you asked me, I told you so. I may have been imprudent; still, I saw it, and I said it."

"But this is second sight!" I cried, drawing away. "Do you pretend to prevision?"

"No, not second sight; nothing uncanny, nothing supernatural. But prevision, yes; prevision based, not on omens or auguries, but on solid fact—on what I have seen and noticed."

"Explain yourself, oh, prophetess!"

She let the point of her parasol make a curved trail on the gravel, and followed its serpentine wavings with her eyes. "You know our house surgeon?" she asked at last, looking up of a sudden.

"What, Travers? Oh, intimately."

"Then come to my ward and see. After you have seen, you will perhaps believe me."

Nothing that I could say would get any further explanation out of her just then. "You would laugh at me if I told you," she persisted; "you won't laugh when you have seen it."

We walked on in silence as far as Hyde Park Corner. There my Sphinx tripped lightly up the steps of St. George's Hospital. "Get Mr. Travers's leave," she said, with a nod, and a bright smile, "to visit Nurse Wade's ward. Then come up to me there in five minutes."

I explained to my friend the house surgeon that I wished to see certain cases in the accident ward of which I had heard; he smiled a restrained smile—"Nurse Wade, no doubt!" but, of course, gave me permission to go up and look at them. "Stop a minute," he added, "and I'll come with you." When we got there, my witch had already changed her dress, and was waiting for us demurely in the neat dove-coloured gown and smooth white apron of the hospital nurses. She looked even prettier and more meaningful so than in her ethereal outside summer-cloud muslin.

"Come over to this bed," she said at once to Travers and myself, without the least air of mystery. "I will show you what I mean by it."

"Nurse Wade has remarkable insight," Travers whispered to me as we went.

"I can believe it," I answered.

"Look at this woman," she went on, aside, in a low voice—"no, not the first bed; the one beyond it; Number 60. I don't want the patient to know you are watching her. Do you observe anything odd about her appearance?"

"She is somewhat the same type," I began, "as Mrs.—"

Before I could get out the words "Le Geyt," her warning eye and puckering forehead had stopped me. "As the lady we were discussing," she interposed, with a quiet wave of one hand. "Yes, in some points very much so. You notice in particular her scanty hair—so thin and poor—though she is young and good-looking?"

"It is certainly rather a feeble crop for a woman of her age," I admitted. "And pale at that, and washy."

"Precisely. It's done up behind about as big as a nutmeg. . . . Now, observe the contour of her back as she sits up there; it is curiously curved, isn't it?"

"Very," I replied. "Not exactly a stoop, nor yet quite a hunch, but certainly an odd spinal configuration."

"Like our friend's, once more?"

"Like our friend's, exactly!"

Hilda Wade looked away, lest she should attract the patient's attention. "Well, that woman was brought in here, half-dead, assaulted by her husband," she went on, with a note of unobtrusive demonstration.

"We get a great many such cases," Travers put in, with true medical unconcern, "very interesting cases; and Nurse Wade has pointed out to me the singular fact that in almost all instances the patients resemble one another physically."

"Incredible!" I cried. "I can understand that there might well be a type of men who assault their wives, but not, surely, a type of women who get assaulted."

"That is because you know less about it than Nurse Wade," Travers answered, with an annoying smile of superior knowledge.

Our instructress moved on to another bed, laying one gentle hand as she passed on a patient's forehead. The patient glanced gratitude. "That one again," she said once more, half indicating a cot at a little distance: "Number 74. She has much the same thin hair—sparse, weak, and colourless. She has much the same curved back, and much the same aggressive, self-assertive features. Looks capable, doesn't she? A born housewife! . . . Well, she, too, was knocked down and kicked half-dead the other night by her husband."

"It is certainly odd," I answered, "how very much they both recall—"

"Our friend at lunch! Yes, extraordinary. See here"; she pulled out a pencil and drew the quick outline of a face in her note-book. "*That* is what is central and essential to the type. They have *this* sort of profile. Women with faces like that *always* get assaulted."

Travers glanced over her shoulder. "Quite true," he assented, with his *bourgeois* nod. "Nurse Wade in her time has shown me dozens of them. Round dozens: bakers' dozens! They all belong to that species. In fact, when a woman of this type is brought in to us wounded now, I ask at once, 'Husband?' and the invariable answer comes pat: 'Well, yes, sir; we had some words together.' The effect of words, my dear fellow, is something truly surprising."

"They can pierce like a dagger," I mused.

"And leave an open wound behind that requires dressing," Travers added, unsuspecting. Practical man, Travers!

"But *why* do they get assaulted—the women of this type?" I asked, still bewildered.

"Number 87 has her mother just come to see her," my sorceress interposed. "*She's* an assault case; brought in last night; badly kicked and bruised about the head and shoulders. Speak to the mother. She'll explain it all to you."

Travers and I moved over to the cot her hand scarcely indicated. "Well, your daughter looks pretty comfortable this afternoon, in spite of the little fuss," Travers began, tentatively.

"Yus, she's a bit tidy, thanky," the mother answered, smoothing her soiled black gown, grown green with long service. "She'll git on naow, please Gord. But Joe most did for 'er."

"How did it all happen?" Travers asked, in a jaunty tone, to draw her out.

"Well, it was like this, sir, yer see. My daughter, she's a lidy as keeps 'erself *to* 'erself, as the sayin' is, an' 'olds 'er 'ead up. She keeps up a proper pride, an' minds 'er 'ouse an' 'er little uns. She ain't no gadabaht. But she *'ave* a tongue, she 'ave"; the mother lowered her voice cautiously, lest the "lidy" should hear. "I don't deny it that she *'ave* a tongue, at times, through myself 'avin' suffered from it. And when she *do* go on, Lord bless you, why, there ain't no stoppin' of 'er."

"Oh, she has a tongue, has she?" Travers replied, surveying the "case" critically. "Well, you know, she looks like it."

"So she do, sir; so she do. An' Joe, 'e's a man as wouldn't 'urt a biby—not when 'e's sober, Joe wouldn't. But 'e'd bin aht; that's where it is; an' 'e cum 'ome lite, a bit fresh, through 'avin' bin at the friendly lead; an' my daughter, yer see, she up an' give it to 'im. My word, she *did* give it to 'im! An' Joe, 'e's a peaceable man when 'e ain't a bit fresh; 'e's more like a friend to 'er than an 'usband, Joe is; but 'e lost 'is temper that time, as yer may say, by reason o' bein' fresh, an' 'e knocked 'er abaht a little, an' knocked 'er teeth aht. So we brought 'er to the orspital."

The injured woman raised herself up in bed with a vindictive scowl, displaying as she did so the same whale-like curved back as in the other "cases." "But we've sent 'im to the lockup," she continued, the scowl giving way fast to a radiant joy of victory as she contemplated her triumph "an' wot's more, I 'ad the last word of 'im. An' 'e'll git six month for this, the neighbours says; an' when he comes aht again, my Gord, won't 'e ketch it!"

"You look capable of punishing him for it," I answered, and as I spoke, I shuddered; for I saw her expression was precisely the expression Mrs. Le Geyt's face had worn for a passing second when her husband accidentally trod on her dress as we left the dining-room.

My witch moved away. We followed. "Well, what do you say to it now?" she asked, gliding among the beds with noiseless feet and ministering fingers.

"Say to it?" I answered. "That it is wonderful, wonderful. You have quite convinced me."

"You would think so," Travers put in, "if you had been in this ward as often as I have, and observed their faces. It's a dead certainty. Sooner or later, that type of woman is cock-sure to be assaulted."

"In a certain rank of life, perhaps," I answered, still loth to believe it; "but not surely in ours. Gentlemen do not knock down their wives and kick their teeth out."

My Sibyl smiled. "No; there class tells," she admitted. "They take longer about it, and suffer more provocation. They curb their tempers. But in the end, one day, they are goaded beyond endurance; and then—a convenient knife—a rusty old sword—a pair of scissors—anything that comes handy, like that dagger this morning. One wild blow—half unpremeditated—and . . . the thing is done! Twelve good men and true will find it wilful murder."

I felt really perturbed. "But can we do nothing," I cried, "to warn poor Hugo?"

"Nothing, I fear," she answered. "After all, character must work itself out in its interactions with character. He has married that woman, and he must take the consequences. Does not each of us in life suffer perforce the Nemesis of his own temperament?"

"Then is there not also a type of men who assault their wives?"

"That is the odd part of it—no. All kinds, good and bad, quick and slow, can be driven to it at last. The quick-tempered stab or kick; the slow devise some deliberate means of ridding themselves of their burden."

"But surely we might caution Le Geyt of his danger!"

"It is useless. He would not believe us. We cannot be at his elbow to hold back his hand when the bad moment comes. Nobody will be there, as a matter of fact; for women of this temperament—born naggers, in short, since that's what it comes to—when they are also ladies, graceful and gracious as she is; never nag at all before outsiders. To the world, they are bland; everybody says, 'What charming talkers!' They are 'angels abroad, devils at home,' as the proverb puts it. Some night she will provoke him when they are alone, till she has reached his utmost limit of endurance—and then," she drew one hand across her dove-like throat, "it will be all finished."

"You think so?"

"I am sure of it. We human beings go straight like sheep to our natural destiny."

"But—that is fatalism."

"No, not fatalism: insight into temperament. Fatalists believe that your life is arranged for you beforehand from without; willy-nilly, you *must* act so. I only believe that in this jostling world your life is mostly determined by your own character, in its interaction with the characters of those who surround you. Temperament works itself out. It is your own acts and deeds that make up Fate for you."

For some months after this meeting neither Hilda Wade nor I saw anything more of the Le Geyts. They left town for Scotland at the end of the season; and when all the grouse had been duly slaughtered and all the salmon duly hooked, they went on to Leicestershire for the opening of fox-hunting; so it was not till after Christmas that they returned to Campden Hill. Meanwhile, I had spoken to Dr. Sebastian about Miss Wade, and on my recommendation he had found her a vacancy at our hospital. "A most intelligent girl, Cumberledge," he remarked to me with a rare burst of approval—for the Professor was always critical—after she had been at work for some weeks at St. Nathaniel's. "I am glad you introduced her here. A nurse with brains is such a valuable accessory—unless, of course, she takes to *thinking*. But Nurse Wade never *thinks*; she is a useful instrument—does what she's told, and carries out one's orders implicitly."

"She knows enough to know when she doesn't know," I answered, "which is really the rarest kind of knowledge."

"Unrecorded among young doctors!" the Professor retorted, with his sardonic smile. "They think they understand the human body from top to toe, when, in reality—well, they might do the measles!"

Early in January, I was invited again to lunch with the Le Geyts. Hilda Wade was invited, too. The moment we entered the house, we were both of us aware that some grim change had come over it.

Le Geyt met us in the hall, in his old genial style, it is true; but still with a certain reserve, a curious veiled timidity which we had not known in him. Big and good-humoured as he was, with kindly eyes beneath the shaggy eyebrows, he seemed strangely subdued now; the boyish buoyancy had gone out of him. He spoke rather lower than was his natural key, and welcomed us warmly, though less effusively than of old. An irreproachable housemaid, in a spotless cap, ushered us into the transfigured drawing-room. Mrs. Le Geyt, in a pretty cloth dress, neatly tailor-made, rose to meet us, beaming the vapid smile of the perfect hostess—that impartial smile which falls, like the rain from Heaven, on good and bad indifferently. "*So* charmed to see you again, Dr. Cumberledge!" she bubbled out, with a cheerful air—she was always cheerful, mechanically cheerful, from a sense of duty. "It *is* such a pleasure to meet dear Hugo's old friends! *And* Miss Wade, too; how delightful! You look so well, Miss Wade! Oh, you're both at St. Nathaniel's now, aren't you? So you can come together. What a privilege for you, Dr. Cumberledge, to have such a clever assistant—or, rather, fellow-worker. It must be a great life, yours, Miss Wade; such a sphere of usefulness! If we can only feel we are *doing good*—that is the main matter. For my own part, I like to be mixed up with every good work that's going on in my neighbourhood. I'm the soup-kitchen, you know, and I'm visitor at the workhouse; and I'm the Dorcas Society, and the Mutual Improvement Class; and the Prevention of Cruelty to Animals and to Children, and I'm sure I don't know how much else; so that, what with all that, and what with dear Hugo and the darling children"—she glanced affectionately at Maisie and Ettie, who sat bolt upright, very mute and still, in their best and stiffest frocks, on two stools in the corner—"I can hardly find time for my social duties."

"Oh, dear Mrs. Le Geyt," one of her visitors said with effusion, from beneath a nodding bonnet—she was the wife of a rural dean from Staffordshire—"*Everybody* is agreed that *your* social duties are performed to a marvel. They are the envy of Kensington. We all of us wonder, indeed, how one woman can find time for all of it!"

Our hostess looked pleased. "Well, yes," she answered, gazing down at her fawn-coloured dress with a half-suppressed smile of self-satisfaction, "I flatter myself I *can* get through about as much work in a day as anybody!" Her eye wandered round her rooms with a modest air of placid self-approval which was almost comic. Everything in them was as well-kept and as well-polished as good servants, thoroughly drilled, could make it. Not a stain or a speck anywhere. A miracle of neatness. Indeed, when I carelessly drew the Norwegian dagger from its scabbard, as we waited for lunch, and found that it stuck in the sheath, I almost started to discover that rust could intrude into that orderly household.

I recollected then how Hilda Wade had pointed out to me during those six months at St. Nathaniel's that the women whose husbands assaulted them were almost always "notable housewives," as they say in America—good souls who prided themselves not a little on their skill in management. They were capable, practical mothers of families, with a boundless belief in themselves, a sincere desire to do their duty, as far as they understood it, and a habit of impressing their virtues upon others which was quite beyond all human endurance. Placidity was their note; provoking placidity. I felt sure it must have been of a woman of this type that the famous phrase was coined—"*Elle a toutes les vertus—et elle est insupportable.*"

"Clara, dear," the husband said, "shall we go in to lunch?"

"You dear, stupid boy! Are we not all waiting for *you* to give your arm to Lady Maitland?"

The lunch was perfect, and it was perfectly served. The silver glowed; the linen was marked with H. C. Le G. in a most artistic monogram. I noticed that the table decorations were extremely pretty. Somebody complimented our hostess upon them. Mrs. Le Geyt nodded and smiled—"*I* arranged them. Dear Hugo, in his blundering way—the big darling—forgot to get me the orchids I had ordered. So I had to make shift with what few things our own wee conservatory afforded. Still, with a little taste and a little ingenuity—" She surveyed her handiwork with just pride, and left the rest to our imaginations.

"Only you ought to explain, Clara—" Le Geyt began, in a deprecatory tone.

"Now, you darling old bear, we won't harp on that twice-told tale again," Clara interrupted, with a knowing smile. *"Point de réchauffés!* Let us leave one another's misdeeds and one another's explanations for their proper sphere—the family circle. The orchids did *not* turn up, that is the point; and I managed to make shift with the plumbago and the geraniums. Maisie, my sweet, *not* that pudding, *if* you please; too rich for you, darling. I know your digestive capacities better than you do. I have told you fifty times it doesn't agree with you. A small slice of the other one!"

"Yes, mamma," Maisie answered, with a cowed and cowering air. I felt sure she would have murmured, "Yes, mamma," in the selfsame tone if the second Mrs. Le Geyt had ordered her to hang herself.

"I saw you out in the park, yesterday, on your bicycle, Ettie," Le Geyt's sister, Mrs. Mallet, put in. "But do you know, dear, I didn't think your jacket was half warm enough."

"Mamma doesn't like me to wear a warmer one," the child answered, with a visible shudder of recollection, "though I should love to, Aunt Lina."

"My precious Ettie, what nonsense—for a violent exercise like bicycling! Where one gets so hot! So unbecomingly hot! You'd be simply stifled, darling." I caught a darted glance which accompanied the words and which made Ettie recoil into the recesses of her pudding.

"But yesterday was so cold, Clara," Mrs. Mallet went on, actually venturing to oppose the infallible authority. "A nipping morning. And such a flimsy coat! Might not the dear child be allowed to judge for herself in a matter purely of her own feelings?"

Mrs. Le Geyt, with just the shadow of a shrug, was all sweet reasonableness. She smiled more suavely than ever. "Surely, Lina," she remonstrated, in her frankest and most convincing tone, "*I* must know best what is good for dear Ettie, when I have been watching her daily for more than six months past, and taking the greatest pains to understand both her constitution and her

disposition. She needs hardening, Ettie does. Hardening. Don't you
agree with me, Hugo?"

Le Geyt shuffled uneasily in his chair. Big man as he was, with
his great black beard and manly bearing, I could see he was afraid
to differ from her overtly. "Well,—m—perhaps, Clara," he began,
peering from under the shaggy eyebrows, "it would be best for a
delicate child like Ettie—"

Mrs. Le Geyt smiled a compassionate smile. "Ah, I forgot," she
cooed, sweetly. "Dear Hugo never *can* understand the upbringing
of children. It is a sense denied him. We women know"—with a
sage nod. "They were wild little savages when I took them in hand
first—weren't you, Maisie? Do you remember, dear, how you broke
the looking-glass in the boudoir, like an untamed young monkey?
Talking of monkeys, Mr. Cotswould, *have* you seen those delightful, clever, amusing French pictures at that place in Suffolk Street?
There's a man there—a Parisian—I forget his honoured name—
Leblanc, or Lenoir, or Lebrun, or something—but he's a most humorous artist, and he paints monkeys and storks and all sorts of
queer beasties *almost* as quaintly and expressively as you do. Mind,
I say *almost*, for I never will allow that any Frenchman could do
anything *quite* so good, quite so funnily mock-human, as your
marabouts and professors."

"What a charming hostess Mrs. Le Geyt makes," the painter
observed to me, after lunch. "Such tact! Such discrimination! . . .
And, what a devoted stepmother!"

"She is one of the local secretaries of the Society for the Prevention of Cruelty to Children," I said, drily.

"And charity begins at home," Hilda Wade added, in a significant aside.

We walked home together as far as Stanhope Gate. Our sense
of doom oppressed us. "And yet," I said, turning to her, as we left
the doorstep, "I don't doubt Mrs. Le Geyt really believes she *is* a
model stepmother!"

"Of course she believes it," my witch answered. "She has no
more doubt about that than about anything else. Doubts are not in
her line. She does everything exactly as it ought to be done—who

should know, if not she?—and therefore she is never afraid of criti-
cism. Hardening, indeed! that poor slender, tender, shrinking little
Ettie! A frail exotic. She would harden her into a skeleton if she
had her way. Nothing's much harder than a skeleton, I suppose,
except Mrs. Le Geyt's manner of training one."

"I should be sorry to think," I broke in, "that that sweet little
floating thistle-down of a child I once knew was to be done to death
by her."

"Oh, as for that, she will *not* be done to death," Hilda answered,
in her confident way. "Mrs. Le Geyt won't live long enough."

I started. "You think not?"

"I don't think, I am sure of it. We are at the fifth act now. I
watched Mr. Le Geyt closely all through lunch, and I'm more confident than ever that the end is coming. He is temporarily crushed;
but he is like steam in a boiler, seething, seething, seething. One
day she will sit on the safety-valve, and the explosion will come.
When it comes"—she raised aloft one quick hand in the air as if
striking a dagger home—"good-bye to her!"

For the next few months I saw much of Le Geyt; and the more I
saw of him, the more I saw that my witch's prognosis was essentially correct. They never quarrelled; but Mrs. Le Geyt, in her unobtrusive way, held a quiet hand over her husband which became
increasingly apparent. In the midst of her fancy-work (those busy
fingers were never idle) she kept her eyes well fixed on him. Now
and again I saw him glance at his motherless girls with what looked
like a tender, protecting regret; especially when "Clara" had been
most openly drilling them; but he dared not interfere. She was
crushing their spirit, as she was crushing their father's—and all,
bear in mind, for the best of motives! She had their interest at
heart; she wanted to do what was right for them. Her manner to
him and to them was always honey-sweet—in all externals; yet one
could somehow feel it was the velvet glove that masked the iron
hand; not cruel, not harsh even, but severely, irresistibly, unflinch-
ingly crushing. "Ettie, my dear, get your brown hat at once. What's
that? Going to rain? I did not ask you, my child, for *your* opinion on
the weather. My own suffices. A headache? Oh, nonsense! Headaches

are caused by want of exercise. Nothing so good for a touch of head-ache as a nice brisk walk in Kensington Gardens. Maisie, don't hold your sister's hand like that; it is imitation sympathy! You are aiding and abetting her in setting my wishes at naught. Now, no long faces! What *I* require is *cheerful* obedience."

A bland, autocratic martinet: smiling, inexorable! Poor, pale Ettie grew thinner and wanner under her law daily, while Maisie's temper, naturally docile, was being spoiled before one's eyes by persistent, needless thwarting.

As spring came on, however, I began to hope that things were really mending. Le Geyt looked brighter; some of his own care-less, happy-go-lucky self came back again at intervals. He told me once, with a wistful sigh, that he thought of sending the children to school in the country—it would be better for them, he said, and would take a little work off dear Clara's shoulders; for never even to me was he disloyal to Clara. I encouraged him in the idea. He went on to say that the great difficulty in the way was . . . Clara. She was SO conscientious; she thought it her duty to look after the children herself, and couldn't bear to delegate any part of that duty to others. Besides, she had such an excellent opinion of the Kensington High School!

When I told Hilda Wade of this, she set her teeth together and answered at once: "That settles it! The end is very near. *He* will insist upon their going, to save them from that woman's ruthless kindness; and *she* will refuse to give up any part of what she calls her duty. *He* will reason with her; he will plead for his children; *she* will be adamant. Not angry—it is never the way of that temperament to get angry—just calmly, sedately, and insupportably provoking. When she goes too far, he will flare up at last; some taunt will rouse him; the explosion will come; and . . . the children will go to their Aunt Lina, whom they dote upon. When all is said and done, it is the poor man I pity!"

"You said within twelve months."

"That was a bow drawn at a venture. It may be a little sooner; it may be a little later. But—next week or next month—it is coming: it is coming!"

June smiled upon us once more; and on the afternoon of the 13th, the anniversary of our first lunch together at the Le Geyts, I was up at my work in the accident ward at St. Nathaniel's. "Well, the ides of June have come, Sister Wade!" I said, when I met her, parodying Caesar.

"But not yet gone," she answered; and a profound sense of foreboding spread over her speaking face as she uttered the words.

Her oracle disquieted me. "Why, I dined there last night," I cried; "and all seemed exceptionally well."

"The calm before the storm, perhaps," she murmured.

Just at that moment I heard a boy crying in the street: "*Pall Mall Gazette*; 'ere y'are; speshul edishun! Shocking tragedy at the West-end! Orful murder! 'Ere y'are! Spechul *Globe! Pall Mall*, extry speshul!"

A weird tremor broke over me. I walked down into the street and bought a paper. There it stared me in the face on the middle page: "Tragedy at Campden Hill: Well-known Barrister Murders his Wife. Sensational Details."

I looked closer and read. It was as I feared. The Le Geyts! After I left their house, the night before, husband and wife must have quarrelled, no doubt over the question of the children's schooling; and at some provoking word, as it seemed, Hugo must have snatched up a knife—"a little ornamental Norwegian dagger," the report said, "which happened to lie close by on the cabinet in the drawing-room," and plunged it into his wife's heart. "The unhappy lady died instantaneously, by all appearances, and the dastardly crime was not discovered by the servants till eight o'clock this morning. Mr. Le Geyt is missing."

I rushed up with the news to Nurse Wade, who was at work in the accident ward. She turned pale, but bent over her patient and said nothing.

"It is fearful to think!" I groaned out at last; "for us who know all—that poor Le Geyt will be hanged for it! Hanged for attempting to protect his children!"

"He will *not* be hanged," my witch answered, with the same unquestioning confidence as ever.

"Why not?" I asked, astonished once more at this bold prediction.

She went on bandaging the arm of the patient whom she was attending. "Because . . . he will commit suicide," she replied, without moving a muscle.

"How do you know that?"

She stuck a steel safety-pin with deft fingers into the roll of lint. "When I have finished my day's work," she answered slowly, still continuing the bandage, "I may perhaps find time to tell you."

THE EPISODE OF THE MAN
WHO WOULD NOT COMMIT SUICIDE

After my poor friend Le Geyt had murdered his wife, in a sudden access of uncontrollable anger, under the deepest provocation, the police naturally began to inquire for him. It is a way they have; the police are no respecters of persons; neither do they pry into the question of motives. They are but poor casuists. A murder is for them a murder, and a murderer a murderer; it is not their habit to divide and distinguish between case and case with Hilda Wade's analytical accuracy.

As soon as my duties at St. Nathaniel's permitted me, on the evening of the discovery, I rushed round to Mrs. Mallet's, Le Geyt's sister. I had been detained at the hospital for some hours, however, watching a critical case; and by the time I reached Great Stanhope Street I found Hilda Wade, in her nurse's dress, there before me. Sebastian, it seemed, had given her leave out for the evening. She was a supernumerary nurse, attached to his own observation-cots as special attendant for scientific purposes, and she could generally get an hour or so whenever she required it.

Mrs. Mallet had been in the breakfast-room with Hilda before I arrived; but as I reached the house she rushed upstairs to wash her red eyes and compose herself a little before the strain of meeting me; so I had the opportunity for a few words alone first with my prophetic companion.

"You said just now at Nathaniel's," I burst out, "that Le Geyt would not be hanged: he would commit suicide. What did you mean by that? What reason had you for thinking so?"

Hilda sank into a chair by the open window, pulled a flower abstractedly from the vase at her side, and began picking it to pieces, floret after floret, with twitching fingers. She was deeply moved. "Well, consider his family history," she burst out at last, looking up at me with her large brown eyes as she reached the last petal. "Heredity counts. . . . And after such a disaster!"

She said "disaster," not "crime"; I noted mentally the reservation implied in the word.

"Heredity counts," I answered. "Oh, yes. It counts much. But what about Le Geyt's family history?" I could not recall any instance of suicide among his forbears.

"Well—his mother's father was General Faskally, you know," she replied, after a pause, in her strange, oblique manner. "Mr. Le Geyt is General Faskally's eldest grandson."

"Exactly," I broke in, with a man's desire for solid fact in place of vague intuition. "But I fail to see quite what that has to do with it."

"The General was killed in India during the Mutiny."

"I remember, of course—killed, bravely fighting."

"Yes; but it was on a forlorn hope, for which he volunteered, and in the course of which he is said to have walked straight into an almost obvious ambuscade of the enemy's."

"Now, my dear Miss Wade"—I always dropped the title of "Nurse," by request, when once we were well clear of Nathaniel's,— "I have every confidence, you are aware, in your memory and your insight; but I do confess I fail to see what bearing this incident can have on poor Hugo's chances of being hanged or committing suicide."

She picked a second flower, and once more pulled out petal after petal. As she reached the last again, she answered, slowly: "You must have forgotten the circumstances. It was no mere accident. General Faskally had made a serious strategical blunder at Jhansi. He had sacrificed the lives of his subordinates needlessly. He could not bear to face the survivors. In the course of the retreat, he volunteered to go on this forlorn hope, which might equally well have been led by an officer of lower rank; and he was permitted to do so by Sir Colin in command, as a means of retrieving his lost military character. He carried his point, but he carried it recklessly, taking care to be shot through the heart himself in the first onslaught. That was virtual suicide—honourable suicide to avoid disgrace, at a moment of supreme remorse and horror."

"You are right," I admitted, after a minute's consideration. "I see it now—though I should never have thought of it."

"That is the use of being a woman," she answered.

I waited a second once more, and mused. "Still, that is only one doubtful case," I objected.

"There was another, you must remember: his uncle Alfred."

"Alfred Le Geyt?"

"No; *he* died in his bed, quietly. Alfred Faskally."

"What a memory you have!" I cried, astonished. "Why, that was before our time—in the days of the Chartist riots!"

She smiled a certain curious sibylline smile of hers. Her earnest face looked prettier than ever. "I told you I could remember many things that happened before I was born," she answered. "*This* is one of them."

"You remember it directly?"

"How impossible! Have I not often explained to you that I am no diviner? I read no book of fate; I call no spirits from the vasty deep. I simply remember with exceptional clearness what I read and hear. And I have many times heard the story about Alfred Faskally."

"So have I—but I forget it."

"Unfortunately, I *can't* forget. That is a sort of disease with me. . . . He was a special constable in the Chartist riots; and being a very strong and powerful man, like his nephew Hugo, he used his truncheon—his special constable's baton, or whatever you call it— with excessive force upon a starveling London tailor in the mob near Charing Cross. The man was hit on the forehead—badly hit, so that he died almost immediately of concussion of the brain. A woman rushed out of the crowd at once, seized the dying man, laid his head on her lap, and shrieked out in a wildly despairing voice that he was her husband, and the father of thirteen children. Alfred Faskally, who never meant to kill the man, or even to hurt him, but who was laying about him roundly, without realising the terrific force of his blows, was so horrified at what he had done when he heard the woman's cry, that he rushed off straight to Waterloo Bridge in an agony of remorse and—flung himself over. He was drowned instantly."

"I recall the story now," I answered; "but, do you know, as it was told me, I think they said the mob *threw* Faskally over in their desire for vengeance."

"That is the official account, as told by the Le Geyts and the Faskallys; they like to have it believed their kinsman was murdered, not that he committed suicide. But my grandfather"—I started; during the twelve months that I had been brought into daily relations with Hilda Wade, that was the first time I had heard her mention any member of her own family, except once her mother— "my grandfather, who knew him well, and who was present in the crowd at the time, assured me many times that Alfred Faskally really jumped over of his own accord, *not* pursued by the mob, and that his last horrified words as he leaped were, 'I never meant it! I never meant it!' However, the family have always had luck in their suicides. The jury believed the throwing-over story, and found a verdict of 'wilful murder' against some person or persons unknown."

"Luck in their suicides! What a curious phrase! And you say, *always*. Were there other cases, then?"

"Constructively, yes; one of the Le Geyts, you must recollect, went down with his ship (just like his uncle, the General, in India) when he might have quitted her. It is believed he had given a mistaken order. You remember, of course; he was navigating lieutenant. Another, Marcus, was *said* to have shot himself by accident while cleaning his gun—after a quarrel with his wife. But you have heard all about it. 'The wrong was on my side,' he moaned, you know, when they picked him up, dying, in the gun-room. And one of the Faskally girls, his cousin, of whom his wife was jealous— that beautiful Linda—became a Catholic, and went into a convent at once on Marcus's death; which, after all, in such cases, is merely a religious and moral way of committing suicide—I mean, for a woman who takes the veil just to cut herself off from the world, and who has no vocation, as I hear she had not."

She filled me with amazement. "That is true," I exclaimed, "when one comes to think of it. It shows the same temperament in fibre. . . . But I should never have thought of it."

"No? Well, I believe it is true, for all that. In every case, one sees they choose much the same way of meeting a reverse, a blunder, an unpremeditated crime. The brave way is to go through with it, and face the music, letting what will come; the cowardly way is to hide one's head incontinently in a river, a noose, or a convent cell."

"Le Geyt is not a coward," I interposed, with warmth.

"No, not, a coward—a manly spirited, great-hearted gentleman—but still, not quite of the bravest type. He lacks one element. The Le Geyts have physical courage—enough and to spare—but their moral courage fails them at a pinch. They rush into suicide or its equivalent at critical moments, out of pure boyish impulsiveness."

A few minutes later, Mrs. Mallet came in. She was not broken down—on the contrary, she was calm—stoically, tragically, pitiably calm; with that ghastly calmness which is more terrible by far than the most demonstrative grief. Her face, though deadly white, did not move a muscle. Not a tear was in her eyes. Even her bloodless hands hardly twitched at the folds of her hastily assumed black gown. She clenched them after a minute when she had grasped mine silently; I could see that the nails dug deep into the palms in her painful resolve to keep herself from collapsing.

Hilda Wade, with infinite sisterly tenderness, led her over to a chair by the window in the summer twilight, and took one quivering hand in hers. "I have been telling Dr. Cumberledge, Lina, about what I most fear for your dear brother, darling; and . . . I think . . . he agrees with me."

Mrs. Mallet turned to me, with hollow eyes, still preserving her tragic calm. "I am afraid of it, too," she said, her drawn lips tremulous. "Dr. Cumberledge, we must get him back! We must induce him to face it!"

"And yet," I answered, slowly, turning it over in my own mind; "he has run away at first. Why should he do that if he means—to commit suicide?" I hated to utter the words before that broken soul; but there was no way out of it.

Hilda interrupted me with a quiet suggestion. "How do you know he has run away?" she asked. "Are you not taking it for granted that, if he meant suicide, he would blow his brains out in his own house? But surely that would not be the Le Geyt way. They are gentle-natured folk; they would never blow their brains out or cut their throats. For all we know, he may have made straight for Waterloo Bridge,"—she framed her lips to the unspoken words, unseen by Mrs. Mallet,—"like his uncle Alfred."

"That is true," I answered, lip-reading. "I never thought of that either."

"Still, I do not attach importance to this idea," she went on. "I have some reason for thinking he has run away . . . elsewhere; and if so, our first task must be to entice him back again."

"What are your reasons?" I asked, humbly. Whatever they might be, I knew enough of Hilda Wade by this time to know that she had probably good grounds for accepting them.

"Oh, they may wait for the present," she answered. "Other things are more pressing. First, let Lina tell us what she thinks of most moment."

Mrs. Mallet braced herself up visibly to a distressing effort. "You have seen the body, Dr. Cumberledge?" she faltered.

"No, dear Mrs. Mallet, I have not. I came straight from Nathaniel's. I have had no time to see it."

"Dr. Sebastian has viewed it by my wish—he has been so kind—and he will be present as representing the family at the post-mortem. He notes that the wound was inflicted with a dagger—a small ornamental Norwegian dagger, which always lay, as I know, on the little what-not by the blue sofa."

I nodded assent. "Exactly; I have seen it there."

"It was blunt and rusty—a mere toy knife—not at all the sort of weapon a man would make use of who designed to commit a deliberate murder. The crime, if there *was* a crime (which we do not admit), must therefore have been wholly unpremeditated."

I bowed my head. "For us who knew Hugo that goes without saying."

She leaned forward eagerly. "Dr. Sebastian has pointed out to me a line of defence which would probably succeed—if we could only induce poor Hugo to adopt it. He has examined the blade and scabbard, and finds that the dagger fits its sheath very tight, so that it can only be withdrawn with considerable violence. The blade sticks." (I nodded again.) "It needs a hard pull to wrench it out. . . . He has also inspected the wound, and assures me its character is such that it *might* have been self-inflicted." She paused now and again, and brought out her words with difficulty. "Self-inflicted, he suggests; therefore, that *this* may have happened. It is admitted—*will* be admitted—the servants overheard it—we can make no reservation there—a difference of opinion, an altercation, even, took place between Hugo and Clara that evening"—she started suddenly—"why, it was only last night—it seems like ages—an altercation about the children's schooling. Clara held strong views on the subject of the children"—her eyes blinked hard—"which Hugo did not share. We throw out the hint, then, that Clara, during the course of the dispute—we must call it a dispute—accidentally took up this dagger and toyed with it. You know her habit of toying, when she had no knitting or needlework. In the course of playing with it (we suggest) she tried to pull the knife out of its sheath; failed; held it up, so, point upward; pulled again; pulled harder—with a jerk, at last the sheath came off; the dagger sprang up; it wounded Clara fatally. Hugo, knowing that they had disagreed, knowing that the servants had heard, and seeing her fall suddenly dead before him, was seized with horror—the Le Geyt impulsiveness!—lost his head; rushed out; fancied the accident would be mistaken for murder. But why? A Q.C., don't you know! Recently married! Most attached to his wife. It is plausible, isn't it?"

"So plausible," I answered, looking it straight in the face, "that . . . it has but one weak point. We might make a coroner's jury or even a common jury accept it, on Sebastian's expert evidence. Sebastian can work wonders; but we could never make—"

Hilda Wade finished the sentence for me as I paused: "Hugo Le Geyt consent to advance it."

I lowered my head. "You have said it," I answered.

"Not for the children's sake?" Mrs. Mallet cried, with clasped hands.

"Not for the children's sake, even," I answered. "Consider for a moment, Mrs. Mallet: *is* it true? Do you yourself *believe* it?"

She threw herself back in her chair with a dejected face. "Oh, as for that," she cried, wearily, crossing her hands, "before you and Hilda, who know all, what need to prevaricate? How *can* I believe it? We understand how it came about. That woman! That woman!"

"The real wonder is," Hilda murmured, soothing her white hand, "that he contained himself so long!"

"Well, we all know Hugo," I went on, as quietly as I was able; "and, knowing Hugo, we know that he might be urged to commit this wild act in a fierce moment of indignation—righteous indignation on behalf of his motherless girls, under tremendous provocation. But we also know that, having once committed it, he would never stoop to disown it by a subterfuge."

The heart-broken sister let her head drop faintly. "So Hilda told me," she murmured; "and what Hilda says in these matters is almost always final."

We debated the question for some minutes more. Then Mrs. Mallet cried at last: "At any rate, he has fled for the moment, and his flight alone brings the worst suspicion upon him. That is our chief point. We must find out where he is; and if he has gone right away, we must bring him back to London."

"Where do you think he has taken refuge?"

"The police, Dr. Sebastian has ascertained, are watching the railway stations, and the ports for the Continent."

"Very like the police!" Hilda exclaimed, with more than a touch of contempt in her voice. "As if a clever man-of-the-world like Hugo Le Geyt would run away by rail, or start off to the Continent! Every Englishman is noticeable on the Continent. It would be sheer madness!"

"You think he has not gone there, then?" I cried, deeply interested.

"Of course not. That is the point I hinted at just now. He has defended many persons accused of murder, and he often spoke to me of their incredible folly, when trying to escape, in going by rail, or in setting out from England for Paris. An Englishman, he used to say, is least observed in his own country. In this case, I think I *know* where he has gone, how he went there."

"Where, then?"

"*Where* comes last; *how* first. It is a question of inference."

"Explain. We know your powers."

"Well, I take it for granted that he killed her—we must not mince matters—about twelve o'clock; for after that hour, the servants told Lina, there was quiet in the drawing-room. Next, I conjecture, he went upstairs to change his clothes: he could not go forth on the world in an evening suit; and the housemaid says his black coat and trousers were lying as usual on a chair in his dressing-room—which shows at least that he was not unduly flurried. After that, he put on another suit, no doubt—*what* suit I hope the police will not discover too soon; for I suppose you must just accept the situation that we are conspiring to defeat the ends of justice."

"No, no!" Mrs. Mallet cried. "To bring him back voluntarily, that he may face his trial like a man!"

"Yes, dear. That is quite right. However, the next thing, of course, would be that he would shave in whole or in part. His big black beard was so very conspicuous; he would certainly get rid of that before attempting to escape. The servants being in bed, he was not pressed for time; he had the whole night before him. So, of course, he shaved. On the other hand, the police, you may be sure, will circulate his photograph—we must not shirk these points"—for Mrs. Mallet winced again—"will circulate his photograph, *beard and all*; and that will really be one of our great safeguards; for the bushy beard so masks the face that, without it, Hugo would be scarcely recognisable. I conclude, therefore, that he must have shorn himself *before* leaving home; though naturally I did not make the police a present of the hint by getting Lina to ask any questions in that direction of the housemaid."

"You are probably right," I answered. "But would he have a razor?"

"I was coming to that. No; certainly he would not. He had not shaved for years. And they kept no men-servants; which makes it difficult for him to borrow one from a sleeping man. So what he would do would doubtless be to cut off his beard, or part of it, quite close, with a pair of scissors, and then get himself properly shaved next morning in the first country town he came to."

"The first country town?"

"Certainly. That leads up to the next point. We must try to be cool and collected." She was quivering with suppressed emotion herself, as she said it, but her soothing hand still lay on Mrs. Mallet's. "The next thing is—he would leave London."

"But not by rail, you say?"

"He is an intelligent man, and in the course of defending others has thought about this matter. Why expose himself to the needless risk and observation of a railway station? No; I saw at once what he would do. Beyond doubt, he would cycle. He always wondered it was not done oftener, under similar circumstances."

"But has his bicycle gone?"

"Lina looked. It has not. I should have expected as much. I told her to note that point very unobtrusively, so as to avoid giving the police the clue. She saw the machine in the outer hall as usual."

"He is too good a criminal lawyer to have dreamt of taking his own," Mrs. Mallet interposed, with another effort.

"But where could he have hired or bought one at that time of night?" I exclaimed.

"Nowhere—without exciting the gravest suspicion. Therefore, I conclude, he stopped in London for the night, sleeping at an hotel, without luggage, and paying for his room in advance. It is frequently done, and if he arrived late, very little notice would be taken of him. Big hotels about the Strand, I am told, have always a dozen such casual bachelor guests every evening."

"And then?"

"And then, this morning, he would buy a new bicycle—a different make from his own, at the nearest shop; would rig himself out, at some ready-made tailor's, with a fresh tourist suit—probably an ostentatiously tweedy bicycling suit; and, with that in his luggage-carrier, would make straight on his machine for the country. He could change in some copse, and bury his own clothes, avoiding the blunders he has seen in others. Perhaps he might ride for the first twenty or thirty miles out of London to some minor side-station, and then go on by train towards his destination, quitting the rail again at some unimportant point where the main west road crosses the Great Western or the South-Western line."

"Great Western or South-Western? Why those two in particular? Then, you have settled in your own mind which direction he has taken?"

"Pretty well. I judge by analogy. Lina, your brother was brought up in the West Country, was he not?"

Mrs. Mallet gave a weary nod. "In North Devon," she answered; "on the wild stretch of moor about Hartland and Clovelly."

Hilda Wade seemed to collect herself. "Now, Mr. Le Geyt is essentially a Celt—a Celt in temperament," she went on; "he comes by origin and ancestry from a rough, heather-clad country; he belongs to the moorland. In other words, his type is the mountaineer's. But a mountaineer's instinct in similar circumstances is—what? Why, to fly straight to his native mountains. In an agony of terror, in an access of despair, when all else fails, he strikes a bee-line for the hills he loves; rationally or irrationally, he seems to think he can hide there. Hugo Le Geyt, with his frank boyish nature, his great Devonian frame, is sure to have done so. I know his mood. He has made for the West Country!"

"You are, right, Hilda," Mrs. Mallet exclaimed, with conviction. "I'm quite sure, from what I know of Hugo, that to go to the West would be his first impulse."

"And the Le Geyts are always governed by first impulses," my character-reader added.

She was quite correct. From the time we two were at Oxford together—I as an undergraduate, he as a don—I had always noticed that marked trait in my dear old friend's temperament.

After a short pause, Hilda broke the silence again. "The sea again; the sea! The Le Geyts love the water. Was there any place on the sea where he went much as a boy—any lonely place, I mean, in that North Devon district?"

Mrs. Mallet reflected a moment. "Yes, there was a little bay—a mere gap in high cliffs, with some fishermen's huts and a few yards of beach—where he used to spend much of his holidays. It was a weird-looking break in a grim sea-wall of dark-red rocks, where the tide rose high, rolling in from the Atlantic."

"The very thing! Has he visited it since he grew up?"

"To my knowledge, never."

Hilda's voice had a ring of certainty. "Then *that* is where we shall find him, dear! We must look there first. He is sure to revisit just such a solitary spot by the sea when trouble overtakes him."

Later in the evening, as we were walking home towards Nathaniel's together, I asked Hilda why she had spoken throughout with such unwavering confidence. "Oh, it was simple enough," she answered. "There were two things that helped me through, which I didn't like to mention in detail before Lina. One was this: the Le Geyts have all of them an instinctive horror of the sight of blood; therefore, they almost never commit suicide by shooting themselves or cutting their throats. Marcus, who shot himself in the gun-room, was an exception to both rules; he never minded blood; he could cut up a deer. But Hugo refused to be a doctor, because he could not stand the sight of an operation; and even as a sportsman he never liked to pick up or handle the game he had shot himself; he said it sickened him. He rushed from that room last night, I feel sure, in a physical horror at the deed he had done; and by now he is as far as he can get from London. The sight of his act drove him away; not craven fear of an arrest. If the Le Geyts kill themselves—a seafaring race on the whole—their impulse is to trust to water."

"And the other thing?"

"Well, that was about the mountaineer's homing instinct. I have often noticed it. I could give you fifty instances, only I didn't like to speak of them before Lina. There was Williams, for example, the Dolgelly man who killed a game-keeper at Petworth in a poaching affray; he was taken on Cader Idris, skulking among rocks, a week later. Then there was that unhappy young fellow, Mackinnon, who shot his sweetheart at Leicester; he made, straight as the crow flies, for his home in the Isle of Skye, and there drowned himself in familiar waters. Lindner, the Tyrolese, again, who stabbed the American swindler at Monte Carlo, was tracked after a few days to his native place, St. Valentin, in the Zillerthal. It is always so. Mountaineers in distress fly to their mountains. It is a part of their nostalgia. I know it from within, too: if *I* were in poor Hugo LeGeyt's place, what do you think I would do? Why, hide myself at once in the greenest recesses of our Carnarvonshire mountains."

"What an extraordinary insight into character you have!" I cried. "You seem to divine what everybody's action will be under given circumstances."

She paused, and held her parasol half poised in her hand. "Character determines action," she said, slowly, at last. "That is the secret of the great novelists. They put themselves behind and within their characters, and so make us feel that every act of their personages is not only natural but even—given the conditions—inevitable. We recognise that their story is the sole logical outcome of the interaction of their *dramatis personae*. Now, *I* am not a great novelist; I cannot create and imagine characters and situations. But I have something of the novelist's gift; I apply the same method to the real life of the people around me. I try to throw myself into the person of others, and to feel how their character will compel them to act in each set of circumstances to which they may expose themselves."

"In one word," I said, "you are a psychologist."

"A psychologist," she assented; "I suppose so; and the police—well, the police are not; they are at best but bungling materialists. They require a *clue*. What need of a *clue* if you can interpret character?"

So certain was Hilda Wade of her conclusions, indeed, that Mrs. Mallet begged me next day to take my holiday at once—which I could easily do—and go down to the little bay in the Hartland district of which she had spoken, in search of Hugo. I consented. She herself proposed to set out quietly for Bideford, where she could be within easy reach of me, in order to hear of my success or failure; while Hilda Wade, whose summer vacation was to have begun in two days' time, offered to ask for an extra day's leave so as to accompany her. The broken-hearted sister accepted the offer; and, secrecy being above all things necessary, we set off by different routes: the two women by Waterloo, myself by Paddington.

We stopped that night at different hotels in Bideford; but next morning, Hilda rode out on her bicycle, and accompanied me on mine for a mile or two along the tortuous way towards Hartland. "Take nothing for granted," she said, as we parted; "and be prepared to find poor Hugo Le Geyt's appearance greatly changed. He has eluded the police and their 'clues' so far; therefore, I imagine he must have largely altered his dress and exterior."

"I will find him," I answered, "if he is anywhere within twenty miles of Hartland."

She waved her hand to me in farewell. I rode on after she left me towards the high promontory in front, the wildest and least-visited part of North Devon. Torrents of rain had fallen during the night; the slimy cart-ruts and cattle-tracks on the moor were brimming with water. It was a lowering day. The clouds drifted low. Black peat-bogs filled the hollows; grey stone homesteads, lonely and forbidding, stood out here and there against the curved sky-line. Even the high road was uneven and in places flooded. For an hour I passed hardly a soul. At last, near a crossroad with a defaced finger-post, I descended from my machine, and consulted my ordnance map, on which Mrs. Mallet had marked ominously, with a cross of red rink, the exact position of the little fishing hamlet where Hugo used to spend his holidays. I took the turning which seemed to me most likely to lead to it; but the tracks were so confused, and the run of the lanes so uncertain—let alone the map being some years out of date—that I soon felt I had lost my bearings. By a little wayside inn, half hidden in a deep combe, with bog on every side, I descended and asked for a bottle of ginger-beer;

for the day was hot and close, in spite of the packed clouds. As they were opening the bottle, I inquired casually the way to the Red Gap bathing-place.

The landlord gave me directions which confused me worse than ever, ending at last with the concise remark: "An' then, zur, two or dree more turns to the right an' to the left 'ull bring 'ee right up alongzide o' ut."

I despaired of finding the way by these unintelligible sailing-orders; but just at that moment, as luck would have it, another cyclist flew past—the first soul I had seen on the road that morning. He was a man with the loose-knit air of a shop assistant, badly got up in a rather loud and obtrusive tourist suit of brown home-spun, with baggy knickerbockers and thin thread stockings. I judged him a gentleman on the cheap at sight. "Very Stylish; this Suit Complete, only thirty-seven and sixpence!" The landlady glanced out at him with a friendly nod. He turned and smiled at her, but did not see me; for I stood in the shade behind the half-open door. He had a short black moustache and a not unpleasing, careless face. His features, I thought, were better than his garments.

However, the stranger did not interest me just then I was far too full of more important matters. "Why don't 'ee taäke an' vollow thik ther gen'leman, zur?" the landlady said, pointing one large red hand after him. "Ur do go down to Urd Gap to zwim every marnin'. Mr. Jan Smith, o' Oxford, they do call un. 'Ee can't go wrong if 'ee do vollow un to the Gap. Ur's lodgin' up to wold Varmer Moore's, an' ur's that vond o' the zay, the vishermen do tell me, as wasn't never any gen'leman like un."

I tossed off my ginger-beer, jumped on to my machine, and fol-lowed the retreating brown back of Mr. John Smith, of Oxford—surely a most non-committing name—round sharp corners and over rutty lanes, tire-deep in mud, across the rusty-red moor, till, all at once, at a turn, a gap of stormy sea appeared wedge-shape between two shelving rock-walls.

It was a lonely spot. Rocks hemmed it in; big breakers walled it. The sou'-wester roared through the gap. I rode down among

loose stones and water-worn channels in the solid grit very carefully. But the man in brown had torn over the wild path with reckless haste, zigzagging madly, and was now on the little three-cor-
nered patch of beach, undressing himself with a sort of careless
glee, and flinging his clothes down anyhow on the shingle beside
him. Something about the action caught my eye. That movement
of the arm! It was not—it could not be—no, no, not Hugo!

A very ordinary person; and Le Geyt bore the stamp of a born
gentleman.

He stood up bare at last. He flung out his arms, as if to welcome the boisterous wind to his naked bosom. Then, with a sudden burst of recognition, the man stood revealed. We had bathed
together a hundred times in London and elsewhere. The face, the
clad figure, the dress, all were different. But the body—the actual
frame and make of the man—the well-knit limbs, the splendid
trunk—no disguise could alter. It was Le Geyt himself—big, powerful, vigorous.

That ill-made suit, those baggy knickerbockers, the slouched
cap, the thin thread stockings, had only distorted and hidden his
figure. Now that I saw him as he was, he came out the same bold
and manly form as ever.

He did not notice me. He rushed down with a certain wild joy
into the turbulent water, and, plunging in with a loud cry, buf-
feted the huge waves with those strong curving arms of his. The
sou'-wester was rising. Each breaker as it reared caught him on its
crest and tumbled him over like a cork, but like a cork he rose again.
He was swimming now, arm over arm, straight out seaward. I saw
the lifted hands between the crest and the trough. For a moment I
hesitated whether I ought to strip and follow him. Was he doing as
so many others of his house had done—courting death from the
water?

But some strange hand restrained me. Who was I that I should
stand between Hugo Le Geyt and the ways of Providence?

The Le Geyts loved ever the ordeal by water.

Presently, he turned again. Before he turned, I had taken the
opportunity to look hastily at his clothes. Hilda Wade had surmised

aright once more. The outer suit was a cheap affair from a big ready-made tailor's in St. Martin's Lane—turned out by the thousand; the underclothing, on the other hand, was new and unmarked, but fine in quality—bought, no doubt, at Bideford. An eerie sense of doom stole over me. I felt the end was near. I withdrew behind a big rock, and waited there unseen till Hugo had landed. He began to dress again, without troubling to dry himself. I drew a deep breath of relief. Then this was not suicide!

By the time he had pulled on his vest and drawers, I came out suddenly from my ambush and faced him. A fresh shock awaited me. I could hardly believe my eyes. It was *not* Le Geyt—no, nor anything like him!

Nevertheless, the man rose with a little cry and advanced, half crouching, towards me. "*You* are not hunting me down—with the police?" he exclaimed, his neck held low and his forehead wrinkling.

The voice—the voice was Le Geyt's. It was an unspeakable mystery. "Hugo," I cried, "dear Hugo—hunting you down?—*could* you imagine it?"

He raised his head, strode forward, and grasped my hand. "Forgive me, Cumberledge," he cried. "But a proscribed and hounded man! If you knew what a relief it is to me to get out on the water!"

"You forget all there?"

"I forget *it*—the red horror!"

"You meant just now to drown yourself?"

"No! If I had meant it I would have done it. . . . Hubert, for my children's sake, I *will* not commit suicide!"

"Then listen!" I cried. I told him in a few words of his sister's scheme—Sebastian's defence—the plausibility of the explanation—the whole long story. He gazed at me moodily. Yet it was not Hugo!

"No, no," he said, shortly; and as he spoke it was *he*. "I have done it; I have killed her; I will not owe my life to a falsehood."

"Not for the children's sake?"

He dashed his hand down impatiently. "I have a better way for the children. I will save them still. . . . Hubert, you are not afraid to speak to a murderer?"

"Dear Hugo—I know all; and to know all is to forgive all."

He grasped my hand once more. "Know *all!*" he cried, with a despairing gesture. "Oh, no; no one knows *all* but myself; not even the children. But the children know much; *they* will forgive me. Lina knows something; *she* will forgive me. You know a little; *you* forgive me. The world can never know. It will brand my darlings as a murderer's children."

"It was the act of a minute," I interposed. "And—though she is dead, poor lady, and one must speak no ill of her—we can at least gather dimly, for your children's sake, how deep was the provocation."

He gazed at me fixedly. His voice was like lead. "For the children's sake—yes," he answered, as in a dream. "It was all for the children! I have killed her—murdered her—she has paid her penalty; and, poor dead soul, I will utter no word against her—the woman I have murdered! But one thing I will say: If omniscient justice sends me for this to eternal punishment, I can endure it gladly, like a man, knowing that so I have redeemed my Marian's motherless girls from a deadly tyranny."

It was the only sentence in which he ever alluded to her.

I sat down by his side and watched him closely. Mechanically, methodically, he went on with his dressing. The more he dressed, the less could I believe it was Hugo. I had expected to find him close-shaven; so did the police, by their printed notices. Instead of that, he had shaved his beard and whiskers, but only trimmed his moustache; trimmed it quite short, so as to reveal the boyish corners of the mouth—a trick which entirely altered his rugged expression. But that was not all; what puzzled me most was the eyes—they were not Hugo's. At first I could not imagine why. By degrees the truth dawned upon me. His eyebrows were naturally thick and shaggy—great overhanging growth, interspersed with many of those stiff long hairs to which Darwin called attention in certain men as surviving traits from a monkey-like ancestor. In order to disguise himself, Hugo had pulled out all these coarser hairs, leaving nothing on his brows but the soft and closely pressed coat of down which underlies the longer bristles in all such cases. This had wholly altered the expression of the eyes, which no longer looked out keenly from their cavernous penthouse; but being deprived of their relief, had acquired a much more ordinary and less individual aspect. From a good-natured but shaggy giant, my old friend was transformed by his shaving and his costume into a well-fed and well-grown, but not very colossal, commercial gentleman. Hugo was scarcely six feet high, indeed, though by his broad shoulders and bushy beard he had always impressed one with such a sense of size; and now that the hirsuteness had been got rid of, and the dress altered, he hardly struck one as taller or bigger than the average of his fellows.

We sat for some minutes and talked. Le Geyt would not speak of Clara; and when I asked him his intentions, he shook his head moodily. "I shall act for the best," he said—"what of best is left—to guard the dear children. It was a terrible price to pay for their redemption; but it was the only one possible, and, in a moment of wrath, I paid it. Now, I have to pay, in turn, myself. I do not shirk it."

"You will come back to London, then, and stand your trial?" I asked, eagerly.

"Come back *to London?*" he cried, with a face of white panic. Hitherto he had seemed to me rather relieved in expression than otherwise; his countenance had lost its worn and anxious look; he was no longer watching each moment over his children's safety. "Come back . . . *to London* . . . and face my trial! Why, did you think, Hubert, 'twas the court or the hanging I was shirking? No, no; not that; but *it*—the red horror! I must get away from *it* to the sea—to the water—to wash away the stain—as far from *it*—that red pool—as possible!"

I answered nothing. I left him to face his own remorse in silence.

At last he rose to go, and held one foot undecided on his bicycle.

"I leave myself in Heaven's hands," he said, as he lingered. "*It* will requite. . . . The ordeal is by water."

"So I judged," I answered.

"Tell Lina this from me," he went on, still loitering: "that if she will trust me, I will strive to do the best that remains for my darlings. I will do it, Heaven helping. She will know *what*, to-morrow."

He mounted his machine and sailed off. My eyes followed him up the path with sad forebodings.

All day long I loitered about the Gap. It consisted of two bays—
the one I had already seen, and another, divided from it by a saw-
edge of rock. In the further cove crouched a few low stone cottages.
A broad-bottomed sailing boat lay there, pulled up high on the
beach. About three o'clock, as I sat and watched, two men began
to launch it. The sea ran high; tide coming in; the sou'-wester still
increasing in force to a gale; at the signal-staff on the cliff, the
danger-cone was hoisted. White spray danced in air. Big black
clouds rolled up seething from windward; low thunder rumbling;
a storm threatened.

One of the men was Le Geyt, the other a fisherman.

He jumped in, and put off through the surf with an air of triumph. He was a splendid sailor. His boat leapt through the breakers and flew before the wind with a mere rag of canvas. "Dangerous weather to be out!" I exclaimed to the fisherman, who stood
with hands buried in his pockets, watching him.

"Ay that ur be, zur!" the man answered. "Doan't like the look o'
ut. But thik there gen'leman, 'ee's one o' Oxford, 'ee do tell me;
and they'm a main venturesome lot, they college volk. 'Ee's off by
'isself droo the starm, all so var as Lundy!"

"Will he reach it?" I asked, anxiously, having my own idea on
the subject.

"Doan't seem like ut, zur, do ut? Ur must, an' ur mustn't, an'
yit again ur must. Powerful 'ard place ur be to maake in a starm, to
be zure, Lundy. Zaid the Lord 'ould dezide. But ur 'ouldn't be
warned, ur 'ouldn't; an' voolhardy volk, as the zayin' is, must go
their own voolhardy waay to perdition!"

It was the last I saw of Le Geyt alive. Next morning the lifeless
body of "the man who was wanted for the Campden Hill mystery"
was cast up by the waves on the shore of Lundy. The Lord had decided.

Hugo had not miscalculated. "Luck in their suicides," Hilda
Wade said; and, strange to say, the luck of the Le Geyts stood him
in good stead still. By a miracle of fate, his children were not
branded as a murderer's daughters. Sebastian gave evidence at the
inquest on the wife's body: "Self-inflicted—a recoil—accidental—I

am *sure* of it." His specialist knowledge—his assertive certainty, combined with that arrogant, masterful manner of his, and his keen, eagle eye, overbore the jury. Awed by the great man's look, they brought in a submissive verdict of "Death by misadventure." The coroner thought it a most proper finding. Mrs. Mallet had made the most of the innate Le Geyt horror of blood. The newspapers charitably surmised that the unhappy husband, crazed by the instantaneous unexpectedness of his loss, had wandered away like a madman to the scenes of his childhood, and had there been drowned by accident while trying to cross a stormy sea to Lundy, under some wild impression that he would find his dead wife alive on the island. Nobody whispered *murder*. Everybody dwelt on the utter absence of motive—a model husband!—such a charming young wife, and such a devoted stepmother. We three alone knew—we three, and the children.

On the day when the jury brought in their verdict at the adjourned inquest on Mrs. Le Geyt, Hilda Wade stood in the room, trembling and white-faced, awaiting their decision. When the foreman uttered the words, "Death by misadventure," she burst into tears of relief. "He did well!" she cried to me, passionately. "He did well, that poor father! He placed his life in the hands of his Maker, asking only for mercy to his innocent children. And mercy has been shown to him and to them. He was taken gently in the way he wished. It would have broken my heart for those two poor girls if the verdict had gone otherwise. He knew how terrible a lot it is to be called a murderer's daughter."

I did not realise at the time with what profound depth of personal feeling she said it.

THE EPISODE OF THE
NEEDLE THAT DID NOT MATCH

"Sebastian is a great man," I said to Hilda Wade, as I sat one afternoon over a cup of tea she had brewed for me in her own little sitting-room. It is one of the alleviations of an hospital doctor's lot that he may drink tea now and again with the Sister of his ward. "Whatever else you choose to think of him, you must admit he is a very great man."

I admired our famous Professor, and I admired Hilda Wade: 'twas a matter of regret to me that my two admirations did not seem in return sufficiently to admire one another. "Oh, yes," Hilda answered, pouring out my second cup; "he is a very great man. I never denied that. The greatest man, on the whole, I think, that I have ever come across."

"And he has done splendid work for humanity," I went on, growing enthusiastic.

"Splendid work! Yes, splendid! (Two lumps, I believe?) He has done more, I admit, for medical science than any other man I ever met."

I gazed at her with a curious glance. "Then why, dear lady, do you keep telling me he is cruel?" I inquired, toasting my feet on the fender. "It seems contradictory."

She passed me the muffins, and smiled her restrained smile.

"Does the desire to do good to humanity in itself imply a benevolent disposition?" she answered, obliquely.

"Now you are talking in paradox. Surely, if a man works all his life long for the good of mankind, that shows he is devoured by sympathy for his species."

"And when your friend Mr. Bates works all his life long at observing, and classifying lady-birds, I suppose that shows he is devoured by sympathy for the race of beetles!"

I laughed at her comical face, she looked at me so quizzically. "But then," I objected, "the cases are not parallel. Bates kills and collects his lady-birds; Sebastian cures and benefits humanity."

Hilda smiled her wise smile once more, and fingered her apron. "Are the cases so different as you suppose?" she went on, with her quick glance. "Is it not partly accident? A man of science, you see, early in life, takes up, half by chance, this, that, or the other particular form of study. But what the study is in itself, I fancy, does not greatly matter; do not mere circumstances as often as not determine it? Surely it is the temperament, on the whole, that tells: the temperament that is or is not scientific."

"How do you mean? You *are* so enigmatic!"

"Well, in a family of the scientific temperament, it seems to me, one brother may happen to go in for butterflies—may he not?—and another for geology, or for submarine telegraphs. Now, the man who happens to take up butterflies does not make a fortune out of his hobby—there is no money in butterflies; so we say, accordingly, he is an unpractical person, who cares nothing for business, and who is only happy when he is out in the fields with a net, chasing emperors and tortoise-shells. But the man who happens to fancy submarine telegraphy most likely invents a lot of new improvements, takes out dozens of patents, finds money flow in upon him as he sits in his study, and becomes at last a peer and a millionaire; so then we say, What a splendid business head he has got, to be sure, and how immensely he differs from his poor woolgathering brother, the entomologist, who can only invent new ways of hatching out wire-worms! Yet all may really depend on the first chance direction which led one brother as a boy to buy a butterfly net, and sent the other into the school laboratory to dabble with an electric wheel and a cheap battery."

"Then you mean to say it is chance that has made Sebastian?"

Hilda shook her pretty head. "By no means. Don't be so stupid. We both know Sebastian has a wonderful brain. Whatever was the work he undertook with that brain in science, he would carry it out consummately. He is a born thinker. It is like this, don't you know." She tried to arrange her thoughts. "The particular branch of science to which Mr. Hiram Maxim's mind happens to have been directed was the making of machine-guns—and he slays his thousands. The particular branch to which Sebastian's mind happens to have been directed was medicine—and he cures as many as Mr. Maxim kills. It is a turn of the hand that makes all the difference."

"I see," I said. "The aim of medicine happens to be a benevolent one."

"Quite so; that's just what I mean. The aim is benevolent; and Sebastian pursues that aim with the single-minded energy of a lofty, gifted, and devoted nature—but not a good one!"

"Not good?"

"Oh, no. To be quite frank, he seems to me to pursue it ruthlessly, cruelly, unscrupulously. He is a man of high ideals, but without principle. In that respect he reminds one of the great spirits of the Italian Renaissance—Benvenuto Cellini and so forth—men who could pore for hours with conscientious artistic care over the detail of a hem in a sculptured robe, yet could steal out in the midst of their disinterested toil to plunge a knife in the back of a rival."

"Sebastian would not do that," I cried. "He is wholly free from the mean spirit of jealousy."

"No, Sebastian would not do that. You are quite right there; there is no tinge of meanness in the man's nature. He likes to be first in the field; but he would acclaim with delight another man's scientific triumph—if another anticipated him; for would it not mean a triumph for universal science?—and is not the advancement of science Sebastian's religion? But . . . he would do almost as much, or more. He would stab a man without remorse, if he thought that by stabbing him he could advance knowledge."

I recognised at once the truth of her diagnosis. "Nurse Wade," I cried, "you are a wonderful woman! I believe you are right; but—how did you come to think of it?"

A cloud passed over her brow. "I have reason to know it," she answered, slowly. Then her voice changed. "Take another muffin."

I helped myself and paused. I laid down my cup, and gazed at her. What a beautiful, tender, sympathetic face! And yet, how able! She stirred the fire uneasily. I looked and hesitated. I had often wondered why I never dared ask Hilda Wade one question that was nearest my heart. I think it must have been because I respected her so profoundly. The deeper your admiration and respect for a woman, the harder you find it in the end to ask her. At last I *almost* made up my mind. "I cannot think," I began, "what can have induced a girl like you, with means and friends, with brains and"— I drew back, then I plumped it out—"beauty, to take to such a life as this—a life which seems, in many ways, so unworthy of you!"

She stirred the fire more pensively than ever, and rearranged the muffin-dish on the little wrought-iron stand in font of the grate. "And yet," she murmured, looking down, "what life can be better than the service of one's kind? You think it a great life for Sebastian!"

"Sebastian! He is a man. That is different; quite different. But a woman! Especially *you*, dear lady, for whom one feels that nothing is quite high enough, quite pure enough, quite good enough. I cannot imagine how—"

She checked me with one wave of her gracious hand. Her movements were always slow and dignified. "I have a Plan in my life," she answered earnestly, her eyes meeting mine with a sincere, frank gaze; "a Plan to which I have resolved to sacrifice everything. It absorbs my being. Till that Plan is fulfilled—" I saw the tears were gathering fast on her lashes. She suppressed them with an effort. "Say no more," she added, faltering. "Infirm of purpose! I *will* not listen."

I leant forward eagerly, pressing my advantage. The air was electric. Waves of emotion passed to and fro. "But surely," I cried, "you do not mean to say—"

She waved me aside once more. "I will not put my hand to the plough, and then look back," she answered, firmly. "Dr. Cumberledge, spare me. I came to Nathaniel's for a purpose. I told you at the time what that purpose was—in part: to be near Sebastian. I want to be near him . . . for an object I have at heart. Do not ask me to reveal it; do not ask me to forego it. I am a woman, therefore weak. But I need your aid. Help me, instead of hindering me."

"Hilda," I cried, leaning forward, with quiverings of my heart, "I will help you in whatever way you will allow me. But let me at any rate help you with the feeling that I am helping one who means in time—"

At that moment, as unkindly fate would have it, the door opened, and Sebastian entered.

"Nurse Wade," he began, in his iron voice, glancing about him with stern eyes, "where are those needles I ordered for that operation? We must be ready in time before Nielsen comes. . . . Cumberledge, I shall want you."

The golden opportunity had come and gone. It was long before I found a similar occasion for speaking to Hilda.

Every day after that the feeling deepened upon me that Hilda was there to watch Sebastian. *Why*, I did not know; but it was growing certain that a life-long duel was in progress between these two— a duel of some strange and mysterious import.

The first approach to a solution of the problem which I obtained came a week or two later. Sebastian was engaged in observing a case where certain unusual symptoms had suddenly supervened. It was a case of some obscure affection of the heart. I will not trouble you here with the particular details. We all suspected a tendency to aneurism. Hilda Wade was in attendance, as she always was on Sebastian's observation cases. We crowded round, watching. The Professor himself leaned over the cot with some medicine for external application in a basin. He gave it to Hilda to hold. I noticed that as she held it her fingers trembled, and that her eyes were fixed harder than ever upon Sebastian. He turned round to his students. "Now this," he began, in a very unconcerned voice, as if the patient were a toad, "is a most unwonted turn for the disease to take. It occurs very seldom. In point of fact, I have only observed the symptom once before; and then it was fatal. The patient in that instance"—he paused dramatically—"was the notorious poisoner, Dr. Yorke-Bannerman."

As he uttered the words, Hilda Wade's hands trembled more than ever, and with a little scream she let the basin fall, breaking it into fragments.

Sebastian's keen eyes had transfixed her in a second. "How did you manage to do that?" he asked, with quiet sarcasm, but in a tone full of meaning.

"The basin was heavy," Hilda faltered. "My hands were trembling—and it somehow slipped through them. I am not . . . quite myself . . . not quite well this afternoon. I ought not to have attempted it."

The Professor's deep-set eyes peered out like gleaming lights from beneath their overhanging brows. "No; you ought not to have attempted it," he answered, withering her with a glance. "You might have let the thing fall on the patient and killed him. As it is, can't you see you have agitated him with the flurry? Don't stand there holding your breath, woman: repair your mischief. Get a cloth and wipe it up, and give *me* the bottle."

With skilful haste he administered a little sal volatile and nux vomica to the swooning patient; while Hilda set about remedying the damage. "That's better," Sebastian said, in a mollified tone, when she had brought another basin. There was a singular note of cloaked triumph in his voice. "Now, we'll begin again. . . . I was just saying, gentlemen, before this accident, that I had seen only *one* case of this peculiar form of the tendency before; and that case was the notorious"—he kept his glittering eyes fixed harder on Hilda than ever—"the notorious Dr. Yorke-Bannerman."

I was watching Hilda, too. At the words, she trembled violently all over once more, but with an effort restrained herself. Their looks met in a searching glance. Hilda's air was proud and fearless: in Sebastian's, I fancied I detected, after a second, just a tinge of wavering.

"You remember Yorke-Bannerman's case," he went on. "He committed a murder—"

"Let *me* take the basin!" I cried, for I saw Hilda's hands giving way a second time, and I was anxious to spare her.

"No, thank you," she answered low, but in a voice that was full of suppressed defiance. "I will wait and hear this out. I *prefer* to stop here."

As for Sebastian, he seemed now not to notice her, though I was aware all the time of a sidelong glance of his eye, parrot-wise, in her direction. "He committed a murder," he went on, "by means of aconitine—then an almost unknown poison; and, after committing it, his heart being already weak, he was taken himself with symptoms of aneurism in a curious form, essentially similar to these; so that he died before the trial—a lucky escape for him."

He paused rhetorically once more; then he added in the same tone: "Mental agitation and the terror of detection no doubt accelerated the fatal result in that instance. He died at once from the shock of the arrest. It was a natural conclusion. Here we may hope for a more successful issue."

He spoke to the students, of course, but I could see for all that that he was keeping his falcon eye fixed hard on Hilda's face. I glanced aside at her. She never flinched for a second. Neither said anything directly to the other; still, by their eyes and mouths, I knew some strange passage of arms had taken place between them. Sebastian's tone was one of provocation, of defiance, I might almost say of challenge. Hilda's air I took rather for the air of calm and resolute, but assured, resistance. He expected her to answer; she said nothing. Instead of that, she went on holding the basin now with fingers that *would* not tremble. Every muscle was strained. Every tendon was strung. I could see she held herself in with a will of iron.

The rest of the episode passed off quietly. Sebastian, having delivered his bolt, began to think less of Hilda and more of the patient. He went on with his demonstration. As for Hilda, she gradually relaxed her muscles, and, with a deep-drawn breath, resumed her natural attitude. The tension was over. They had had their little skirmish, whatever it might mean, and had it out; now, they called a truce over the patient's body.

When the case had been disposed of, and the students dismissed, I went straight into the laboratory to get a few surgical instruments I had chanced to leave there. For a minute or two, I mislaid my clinical thermometer, and began hunting for it behind a wooden partition in the corner of the room by the place for washing test-tubes. As I stooped down, turning over the various objects

about the tap in my search, Sebastian's voice came to me. He had
paused outside the door, and was speaking in his calm, clear tone,
very low, to Hilda. "So *now* we understand one another, Nurse
Wade," he said, with a significant sneer. "I know whom I have to
deal with!"

"And *I* know, too," Hilda answered, in a voice of placid confidence.

"Yet you are not afraid?"

"It is not *I* who have cause for fear. The accused may tremble,
not the prosecutor."

"What! You threaten?"

"No; I do not threaten. Not in words, I mean. My presence here
is in itself a threat, but I make no other. You know now, unfortunately, *why* I have come. That makes my task harder. But I will
not give it up. I will wait and conquer."

Sebastian answered nothing. He strode into the laboratory
alone, tall, grim, unbending, and let himself sink into his easy chair,
looking up with a singular and somewhat sinister smile at his
bottles of microbes. After a minute he stirred the fire, and bent his
head forward, brooding. He held it between his hands, with his
elbows on his knees, and gazed moodily straight before him into the
glowing caves of white-hot coal in the fireplace. That sinister smile
still played lambent around the corners of his grizzled moustaches.

I moved noiselessly towards the door, trying to pass behind him
unnoticed. But, alert as ever, his quick ears detected me. With a
sudden start, he raised his head and glanced round. "What! you
here?" he cried, taken aback. For a second he appeared almost to
lose his self-possession.

"I came for my clinical," I answered, with an unconcerned air.
"I have somehow managed to mislay it in the laboratory."

My carefully casual tone seemed to reassure him. He peered
about him with knit brows. "Cumberledge," he asked at last, in a
suspicious voice, "did you hear that woman?"

"The woman in 93? Delirious?"

"No, no. Nurse Wade?"

"Hear her?" I echoed, I must candidly admit with intent to deceive. "When she broke the basin?"

His forehead relaxed. "Oh! it is nothing," he muttered, hastily. "A mere point of discipline. She spoke to me just now, and I thought her tone unbecoming in a subordinate. . . . Like Korah and his crew, she takes too much upon her. . . . We must get rid of her, Cumberledge; we must get rid of her. She is a dangerous woman!"

"She is the most intelligent nurse we have ever had in the place, sir," I objected, stoutly.

He nodded his head twice. "Intelligent—*je vous l'accorde*; but dangerous—dangerous!"

Then he turned to his papers, sorting them out one by one with a preoccupied face and twitching fingers. I recognised that he desired to be left alone, so I quitted the laboratory.

I cannot quite say *why*, but ever since Hilda Wade first came to Nathaniel's my enthusiasm for Sebastian had been cooling continuously. Admiring his greatness still, I had doubts as to his goodness. That day I felt I positively mistrusted him. I wondered what his passage of arms with Hilda might mean. Yet, somehow, I was shy of alluding to it before her.

One thing, however, was clear to me now—this great campaign that was being waged between the nurse and the Professor had reference to the case of Dr. Yorke-Bannerman.

For a time, nothing came of it; the routine of the hospital went on as usual. The patient with the suspected predisposition to aneurism kept fairly well for a week or two, and then took a sudden turn for the worse, presenting at times most unwonted symptoms. He died unexpectedly. Sebastian, who had watched him every hour, regarded the matter as of prime importance. "I'm glad it happened here," he said, rubbing his hands. "A grand opportunity. I wanted to catch an instance like this before that fellow in Paris had time to anticipate me. They're all on the lookout. Von Strahlendorff, of Vienna, has been waiting for just such a patient for years. So have I. Now fortune has favoured me. Lucky for us he died! We shall find out everything."

We held a post-mortem, of course, the condition of the blood being what we most wished to observe; and the autopsy revealed some unexpected details. One remarkable feature consisted in a certain undescribed and impoverished state of the contained bodies which Sebastian, with his eager zeal for science, desired his students to see and identify. He said it was likely to throw much light on other ill-understood conditions of the brain and nervous system, as well as on the peculiar faint odour of the insane, now so well recognised in all large asylums. In order to compare this abnormal state with the aspect of the healthy circulating medium, he proposed to examine a little good living blood side by side with the morbid specimen under the microscope. Nurse Wade was in attendance in the laboratory, as usual. The Professor, standing by the instrument, with one hand on the brass screw, had got the diseased drop ready arranged for our inspection beforehand, and was gloating over it himself with scientific enthusiasm. "Grey corpuscles, you will observe," he said, "almost entirely deficient. Red, poor in number, and irregular in outline. Plasma, thin. Nuclei, feeble. A state of body which tells severely against the due rebuilding of the wasted tissues. Now compare with typical normal specimen." He removed his eye from the microscope, and wiped a glass slide with a clean cloth as he spoke. "Nurse Wade, we know of old the purity and vigour of your circulating fluid. You shall have the honour of advancing science once more. Hold up your finger."

Hilda held up her forefinger unhesitatingly. She was used to such requests; and, indeed, Sebastian had acquired by long experience the faculty of pinching the finger-tip so hard, and pressing the point of a needle so dexterously into a minor vessel, that he could draw at once a small drop of blood without the subject even feeling it.

The Professor nipped the last joint between his finger and thumb for a moment till it was black at the end; then he turned to the saucer at his side, which Hilda herself had placed there, and chose from it, cat-like, with great deliberation and selective care, a particular needle. Hilda's eyes followed his every movement as closely and as fearlessly as ever. Sebastian's hand was raised, and he was just about to pierce the delicate white skin, when, with a sudden, quick scream of terror, she snatched her hand away hastily.

The Professor let the needle drop in his astonishment. "What did you do that for?" he cried, with an angry dart of the keen eyes. "This is not the first time I have drawn your blood. You *knew* I would not hurt you."

Hilda's face had grown strangely pale. But that was not all. I believe I was the only person present who noticed one unobtrusive piece of sleight-of-hand which she hurriedly and skilfully executed. When the needle slipped from Sebastian's hand, she leant forward even as she screamed, and caught it, unobserved, in the folds of her apron. Then her nimble fingers closed over it as if by magic, and conveyed it with a rapid movement at once to her pocket. I do not think even Sebastian himself noticed the quick forward jerk of her eager hands, which would have done honour to a conjurer. He was too much taken aback by her unexpected behaviour to observe the needle.

Just as she caught it, Hilda answered his question in a somewhat flurried voice. "I—I was afraid," she broke out, gasping. "One gets these little accesses of terror now and again. I—I feel rather weak. I don't think I will volunteer to supply any more normal blood this morning."

Sebastian's acute eyes read her through, as so often. With a trenchant dart he glanced from her to me. I could see he began to suspect a confederacy. "That will do," he went on, with slow deliberateness. "Better so. Nurse Wade, I don't know what's beginning to come over you. You are losing your nerve—which is fatal in a nurse. Only the other day you let fall and broke a basin at a most critical moment; and now, you scream aloud on a trifling apprehension." He paused and glanced around him. "Mr. Callaghan," he said, turning to our tall, red-haired Irish student, "*your* blood is good normal, and *you* are not hysterical." He selected another needle with studious care. "Give me your finger."

As he picked out the needle, I saw Hilda lean forward again, alert and watchful, eyeing him with a piercing glance; but, after a second's consideration, she seemed to satisfy herself, and fell back without a word. I gathered that she was ready to interfere, had occasion demanded. But occasion did not demand; and she held her peace quietly.

The rest of the examination proceeded without a hitch. For a minute or two, it is true, I fancied that Sebastian betrayed a certain suppressed agitation—a trifling lack of his accustomed perspicuity and his luminous exposition. But, after meandering for a while through a few vague sentences, he soon recovered his wonted calm; and as he went on with his demonstration, throwing himself eagerly into the case, his usual scientific enthusiasm came back to him undiminished. He waxed eloquent (after his fashion) over the "beautiful" contrast between Callaghan's wholesome blood, "rich in the vivifying architectonic grey corpuscles which rebuild worn tissues," and the effete, impoverished, unvitalised fluid which stagnated in the sluggish veins of the dead patient. The carriers of oxygen had neglected their proper task; the granules whose duty it was to bring elaborated food-stuffs to supply the waste of brain and nerve and muscle had forgotten their cunning. The bricklayers of the bodily fabric had gone out on strike; the weary scavengers had declined to remove the useless by-products. His vivid tongue, his picturesque fancy, ran away with him. I had never heard him talk better or more incisively before; one could feel sure, as he spoke, that the arteries of his own acute and teeming brain at that moment of exaltation were by no means deficient in those energetic and highly vital globules on whose reparative worth he so eloquently descanted. "Sure, the Professor makes annywan see right inside wan's own vascular system," Callaghan whispered aside to me, in unfeigned admiration.

The demonstration ended in impressive silence. As we streamed out of the laboratory, aglow with his electric fire, Sebastian held me back with a bent motion of his shrivelled forefinger. I stayed behind unwillingly. "Yes, sir?" I said, in an interrogative voice.

The Professor's eyes were fixed intently on the ceiling. His look was one of rapt inspiration. I stood and waited. "Cumberledge," he said at last, coming back to earth with a start, "I see it more plainly each day that goes. We must get rid of that woman."

"Of Nurse Wade?" I asked, catching my breath.

He roped the grizzled moustache, and blinked the sunken eyes. "She has lost nerve," he went on, "lost nerve entirely. I shall suggest that she be dismissed. Her sudden failures of stamina are most embarrassing at critical junctures."

"Very well, sir," I answered, swallowing a lump in my throat. To say the truth, I was beginning to be afraid on Hilda's account. That morning's events had thoroughly disquieted me.

He seemed relieved at my unquestioning acquiescence. "She is a dangerous edged-tool; that's the truth of it," he went on, still twirling his moustache with a preoccupied air, and turning over his stock of needles. "When she's clothed and in her right mind, she is a valuable accessory—sharp and trenchant like a clean, bright lancet; but when she allows one of these causeless hysterical fits to override her tone, she plays one false at once—like a lancet that slips, or grows dull and rusty." He polished one of the needles on a soft square of new chamois-leather while he spoke, as if to give point and illustration to his simile.

I went out from him, much perturbed. The Sebastian I had once admired and worshipped was beginning to pass from me; in his place I found a very complex and inferior creation. My idol had feet of clay. I was loth to acknowledge it.

I stalked along the corridor moodily towards my own room. As I passed Hilda Wade's door, I saw it half ajar. She stood a little within, and beckoned me to enter.

I passed in and closed the door behind me. Hilda looked at me with trustful eyes. Resolute still, her face was yet that of a hunted creature. "Thank Heaven, I have *one* friend here, at least!" she said, slowly seating herself. "You saw me catch and conceal the needle?"

"Yes, I saw you."

She drew it forth from her purse, carefully but loosely wrapped up in a small tag of tissue-paper. "Here it is!" she said, displaying it. "Now, I want you to test it."

"In a culture?" I asked; for I guessed her meaning.

She nodded. "Yes, to see what that man has done to it."

"What do you suspect?"

She shrugged her graceful shoulders half imperceptibly.

"How should I know? Anything!"

I gazed at the needle closely. "What made you distrust it?" I inquired at last, still eyeing it.

She opened a drawer, and took out several others. "See here," she said, handing me one; "*These* are the needles I keep in anti-septic wool—the needles with which I always supply the Profes-sor. You observe their shape—the common surgical patterns. Now, look at *this* needle, with which the Professor was just going to prick my finger! You can see for yourself at once it is of bluer steel and of a different manufacture."

"That is quite true," I answered, examining it with my pocket lens, which I always carry. "I see the difference. But how did you detect it?"

"From his face, partly; but partly, too, from the needle itself. I had my suspicions, and I was watching him closely. Just as he raised the thing in his hand, half concealing it, so, and showing only the point, I caught the blue gleam of the steel as the light glanced off it. It was not the kind I knew. Then I withdrew my hand at once, feeling sure he meant mischief."

"That was wonderfully quick of you!"

"Quick? Well, yes. Thank Heaven, my mind works fast; my per-ceptions are rapid. Otherwise—" she looked grave. "One second more, and it would have been too late. The man might have killed me."

"You think it is poisoned, then?"

Hilda shook her head with confident dissent. "Poisoned? Oh, no. He is wiser now. Fifteen years ago, he used poison. But science has made gigantic strides since then. He would not needlessly ex-pose himself to-day to the risks of the poisoner."

"Fifteen years ago he used poison?"

She nodded, with the air of one who knows. "I am not speaking at random," she answered. "I say what I know. Some day I will ex-plain. For the present, it is enough to tell you I know it."

"And what do you suspect now?" I asked, the weird sense of her strange power deepening on me every second.

She held up the incriminated needle again.

"Do you see this groove?" she asked, pointing to it with the tip of another.

I examined it once more at the light with the lens. A longitudinal groove, apparently ground into one side of the needle, lengthwise, by means of a small grinding-stone and emery powder, ran for a quarter of an inch above the point. This groove seemed to me to have been produced by an amateur, though he must have been one accustomed to delicate microscopic manipulation; for the edges under the lens showed slightly rough, like the surface of a file on a small scale: not smooth and polished, as a needle-maker would have left them. I said so to Hilda.

"You are quite right," she answered. "That is just what it shows. I feel sure Sebastian made that groove himself. He could have bought grooved needles, it is true, such as they sometimes use for retaining small quantities of lymphs and medicines; but we had none in stock, and to buy them would be to manufacture evidence against himself, in case of detection. Besides, the rough, jagged edge would hold the material he wished to inject all the better, while its saw-like points would tear the flesh, imperceptibly, but minutely, and so serve his purpose."

"Which was?"

"Try the needle, and judge for yourself. I prefer you should find out. You can tell me to-morrow."

"It was quick of you to detect it!" I cried, still turning the suspicious object over. "The difference is so slight."

"Yes; but you tell me my eyes are as sharp as the needle. Besides, I had reason to doubt; and Sebastian himself gave me the clue by selecting his instrument with too great deliberation. He had put it there with the rest, but it lay a little apart; and as he picked it up gingerly, I began to doubt. When I saw the blue gleam, my doubt was at once converted into certainty. Then his eyes, too, had the look which I know means victory. Benign or baleful, it goes with his triumphs. I have seen that look before, and when once it lurks scintillating in the luminous depths of his gleaming eyeballs, I recognise at once that, whatever his aim, he has succeeded in it."

"Still, Hilda, I am loth—"

She waved her hand impatiently. "Waste no time," she cried, in an authoritative voice. "If you happen to let that needle rub carelessly against the sleeve of your coat you may destroy the evidence. Take it at once to your room, plunge it into a culture, and lock it up safe at a proper temperature—where Sebastian cannot get at it—till the consequences develop."

I did as she bid me. By this time, I was not wholly unprepared for the result she anticipated. My belief in Sebastian had sunk to zero, and was rapidly reaching a negative quantity.

At nine the next morning, I tested one drop of the culture under the microscope. Clear and limpid to the naked eye, it was alive with small objects of a most suspicious nature, when properly magnified. I knew those hungry forms. Still, I would not decide offhand on my own authority in a matter of such moment. Sebas-tian's character was at stake—the character of the man who led the profession. I called in Callaghan, who happened to be in the ward, and asked him to put his eye to the instrument for a moment. He was a splendid fellow for the use of high powers, and I had magnified the culture 300 diameters. "What do you call those?" I asked, breathless.

He scanned them carefully with his experienced eye. "Is it the microbes ye mean?" he answered. "An' what 'ud they be, then, if it wasn't the bacillus of pyaemia?"

"Blood-poisoning!" I ejaculated, horror-struck.

"Aye; blood-poisoning: that's the English of it."

I assumed an air of indifference. "I made them that myself," I rejoined, as if they were mere ordinary experimental germs; "but I wanted confirmation of my own opinion. You're sure of the bacillus?"

"An' haven't I been keeping swarms of those very same bacteria under close observation for Sebastian for seven weeks past? Why, I know them as well as I know me own mother."

"Thank you," I said. "That will do." And I carried off the microscope, bacilli and all, into Hilda Wade's sitting-room. "Look yourself!" I cried to her.

She stared at them through the instrument with an unmoved face. "I thought so," she answered shortly. "The bacillus of pyaemia. A most virulent type. Exactly what I expected."

"You anticipated that result?"

"Absolutely. You see, blood-poisoning matures quickly, and kills almost to a certainty. Delirium supervenes so soon that the patient has no chance of explaining suspicions. Besides, it would all seem so very natural! Everybody would say: 'She got some slight wound, which microbes from some case she was attending contaminated.' You may be sure Sebastian thought out all that. He plans with consummate skill. He had designed everything."

I gazed at her, uncertain. "And what will you *do?*" I asked. "Expose him?"

She opened both her palms with a blank gesture of helplessness. "It is useless!" she answered. "Nobody would believe me. Consider the situation. *You* know the needle I gave you was the one Sebastian meant to use—the one he dropped and I caught— *because* you are a friend of mine, and because you have learned to trust me. But who else would credit it? I have only my word against his—an unknown nurse's against the great Professor's. Everybody would say I was malicious or hysterical. Hysteria is always an easy stone to fling at an injured woman who asks for justice. They would declare I had trumped up the case to forestall my dismissal. They would set it down to spite. We can do nothing against him. Remember, on his part, the utter absence of overt motive."

"And you mean to stop on here, in close attendance on a man who has attempted your life?" I cried, really alarmed for her safety.

"I am not sure about that," she answered. "I must take time to think. My presence at Nathaniel's was necessary to my Plan. The Plan fails for the present. I have now to look round and reconsider my position."

"But you are not safe here now," I urged, growing warm. "If Sebastian really wishes to get rid of you, and is as unscrupulous as you suppose, with his gigantic brain he can soon compass his end. What he plans he executes. You ought not to remain within the Professor's reach one hour longer."

"I have thought of that, too," she replied, with an almost unearthly calm. "But there are difficulties either way. At any rate, I am glad he did not succeed this time. For, to have killed me now,

would have frustrated my Plan"—she clasped her hands—"my Plan
is ten thousand times dearer than life to me!"

"Dear lady!" I cried, drawing a deep breath, "I implore you in
this strait, listen to what I urge. Why fight your battle alone? Why
refuse assistance? I have admired you so long—I am so eager to
help you. If only you will allow me to call you—"

Her eyes brightened and softened. Her whole bosom heaved. I
felt in a flash she was not wholly indifferent to me. Strange trem-
ors in the air seemed to play about us. But she waved me aside
once more. "Don't press me," she said, in a very low voice. "Let me
go my own way. It is hard enough already, this task I have under-
taken, without *your* making it harder. . . . Dear friend, dear friend,
you don't quite understand. There are *two* men at Nathaniel's
whom I desire to escape—because they both alike stand in the way
of my Purpose." She took my hands in hers. "Each in a different
way," she murmured once more. "But each I must avoid. One is
Sebastian. The other—" she let my hand drop again, and broke off
suddenly. "Dear Hubert," she cried, with a catch, "I cannot help it:
forgive me!"

It was the first time she had ever called me by my Christian
name. The mere sound of the word made me unspeakably happy.

Yet she waved me away. "Must I go?" I asked, quivering.

"Yes, yes: you must go. I cannot stand it. I must think this thing
out, undisturbed. It is a very great crisis."

That afternoon and evening, by some unhappy chance, I was
fully engaged in work at the hospital. Late at night a letter arrived
for me. I glanced at it in dismay. It bore the Basingstoke postmark.
But, to my alarm and surprise, it was in Hilda's hand. What could
this change portend? I opened it, all tremulous.

"Dear Hubert,—" I gave a sigh of relief. It was no longer "Dear
Dr. Cumberledge" now, but "Hubert." That was something gained,
at any rate. I read on with a beating heart. What had Hilda to say
to me?

"Dear Hubert,—By the time this reaches you, I
shall be far away, irrevocably far, from London. With

deep regret, with fierce searchings of spirit, I have come to the conclusion that, for the Purpose I have in view, it would be better for me at once to leave Nathaniel's. Where I go, or what I mean to do, I do not wish to tell you. Of your charity, I pray, refrain from asking me. I am aware that your kindness and generosity deserve better recognition. But, like Sebastian himself, I am the slave of my Purpose. I have lived for it all these years, and it is still very dear to me. To tell you my plans would interfere with that end. Do not, therefore, suppose I am insensible to your goodness. . . . Dear Hubert, spare me—I dare not say more, lest I say too much. I dare not trust myself. But one thing I *must* say. I am flying from *you* quite as much as from Sebastian. Flying from my own heart, quite as much as from my enemy. Some day, perhaps, if I accomplish my object, I may tell you all. Meanwhile, I can only beg of you of your kindness to trust me. We shall not meet again, I fear, for years. But I shall never forget you—you, the kind counsellor, who have half turned me aside from my life's Purpose. One word more, and I should falter.— In very great haste, and amid much disturbance, yours ever affectionately and gratefully,

"Hilda."

It was a hurried scrawl in pencil, as if written in a train. I felt utterly dejected. Was Hilda, then, leaving England?

Rousing myself after some minutes, I went straight to Sebastian's rooms, and told him in brief terms that Nurse Wade had disappeared at a moment's notice, and had sent a note to tell me so.

He looked up from his work, and scanned me hard, as was his wont. "That is well," he said at last, his eyes glowing deep; "she was getting too great a hold on you, that young woman!"

"She retains that hold upon me, sir," I answered curtly.

"You are making a grave mistake in life, my dear Cumberledge," he went on, in his old genial tone, which I had almost forgotten. "Before you go further, and entangle yourself more deeply, I think it is only right that I should undeceive you as to this girl's true position. She is passing under a false name, and she comes of a tainted stock. . . . Nurse Wade, as she chooses to call herself, is a daughter of the notorious murderer, Yorke-Bannerman."

My mind leapt back to the incident of the broken basin. Yorke-Bannerman's name had profoundly moved her. Then I thought of Hilda's face. Murderers, I said to myself, do not beget such daughters as that. Not even accidental murderers, like my poor friend Le Geyt. I saw at once the prima facie evidence was strongly against her. But I had faith in her still. I drew myself up firmly, and stared him back full in the face. "I do not believe it," I answered, shortly.

"You do not believe it? I tell you it is so. The girl herself as good as acknowledged it to me."

I spoke slowly and distinctly. "Dr. Sebastian," I said, confronting him, "let us be quite clear with one another. I have found you out. I know how you tried to poison that lady. To poison her with bacilli which *I* detected. I cannot trust your word; I cannot trust your inferences. Either she is not Yorke-Bannerman's daughter at all, or else . . . Yorke-Bannerman was *not* a murderer. . . ." I watched his face closely. Conviction leaped upon me. "And someone else was," I went on. "I might put a name to him."

With a stern white face, he rose and opened the door. He pointed to it slowly. "This hospital is not big enough for you and me abreast," he said, with cold politeness. "One or other of us must go. Which, I leave to your good sense to determine."

Even at that moment of detection and disgrace, in one man's eyes, at least, Sebastian retained his full measure of dignity.

THE EPISODE OF THE LETTER
WITH THE BASINGSTOKE POSTMARK

I have a vast respect for my grandfather. He was a man of forethought. He left me a modest little income of seven hundred a-year, well invested. Now, seven hundred a-year is not exactly wealth; but it is an unobtrusive competence; it permits a bachelor to move about the world and choose at will his own profession. *I* chose medicine; but I was not wholly dependent upon it. So I honoured my grandfather's wise disposition of his worldly goods; though, oddly enough, my cousin Tom (to whom he left his watch and five hundred pounds) speaks *most* disrespectfully of his character and intellect.

Thanks to my grandfather's silken-sailed barque, therefore, when I found myself practically dismissed from Nathaniel's I was not thrown on my beam-ends, as most young men in my position would have been; I had time and opportunity for the favourite pastime of looking about me. Of course, had I chosen, I might have fought the case to the bitter end against Sebastian; he could not dismiss me—that lay with the committee. But I hardly cared to fight. In the first place, though I had found him out as a man, I still respected him as a great teacher; and in the second place (which is always more important), I wanted to find and follow Hilda.

To be sure, Hilda, in that enigmatic letter of hers, had implored me not to seek her out; but I think you will admit there is one request which no man can grant to the girl he loves—and that is the request to keep away from her. If Hilda did not want *me*, I wanted Hilda; and, being a man, I meant to find her.

My chances of discovering her whereabouts, however, I had to confess to myself (when it came to the point) were extremely slender. She had vanished from my horizon, melted into space. My sole hint of a clue consisted in the fact that the letter she sent me had been posted at Basingstoke. Here, then, was my problem: given an envelope with the Basingstoke postmark, to find in what part of Europe, Asia, Africa, or America the writer of it might be discovered. It opened up a fine field for speculation.

When I set out to face this broad puzzle, my first idea was: "I must ask Hilda." In all circumstances of difficulty, I had grown accustomed to submitting my doubts and surmises to her acute intelligence; and her instinct almost always supplied the right solution. But now Hilda was gone; it was Hilda herself I wished to track through the labyrinth of the world. I could expect no assistance in tracking her from Hilda.

"Let me think," I said to myself, over a reflective pipe, with feet poised on the fender. "How would Hilda herself have approached this problem? Imagine I'm Hilda. I must try to strike a trail by applying her own methods to her own character. She would have attacked the question, no doubt,"—here I eyed my pipe wisely,—"from the psychological side. She would have asked herself"—I stroked my chin—"what such a temperament as hers was likely to do under such-and-such circumstances. And she would have answered it aright. But then"—I puffed away once or twice—"*she* is Hilda."

When I came to reconnoitre the matter in this light, I became at once aware how great a gulf separated the clumsy male intelligence from the immediate and almost unerring intuitions of a clever woman. I am considered no fool; in my own profession, I may venture to say, I was Sebastian's favourite pupil. Yet, though I asked myself over and over again where Hilda would be likely to go—Canada, China, Australia—as the outcome of her character, in these given conditions, I got no answer. I stared at the fire and reflected. I smoked two successive pipes, and shook out the ashes. "Let me consider how Hilda's temperament would work," I said, looking sagacious. I said it several times—but there I stuck. I went no further. The solution would not come. I felt that in order to play Hilda's part, it was necessary first to have Hilda's head-piece. Not every man can bend the bow of Ulysses.

As I turned the problem over in my mind, however, one phrase at last came back to me—a phrase which Hilda herself had let fall when we were debating a very similar point about poor Hugo Le Geyt: "If I were in his place, what do you think I would do?—why, hide myself at once in the greenest recesses of our Carnarvonshire mountains."

She must have gone to Wales, then. I had her own authority for saying so. . . . And yet—Wales? Wales? I pulled myself up with a jerk. In that case, how did she come to be passing by Basingstoke?

Was the postmark a blind? Had she hired someone to take the letter somewhere for her, on purpose to put me off on a false track? I could hardly think so. Besides, the time was against it. I saw Hilda at Nathaniel's in the morning; the very same evening I received the envelope with the Basingstoke postmark.

"If I were in his place." Yes, true; but, now I come to think on it, *were* the positions really parallel? Hilda was not flying for her life from justice; she was only endeavouring to escape Sebastian— and myself. The instances she had quoted of the mountaineer's curious homing instinct—the wild yearning he feels at moments of great straits to bury himself among the nooks of his native hills— were they not all instances of murderers pursued by the police? It was abject terror that drove these men to their burrows. But Hilda was not a murderer; she was not dogged by remorse, despair, or the myrmidons of the law; it was murder she was avoiding, not the punishment of murder. That made, of course, an obvious differ- ence. "Irrevocably far from London," she said. Wales is a suburb. I gave up the idea that it was likely to prove her place of refuge from the two men she was bent on escaping. Hong-Kong, after all, seemed more probable than Llanberis.

That first failure gave me a clue, however, as to the best way of applying Hilda's own methods. "What would such a person do under the circumstances?" that was her way of putting the question. Clearly, then, I must first decide what *were* the circumstances. Was

Sebastian speaking the truth? Was Hilda Wade, or was she not, the daughter of the supposed murderer, Dr. Yorke-Bannerman?

I looked up as much of the case as I could, in unobtrusive ways, among the old law-reports, and found that the barrister who had had charge of the defence was my father's old friend, Mr. Horace Mayfield, a man of elegant tastes, and the means to gratify them.

I went to call on him on Sunday evening at his artistically luxurious house in Onslow Gardens. A sedate footman answered the bell. Fortunately, Mr. Mayfield was at home, and, what is rarer, disengaged. You do not always find a successful Q.C. at his ease among his books, beneath the electric light, ready to give up a vacant hour to friendly colloquy.

"Remember Yorke-Bannerman's case?" he said, a huge smile breaking slowly like a wave over his genial fat face—Horace Mayfield resembles a great good-humoured toad, with bland manners and a capacious double chin—"I should just say I *did!* Bless my soul—why, yes," he beamed, "I was Yorke-Bannerman's counsel. Excellent fellow, Yorke-Bannerman—most unfortunate end, though—precious clever chap, too! Had an astounding memory. Recollected every symptom of every patient he ever attended. And *such* an eye! Diagnosis? It was clairvoyance! A gift—no less. Knew what was the matter with you the moment he looked at you."

That sounded like Hilda. The same surprising power of recalling facts; the same keen faculty for interpreting character or the signs of feeling. "He poisoned somebody, I believe," I murmured, casually. "An uncle of his, or something."

Mayfield's great squat face wrinkled; the double chin, folding down on the neck, became more ostentatiously double than ever. "Well, I can't admit that," he said, in his suave voice, twirling the string of his eye-glass. "I was Yorke-Bannerman's advocate, you see; and therefore I was paid not to admit it. Besides, he was a friend of mine, and I always liked him. But I *will* allow that the case *did* look a trifle black against him."

"Ha? Looked black, did it?" I faltered.

The judicious barrister shrugged his shoulders. A genial smile spread oilily once more over his smooth face. "None of my business to say so," he answered, puckering the corners of his eyes. "Still, it was a long time ago; and the circumstances certainly *were* suspicious. Perhaps, on the whole, Hubert, it was just as well the poor fellow died before the trial came off; otherwise"—he pouted his lips—"I might have had my work cut out to save him." And he eyed the blue china gods on the mantelpiece affectionately.

"I believe the Crown urged money as the motive?" I suggested.

Mayfield glanced inquiry at me. "Now, why do you want to know all this?" he asked, in a suspicious voice, coming back from his dragons. "It is irregular, very, to worm information out of an innocent barrister in his hours of ease about a former client. We are a guileless race, we lawyers; don't abuse our confidence."

He seemed an honest man, I thought, in spite of his mocking tone. I trusted him, and made a clean breast of it. "I believe," I answered, with an impressive little pause, "I want to marry Yorke-Bannerman's daughter."

He gave a quick start. "What, Maisie?" he exclaimed.

I shook my head. "No, no; that is not the name," I replied.

He hesitated a moment. "But there *is* no other," he hazarded cautiously at last. "I knew the family."

"I am not sure of it," I went on. "I have merely my suspicions. I am in love with a girl, and something about her makes me think she is probably a Yorke-Bannerman."

"But, my dear Hubert, if that is so," the great lawyer went on, waving me off with one fat hand, "it must be at once apparent to you that *I* am the last person on earth to whom you ought to apply for information. Remember my oath. The practice of our clan: the seal of secrecy!"

I was frank once more. "I do not know whether the lady I mean is or is not Yorke-Bannerman's daughter," I persisted. "She may be, and she may not. She gives another name—that's certain. But whether she is or isn't, one thing I know—I mean to marry her. I believe in her; I trust her. I only seek to gain this information now because I don't know where she is—and I want to track her."

He crossed his big hands with an air of Christian resignation, and looked up at the panels of the coffered ceiling. "In that," he answered, "I may honestly say, I can't help you. Humbug apart, I have not known Mrs. Yorke-Bannerman's address—or Maisie's either— ever since my poor friend's death. Prudent woman, Mrs. Yorke-Bannerman! She went away, I believe, to somewhere in North Wales, and afterwards to Brittany. But she probably changed her name; and—she did not confide in me."

I went on to ask him a few questions about the case, premising that I did so in the most friendly spirit. "Oh, I can only tell you what is publicly known," he answered, beaming, with the usual professional pretence of the most sphinx-like reticence. "But the plain facts, as universally admitted, were these. I break no confidence. Yorke-Bannerman had a rich uncle from whom he had expectations—a certain Admiral Scott Prideaux. This uncle had lately made a will in Yorke-Bannerman's favour; but he was a cantankerous old chap—naval, you know autocratic—crusty—given to changing his mind with each change of the wind, and easily offended by his relations—the sort of cheerful old party who makes a new will once every month, disinheriting the nephew he last dined with. Well, one day the Admiral was taken ill, at his own house, and Yorke-Bannerman attended him. *Our* contention was—I speak now as my old friend's counsel—that Scott Prideaux, getting as tired of life as we were all tired of him, and weary of this recurrent worry of will-making, determined at last to clear out for good from a world where he was so little appreciated, and, therefore, tried to poison himself."

"With aconitine?" I suggested, eagerly.

"Unfortunately, yes; he made use of aconitine for that otherwise laudable purpose. Now, as ill luck would have it"—Mayfield's wrinkles deepened—"Yorke-Bannerman and Sebastian, then two rising doctors engaged in physiological researches together, had just been occupied in experimenting upon this very drug—testing the use of aconitine. Indeed, you will no doubt remember"—he crossed his fat hands again comfortably—"it was these precise researches on a then little-known poison that first brought Sebastian prominently before the public. What was the consequence?" His smooth, persuasive voice flowed on as if I were a concentrated jury.

"The Admiral grew rapidly worse, and insisted upon calling in a second opinion. No doubt he didn't like the aconitine when it came to the pinch—for it *does* pinch, I can tell you—and repented him of his evil. Yorke-Bannerman suggested Sebastian as the second opinion; the uncle acquiesced; Sebastian was called in, and, of course, being fresh from his researches, immediately recognised the symptoms of aconitine poisoning."

"What! Sebastian found it out?" I cried, starting.

"Oh, yes! Sebastian. He watched the case from that point to the end; and the oddest part of it all was this—that though he communicated with the police, and himself prepared every morsel of food that the poor old Admiral took from that moment forth, the symptoms continually increased in severity. The police contention was that Yorke-Bannerman somehow managed to put the stuff into the milk beforehand; my own theory was—as counsel for the accused"—he blinked his fat eyes—"that old Prideaux had concealed a large quantity of aconitine in the bed, before his illness, and went on taking it from time to time—just to spite his nephew."

"And you *believe* that, Mr. Mayfield?"

The broad smile broke concentrically in ripples over the great lawyer's face. His smile was Mayfield's main feature. He shrugged his shoulders and expanded his big hands wide open before him. "My dear Hubert," he said, with a most humorous expression of countenance, "you are a professional man yourself; therefore you know that every profession has its own little courtesies—its own small fictions. I was Yorke-Bannerman's counsel, as well as his friend. 'Tis a point of honour with us that no barrister will ever admit a doubt as to a client's innocence—is he not paid to maintain it?—and to my dying day I will constantly maintain that old Prideaux poisoned himself. Maintain it with that dogged and meaningless obstinacy with which we always cling to whatever is least provable. . . . Oh, yes! He poisoned himself; and Yorke-Bannerman was innocent. . . . But still, you know, it *was* the sort of case where an acute lawyer, with a reputation to make, would prefer to be for the Crown rather than for the prisoner."

"But it was never tried," I ejaculated.

"No, happily for us, it was never tried. Fortune favoured us. Yorke-Bannerman had a weak heart, a conveniently weak heart, which the inquest sorely affected; and besides, he was deeply angry at what he persisted in calling Sebastian's defection. He evidently thought Sebastian ought to have stood by him. His colleague preferred the claims of public duty—as he understood them, I mean—to those of private friendship. It was a very sad case—for Yorke-Bannerman was really a charming fellow. But I confess I *was* relieved when he died unexpectedly on the morning of his arrest. It took off my shoulders a most serious burden."

"You think, then, the case would have gone against him?"

"My dear Hubert," his whole face puckered with an indulgent smile, "of course the case must have gone against us. Juries are fools; but they are not such fools as to swallow everything—like ostriches: to let me throw dust in their eyes about so plain an issue. Consider the facts, consider them impartially. Yorke-Bannerman had easy access to aconitine; had whole ounces of it in his possession; he treated the uncle from whom he was to inherit; he was in temporary embarrassments—that came out at the inquest; it was known that the Admiral had just made a twenty-third will in his favour, and that the Admiral's wills were liable to alteration every time a nephew ventured upon an opinion in politics, religion, science, navigation, or the right card at whist, differing by a shade from that of the uncle. The Admiral died of aconitine poisoning; and Sebastian observed and detailed the symptoms. Could anything be plainer—I mean, could any combination of fortuitous circumstances"—he blinked pleasantly again—"be more adverse to an advocate sincerely convinced of his client's innocence—as a professional duty?" And he gazed at me comically.

The more he piled up the case against the man who I now felt sure was Hilda's father, the less did I believe him. A dark conspiracy seemed to loom up in the background. "Has it ever occurred to you," I asked, at last, in a very tentative tone, "that perhaps—I throw out the hint as the merest suggestion—perhaps it may have been Sebastian who—"

He smiled this time till I thought his smile would swallow him.

"If Yorke-Bannerman had *not* been my client," he mused aloud, "I might have been inclined to suspect rather that Sebastian aided him to avoid justice by giving him something violent to take, if he wished it: something which might accelerate the inevitable action of the heart-disease from which he was suffering. Isn't *that* more likely?"

I saw there was nothing further to be got out of Mayfield. His opinion was fixed; he was a placid ruminant. But he had given me already much food for thought. I thanked him for his assistance, and returned on foot to my rooms at the hospital.

I was now, however, in a somewhat different position for tracking Hilda from that which I occupied before my interview with the famous counsel. I felt certain by this time that Hilda Wade and Maisie Yorke-Bannerman were one and the same person. To be sure, it gave me a twinge to think that Hilda should be masquerading under an assumed name; but I waived that question for the moment, and awaited her explanations. The great point now was to find Hilda. She was flying from Sebastian to mature a new plan. But whither? I proceeded to argue it out on her own principles; oh, how lamely! The world is still so big! Mauritius, the Argentine, British Columbia, New Zealand!

The letter I had received bore the Basingstoke postmark. Now a person may be passing Basingstoke on his way either to Southampton or Plymouth, both of which are ports of embarcation for various foreign countries. I attached importance to that clue. Something about the tone of Hilda's letter made me realise that she intended to put the sea between us. In concluding so much, I felt sure I was not mistaken. Hilda had too big and too cosmopolitan a mind to speak of being "irrevocably far from London," if she were only going to some town in England, or even to Normandy, or the Channel Islands. "Irrevocably far" pointed rather to a destination outside Europe altogether—to India, Africa, America: not to Jersey, Dieppe, or Saint-Malo.

Was it Southampton or Plymouth to which she was first bound?—that was the next question. I inclined to Southampton.

For the sprawling lines (so different from her usual neat hand) were written hurriedly in a train, I could see; and, on consulting Bradshaw, I found that the Plymouth expresses stop longest at Salisbury, where Hilda would, therefore, have been likely to post her note if she were going to the far west; while some of the Southampton trains stop at Basingstoke, which is, indeed, the most convenient point on that route for sending off a letter. This was mere blind guesswork, to be sure, compared with Hilda's immediate and unerring intuition; but it had some probability in its favour, at any rate. Try both: of the two, she was likelier to be going to Southampton.

My next move was to consult the list of outgoing steamers. Hilda had left London on a Saturday morning. Now, on alternate Saturdays, the steamers of the Castle line sail from Southampton, where they call to take up passengers and mails. Was this one of those alternate Saturdays? I looked at the list of dates: it was. That told further in favour of Southampton. But did any steamer of any passenger line sail from Plymouth on the same day? None, that I could find. Or from Southampton elsewhere? I looked them all up. The Royal Mail Company's boats start on Wednesdays; the North German Lloyd's on Wednesdays and Sundays. Those were the only likely vessels I could discover. Either, then, I concluded, Hilda meant to sail on Saturday by the Castle line for South Africa, or else on Sunday by North German Lloyd for some part of America.

How I longed for one hour of Hilda to help me out with her almost infallible instinct. I realised how feeble and fallacious was my own groping in the dark. Her knowledge of temperament would have revealed to her at once what I was trying to discover, like the police she despised, by the clumsy "clues" which so roused her sarcasm.

However, I went to bed and slept on it. Next morning I determined to set out for Southampton on a tour of inquiry to all the steamboat agencies. If that failed, I could go on to Plymouth.

But, as chance would have it, the morning post brought me an unexpected letter, which helped me not a little in unravelling the problem. It was a crumpled letter, written on rather soiled paper, in an uneducated hand, and it bore, like Hilda's, the Basingstoke postmark.

"Charlotte Churtwood sends her duty to Dr. Cumberledge," it said, with somewhat uncertain spelling, "and I am very sorry that I was not able to Post the letter to you in London, as the lady ast me, but after her train ad left has I was stepping into mine the Ingine started and I was knocked down and badly hurt and the lady gave me a half-sovering to Post it in London has soon as I got there but bein unable to do so I now return it dear sir not knowing the lady's name and adress she having trusted me through seeing me on the platform, and perhaps you can send it back to her, and was very sorry I could not Post it were she ast me, but time bein an objeck put it in the box in Basingstoke station and now inclose post office order for ten Shillings whitch dear sir kindly let the young lady have from your obedient servant,

"Charlotte Churtwood."

In the corner was the address: "11, Chubb's Cottages, Basingstoke."

The happy accident of this letter advanced things for me greatly—though it also made me feel how dependent I was upon happy accidents, where Hilda would have guessed right at once by mere knowledge of character. Still, the letter explained many things which had hitherto puzzled me. I had felt not a little surprise that Hilda, wishing to withdraw from me and leave no traces, should have sent off her farewell letter from Basingstoke—so as to let me see at once in what direction she was travelling. Nay, I even wondered at times whether she had really posted it herself at Basingstoke, or given it to somebody who chanced to be going there to post for her as a blind. But I did not think she would deliberately deceive me; and, in my opinion, to get a letter posted at Basingstoke would be deliberate deception, while to get it posted in London was mere vague precaution. I understood now that she had written it in the train, and then picked out a likely person as she passed to take it to Waterloo for her.

Of course, I went straight down to Basingstoke, and called at once at Chubb's Cottages. It was a squalid little row on the outskirts of the town. I found Charlotte Churtwood herself exactly such a girl as Hilda, with her quick judgment of character, might have hit upon for such a purpose. She was a conspicuously honest and transparent country servant, of the lumpy type, on her way to London to take a place as housemaid. Her injuries were severe, but not dangerous. "The lady saw me on the platform," she said, "and beckoned to me to come to her. She ast me where I was going, and I says, 'To London, miss.' Says she, smiling kind-like, 'Could you post a letter for me, certain sure?' Says I, 'You can depend upon me.' An' then she give me the arf-sovering, an' says, says she, 'Mind, it's *very* par-tickler; if the gentleman don't get it, 'e'll fret 'is 'eart out.' An' through 'aving a young man o' my own, as is a groom at Andover, o' course I understood 'er, sir. An' then, feeling all full of it, as yu may say, what with the arf-sovering, and what with one thing and what with another, an' all of a fluster with not being used to travelling, I run up, when the train for London come in, an' tried to scramble into it, afore it 'ad quite stopped moving. An' a guard, 'e rushes up, an' 'Stand back!' says 'e; 'wait till the train stops,' says 'e, an' waves his red flag at me. But afore I could stand back, with one foot on the step, the train sort of jumped away from me, and knocked me down like this; and they say it'll be a week now afore I'm well enough to go on to London. But I posted the letter all the same, at Basingstoke station, as they was carrying me off; an' I took down the address, so as to return the arf-sovering." Hilda was right, as always. She had chosen instinctively the trustworthy person,—chosen her at first sight, and hit the bull's-eye.

"Do you know what train the lady was in?" I asked, as she paused. "Where was it going, did you notice?"

"It was the Southampton train, sir. I saw the board on the carriage."

That settled the question. "You are a good and an honest girl," I said, pulling out my purse; "and you came to this misfortune through trying—too eagerly—to help the young lady. A ten-pound note is not overmuch as compensation for your accident. Take it, and get well. I should be sorry to think you lost a good place through your anxiety to help us."

The rest of my way was plain sailing now. I hurried on straight to Southampton. There my first visit was to the office of the Castle line. I went to the point at once. Was there a Miss Wade among the passengers by the *Dunottar Castle*?

No; nobody of that name on the list.

Had any lady taken a passage at the last moment?

The clerk perpended. Yes; a lady had come by the mail train from London, with no heavy baggage, and had gone on board direct, taking what cabin she could get. A young lady in grey. Quite unprepared. Gave no name. Called away in a hurry.

What sort of lady?

Youngish; good-looking; brown hair and eyes, the clerk thought; a sort of creamy skin; and a—well, a mesmeric kind of glance that seemed to go right through you.

"That will do," I answered, sure now of my quarry. "To which port did she book?"

"To Cape Town."

"Very well," I said, promptly. "You may reserve me a good berth in the next outgoing steamer."

It was just like Hilda's impulsive character to rush off in this way at a moment's notice; and just like mine to follow her. But it piqued me a little to think that, but for the accident of an accident, I might never have tracked her down. If the letter had been posted in London as she intended, and not at Basingstoke, I might have sought in vain for her from then till Doomsday.

Ten days later, I was afloat on the Channel, bound for South Africa.

I always admired Hilda's astonishing insight into character and motive; but I never admired it quite so profoundly as on the glorious day when we arrived at Cape Town. I was standing on deck,

looking out for the first time in my life on that tremendous view—
the steep and massive bulk of Table Mountain,—a mere lump of
rock, dropped loose from the sky, with the long white town spread
gleaming at its base, and the silver-tree plantations that cling to
its lower slopes and merge by degrees into gardens and vineyards—
when a messenger from the shore came up to me tentatively.

"Dr. Cumberledge?" he said, in an inquiring tone.

I nodded. "That is my name."

"I have a letter for you, sir."

I took it, in great surprise. Who on earth in Cape Town could
have known I was coming? I had not a friend to my knowledge in
the colony. I glanced at the envelope. My wonder deepened. That
prescient brain! It was Hilda's handwriting.

I tore it open and read:

> "My Dear Hubert,—I *know* you will come; I *know*
> you will follow me. So I am leaving this letter at
> Donald Currie & Co.'s office, giving their agent in-
> structions to hand it to you as soon as you reach Cape
> Town. I am quite sure you will track me so far at
> least; I understand your temperament. But I beg you,
> I implore you, to go no further. You will ruin my plan
> if you do. And I still adhere to it. It is good of you to
> come so far; I cannot blame you for that. I know your
> motives. But do not try to find me out. I warn you,
> beforehand, it will be quite useless. I have made up
> my mind. I have an object in life, and, dear as you
> are to me—*that* I will not pretend to deny—I can
> never allow even *you* to interfere with it. So be
> warned in time. Go back quietly by the next steamer.
> "Your ever attached and grateful,
> "Hilda."

I read it twice through with a little thrill of joy. Did any man
ever court so strange a love? Her very strangeness drew me. But
go back by the next steamer! I felt sure of one thing: Hilda was far

too good a judge of character to believe that I was likely to obey that mandate.

I will not trouble you with the remaining stages of my quest. Except for the slowness of South African mail coaches, they were comparatively easy. It is not so hard to track strangers in Cape Town as strangers in London. I followed Hilda to her hotel, and from her hotel up country, stage after stage—jolted by rail, worse jolted by mule-waggon—inquiring, inquiring, inquiring—till I learned at last she was somewhere in Rhodesia.

That is a big address; but it does not cover as many names as it covers square miles. In time I found her. Still, it took time; and before we met, Hilda had had leisure to settle down quietly to her new existence. People in Rhodesia had noted her coming, as a new portent, because of one strange peculiarity. She was the only woman of means who had ever gone up of her own free will to Rhodesia. Other women had gone there to accompany their husbands, or to earn their livings; but that a lady should freely select that half-baked land as a place of residence—a lady of position, with all the world before her where to choose—that puzzled the Rhodesians. So she was a marked person. Most people solved the vexed problem, indeed, by suggesting that she had designs against the stern celibacy of a leading South African politician. "Depend upon it," they said, "it's Rhodes she's after." The moment I arrived at Salisbury, and stated my object in coming, all the world in the new town was ready to assist me. The lady was to be found (vaguely speaking) on a young farm to the north—a budding farm, whose general direction was expansively indicated to me by a wave of the arm, with South African uncertainty.

I bought a pony at Salisbury—a pretty little seasoned sorrel mare—and set out to find Hilda. My way lay over a brand-new road, or what passes for a road in South Africa—very soft and lumpy, like an English cart-track. I am a fair cross-country rider in our own Midlands, but I never rode a more tedious journey than that one. I had crawled several miles under a blazing sun along the shadeless new track, on my African pony, when, to my surprise I saw, of all sights in the world, a bicycle coming towards me.

I could hardly believe my eyes. Civilisation indeed! A bicycle in these remotest wilds of Africa!

I had been picking my way for some hours through a desolate plateau—the high veldt—about five thousand feet above the sea level, and entirely treeless. In places, to be sure, a few low bushes of prickly aspect rose in tangled clumps; but for the most part the arid table-land was covered by a thick growth of short brown grass, about nine inches high, burnt up in the sun, and most wearisome to look at. The distressing nakedness of a new country confronted me. Here and there a bald farm or two had been literally pegged out—the pegs were almost all one saw of them as yet; the fields were in the future. Here and there, again, a scattered range of low granite hills, known locally as kopjes—red, rocky prominences, flaunting in the sunshine—diversified the distance. But the road itself, such as it was, lay all on the high plain, looking down now and again into gorges or kloofs, wooded on their slopes with scrubby trees, and comparatively well-watered. In the midst of all this crude, unfinished land, the mere sight of a bicycle, bumping over the rubbly road, was a sufficient surprise; but my astonishment reached a climax when I saw, as it drew near, that it was ridden by a woman!

One moment later I had burst into a wild cry, and rode forward to her hurriedly. "Hilda!" I shouted aloud, in my excitement: "Hilda!"

She stepped lightly from her pedals, as if it had been in the park: head erect and proud; eyes liquid, lustrous. I dismounted, trembling, and stood beside her. In the wild joy of the moment, for the first time in my life, I kissed her fervently. Hilda took the kiss, unreproving. She did not attempt to refuse me.

"So you have come at last!" she murmured, with a glow on her face, half nestling towards me, half withdrawing, as if two wills tore her in different directions. "I have been expecting you for some days; and, somehow, to-day, I was almost certain you were coming!"

"Then you are not angry with me?" I cried. "You remember, you forbade me!"

"Angry with you? Dear Hubert, could I ever be angry with you, especially for thus showing me your devotion and your trust? I am never angry with you. When one knows, one understands. I have thought of you so often; sometimes, alone here in this raw new land, I have longed for you to come. It is inconsistent of me, of course; but I am so solitary, so lonely!"

"And yet you begged me not to follow you!"

She looked up at me shyly—I was not accustomed to see Hilda shy. Her eyes gazed deep into mine beneath the long, soft lashes. "I begged you not to follow me," she repeated, a strange gladness in her tone. "Yes, dear Hubert, I begged you—and I meant it. Cannot you understand that sometimes one hopes a thing may never happen—and is supremely happy because it happens, in spite of one? I have a purpose in life for which I live: I live for it still. For its sake I told you you must not come to me. Yet you *have* come, against my orders; and—" she paused, and drew a deep sigh—"oh, Hubert, I thank you for daring to disobey me!"

I clasped her to my bosom. She allowed me, half resisting. "I am too weak," she murmured. "Only this morning, I made up my mind that when I saw you I would implore you to return at once. And now that you are here—" she laid her little hand confidingly in mine—"see how foolish I am!—I cannot dismiss you."

"Which means to say, Hilda, that, after all, you are still a woman!"

"A woman; oh, yes; very much a woman! Hubert, I love you; I half wish I did not."

"Why, darling?" I drew her to me.

"Because—if I did not, I could send you away—so easily! As it is—I cannot let you stop—and . . . I cannot dismiss you."

"Then divide it," I cried gaily; "do neither; come away with me!"

"No, no; nor that, either. I will not stultify my whole past life. I will not dishonour my dear father's memory."

I looked around for something to which to tether my horse. A bridle is in one's way—when one has to discuss important business. There was really nothing about that seemed fit for the purpose. Hilda saw what I sought, and pointed mutely to a stunted bush beside a big granite boulder which rose abruptly from the dead level of the grass, affording a little shade from that sweltering sunlight. I tied my mare to the gnarled root—it was the only part big enough—and sat down by Hilda's side, under the shadow of a great rock in a thirsty land. I realised at that moment the force and appropriateness of the Psalmist's simile. The sun beat fiercely on the seeding grasses. Away on the southern horizon we could faintly perceive the floating yellow haze of the prairie fires lit by the Mashonas.

"Then you knew I would come?" I began, as she seated herself on the burnt-up herbage, while my hand stole into hers, to nestle there naturally.

She pressed it in return. "Oh, yes; I knew you would come," she answered, with that strange ring of confidence in her voice. "Of course you got my letter at Cape Town?"

"I did, Hilda—and I wondered at you more than ever as I read it. But if you *knew* I would come, why write to prevent me?"

Her eyes had their mysterious far-away air. She looked out upon infinity. "Well, I wanted to do my best to turn you aside," she said, slowly. "One must always do one's best, even when one feels and believes it is useless. That surely is the first clause in a doctor's or a nurse's rubric."

"But *why* didn't you want me to come?" I persisted. "Why fight against your own heart? Hilda, I am sure—I *know* you love me."

Her bosom rose and fell. Her eyes dilated. "Love you?" she cried, looking away over the bushy ridges, as if afraid to trust herself. "Oh, yes, Hubert, I love you! It is not for that that I wish to avoid you. Or, rather, it is just because of that. I cannot endure to spoil your life—by a fruitless affection."

"Why fruitless?" I asked, leaning forward.

She crossed her hands resignedly. "You know all by this time," she answered. "Sebastian would tell you, of course, when you went to announce that you were leaving Nathaniel's. He could not do otherwise; it is the outcome of his temperament—an integral part of his nature."

"Hilda," I cried, "you are a witch! How *could* you know that? I can't imagine."

She smiled her restrained, Chaldean smile. "Because I *know* Sebastian," she answered, quietly. "I can read that man to the core. He is simple as a book. His composition is plain, straightforward, quite natural, uniform. There are no twists and turns in him. Once learn the key, and it discloses everything, like an open sesame. He has a gigantic intellect, a burning thirst for knowledge; one love, one hobby—science; and no moral instincts. He goes straight for his ends; and whatever comes in his way," she dug her little heel in the brown soil, "he tramples on it as ruthlessly as a child will trample on a worm or a beetle."

"And yet," I said, "he is so great."

"Yes, great, I grant you; but the easiest character to unravel that I have ever met. It is calm, austere, unbending, yet not in the least degree complex. He has the impassioned temperament, pushed to its highest pitch; the temperament that runs deep, with irresistible force; but the passion that inspires him, that carries him away headlong, as love carries some men, is a rare and abstract one—the passion of science."

I gazed at her as she spoke, with a feeling akin to awe. "It must destroy the plot-interest of life for you, Hilda," I cried—out there in the vast void of that wild African plateau—"to foresee so well what each person will do—how each will act under such given circumstances."

She pulled a bent of grass and plucked off its dry spikelets one by one. "Perhaps so," she answered, after a meditative pause; "though, of course, all natures are not equally simple. Only with great souls can you be sure beforehand like that, for good or for evil. It is essential to anything worth calling character that one should be able to predict in what way it will act under given circumstances—to feel certain, 'This man will do nothing small or mean,' 'That one could never act dishonestly, or speak deceitfully.' But smaller natures are more complex. They defy analysis, because their motives are not consistent."

"Most people think to be complex is to be great," I objected.

She shook her head. "That is quite a mistake," she answered. "Great natures are simple, and relatively predictable, since their motives balance one another justly. Small natures are complex, and hard to predict, because small passions, small jealousies, small discords and perturbations come in at all moments, and override for a time the permanent underlying factors of character. Great natures, good or bad, are equally poised; small natures let petty motives intervene to upset their balance."

"Then you knew I would come," I exclaimed, half pleased to find I belonged inferentially to her higher category.

Her eyes beamed on me with a beautiful light. "Knew you would come? Oh, yes. I begged you not to come; but I felt sure you were too deeply in earnest to obey me. I asked a friend in Cape Town to telegraph your arrival; and almost ever since the telegram reached me I have been expecting you and awaiting you."

"So you believed in me?"

"Implicitly—as you in me. That is the worst of it, Hubert. If you did *not* believe in me, I could have told you all—and then, you would have left me. But, as it is, you *know* all—and yet, you want to cling to me."

"You know I know all—because Sebastian told me?"

"Yes; and I think I even know how you answered him."

"How?"

She paused. The calm smile lighted up her face once more. Then she drew out a pencil. "You think life must lack plot-interest for me," she began, slowly, "because, with certain natures, I can partially guess beforehand what is coming. But have you not observed that, in reading a novel, part of the pleasure you feel arises from your conscious anticipation of the end, and your satisfaction in seeing that you anticipated correctly? Or part, sometimes, from the occasional unexpectedness of the real *dénouement?* Well, life is like that. I enjoy observing my successes, and, in a way, my failures. Let me show you what I mean. I think I know what you said to Sebastian—not the words, of course, but the purport; and I will write it down now for you. Set down *your* version, too. And then we will compare them."

It was a crucial test. We both wrote for a minute or two. Somehow, in Hilda's presence, I forgot at once the strangeness of the scene, the weird oddity of the moment. That sombre plain disappeared for me. I was only aware that I was with Hilda once more—and therefore in Paradise. Pison and Gihon watered the desolate land. Whatever she did seemed to me supremely right. If she had proposed to me to begin a ponderous work on Medical Jurisprudence, under the shadow of the big rock, I should have begun it incontinently.

She handed me her slip of paper; I took it and read: "Sebastian told you I was Dr. Yorke-Bannerman's daughter. And you answered, 'If so, Yorke-Bannerman was innocent, and *you* are the poisoner.' Is not that correct?"

I handed her in answer my own paper. She read it with a faint flush. When she came to the words: "Either she is not Yorke-Bannerman's daughter; or else, Yorke-Bannerman was not a poisoner, and someone else was—I might put a name to him," she rose to her feet with a great rush of long-suppressed feeling, and clasped me passionately. "My Hubert!" she cried, "I read you aright. I knew it! I was sure of you!"

I folded her in my arms, there, on the rusty-red South African desert. "Then, Hilda dear," I murmured, "you will consent to marry me?"

The words brought her back to herself. She unfolded my arms with slow reluctance. "No, dearest," she said, earnestly, with a face where pride fought hard against love. "That is *why*, above all things, I did not want you to follow me. I love you; I trust you: you love me; you trust me. But I never will marry anyone till I have succeeded in clearing my father's memory. I *know* he did not do it; I *know* Sebastian did. But that is not enough. I must prove it, I must prove it!"

"I believe it already," I answered. "What need, then, to prove it?"

"To you, Hubert? Oh, no; not to you. There I am safe. But to the world that condemned him—condemned him untried. I must vindicate him; I must clear him!"

I bent my face close to hers. "But may I not marry you first?" I asked—"and after that, I can help you to clear him."

She gazed at me fearlessly. "No, no!" she cried, clasping her hands; "much as I love you, dear Hubert, I cannot consent to it. I am too proud!—too proud! I will not allow the world to say—not even to say falsely"—her face flushed crimson; her voice dropped low—"I will not allow them to say those hateful words, 'He married a murderer's daughter.'"

I bowed my head. "As you will, my darling," I answered. "I am content to wait. I trust you in this, too. Some day, we will prove it."

And all this time, preoccupied as I was with these deeper concerns, I had not even asked where Hilda lived, or what she was doing!

THE EPISODE OF THE
STONE THAT LOOKED ABOUT IT

Hilda took me back with her to the embryo farm where she had pitched her tent for the moment; a rough, wild place. It lay close to the main road from Salisbury to Chimoio.

Setting aside the inevitable rawness and newness of all things Rhodesian, however, the situation itself was not wholly unpicturesque. A ramping rock or tor of granite, which I should judge at a rough guess to extend to an acre in size, sprang abruptly from the brown grass of the upland plain. It rose like a huge boulder. Its summit was crowned by the covered grave of some old Kaffir chief—a rude cairn of big stones under a thatched awning. At the foot of this jagged and cleft rock the farmhouse nestled—four square walls of wattle-and-daub, sheltered by its mass from the sweeping winds of the South African plateau. A stream brought water from a spring close by: in front of the house—rare sight in that thirsty land—spread a garden of flowers. It was an oasis in the desert. But the desert itself stretched grimly all round. I could never quite decide how far the oasis was caused by the water from the spring, and how far by Hilda's presence.

"Then you live here?" I cried, gazing round—my voice, I suppose, betraying my latent sense of the unworthiness of the position.

"For the present," Hilda answered, smiling. "You know, Hubert, I have no abiding city anywhere, till my Purpose is fulfilled. I came here because Rhodesia seemed the farthest spot on earth where a white woman just now could safely penetrate—in order to get away from you and Sebastian."

"That is an unkind conjunction!" I exclaimed, reddening.

"But I mean it," she answered, with a wayward little nod. "I wanted breathing-space to form fresh plans. I wanted to get clear away for a time from all who knew me. And this promised best. . . . But nowadays, really, one is never safe from intrusion anywhere."

"You are cruel, Hilda!"

"Oh, no. You deserve it. I asked you not to come—and you came in spite of me. I have treated you very nicely under the circumstances, I think. I have behaved like an angel. The question is now, what ought I to do next? You have upset my plans so."

"Upset your plans? How?"

"Dear Hubert,"—she turned to me with an indulgent smile,—"for a clever man, you are really *too* foolish! Can't you see that you have betrayed my whereabouts to Sebastian? *I* crept away secretly, like a thief in the night, giving no name or place; and, having the world to ransack, he might have found it hard to track me; for *he* had not *your* clue of the Basingstoke letter—nor your reason for seeking me. But now that *you* have followed me openly, with your name blazoned forth in the company's passenger-lists, and your traces left plain in hotels and stages across the map of South Africa—why, the spoor is easy. If Sebastian cares to find us, he can follow the scent all through without trouble."

"I never thought of that!" I cried, aghast.

She was forbearance itself. "No, I knew you would never think of it. You are a man, you see. I counted that in. I was afraid from the first you would wreck all by following me."

I was mutely penitent. "And yet, you forgive me, Hilda?"

Her eyes beamed tenderness. "To know all, is to forgive all," she answered. "I have to remind you of that so often! How can I help forgiving, when I know *why* you came—what spur it was that drove you? But it is the future we have to think of now, not the past. And I must wait and reflect. I have *no* plan just at present."

"What are you doing at this farm?" I gazed round at it, dissatisfied.

"I board here," Hilda answered, amused at my crestfallen face. "But, of course, I cannot be idle; so I have found work to do. I ride out on my bicycle to two or three isolated houses about, and give lessons to children in this desolate place, who would otherwise grow up ignorant. It fills my time, and supplies me with something besides myself to think about."

"And what am *I* to do?" I cried, oppressed with a sudden sense of helplessness.

She laughed at me outright. "And is this the first moment that that difficulty has occurred to you?" she asked, gaily. "You have hurried all the way from London to Rhodesia without the slightest idea of what you mean to do now you have got here?"

I laughed at myself in turn. "Upon my word, Hilda," I cried, "I set out to find you. Beyond the desire to find you, I had no plan in my head. That was an end in itself. My thoughts went no farther."

She gazed at me half saucily. "Then don't you think, sir, the best thing you can do, now you *have* found me, is—to turn back and go home again?"

"I am a man," I said, promptly, taking a firm stand. "And you are a judge of character. If you really mean to tell me you think *that* likely—well, I shall have a lower opinion of your insight into men than I have been accustomed to harbour."

Her smile was not wholly without a touch of triumph.

"In that case," she went on, "I suppose the only alternative is for you to remain here."

"That would appear to be logic," I replied. "But what can I do? Set up in practice?"

"I don't see much opening," she answered. "If you ask my advice, I should say there is only one thing to be done in Rhodesia just now—turn farmer."

"It *is* done," I answered, with my usual impetuosity. "Since *you* say the word, I am a farmer already. I feel an interest in oats that is simply absorbing. What steps ought I to take first in my present condition?"

She looked at me, all brown with the dust of my long ride. "I would suggest," she said slowly, "a good wash, and some dinner."

"Hilda," I cried, surveying my boots, or what was visible of them, "that is *really* clever of you. A wash and some dinner! So practical, so timely! The very thing! I will see to it."

Before night fell, I had arranged everything. I was to buy the next farm from the owner of the one where Hilda lodged; I was also to learn the rudiments of South African agriculture from him for a valuable consideration; and I was to lodge in his house while my own was building. He gave me his views on the cultivation of oats. He gave them at some length—more length than perspicuity. I knew nothing about oats, save that they were employed in the manufacture of porridge—which I detest; but I was to be near Hilda once more, and I was prepared to undertake the superintendence of the oat from its birth to its reaping if only I might be allowed to live so close to Hilda.

The farmer and his wife were Boers, but they spoke English. Mr. Jan Willem Klaas himself was a fine specimen of the breed—tall, erect, broad-shouldered, and genial. Mrs. Klaas, his wife, was mainly suggestive, in mind and person, of suet-pudding. There was one prattling little girl of three years old, by name Sannie, a most engaging child; and also a chubby baby.

"You are betrothed, of course?" Mrs. Klaas said to Hilda before me, with the curious tactlessness of her race, when we made our first arrangement.

Hilda's face flushed. "No; we are nothing to one another," she answered—which was only true formally. "Dr. Cumberledge had a post at the same hospital in London where I was a nurse; and he thought he would like to try Rhodesia. That is all."

Mrs. Klaas gazed from one to other of us suspiciously. "You English are strange!" she answered, with a complacent little shrug. "But there—from Europe! Your ways, we know, are different."

Hilda did not attempt to explain. It would have been impossible to make the good soul understand. Her horizon was so simple. She was a harmless housewife, given mostly to dyspepsia and the care of her little ones. Hilda had won her heart by unfeigned admiration for the chubby baby. To a mother, that covers a multitude of eccentricities, such as one expects to find in incomprehensible English. Mrs. Klaas put up with me because she liked Hilda.

We spent some months together on Klaas's farm. It was a dreary place, save for Hilda. The bare daub-and-wattle walls; the clumps of misshapen and dusty prickly-pears that girt round the thatched huts of the Kaffir workpeople; the stone-penned sheep-kraals, and the corrugated iron roof of the bald stable for the waggon oxen— all was as crude and ugly as a new country can make things. It seemed to me a desecration that Hilda should live in such an unfinished land—Hilda, whom I imagined as moving by nature through broad English parks, with Elizabethan cottages and immemorial oaks—Hilda, whose proper atmosphere seemed to be one of coffee-coloured laces, ivy-clad abbeys, lichen-incrusted walls— all that is beautiful and gracious in time-honoured civilisations.

Nevertheless, we lived on there in a meaningless sort of way— I hardly knew why. To me it was a puzzle. When I asked Hilda, she shook her head with her sibylline air and answered, confidently: "You do not understand Sebastian as well as I do. We have to wait for *him*. The next move is his. Till he plays his piece, I cannot tell how I may have to checkmate him."

So we waited for Sebastian to advance a pawn. Meanwhile, I toyed with South African farming—not very successfully, I must admit. Nature did not design me for growing oats. I am no judge of oxen, and my views on the feeding of Kaffir sheep raised broad smiles on the black faces of my Mashona labourers.

I still lodged at Tant Mettie's, as everybody called Mrs. Klaas; she was courtesy aunt to the community at large, while Oom Jan Willem was its courtesy uncle. They were simple, homely folk, who lived up to their religious principles on an unvaried diet of stewed ox-beef and bread; they suffered much from chronic dyspepsia, due in part, at least, no doubt, to the monotony of their food, their life, their interests. One could hardly believe one was still in the nineteenth century; these people had the calm, the local seclusion of the prehistoric epoch. For them, Europe did not exist; they knew it merely as a place where settlers came from. What the Czar intended, what the Kaiser designed, never disturbed their rest. A sick ox, a rattling tile on the roof, meant more to their lives than war in Europe. The one break in the sameness of their daily routine was family prayers; the one weekly event, going to church at Salisbury. Still, they had a single enthusiasm. Like everybody else for fifty

miles around, they believed profoundly in the "future of Rhodesia."
When I gazed about me at the raw new land—the weary flat of red
soil and brown grasses—I felt at least that, with a present like that,
it had need of a future.

I am not by disposition a pioneer; I belong instinctively to the
old civilisations. In the midst of rudimentary towns and incipient
fields, I yearn for grey houses, a Norman church, an English
thatched cottage.

However, for Hilda's sake, I braved it out, and continued to
learn the A B C of agriculture on an unmade farm with great assi-
duity from Oom Jan Willem.

We had been stopping some months at Klaas's together when
business compelled me one day to ride in to Salisbury. I had ordered
some goods for my farm from England which had at last arrived. I
had now to arrange for their conveyance from the town to my plot
of land—a portentous matter. Just as I was on the point of leaving
Klaas's, and was tightening the saddle-girth on my sturdy little
pony, Oom Jan Willem himself sidled up to me with a mysterious
air, his broad face all wrinkled with anticipatory pleasure. He
placed a sixpence in my palm, glancing about him on every side as
he did so, like a conspirator.

"What am I to buy with it?" I asked, much puzzled, and suspecting tobacco. Tant Mettie declared he smoked too much for a
church elder.

He put his finger to his lips, nodded, and peered round. "Lolli-
pops for Sannie," he whispered low, at last, with a guilty smile.
"But"—he glanced about him again—"give them to me, please, when
Tant Mettie isn't looking." His nod was all mystery.

"You may rely on my discretion," I replied, throwing the time-
honoured prejudices of the profession to the winds, and well pleased
to aid and abet the simple-minded soul in his nefarious designs
against little Sannie's digestive apparatus. He patted me on the
back. "*Peppermint* lollipops, mind!" he went on, in the same solemn undertone. "Sannie likes them best—peppermint."

I put my foot in the stirrup, and vaulted into my saddle. "They
shall not be forgotten," I answered, with a quiet smile at this pretty

little evidence of fatherly feeling. I rode off. It was early morning, before the heat of the day began. Hilda accompanied me part of the way on her bicycle. She was going to the other young farm, some eight miles off, across the red-brown plateau, where she gave lessons daily to the ten-year old daughter of an English settler. It was a labour of love; for settlers in Rhodesia cannot afford to pay for what are beautifully described as "finishing governesses"; but Hilda was of the sort who cannot eat the bread of idleness. She had to justify herself to her kind by finding some work to do which should vindicate her existence.

I parted from her at a point on the monotonous plain where one rubbly road branched off from another. Then I jogged on in the full morning sun over that scorching plain of loose red sand all the way to Salisbury. Not a green leaf or a fresh flower anywhere. The eye ached at the hot glare of the reflected sunlight from the sandy level.

My business detained me several hours in the half-built town, with its flaunting stores and its rough new offices; it was not till towards afternoon that I could get away again on my sorrel, across the blazing plain once more to Klaas's.

I moved on over the plateau at an easy trot, full of thoughts of Hilda. What could be the step she expected Sebastian to take next? She did not know, herself, she had told me; there, her faculty failed her. But *some* step he *would* take; and till he took it she must rest and be watchful.

I passed the great tree that stands up like an obelisk in the midst of the plain beyond the deserted Matabele village. I passed the low clumps of dry karroo-bushes by the rocky kopje. I passed the fork of the rubbly roads where I had parted from Hilda. At last, I reached the long, rolling ridge which looks down upon Klaas's, and could see in the slant sunlight the mud farmhouse and the corrugated iron roof where the oxen were stabled.

The place looked more deserted, more dead-alive than ever. Not a black boy moved in it. Even the cattle and Kaffir sheep were nowhere to be seen. . . . But then it was always quiet; and perhaps I noticed the obtrusive air of solitude and sleepiness even more than usual, because I had just returned from Salisbury. All things are comparative. After the lost loneliness of Klaas's farm, even brand-new Salisbury seemed busy and bustling.

I hurried on, ill at ease. But Tant Mettie would, doubtless, have a cup of tea ready for me as soon as I arrived, and Hilda would be waiting at the gate to welcome me.

I reached the stone enclosure, and passed up through the flower-garden. To my great surprise, Hilda was not there. As a rule, she came to meet me, with her sunny smile. But perhaps she was tired, or the sun on the road might have given her a headache. I dismounted from my mare, and called one of the Kaffir boys to take her to the stable. Nobody answered. . . . I called again. Still silence. . . . I tied her up to the post, and strode over to the door, astonished at the solitude. I began to feel there was something weird and uncanny about this homecoming. Never before had I known Klaas's so entirely deserted.

I lifted the latch and opened the door. It gave access at once to the single plain living-room. There, all was huddled. For a moment my eyes hardly took in the truth. There are sights so sickening that the brain at the first shock wholly fails to realise them.

On the stone slab floor of the low living-room Tant Mettie lay dead. Her body was pierced through by innumerable thrusts, which I somehow instinctively recognised as assegai wounds. By her side lay Sannie, the little prattling girl of three, my constant playmate, whom I had instructed in cat's-cradle, and taught the tales of Cinderella and Red Riding Hood. My hand grasped the lollipops in my pocket convulsively. She would never need them. Nobody else was about. What had become of Oom Jan Willem—and the baby?

I wandered out into the yard, sick with the sight I had already seen. There Oom Jan Willem himself lay stretched at full length; a bullet had pierced his left temple; his body was also riddled through with assegai thrusts.

I saw at once what this meant. A rising of the Matabele!

I had come back from Salisbury, unknowing it, into the midst of a revolt of bloodthirsty savages.

Yet, even if I had known, I must still have hurried home with all speed to Klaas's—to protect Hilda.

Hilda? Where was Hilda? A breathless sinking crept over me.

I staggered out into the open. It was impossible to say what horror might not have happened. The Matabele might even now be lurking about the kraal—for the bodies were hardly cold. But Hilda? Hilda? Whatever came, I must find Hilda.

Fortunately, I had my loaded revolver in my belt. Though we had not in the least anticipated this sudden revolt—it broke like a thunder-clap from a clear sky—the unsettled state of the country made even women go armed about their daily avocations.

I strode on, half maddened. Beside the great block of granite which sheltered the farm there rose one of those rocky little hillocks of loose boulders which are locally known in South Africa by the Dutch name of kopjes. I looked out upon it drearily. Its round brown ironstones lay piled irregularly together, almost as if placed there in some earlier age by the mighty hands of prehistoric giants. My gaze on it was blank. I was thinking, not of it, but of Hilda, Hilda.

I called the name aloud: "Hilda! Hilda! Hilda!"

As I called, to my immense surprise, one of the smooth round boulders on the hillside seemed slowly to uncurl, and to peer about it cautiously. Then it raised itself in the slant sunlight, put a hand to its eyes, and gazed out upon me with a human face for a moment. After that it descended, step by step, among the other stones, with a white object in its arms. As the boulder uncurled and came to life, I was aware, by degrees . . . yes, yes, it was Hilda, with Tant Mettie's baby!

In the fierce joy of that discovery I rushed forward to her, trembling, and clasped her in my arms. I could find no words but "Hilda! Hilda!"

"Arc they gone?" she asked, staring about her with a terrified air, though still strangely preserving her wonted composure of manner.

"Who gone? The Matabele?"

"Yes, yes!"

"Did you see them, Hilda?"

"For a moment—with black shields and assegais, all shouting madly. You have been to the house, Hubert? You know what has happened?"

"Yes, yes, I know—a rising. They have massacred the Klaases."

She nodded. "I came back on my bicycle, and, when I opened the door, found Tant Mettie and little Sannie dead. Poor, sweet little Sannie! Oom Jan was lying shot in the yard outside. I saw the cradle overturned, and looked under it for the baby. They did not kill her—perhaps did not notice her. I caught her up in my arms, and rushed out to my machine, thinking to make for Salisbury, and give the alarm to the men there. One must try to save others—and *you* were coming, Hubert! Then I heard horses' hoofs—the Matabele returning. They dashed back, mounted,—stolen horses from other farms,—they have taken poor Oom Jan's,—and they have gone on, shouting, to murder elsewhere! I flung down my machine among the bushes as they came,—I hope they have not seen it,— and I crouched here between the boulders, with the baby in my arms, trusting for protection to the colour of my dress, which is just like the ironstone."

"It is a perfect deception," I answered, admiring her instinctive cleverness even then. "I never so much as noticed you."

"No, nor the Matabele either, for all their sharp eyes. They passed by without stopping. I clasped the baby hard, and tried to keep it from crying—if it had cried, all would have been lost; but they passed just below, and swept on toward Rozenboom's. I lay still for a while, not daring to look out. Then I raised myself warily, and tried to listen. Just at that moment, I heard a horse's hoofs ring out once more. I couldn't tell, of course, whether it was *you* returning, or one of the Matabele, left behind by the others. So I crouched again. . . . Thank God, you are safe, Hubert!"

All this took a moment to say, or was less said than hinted. "Now, what must we do?" I cried. "Bolt back again to Salisbury?"

"It is the only thing possible—if my machine is unhurt. They may have taken it . . . or ridden over and broken it."

We went down to the spot, and picked it up where it lay, half-concealed among the brittle, dry scrub of milk-bushes. I examined the bearings carefully; though there were hoof-marks close by, it had received no hurt. I blew up the tire, which was somewhat flabby, and went on to untie my sturdy pony. The moment I looked at her I saw the poor little brute was wearied out with her two long rides in the sweltering sun. Her flanks quivered. "It is no use," I cried, patting her, as she turned to me with appealing eyes that asked for water. "She *can't* go back as far as Salisbury; at least, till she has had a feed of corn and a drink. Even then, it will be rough on her."

"Give her bread," Hilda suggested. "That will hearten her more than corn. There is plenty in the house; Tant Mettie baked this morning."

I crept in reluctantly to fetch it. I also brought out from the dresser a few raw eggs, to break into a tumbler and swallow whole; for Hilda and I needed food almost as sorely as the poor beast herself. There was something gruesome in thus rummaging about for bread and meat in the dead woman's cupboard, while she herself lay there on the floor; but one never realises how one will act in these great emergencies until they come upon one. Hilda, still calm with unearthly calmness, took a couple of loaves from my hand, and began feeding the pony with them. "Go and draw water for her," she said, simply, "while I give her the bread; that will save time. Every minute is precious."

I did as I was bid, not knowing each moment but that the insurgents would return. When I came back from the spring with the bucket, the mare had demolished the whole two loaves, and was going on upon some grass which Hilda had plucked for her.

"She hasn't had enough, poor dear," Hilda said, patting her neck. "A couple of loaves are penny buns to her appetite. Let her drink the water, while I go in and fetch out the rest of the baking."

I hesitated. "You *can't* go in there again, Hilda!" I cried. "Wait, and let me do it."

Her white face was resolute. "Yes, I *can*," she answered. "It is a work of necessity; and in works of necessity a woman, I think, should flinch at nothing. Have I not seen already every varied aspect of death at Nathaniel's?" And in she went, undaunted, to that chamber of horrors, still clasping the baby.

The pony made short work of the remaining loaves, which she devoured with great zest. As Hilda had predicted, they seemed to hearten her. The food and drink, with a bucket of water dashed on her hoofs, gave her new vigour like wine. We gulped down our eggs in silence. Then I held Hilda's bicycle. She vaulted lightly on to the seat, white and tired as she was, with the baby in her left arm, and her right hand on the handle-bar.

"I must take the baby," I said.

She shook her head.

"Oh, no. I will not trust her to you."

"Hilda, I insist."

"And I insist, too. It is my place to take her."

"But can you ride so?" I asked, anxiously.

She began to pedal. "Oh, dear, yes. It is quite, quite easy. I shall get there all right—if the Matabele don't burst upon us."

Tired as I was with my long day's work, I jumped into my saddle. I saw I should only lose time if I disputed about the baby. My little horse seemed to understand that something grave had occurred; for, weary as she must have been, she set out with a will once more over that great red level. Hilda pedalled bravely by my side. The road was bumpy, but she was well accustomed to it. I could have ridden faster than she went, for the baby weighted her. Still, we rode for dear life. It was a grim experience.

All round, by this time, the horizon was dim with clouds of black smoke which went up from burning farms and plundered home-steads. The smoke did not rise high; it hung sullenly over the hot plain in long smouldering masses, like the smoke of steamers on foggy days in England. The sun was nearing the horizon; his slant red rays lighted up the red plain, the red sand, the brown-red grasses, with a murky, spectral glow of crimson. After those red pools of blood, this universal burst of redness appalled one. It seemed as though all nature had conspired in one unholy league with the Matabele. We rode on without a word. The red sky grew redder.

"They may have sacked Salisbury!" I exclaimed at last, looking out towards the brand-new town.

"I doubt it," Hilda answered. Her very doubt reassured me.

We began to mount a long slope. Hilda pedalled with difficulty. Not a sound was heard save the light fall of my pony's feet on the soft new road, and the shrill cry of the cicalas. Then, suddenly, we started. What was that noise in our rear? Once, twice, it rang out. The loud *ping* of a rifle!

Looking behind us, we saw eight or ten mounted Matabele! Stalwart warriors they were—half naked, and riding stolen horses. They were coming our way! They had seen us! They were pursuing us!

"Put on all speed!" I cried, in my agony. "Hilda, can you manage it?" She pedalled with a will. But, as we mounted the slope, I saw they were gaining upon us. A few hundred yards were all our start. They had the descent of the opposite hill as yet in their favour.

One man, astride on a better horse than the rest, galloped on in front and came within range of us. He had a rifle in his hand, he pointed it twice, and covered us. But he did not shoot. Hilda gave a cry of relief. "Don't you see?" she exclaimed. "It is Oom Jan Willem's rifle! That was their last cartridge. They have no more ammunition."

I saw she was probably right; for Klaas was out of cartridges, and was waiting for my new stock to arrive from England. If that were correct, they must get near enough to attack us with assegais. They are more dangerous so. I remembered what an old Boer had said to me at Buluwayo: "The Zulu with his assegai is an enemy to be feared; with a gun, he is a bungler."

We pounded on up the hill. It was deadly work, with those brutes at our heels. The child on Hilda's arm was visibly wearying her. It kept on whining. "Hilda," I cried, "that baby will lose your life! You *cannot* go on carrying it."

She turned to me with a flash of her eyes. "What! You are a man," she broke out, "and you ask a woman to save her life by abandoning a baby! Hubert, you shame me!"

I felt she was right. If she had been capable of giving it up, she would not have been Hilda. There was but one other way left.

"Then *you* must take the pony," I called out, "and let me have the bicycle!"

"You couldn't ride it," she called back. "It is a woman's machine, remember."

"Yes, I could," I replied, without slowing. "It is not much too short; and I can bend my knees a bit. Quick, quick! No words! Do as I tell you!"

She hesitated a second. The child's weight distressed her. "We should lose time in changing," she answered, at last, doubtful but still pedalling, though my hand was on the rein, ready to pull up the pony.

"Not if we manage it right. Obey orders! The moment I say 'Halt,' I shall slacken my mare's pace. When you see me leave the saddle, jump off instantly, you, and mount her! I will catch the machine before it falls. Are you ready? Halt, then!"

She obeyed the word without one second's delay. I slipped off, held the bridle, caught the bicycle, and led it instantaneously. Then I ran beside the pony—bridle in one hand, machine in the other—till Hilda had sprung with a light bound into the stirrup. At that, a little leap, and I mounted the bicycle. It was all done nimbly, in less time than the telling takes, for we are both of us naturally quick in our movements. Hilda rode like a man, astride—her short, bicycling skirt, unobtrusively divided in front and at the back, made this easily possible. Looking behind me with a hasty glance, I could see that the savages, taken aback, had reined in to deliberate at our unwonted evolution. I feel sure that the novelty of the iron horse, with a woman riding it, played not a little on their superstitious fears; they suspected, no doubt, this was some ingenious new engine of war devised against them by the unaccountable white man; it might go off unexpectedly in their faces at any moment. Most of them, I observed, as they halted, carried on their backs black ox-hide shields, interlaced with white thongs; they were armed with two or three assegais apiece and a knobkerry.

Instead of losing time by the change, as it turned out, we had actually gained it. Hilda was able to put on my sorrel to her full pace, which I had not dared to do, for fear of outrunning my companion; the wise little beast, for her part, seemed to rise to the occasion, and to understand that we were pursued; for she stepped out bravely. On the other hand, in spite of the low seat and the short crank of a woman's machine, I could pedal up the slope with more force than Hilda, for I am a practised hill-climber; so that in both ways we gained, besides having momentarily disconcerted and checked the enemy. Their ponies were tired, and they rode them full tilt with savage recklessness, making them canter up-hill, and so needlessly fatiguing them. The Matabele, indeed, are unused to horses, and manage them but ill. It is as foot soldiers, creeping stealthily through bush or long grass, that they are really formidable. Only one of their mounts was tolerably fresh, the one which had once already almost overtaken us. As we neared the top of the slope, Hilda, glancing behind her, exclaimed, with a sudden thrill, "He is spurting again, Hubert!"

I drew my revolver and held it in my right hand, using my left for steering. I did not look back; time was far too precious. I set my teeth hard. "Tell me when he draws near enough for a shot," I said, quietly.

Hilda only nodded. Being mounted on the mare, she could see behind her more steadily now than I could from the machine; and her eye was trustworthy. As for the baby, rocked by the heave and fall of the pony's withers, it had fallen asleep placidly in the very midst of this terror!

After a second, I asked once more, with bated breath, "Is he gaining?"

She looked back. "Yes; gaining."

A pause. "And now?"

"Still gaining. He is poising an assegai."

Ten seconds more passed in breathless suspense. The thud of their horses' hoofs alone told me their nearness. My finger was on the trigger. I awaited the word. "Fire!" she said at last, in a calm, unflinching voice. "He is well within distance."

I turned half round and levelled as true as I could at the advancing black man. He rode, nearly naked, showing all his teeth and brandishing his assegai; the long white feathers stuck upright in his hair gave him a wild and terrifying barbaric aspect. It was difficult to preserve one's balance, keep the way on, and shoot, all at the same time; but, spurred by necessity, I somehow did it. I fired three shots in quick succession. My first bullet missed; my second knocked the man over; my third grazed the horse. With a ringing shriek, the Matabele fell in the road, a black writhing mass; his horse, terrified, dashed back with maddened snorts into the midst of the others. Its plunging disconcerted the whole party for a minute.

We did not wait to see the rest. Taking advantage of this momentary diversion in our favour, we rode on at full speed to the top of the slope—I never knew before how hard I could pedal—and began to descend at a dash into the opposite hollow.

The sun had set by this time. There is no twilight in those latitudes. It grew dark at once. We could see now, in the plain all round, where black clouds of smoke had rolled before, one lurid red glare of burning houses, mixed with a sullen haze of tawny light from the columns of prairie fire kindled by the insurgents.

We made our way still onward across the open plain without one word towards Salisbury. The mare was giving out. She strode with a will; but her flanks were white with froth; her breath came short; foam flew from her nostrils.

As we mounted the next ridge, still distancing our pursuers, I saw suddenly, on its crest, defined against the livid red sky like a silhouette, two more mounted black men!

"It's all up, Hilda!" I cried, losing heart at last. "They are on both sides of us now! The mare is spent; we are surrounded!"

She drew rein and gazed at them. For a moment suspense spoke in all her attitude. Then she burst into a sudden deep sigh of relief. "No, no," she cried; "these are friendlies!"

"How do you know?" I gasped. But I believed her.

"They are looking out this way, with hands shading their eyes against the red glare. They are looking away from Salisbury, in the direction of the attack. They are expecting the enemy. They *must* be friendlies! See, see! they have caught sight of us!"

As she spoke, one of the men lifted his rifle and half pointed it. "Don't shoot! don't shoot!" I shrieked aloud. "We are English! English!"

The men let their rifles drop, and rode down towards us. "Who are you?" I cried.

They saluted us, military fashion. "Matabele police, sah," the leader answered, recognising me. "You are flying from Klaas's?"

"Yes," I answered. "They have murdered Klaas, with his wife and child. Some of them are now following us."

The spokesman was a well-educated Cape Town negro. "All right sah," he answered. "I have forty men here right behind de kopje. Let dem come! We can give a good account of dem. Ride on straight wit de lady to Salisbury!"

"The Salisbury people know of this rising, then?" I asked.

"Yes, sah. Dem know since five o'clock. Kaffir boys from Klaas's brought in de news; and a white man escaped from Rozenboom's confirm it. We have pickets all round. You is safe now; you can ride on into Salisbury witout fear of de Matabele."

I rode on, relieved. Mechanically, my feet worked to and fro on the pedals. It was a gentle down-gradient now towards the town. I had no further need for special exertion.

Suddenly, Hilda's voice came wafted to me, as through a mist. "What are you doing, Hubert? You'll be off in a minute!"

I started and recovered my balance with difficulty. Then I was aware at once that one second before I had all but dropped asleep, dog tired, on the bicycle. Worn out with my long day and with the nervous strain, I began to doze off, with my feet still moving round and round automatically, the moment the anxiety of the chase was relieved, and an easy down-grade gave me a little respite.

I kept myself awake even then with difficulty. Riding on through the lurid gloom, we reached Salisbury at last, and found the town already crowded with refugees from the plateau. However, we succeeded in securing two rooms at a house in the long street, and were soon sitting down to a much-needed supper.

As we rested, an hour or two later, in the ill-furnished back room, discussing this sudden turn of affairs with our host and some neighbours—for, of course, all Salisbury was eager for news from the scene of the massacres—I happened to raise my head, and saw, to my great surprise . . . a haggard white face peering in at us through the window.

It peered round a corner, stealthily. It was an ascetic face, very sharp and clear-cut. It had a stately profile. The long and wiry grizzled moustache, the deep-set, hawk-like eyes, the acute, intense, intellectual features, all were very familiar. So was the outer setting of long, white hair, straight and silvery as it fell, and just curled in one wave-like inward sweep where it turned and rested on the stooping shoulders. But the expression on the face was even stranger than the sudden apparition. It was an expression of keen and poignant disappointment—as of a man whom fate has baulked of some well-planned end, his due by right, which mere chance has evaded.

"They say there's a white man at the bottom of all this trouble," our host had been remarking, one second earlier. "The niggers know too much; and where did they get their rifles? People at Rozenboom's believe some black-livered traitor has been stirring up the Matabele for weeks and weeks. An enemy of Rhodes's, of course, jealous of our advance; a French agent, perhaps; but more likely one of these confounded Transvaal Dutchmen. Depend upon it, it's Kruger's doing."

As the words fell from his lips, I saw the face. I gave a quick little start, then recovered my composure.

But Hilda noted it. She looked up at me hastily. She was sitting with her back to the window, and therefore, of course, could not see the face itself, which indeed was withdrawn with a hurried movement, yet with a certain strange dignity, almost before I could feel sure of having seen it. Still, she caught my startled expression, and the gleam of surprise and recognition in my eye. She laid one hand upon my arm. "You have seen him?" she asked quietly, almost below her breath.

"Seen whom?"

"Sebastian."

It was useless denying it to *her*. "Yes, I have seen him," I answered, in a confidential aside.

"Just now—this moment—at the back of the house—looking in at the window upon us?"

"You are right—as always."

She drew a deep breath. "He has played his game," she said low to me, in an awed undertone. "I felt sure it was he. I expected him to play; though what piece, I knew not; and when I saw those poor dead souls, I was certain he had done it—indirectly done it. The Matabele are his pawns. He wanted to aim a blow at *me*; and *this* was the way he chose to aim it."

"Do you think he is capable of that?" I cried. For, in spite of all, I had still a sort of lingering respect for Sebastian. "It seems so reckless—like the worst of anarchists—when he strikes at one head, to involve so many irrelevant lives in one common destruction."

Hilda's face was like a drowned man's.

"To Sebastian," she answered, shuddering, "the End is all; the Means are unessential. Who wills the End, wills the Means; that is the sum and substance of his philosophy of life. From first to last, he has always acted up to it. Did I not tell you once he was a snow-clad volcano?"

"Still, I am loth to believe—" I cried.

She interrupted me calmly. "I knew it," she said. "I expected it. Beneath that cold exterior, the fires of his life burn fiercely still. I told you we must wait for Sebastian's next move; though I confess, even from *him*, I hardly dreamt of this one. But, from the moment when I opened the door on poor Tant Mettie's body, lying there in its red horror, I felt it must be he. And when you started just now, I said to myself in a flash of intuition—'Sebastian has come! He has come to see how his devil's work has prospered.' He sees it has gone wrong. So now he will try to devise some other."

I thought of the malign expression on that cruel white face as it stared in at the window from the outer gloom, and I felt convinced she was right. She had read her man once more. For it was the desperate, contorted face of one appalled to discover that a great crime attempted and successfully carried out has failed, by mere accident, of its central intention.

THE EPISODE OF THE
EUROPEAN WITH THE KAFFIR HEART

Unfashionable as it is to say so, I am a man of peace. I belong to a profession whose province is to heal, not to destroy. Still there *are* times which turn even the most peaceful of us perforce into fighters—times when those we love, those we are bound to protect, stand in danger of their lives; and at moments like that, no man can doubt what is his plain duty. The Matabele revolt was one such moment. In a conflict of race we *must* back our own colour. I do not know whether the natives were justified in rising or not; most likely, yes; for we had stolen their country; but when once they rose, when the security of white women depended upon repelling them, I felt I had no alternative. For Hilda's sake, for the sake of every woman and child in Salisbury, and in all Rhodesia, I was bound to bear my part in restoring order.

For the immediate future, it is true, we were safe enough in the little town; but we did not know how far the revolt might have spread; we could not tell what had happened at Charter, at Buluwayo, at the outlying stations. The Matabele, perhaps, had risen in force over the whole vast area which was once Lo-Bengula's country; if so, their first object would certainly be to cut us off from communication with the main body of English settlers at Buluwayo.

"I trust to you, Hilda," I said, on the day after the massacre at Klaas's, "to divine for us where these savages are next likely to attack us."

She cooed at the motherless baby, raising one bent finger, and then turned to me with a white smile. "Then you ask too much of me," she answered. "Just think what a correct answer would imply! First, a knowledge of these savages' character; next, a knowledge of their mode of fighting. Can't you see that only a person who possessed my trick of intuition, and who had also spent years in warfare among the Matabele, would be really able to answer your question?"

"And yet such questions have been answered before now by people far less intuitive than you," I went on. "Why, I've read somewhere how, when the war between Napoleon the First and the Prussians broke out, in 1806, Jomini predicted that the decisive battle of the campaign would be fought near Jena; and near Jena it was fought. Are not *you* better than many Jominis?"

Hilda tickled the baby's cheek. "Smile, then, baby, smile!" she said, pouncing one soft finger on a gathering dimple. "And who *was* your friend Jomini?"

"The greatest military critic and tactician of his age," I answered. "One of Napoleon's generals. I fancy he wrote a book, don't you know—a book on war—*Des Grandes Opérations Militaires*, or something of that sort."

"Well, there you are, then! That's just it! Your Jomini, or Hominy, or whatever you call him, not only understood Napoleon's temperament, but understood war and understood tactics. It was all a question of the lie of the land, and strategy, and so forth. If *I* had been asked, I could never have answered a quarter as well as Jomini Piccolomini—could I, baby? Jomini would have been worth a good many me's. There, there, a dear, motherless darling! Why, she crows just as if she hadn't lost all her family!"

"But, Hilda, we must be serious. I count upon you to help us in this matter. We are still in danger. Even now these Matabele may attack and destroy us."

She laid the child on her lap, and looked grave. "I know it, Hubert; but I must leave it now to you men. I am no tactician. Don't take *me* for one of Napoleon's generals."

"Still," I said, "we have not only the Matabele to reckon with, recollect. There is Sebastian as well. And, whether you know your Matabele or not, you at least know your Sebastian."

She shuddered. "I know him; yes, I know him. . . . But this case is so difficult. We have Sebastian—complicated by a rabble of savages, whose habits and manners I do not understand. It is *that* that makes the difficulty."

"But Sebastian himself?" I urged. "Take him first, in isolation."

She paused for a full minute, with her chin on her hand and her elbow on the table. Her brow gathered. "Sebastian?" she repeated. "Sebastian?—ah, there I might guess something. Well, of course, having once begun this attempt, and being definitely committed, as it were, to a policy of killing us, he will go through to the bitter end, no matter how many other lives it may cost. That is Sebastian's method."

"You don't think, having once found out that I saw and recognised him, he would consider the game lost, and slink away to the coast again?"

"Sebastian? Oh, no; that is the absolute antipodes of his type and temperament."

"He will never give up because of a temporary check, you think?"

"No, never. The man has a will of sheer steel—it may break, but it will not bend. Besides, consider: he is too deeply involved. You have seen him; you know; and he knows you know. You may bring this thing home to him. Then what is his plain policy? Why, to egg on the natives whose confidence he has somehow gained into making a further attack, and cutting off all Salisbury. If he had succeeded in getting you and me massacred at Klaas's, as he hoped, he would no doubt have slunk off to the coast at once, leaving his black dupes to be shot down at leisure by Rhodes's soldiers."

"I see; but having failed in that?"

"Then he is bound to go through with it, and kill us if he can, even if he has to kill all Salisbury with us. That, I feel sure, is Sebastian's plan. Whether he can get the Matabele to back him up in it or not is a different matter."

"But taking Sebastian himself; alone?"

"Oh, Sebastian himself alone would naturally say: 'Never mind Buluwayo! Concentrate round Salisbury, and kill off all there first; when that is done, then you can move on at your ease and cut them to pieces in Charter and Buluwayo.' You see, he would have no interest in the movement, himself, once he had fairly got rid of us here. The Matabele are only the pieces in his game. It is *me* he wants, not Salisbury. He would clear out of Rhodesia as soon as he had carried his point. But he would have to give some reasonable ground to the Matabele for his first advice; and it seems a reasonable ground to say, 'Don't leave Salisbury in your rear, so as to put yourselves between two fires. Capture the outpost first; that down, march on undistracted to the principal stronghold.'"

"Who is no tactician?" I murmured, half aloud.

She laughed. "That's not tactics, Hubert; that's plain common sense—and knowledge of Sebastian. Still, it comes to nothing. The question is not, 'What would Sebastian wish?' it is, 'Could Sebastian persuade these angry black men to accept his guidance?'"

"Sebastian!" I cried; "Sebastian could persuade the very devil! I know the man's fiery enthusiasm, his contagious eloquence. He thrilled me through, myself, with his electric personality, so that it took me six years—and your aid—to find him out at last. His very abstractness tells. Why, even in this war, you may be sure, he will be making notes all the time on the healing of wounds in tropical climates, contrasting the African with the European constitution."

"Oh, yes; of course. Whatever he does, he will never forget the interests of science. He is true to his lady-love, to whomever else he plays false. That is his saving virtue."

"And he will talk down the Matabele," I went on, "even if he doesn't know their language. But I suspect he does; for, you must remember, he was three years in South Africa as a young man, on a scientific expedition, collecting specimens. He can ride like a trooper; and he knows the country. His masterful ways, his austere face, will cow the natives. Then, again, he has the air of a prophet; and prophets always stir the negro. I can imagine with what air he will bid them drive out the intrusive white men who have usurped their land, and draw them flattering pictures of a new Matabele empire about to arise under a new chief, too strong for these gold-grubbing, diamond-hunting mobs from over sea to meddle with."

She reflected once more. "Do you mean to say anything of our suspicions in Salisbury, Hubert?" she asked at last.

"It is useless," I answered. "The Salisbury folk believe there is a white man at the bottom of this trouble already. They will try to catch him; that's all that is necessary. If we said it was Sebastian, people would only laugh at us. They must understand Sebastian, as you and I understand him, before they would think such a move credible. As a rule in life, if you know anything which other people do not know, better keep it to yourself; you will only get laughed at as a fool for telling it."

"I think so, too. That is why I never say what I suspect or infer from my knowledge of types—except to a few who can understand and appreciate. Hubert, if they all arm for the defence of the town, you will stop here, I suppose, to tend the wounded?"

Her lips trembled as she spoke, and she gazed at me with a strange wistfulness. "No, dearest," I answered at once, taking her face in my hands. "I shall fight with the rest. Salisbury has more need to-day of fighters than of healers."

"I thought you would," she answered, slowly. "And I think you do right." Her face was set white; she played nervously with the baby. "I would not urge you; but I am glad you say so. I want you to stop; yet I could not love you so much if I did not see you ready to play the man at such a crisis."

"I shall give in my name with the rest," I answered.

"Hubert, it is hard to spare you—hard to send you to such danger. But for one other thing, I am glad you are going. . . . They must take Sebastian alive; they must *not* kill him."

"They will shoot him red-handed if they catch him," I answered confidently. "A white man who sides with the blacks in an insurrection!"

"Then *you* must see that they do not do it. They must bring him in alive, and try him legally. For me—and therefore for you— that is of the first importance."

"Why so, Hilda?"

"Hubert, you want to marry me." I nodded vehemently. "Well, you know I can only marry you on one condition—that I have succeeded first in clearing my father's memory. Now, the only man living who can clear it is Sebastian. If Sebastian were to be shot, it could *never* be cleared—and then, law of Medes and Persians, I could never marry you."

"But how can you expect Sebastian, of all men, to clear it, Hilda?" I cried. "He is ready to kill us both, merely to prevent your attempting a revision; is it likely you can force him to confess his crime, still less induce him to admit it voluntarily?"

She placed her hands over her eyes and pressed them hard with a strange, prophetic air she often had about her when she gazed into the future. "I know my man," she answered, slowly, without uncovering her eyes. "I know how I can do it—if the chance ever comes to me. But the chance must come first. It is hard to find. I lost it once at Nathaniel's. I must not lose it again. If Sebastian is killed skulking here in Rhodesia, my life's purpose will have failed; I shall not have vindicated my father's good name; and then, we can never marry."

"So I understand, Hilda, my orders are these: I am to go out and fight for the women and children, if possible; that Sebastian shall be made prisoner alive, and on no account to let him be killed in the open!"

"I give you no orders, Hubert. I tell you how it seems best to me. But if Sebastian is shot dead—then you understand it must be all over between us. I *never* can marry you until, or unless, I have cleared my father."

"Sebastian shall not be shot dead," I cried, with my youthful impetuosity. "He shall be brought in alive, though all Salisbury as one man try its best to lynch him."

I went out to report myself as a volunteer for service. Within the next few hours the whole town had been put in a state of siege, and all available men armed to oppose the insurgent Matabele. Hasty preparations were made for defence. The ox-waggons of settlers were drawn up outside in little circles here and there, so as to form laagers, which acted practically as temporary forts for the protection of the outskirts. In one of these I was posted. With our company were two American scouts, named Colebrook and Doolittle, irregular fighters whose value in South African campaigns had already been tested in the old Matabele war against LoBengula. Colebrook, in particular, was an odd-looking creature—a tall, spare man, bodied like a weasel. He was red-haired, ferret-eyed, and an excellent scout, but scrappier and more inarticulate in his manner of speech than any human being I had ever encountered. His conversation was a series of rapid interjections, jerked out at intervals, and made comprehensible by a running play of gesture and attitude.

"Well, yes," he said, when I tried to draw him out on the Matabele mode of fighting. "Not on the open. Never! Grass, if you like. Or bushes. The eyes of them! The eyes! . . ." He leaned eagerly forward, as if looking for something. "See here, Doctor; I'm telling you. Spots. Gleaming. Among the grass. Long grass. And armed, too. A pair of 'em each. One to throw"—he raised his hand as if lancing something—"the other for close fighting. Assegais, you know. That's the name of it. Only the eyes. Creeping, creeping, creeping. No noise. One raised. Waggons drawn up in laager. Oxen out-spanned in the middle. Trekking all day. Tired out; dog tired. Crawl, crawl, crawl! Hands and knees. Might be snakes. A wriggle. Men sitting about the camp fire. Smoking. Gleam of their eyes! Under the waggons. Nearer, nearer, nearer! Then, the throwing ones in your midst. Shower of 'em. Right and left. 'Halloa! stand by, boys!' Look up; see 'em swarming, black like ants, over the waggons. Inside the laager. Snatch up rifles! All up! Oxen stampeding, men running, blacks sticking 'em like pigs in the back with their assegais. Bad job, the whole thing. Don't care for it, myself. Very tough 'uns to fight. If they once break laager."

"Then you should never let them get to close quarters," I suggested, catching the general drift of his inarticulate swift pictures.

"You're a square man, you are, Doctor! There you touch the spot. Never let 'em get at close quarters. Sentries?—creep past 'em. Outposts?—crawl between. Had Forbes and Wilson like that. Cut 'em off. Perdition! . . . But Maxims will do it! Maxims! Never let 'em get near. Sweep the ground all round. Durned hard, though, to know just *when* they're coming. A night; two nights; all clear; only waste ammunition. Third, they swarm like bees; break laager; all over!"

This was not exactly an agreeable picture of what we had to expect—the more so as our particular laager happened to have no Maxims. However, we kept a sharp lookout for those gleaming eyes in the long grass of which Colebrook warned us; their flashing light was the one thing to be seen, at night above all, when the black bodies could crawl unperceived through the tall dry herbage. On our first night out we had no adventures. We watched by turns outside, relieving sentry from time to time, while those of us who slept within the laager slept on the bare ground with our arms beside us. Nobody spoke much. The tension was too great. Every moment we expected an attack of the enemy.

Next day news reached us by scouts from all the other laagers. None of them had been attacked; but in all there was a deep, half-instinctive belief that the Matabele in force were drawing step by step closer and closer around us. Lo-Bengula's old impis, or native regiments, had gathered together once more under their own indunas—men trained and drilled in all the arts and ruses of savage warfare. On their own ground, and among their native scrub, those rude strategists are formidable. They know the country, and how to fight in it. We had nothing to oppose to them but a handful of the new Matabeleland police, an old regular soldier or two, and a raw crowd of volunteers, most of whom, like myself, had never before really handled a rifle.

That afternoon, the Major in command decided to send out the two American scouts to scour the grass and discover, if possible, how near our lines the Matabele had penetrated. I begged hard to be permitted to accompany them. I wanted, if I could, to get evidence against Sebastian; or, at least, to learn whether he was still directing and assisting the enemy. At first, the scouts laughed at my request; but when I told them privately that I believed I had a clue against the white traitor who had caused the revolt, and that I wished to identify him, they changed their tone, and began to think there might be something in it.

"Experience?" Colebrook asked in his brief shorthand of speech, running his ferret eyes over me.

"None," I answered; "but a noiseless tread and a capacity for crawling through holes in hedges which may perhaps be useful."

He glanced inquiry at Doolittle, who was a shorter and stouter man, with a knack of getting over obstacles by sheer forcefulness.

"Hands and knees!" he said, abruptly, in the imperative mood, pointing to a clump of dry grass with thorny bushes ringed about it.

I went down on my hands and knees, and threaded my way through the long grasses and matted boughs as noiselessly as I could. The two old hands watched me. When I emerged several yards off, much to their surprise, Colebrook turned to Doolittle. "Might answer," he said curtly. "Major says, 'Choose your own men.' Anyhow, if they catch him, nobody's fault but his. Wants to go. Will do it."

We set out through the long grass together, walking erect at first, till we had got some distance from the laager, and then, creeping as the Matabele themselves creep, without displacing the grass-flowers, for a mere wave on top would have betrayed us at once to the quick eyes of those observant savages. We crept on for a mile or so. At last, Colebrook turned to me, one finger on his lips. His ferret eyes gleamed. We were approaching a wooded hill, all interspersed with boulders. "Kaffirs here!" he whispered low, as if he knew by instinct. *How* he knew, I cannot tell; he seemed almost to scent them.

We stole on farther, going more furtively than ever now. I could notice by this time that there were waggons in front, and could hear men speaking in them. I wanted to proceed, but Colebrook held up one warning hand. "Won't do," he said, shortly, in a low tone. "Only myself. Danger ahead! Stop here and wait for me."

Doolittle and myself waited. Colebrook kept on cautiously, squirming his long body in sinuous waves like a lizard's through the grass, and was soon lost to us. No snake could have been lither.

We waited, with ears intent. One minute, two minutes, many minutes passed. We could catch the voices of the Kaffirs in the bush all round. They were speaking freely, but what they said I did not know, as I had picked up only a very few words of the Matabele language.

It seemed hours while we waited, still as mice in our ambush, and alert. I began to think Colebrook must have been lost or killed—so long was he gone—and that we must return without him. At last—we leaned forward—a muffled movement in the grass ahead! A slight wave at the base! Then it divided below, bit by bit, while the tops remained stationary. A weasel-like body slank noiselessly through. Finger on lips once more, Colebrook glided beside us. We turned and crawled back, stifling our very pulses. For many minutes none of us spoke. But we heard in our rear a loud cry and a shaking of assegais; the Kaffirs behind us were yelling frightfully. They must have suspected something—seen some movement in the tufted heads of grass, for they spread abroad, shouting. We halted, holding our breath. After a time, however; the noise died down. They were moving another way. We crept on again, stealthily.

When, at last, after many minutes, we found ourselves beyond a sheltering belt of brushwood, we ventured to rise and speak. "Well?" I asked of Colebrook. "Did you discover anything?"

He nodded assent. "Couldn't see him," he said shortly. "But he's there, right enough. White man. Heard 'em talk of him."

"What did they say?" I asked, eagerly.

"Said he had a white skin, but his heart was a Kaffir's. Great induna; leader of many impis. Prophet, wise weather doctor! Friend of old Moselekatse's. Destroy the white men from over the big water; restore the land to the Matabele. Kill all in Salisbury, especially the white women. Witches—all witches. They give charms to the men; cook lions' hearts for them; make them brave with love-drinks."

"They said that?" I exclaimed, taken aback. "Kill all the white women!"

"Yes. Kill all. White witches, every one. The young ones worst. Word of the great induna."

"And you could not see him?"

"Crept near waggons, close. Fellow himself inside. Heard his voice; spoke English, with a little Matabele. Kaffir boy who was servant at the mission interpreted."

"What sort of voice? Like this?" And I imitated Sebastian's cold, clear-cut tone as well as I was able.

"The man! That's him, Doctor. You've got him down to the ground. The very voice. Heard him giving orders."

That settled the question. I was certain of it now. Sebastian was with the insurgents.

We made our way back to our laager, flung ourselves down, and slept a little on the ground before taking our turn in the fatigues of the night watch. Our horses were loosely tied, ready for any sudden alarm. About midnight, we three were sitting with others about the fire, talking low to one another. All at once Doolittle sprang up, alert and eager. "Look out, boys!" he cried, pointing his hands under the waggons. "What's wriggling in the grass there?"

I looked, and saw nothing. Our sentries were posted outside, about a hundred yards apart, walking up and down till they met, and exchanging "All's well" aloud at each meeting.

"They should have been stationary!" one of our scouts exclaimed, looking out at them. "It's easier for the Matabele to see them so, when they walk up and down, moving against the sky. The Major ought to have posted them where it wouldn't have been so simple for a Kaffir to see them and creep in between them!"

"Too late now, boys!" Colebrook burst out, with a rare effort of articulateness. "Call back the sentries, Major! The blacks have broken line! Hold there! They're in upon us!"

Even as he spoke, I followed his eager pointing hand with my eyes, and just descried among the grass two gleaming objects, seen under the hollow of one of the waggons. Two: then two; then two again; and behind, whole pairs of them. They looked like twin stars; but they were eyes, black eyes, reflecting the starlight and the red glare of the camp-fire. They crept on tortuously in serpentine curves through the long, dry grasses. I could feel, rather than see, that they were Matabele, crawling prone on their bellies, and trailing their snake-like way between the dark jungle. Quick as thought, I raised my rifle and blazed away at the foremost. So did several others. But the Major shouted, angrily: "Who fired? Don't shoot, boys, till you hear the word of command! Back, sentries, to laager! Not a shot till they're safe inside! You'll hit your own people!"

Almost before he said it, the sentries darted back. The Matabele, crouching on hands and knees in the long grass, had passed between them unseen. A wild moment followed. I can hardly describe it; the whole thing was so new to me, and took place so quickly. Hordes of black human ants seemed to surge up all at once over and under the waggons. Assegais whizzed through the air, or gleamed brandished around one. Our men fell back to the centre of the laager, and formed themselves hastily under the Major's orders. Then a pause; a deadly fire. Once, twice, thrice we volleyed. The Matabele fell by dozens—but they came on by hundreds. As fast as we fired and mowed down one swarm, fresh swarms seemed to spring from the earth and stream over the waggons. Others appeared to grow up almost beneath our feet as they wormed their way on their faces along the ground between the wheels, squirmed into the circle, and then rose suddenly, erect and naked, in front of us. Meanwhile, they yelled and shouted, clashing their spears and shields. The oxen bellowed. The rifles volleyed. It was a pandemonium of sound in an orgy of gloom. Darkness, lurid flame, blood, wounds, death, horror!

Yet, in the midst of all this hubbub, I could not help admiring the cool military calm and self-control of our Major. His voice rose clear above the confused tumult. "Steady, boys, steady! Don't fire at random. Pick each your likeliest man, and aim at him deliberately. That's right; easy—easy! Shoot at leisure, and don't waste ammunition!"

He stood as if he were on parade, in the midst of this palpitating turmoil of savages. Some of us, encouraged by his example, mounted the waggons, and shot from the tops at our approaching assailants.

How long the hurly-burly went on, I cannot say. We fired, fired, fired, and Kaffirs fell like sheep; yet more Kaffirs rose fresh from the long grass to replace them. They swarmed with greater ease now over the covered waggons, across the mangled and writhing bodies of their fellows; for the dead outside made an inclined plane for the living to mount by. But the enemy were getting less numerous, I thought, and less anxious to fight. The steady fire told on them. By-and-by, with a little halt, for the first time they wavered. All our men now mounted the waggons, and began to fire on them in regular volleys as they came up. The evil effects of the surprise were gone by this time; we were acting with coolness and obeying orders. But several of our people dropped close beside me, pierced through with assegais.

All at once, as if a panic had burst over them, the Matabele, with one mind, stopped dead short in their advance and ceased fighting. Till that moment, no number of deaths seemed to make any difference to them. Men fell, disabled; others sprang up from the ground by magic. But now, of a sudden, their courage flagged—they faltered, gave way, broke, and shambled in a body. At last, as one man, they turned and fled. Many of them leapt up with a loud cry from the long grass where they were skulking, flung away their big shields with the white thongs interlaced, and ran for dear life, black, crouching figures, through the dense, dry jungle. They held their assegais still, but did not dare to use them. It was a flight, pell-mell—and the devil take the hindmost.

Not until then had I leisure to *think*, and to realise my position. This was the first and only time I had ever seen a battle. I am a bit of a coward, I believe—like most other men—though I have courage enough to confess it; and I expected to find myself terribly afraid when it came to fighting. Instead of that, to my immense surprise, once the Matabele had swarmed over the laager, and were upon us in their thousands, I had no time to be frightened. The absolute necessity for keeping cool, for loading and reloading, for aiming and firing, for beating them off at close quarters—all this so occupied one's mind, and still more one's hands, that one couldn't find room for any personal terrors. "They are breaking over there!" "They will overpower us yonder!" "They are faltering now!" Those thoughts were so uppermost in one's head, and one's arms were so alert, that only after the enemy gave way, and began to run at full pelt, could a man find breathing-space to think of his own safety. Then the thought occurred to me, "I have been through my first fight, and come out of it alive; after all, I was a deal less afraid than I expected!"

That took but a second, however. Next instant, awaking to the altered circumstances, we were after them at full speed; accompanying them on their way back to their kraals in the uplands with a running fire as a farewell attention.

As we broke laager in pursuit of them, by the uncertain starlight we saw a sight which made us boil with indignation. A mounted man turned and fled before them. He seemed their leader, unseen till then. He was dressed like a European—tall, thin, unbending, in a greyish-white suit. He rode a good horse, and sat it well; his air was commanding, even as he turned and fled in the general rout from that lost battle.

I seized Colebrook's arm, almost speechless with anger. "The white man!" I cried. "The traitor!"

He did not answer a word, but with a set face of white rage loosed his horse from where it was tethered among the waggons. At the same moment, I loosed mine. So did Doolittle. Quick as thought, but silently, we led them out all three where the laager was broken. I clutched my mare's mane, and sprang to the stirrup to pursue our enemy. My sorrel bounded off like a bird. The fugitive had a good two minutes start of us; but our horses were fresh, while his had probably been ridden all day. I patted my pony's neck; she responded with a ringing neigh of joy. We tore after the outlaw, all three of us abreast. I felt a sort of fierce delight in the reaction after the fighting. Our ponies galloped wildly over the plain; we burst out into the night, never heeding the Matabele whom we passed on the open in panic-stricken retreat. I noticed that many of them in their terror had even flung away their shields and their assegais.

It was a mad chase across the dark veldt—we three, neck to neck, against that one desperate runaway. We rode all we knew. I dug my heels into my sorrel's flanks, and she responded bravely.

The tables were turned now on our traitor since the afternoon of the massacre. *He* was the pursued, and *we* were the pursuers. We felt we must run him down, and punish him for his treachery.

At a breakneck pace, we stumbled over low bushes; we grazed big boulders; we rolled down the sides of steep ravines; but we kept him in sight all the time, dim and black against the starry sky; slowly, slowly—yes, yes!—we gained upon him. My pony led now. The mysterious white man rode and rode—head bent, neck forward—but never looked behind him. Bit by bit we lessened the distance between us. As we drew near him at last, Doolittle called out to me, in a warning voice: "Take care, Doctor! Have your revolvers ready! He's driven to bay now! As we approach, he'll fire at us!"

Then it came home to me in a flash. I felt the truth of it. "He *dare* not fire!" I cried. "He dare not turn towards us. He cannot show his face! If he did, we might recognise him!"

On we rode, still gaining. "Now, now," I cried, "we shall catch him!"

Even as I leaned forward to seize his rein, the fugitive, without checking his horse, without turning his head, drew his revolver from his belt, and, raising his hand, fired behind him at random. He fired towards us, on the chance. The bullet whizzed past my ear, not hitting anyone. We scattered, right and left, still galloping free and strong. We did not return his fire, as I had told the others of my desire to take him alive. We might have shot his horse; but the risk of hitting the rider, coupled with the confidence we felt of eventually hunting him to earth, restrained us. It was the great mistake we made.

He had gained a little by his shots, but we soon caught it up. Once more I said, "We are on him!"

A minute later, we were pulled up short before an impenetrable thicket of prickly shrubs, through which I saw at once it would have been quite impossible to urge our staggering horses.

The other man, of course, reached it before us, with his mare's last breath. He must have been making for it, indeed, of set purpose; for the second he arrived at the edge of the thicket he slipped off his tired pony, and seemed to dive into the bush as a swimmer dives off a rock into the water.

"We have him now!" I cried, in a voice of triumph. And Colebrook echoed, "We have him!"

We sprang down quickly. "Take him alive, if you can!" I exclaimed, remembering Hilda's advice. "Let us find out who he is, and have him properly tried and hanged at Buluwayo! Don't give him a soldier's death! All he deserves is a murderer's!"

"You stop here," Colebrook said, briefly, flinging his bridle to Doolittle to hold. "Doctor and I follow him. Thick bush. Knows the ways of it. Revolvers ready!"

I handed my sorrel to Doolittle. He stopped behind, holding the three foam-bespattered and panting horses, while Colebrook and I dived after our fugitive into the matted bushes.

The thicket, as I have said, was impenetrable above; but it was burrowed at its base by over-ground runs of some wild animal—not, I think, a very large one; they were just like the runs which rabbits make among gorse and heather, only on a bigger scale—bigger, even, than a fox's or badger's. By crouching and bending our backs, we could crawl through them with difficulty into the scrubby tangle. It was hard work creeping. The runs divided soon. Colebrook felt with his hands on the ground: "I can make out the spoor!" he muttered, after a minute. "He has gone on this way!"

We tracked him a little distance in, crawling at times, and rising now and again where the runs opened out on to the air for a moment. The spoor was doubtful and the tunnels tortuous. I felt the ground from time to time, but could not be sure of the tracks with my fingers; I was not a trained scout, like Colebrook or Doolittle. We wriggled deeper into the tangle. Something stirred once or twice. It was not far from me. I was uncertain whether it was *him*—Sebastian—or a Kaffir earth-hog, the animal which seemed likeliest to have made the burrows. Was he going to clude us, even now? Would he turn upon us with a knife? If so, could we hold him?

At last, when we had pushed our way some distance in, we heard a wild cry from outside. It was Doolittle's voice. "Quick! quick! out again! The man will escape! He has come back on his tracks, and rounded!"

I saw our mistake at once. We had left our companion out there alone, rendered helpless by the care of all three horses.

Colebrook said never a word. He was a man of action. He turned with instinctive haste, and followed our own spoor back again with his hands and knees to the opening in the thicket by which we had first entered.

Before we could reach it, however, two shots rang out clear in the direction where we had left poor Doolittle and the horses. Then a sharp cry broke the stillness—the cry of a wounded man. We redoubled our pace. We knew we were outwitted.

When we reached the open, we saw at once by the uncertain light what had happened. The fugitive was riding away on my own little sorrel,—riding for dear life; not back the way we came from Salisbury, but sideways across the veldt towards Chimoio and the Portuguese seaports. The other two horses, riderless and terrified, were scampering with loose heels over the dark plain. Doolittle was not to be seen; he lay, a black lump, among the black bushes about him.

We looked around for him, and found him. He was severely, I may even say dangerously, wounded. The bullet had lodged in his right side. We had to catch our two horses, and ride them back with our wounded man, leading the fugitive's mare in tow, all blown and breathless. I stuck to the fugitive's mare; it was the one clue we had now against him. But Sebastian, if it *was* Sebastian, had ridden off scot-free. I understood his game at a glance. He had got the better of us once more. He would make for the coast by the nearest road, give himself out as a settler escaped from the massacre, and catch the next ship for England or the Cape, now this *coup* had failed him.

Doolittle had not seen the traitor's face. The man rose from the bush, he said, shot him, seized the pony, and rode off in a second with ruthless haste. He was tall and thin, but erect—that was all the wounded scout could tell us about his assailant. And *that* was not enough to identify Sebastian.

All danger was over. We rode back to Salisbury. The first words Hilda said when she saw me were: "Well, he has got away from you!"

"Yes; how did you know?"

"I read it in your step. But I guessed as much before. He is so very keen; and you started too confident."

THE EPISODE OF THE LADY
WHO WAS VERY EXCLUSIVE

The Matabele revolt gave Hilda a prejudice against Rhodesia. I will confess that I shared it. I may be hard to please; but it somehow sets one against a country when one comes home from a ride to find all the other occupants of the house one lives in massacred. So Hilda decided to leave South Africa. By an odd coincidence, I also decided on the same day to change my residence. Hilda's movements and mine, indeed, coincided curiously. The moment I learned she was going anywhere, I discovered in a flash that I happened to be going there too. I commend this strange case of parallel thought and action to the consideration of the Society for Psychical Research.

So I sold my farm, and had done with Rhodesia. A country with a future is very well in its way; but I am quite Ibsenish in my preference for a country with a past. Oddly enough, I had no difficulty in getting rid of my white elephant of a farm. People seemed to believe in Rhodesia none the less firmly because of this slight disturbance. They treated massacres as necessary incidents in the early history of a colony with a future. And I do not deny that native risings add picturesqueness. But I prefer to take them in a literary form.

"You will go home, of course?" I said to Hilda, when we came to talk it all over.

She shook her head. "To England? Oh, no. I must pursue my Plan. Sebastian will have gone home; he expects me to follow."

"And why don't you?"

"Because—he expects it. You see, he is a good judge of character; he will naturally infer, from what he knows of my temperament, that after this experience I shall want to get back to England and safety. So I should—if it were not that I know he will expect it. As it is, I must go elsewhere; I must draw him after me."

"Where?"

"Why do you ask, Hubert?"

"Because—I want to know where I am going myself. Wherever you go, I have reason to believe, I shall find that I happen to be going also."

She rested her little chin on her hand and reflected a minute. "Does it occur to you," she asked at last, "that people have tongues? If you go on following me like this, they will really begin to talk about us."

"Now, upon my word, Hilda," I cried, "that is the very first time I have ever known you show a woman's want of logic! I do not propose to follow you; I propose to happen to be travelling by the same steamer. I ask you to marry me; you won't; you admit you are fond of me; yet you tell me not to come with you. It is *I* who suggest a course which would prevent people from chattering—by the simple device of a wedding. It is *you* who refuse. And then you turn upon me like this! Admit that you are unreasonable."

"My dear Hubert, have I ever denied that I was a woman?"

"Besides," I went on, ignoring her delicious smile, "I don't intend to *follow* you. I expect, on the contrary, to find myself beside you. When I know where you are going, I shall accidentally turn up on the same steamer. Accidents *will* happen. Nobody can prevent coincidences from occurring. You may marry me, or you may not; but if you don't marry me, you can't expect to curtail my liberty of action, can you? You had better know the worst at once; if you won't take me, you must count upon finding me at your elbow all the world over—till the moment comes when you choose to accept me."

"Dear Hubert, I am ruining your life!"

"An excellent reason, then, for taking my advice, and marrying me instantly! But you wander from the question. Where are you

going? That is the issue now before the house. You persist in evading it."

She smiled, and came back to earth. "Oh, if you *must* know, to
India, by the east coast, changing steamers at Aden."

"Extraordinary!" I cried. "Do you know, Hilda, as luck will have
it, *I* also shall be on my way to Bombay by the very same steamer!"

"But you don't know what steamer it is?"

"No matter. That only makes the coincidence all the odder.
Whatever the name of the ship may be, when you get on board, I
have a presentiment that you will be surprised to find me there."

She looked up at me with a gathering film in her eyes. "Hubert,
you are irrepressible!"

"I am, my dear child; so you may as well spare yourself the
needless trouble of trying to repress me."

If you rub a piece of iron on a loadstone, it becomes magnetic.
So, I think, I must have begun to acquire some part of Hilda's own
prophetic strain; for, sure enough, a few weeks later, we both of us
found ourselves on the German East African steamer *Kaiser Wilhelm*, on our way to Aden—exactly as I had predicted. Which goes
to prove that there is really something after all in presentiments!

"Since you persist in accompanying me," Hilda said to me, as
we sat in our chairs on deck the first evening out, "I see what I
must do. I must invent some plausible and ostensible reason for
our travelling together."

"We are not travelling together," I answered. "We are travelling by the same steamer; that is all—exactly like the rest of our
fellow-passengers. I decline to be dragged into this imaginary part-
nership."

"Now do be serious, Hubert! I am going to invent an object in
life for us."

"What object?"

"How can I tell yet? I must wait and see what turns up. When
we tranship at Aden, and find out what people are going on to
Bombay with us, I shall probably discover some nice married lady
to whom I can attach myself."

"And am I to attach myself to her, too?"

"My dear boy, I never asked you to come. You came unbidden. You must manage for yourself as best you may. But I leave much to the chapter of accidents. We never know what will turn up, till it turns up in the end. Everything comes at last, you know, to him that waits."

"And yet," I put in, with a meditative air, "I have never observed that waiters are so much better off than the rest of the community. They seem to me—"

"Don't talk nonsense. It is *you* who are wandering from the question now. Please return to it."

I returned at once. "So I am to depend on what turns up?"

"Yes. Leave that to me. When we see our fellow-passengers on the Bombay steamer, I shall soon discover some ostensible reason why we two should be travelling through India with one of them."

"Well, you are a witch, Hilda," I answered. "I found that out long ago; but if you succeed between here and Bombay in inventing a Mission, I shall begin to believe you are even more of a witch than I ever thought you."

At Aden we changed into a P. and O. steamer. Our first evening out on our second cruise was a beautiful one; the bland Indian Ocean wore its sweetest smile for us. We sat on deck after dinner. A lady with a husband came up from the cabin while we sat and gazed at the placid sea. I was smoking a quiet digestive cigar. Hilda was seated in her deck chair next to me.

The lady with the husband looked about her for a vacant space on which to place the chair a steward was carrying for her. There was plenty of room on the quarter-deck. I could not imagine why she gazed about her with such obtrusive caution. She inspected the occupants of the various chairs around with deliberate scrutiny through a long-handled tortoise-shell optical abomination. None of them seemed to satisfy her. After a minute's effort, during which she also muttered a few words very low to her husband, she selected an empty spot midway between our group and the most distant group on the other side of us. In other words, she sat as far away from everybody present as the necessarily restricted area of the quarter-deck permitted.

Hilda glanced at me and smiled. I snatched a quick look at the
lady again. She was dressed with an amount of care and a smart-
ness of detail that seemed somewhat uncalled for on the Indian
Ocean. A cruise on a P. and O. steamer is not a garden party. Her
chair was most luxurious, and had her name painted on it, back
and front, in very large letters, with undue obtrusiveness. I read it
from where I sat, "Lady Meadowcroft."

The owner of the chair was tolerably young, not bad looking,
and most expensively attired. Her face had a certain vacant, languid, half ennuyee air which I have learned to associate with women
of the nouveau-riche type—women with small brains and restless
minds, habitually plunged in a vortex of gaiety, and miserable when
left for a passing moment to their own resources.

Hilda rose from her chair, and walked quietly forward towards
the bow of the steamer. I rose, too, and accompanied her. "Well?"
she said, with a faint touch of triumph in her voice when we had
got out of earshot.

"Well, what?" I answered, unsuspecting.

"I told you everything turned up at the end!" she said, confidently. "Look at the lady's nose!"

"It does turn up at the end—certainly," I answered, glancing
back at her. "But I hardly see—"

"Hubert, you are growing dull! You were not so at Nathaniel's.
. . . It is the lady herself who has turned up, not her nose—though
I grant you *that* turns up too—the lady I require for our tour in
India; the not impossible chaperon."

"Her nose tells you that?"

"Her nose, in part; but her face as a whole, too, her dress, her
chair, her mental attitude to things in general."

"My dear Hilda, you can't mean to tell me you have divined her
whole nature at a glance, by magic!"

"Not wholly at a glance. I saw her come on board, you know—
she transhipped from some other line at Aden as we did, and I have
been watching her ever since. Yes, I think I have unravelled her."

"You have been astonishingly quick!" I cried.

"Perhaps—but then, you see, there is so little to unravel! Some books, we all know, you must 'chew and digest'; they can only be read slowly; but some you can glance at, skim, and skip; the mere turning of the pages tells you what little worth knowing there is in them."

"She doesn't *look* profound," I admitted, casting an eye at her meaningless small features as we paced up and down. "I incline to agree you might easily skim her."

"Skim her—and learn all. The table of contents is *so* short. . . . You see, in the first place, she is extremely 'exclusive'; she prides herself on her 'exclusiveness': it, and her shoddy title, are probably all she has to pride herself upon, and she works them both hard. She is a sham great lady."

As Hilda spoke, Lady Meadowcroft raised a feebly querulous voice. "Steward! this won't do! I can smell the engine here. Move my chair. I must go on further."

"If you go on further that way, my lady," the steward answered, good-humouredly, but with a man-servant's deference for any sort of title, "you'll smell the galley, where they're cooking the dinner. I don't know which your ladyship would like best—the engine or the galley."

The languid figure leaned back in the chair with an air of resignation. "I'm sure I don't know why they cook the dinners up so high," she murmured, pettishly, to her husband. "Why can't they stick the kitchens underground—in the hold, I mean—instead of bothering us up here on deck with them?"

The husband was a big, burly, rough-and-ready Yorkshireman—stout, somewhat pompous, about forty, with hair wearing bald on the forehead: the personification of the successful business man. "My dear Emmie," he said, in a loud voice, with a North Country accent, "the cooks have got to live. They've got to live like the rest of us. I can never persuade you that the hands must always be humoured. If you don't humour 'em, they won't work for you. It's a poor tale when the hands won't work. Even with galleys on deck, the life of a sea-cook is not generally thowt an enviable position.

Is not a happy one—not a happy one, as the fellah says in the opera. You must humour your cooks. If you stuck 'em in the hold,
you'd get no dinner at all—that's the long and the short of it."

The languid lady turned away with a sickly, disappointed air.
"Then they ought to have a conscription, or something," she said,
pouting her lips. "The Government ought to take it in hand and
manage it somehow. It's bad enough having to go by these beastly
steamers to India at all, without having one's breath poisoned by—
" the rest of the sentence died away inaudibly in a general murmur
of ineffective grumbling.

"Why do you think she is *exclusive*?" I asked Hilda as we strolled on towards the stern, out of the spoilt child's hearing.

"Why, didn't you notice?—she looked about her when she came
on deck to see whether there was anybody who *was* anybody sitting there, whom she might put her chair near. But the Governor
of Madras hadn't come up from his cabin yet; and the wife of the
chief Commissioner of Oude had three civilians hanging about her
seat; and the daughters of the Commander-in-Chief drew their
skirts away as she passed. So she did the next best thing—sat as
far apart as she could from the common herd: meaning all the rest
of us. If you can't mingle at once with the Best People, you can at
least assert your exclusiveness negatively, by declining to associate with the mere multitude."

"Now, Hilda, that is the first time I have ever known you to
show any feminine ill-nature!"

"Ill-nature! Not at all. I am merely trying to arrive at the lady's
character for my own guidance. I rather like her, poor little thing.
Don't I tell you she will do? So far from objecting to her, I mean to
go the round of India with her."

"You have decided quickly."

"Well, you see, if you insist upon accompanying me, I *must* have
a chaperon; and Lady Meadowcroft will do as well as anybody else.
In fact, being be-ladied, she will do a little better, from the point
of view of Society, though *that* is a detail. The great matter is to fix
upon a possible chaperon at once, and get her well in hand before
we arrive at Bombay."

"But she seems so complaining!" I interposed. "I'm afraid, if you take her on, you'll get terribly bored with her."

"If *she* takes *me* on, you mean. She's not a lady's-maid, though I intend to go with her; and she may as well give in first as last, for I'm going. Now see how nice I am to you, sir! I've provided you, too, with a post in her suite, as you *will* come with me. No, never mind asking me what it is just yet; all things come to him who waits; and if you will only accept the post of waiter, I mean all things to come to you."

"All things, Hilda?" I asked, meaningly, with a little tremor of delight.

She looked at me with a sudden passing tenderness in her eyes. "Yes, all things, Hubert. All things. But we mustn't talk of that—though I begin to see my way clearer now. You shall be rewarded for your constancy at last, dear knight-errant. As to my chaperon, I'm not afraid of her boring me; she bores herself, poor lady; one can see that, just to look at her; but she will be much less bored if she has us two to travel with. What she needs is constant companionship, bright talk, excitement. She has come away from London, where she swims with the crowd; she has no resources of her own, no work, no head, no interests. Accustomed to a whirl of foolish gaieties, she wearies her small brain; thrown back upon herself, she bores herself at once, because she has nothing interesting to tell herself. She absolutely requires somebody else to interest her. She can't even amuse herself with a book for three minutes to-gether. See, she has a yellow-backed French novel now, and she is only able to read five lines at a time; then she gets tired and glances about her listlessly. What she wants is someone gay, laid on, to divert her all the time from her own inanity."

"Hilda, how wonderfully quick you are at reading these things! I see you are right; but I could never have guessed so much myself from such small premises."

"Well, what can you expect, my dear boy? A girl like this, brought up in a country rectory, a girl of no intellect, busy at home with the fowls, and the pastry, and the mothers' meetings—suddenly married offhand to a wealthy man, and deprived of the occupations which were her salvation in life, to be plunged into the whirl of a London season, and stranded at its end for want of the diversions which, by dint of use, have become necessaries of life to her!"

"Now, Hilda, you are practising upon my credulity. You can't possibly tell from her look that she was brought up in a country rectory."

"Of course not. You forget. There my memory comes in. I simply remember it."

"You remember it? How?"

"Why, just in the same way as I remembered your name and your mother's when I was first introduced to you. I saw a notice once in the births, deaths, and marriages—'At St. Alphege's, Millington, by the Rev. Hugh Clitheroe, M.A., father of the bride, Peter Gubbins, Esq., of The Laurels, Middleston, to Emilia Frances, third daughter of the Rev. Hugh Clitheroe, rector of Millington.'"

"Clitheroe—Gubbins; what on earth has that to do with it? That would be Mrs. Gubbins: this is Lady Meadowcroft."

"The same article, as the shopmen say—only under a different name. A year or two later I read a notice in the *Times* that 'I, Ivor de Courcy Meadowcroft, of The Laurels, Middleston, Mayor-elect of the Borough of Middleston, hereby give notice, that I have this day discontinued the use of the name Peter Gubbins, by which I was formerly known, and have assumed in lieu thereof the style and title of Ivor de Courcy Meadowcroft, by which I desire in future to be known.'

"A month or two later, again I happened to light upon a notice in the *Telegraph* that the Prince of Wales had opened a new hospital for incurables at Middleston, and that the Mayor, Mr. Ivor Meadowcroft, had received an intimation of Her Majesty's intention of conferring upon him the honour of knighthood. Now what do you make of it?"

"Putting two and two together," I answered, with my eye on our subject, "and taking into consideration the lady's face and manner, I should incline to suspect that she was the daughter of a poor parson, with the usual large family in inverse proportion to his means. That she unexpectedly made a good match with a very wealthy manufacturer who had raised himself; and that she was puffed up accordingly with a sense of self-importance."

"Exactly. He is a millionaire, or something very like it; and, being an ambitious girl, as she understands ambition, she got him to stand for the mayoralty, I don't doubt, in the year when the Prince of Wales was going to open the Royal Incurables, on purpose to secure him the chance of a knighthood. Then she said, very reasonably, 'I *won't* be Lady Gubbins—Sir Peter Gubbins!' There's an aristocratic name for you!—and, by a stroke of his pen, he straightway dis-Gubbinised himself, and emerged as Sir Ivor de Courcy Meadowcroft."

"Really, Hilda, you know everything about everybody! And what do you suppose they're going to India for?"

"Now, you've asked me a hard one. I haven't the faintest notion. . . . And yet . . . let me think. How is this for a conjecture? Sir Ivor is interested in steel rails, I believe, and in railway plant generally. I'm almost sure I've seen his name in connection with steel rails in reports of public meetings. There's a new Government railway now being built on the Nepaul frontier—one of these strategic railways, I think they call them—it's mentioned in the papers we got at Aden. He *might* be going out for that. We can watch his conversation, and see what part of India he talks about."

"They don't seem inclined to give us much chance of talking," I objected.

"No; they are *very* exclusive. But I'm very exclusive, too. And I mean to give them a touch of my exclusiveness. I venture to predict that, before we reach Bombay, they'll be going down on their knees and imploring us to travel with them."

At table, as it happened, from next morning's breakfast the Meadowcrofts sat next to us. Hilda was on one side of me; Lady Meadowcroft on the other; and beyond her again, bluff Yorkshire Sir Ivor, with his cold, hard, honest blue North Country eyes, and his dignified, pompous English, breaking down at times into a

North Country colloquialism. They talked chiefly to each other.
Acting on Hilda's instructions, I took care not to engage in conversation with our "exclusive" neighbour, except so far as the absolute necessities of the table compelled me. I "troubled her for
the salt" in the most frigid voice. "May I pass you the potato salad?"
became on my lips a barrier of separation. Lady Meadowcroft
marked and wondered. People of her sort are so anxious to ingra-
tiate themselves with "all the Best People" that if they find you are
wholly unconcerned about the privilege of conversation with a
"titled person," they instantly judge you to be a distinguished character. As the days rolled on, Lady Meadowcroft's voice began to
melt by degrees. Once, she asked me, quite civilly, to send round
the ice; she even saluted me on the third day out with a polite
"Good-morning, doctor."

Still, I maintained (by Hilda's advice) my dignified reserve, and
took my seat severely with a cold "Good-morning." I behaved like
a high-class consultant, who expects to be made Physician in Ordinary to Her Majesty.

At lunch that day, Hilda played her first card with delicious
unconsciousness—apparent unconsciousness; for, when she chose,
she was a consummate actress. She played it at a moment when
Lady Meadowcroft, who by this time was burning with curiosity
on our account, had paused from her talk with her husband to listen to us. I happened to say something about some Oriental curios
belonging to an aunt of mine in London. Hilda seized the opportunity. "What did you say was her name?" she asked, blandly.

"Why, Lady Tepping," I answered, in perfect innocence. "She
has a fancy for these things, you know. She brought a lot of them
home with her from Burma."

As a matter of fact, as I have already explained, my poor dear
aunt is an extremely commonplace old Army widow, whose husband happened to get knighted among the New Year's honours for
some brush with the natives on the Shan frontier. But Lady Meadowcroft was at the stage where a title is a title; and the discovery
that I was the nephew of a "titled person" evidently interested her.
I could feel rather than see that she glanced significantly aside at

Sir Ivor, and that Sir Ivor in return made a little movement of his shoulders equivalent to "I told you so."

Now Hilda knew perfectly well that the aunt of whom I spoke *was* Lady Tepping; so I felt sure that she had played this card of malice prepense, to pique Lady Meadowcroft.

But Lady Meadowcroft herself seized the occasion with inartistic avidity. She had hardly addressed us as yet. At the sound of the magic passport, she pricked up her ears, and turned to me suddenly. "Burma?" she said, as if to conceal the true reason for her change of front. "Burma? I had a cousin there once. He was in the Gloucestershire Regiment."

"Indeed?" I answered. My tone was one of utter unconcern in her cousin's history. "Miss Wade, will you take Bombay ducks with your curry?" In public, I thought it wise under the circumstances to abstain from calling her Hilda. It might lead to misconceptions; people might suppose we were more than fellow-travellers.

"You have had relations in Burma?" Lady Meadowcroft persisted.

I manifested a desire to discontinue the conversation. "Yes," I answered, coldly, "my uncle commanded there."

"Commanded there! Really! Ivor, do you hear? Dr. Cumberledge's uncle commanded in Burma." A faint intonation on the word *commanded* drew unobtrusive attention to its social importance. "May I ask what was his name?—my cousin was there, you see." An insipid smile. "We may have friends in common."

"He was a certain Sir Malcolm Tepping," I blurted out, staring hard at my plate.

"Tepping! I think I have heard Dick speak of him, Ivor."

"Your cousin," Sir Ivor answered, with emphatic dignity, "is certain to have mixed with nobbut the highest officials in Burma."

"Yes, I'm sure Dick used to speak of a certain Sir Malcolm. My cousin's name, Dr. Cumberledge, was Maltby—Captain Richard Maltby."

"Indeed," I answered, with an icy stare. "I cannot pretend to the pleasure of having met him."

Be exclusive to the exclusive, and they burn to know you. From that moment forth Lady Meadowcroft pestered us with her endeavours to scrape acquaintance. Instead of trying how far she could place her chair from us, she set it down as near us as politeness permitted. She entered into conversation whenever an opening afforded itself, and we two stood off haughtily. She even ventured to question me about our relation to one another: "Miss Wade is your cousin, I suppose?" she suggested.

"Oh, dear, no," I answered, with a glassy smile. "We are not connected in any way."

"But you are travelling together!"

"Merely as you and I are travelling together—fellow-passengers on the same steamer."

"Still, you have met before."

"Yes, certainly. Miss Wade was a nurse at St. Nathaniel's, in London, where I was one of the house doctors. When I came on board at Cape Town, after some months in South Africa, I found she was going by the same steamer to India." Which was literally true. To have explained the rest would have been impossible, at least to anyone who did not know the whole of Hilda's history.

"And what are you both going to do when you get to India?"

"Really, Lady Meadowcroft," I said, severely, "I have not asked Miss Wade what she is going to do. If you inquire of her point-blank, as you have inquired of me, I dare say she will tell you. For myself, I am just a globe-trotter, amusing myself. I only want to have a look round at India."

"Then you are not going out to take an appointment?"

"By George, Emmie," the burly Yorkshireman put in, with an air of annoyance, "you are cross-questioning Dr. Cumberledge; nowt less than cross-questioning him!"

I waited a second. "No," I answered, slowly. "I have not been practising of late. I am looking about me. I travel for enjoyment."

That made her think better of me. She was of the kind, indeed, who think better of a man if they believe him to be idle.

She dawdled about all day on deck chairs, herself seldom even reading; and she was eager now to drag Hilda into conversation. Hilda resisted; she had found a volume in the library which immensely interested her.

"What *are* you reading, Miss Wade?" Lady Meadowcroft cried at last, quite savagely. It made her angry to see anybody else pleased and occupied when she herself was listless.

"A delightful book!" Hilda answered. "*The Buddhist Praying Wheel*, by William Simpson."

Lady Meadowcroft took it from her and turned the pages over with a languid air. "Looks awfully dull!" she observed, with a faint smile, at last, returning it.

"It's charming," Hilda retorted, glancing at one of the illustrations. "It explains so much. It shows one why one turns round one's chair at cards for luck; and why, when a church is consecrated, the bishop walks three times about it sunwise."

"Our Bishop is a dreadfully prosy old gentleman," Lady Meadowcroft answered, gliding off at a tangent on a personality, as is the wont of her kind; "he had, oh, such a dreadful quarrel with my father over the rules of the St. Alphege Schools at Millington."

"Indeed," Hilda answered, turning once more to her book. Lady Meadowcroft looked annoyed. It would never have occurred to her that within a few weeks she was to owe her life to that very abstruse work, and what Hilda had read in it.

That afternoon, as we watched the flying fish from the ship's side, Hilda said to me abruptly, "My chaperon is an extremely nervous woman."

"Nervous about what?"

"About disease, chiefly. She has the temperament that dreads infection—and therefore catches it."

"Why do you think so?"

"Haven't you noticed that she often doubles her thumb under her fingers—folds her fist across it—so—especially when anybody talks about anything alarming? If the conversation happens to turn on jungle fever, or any subject like that, down goes her thumb instantly, and she clasps her fist over it with a convulsive squeeze. At the same time, too, her face twitches. I know what that trick means. She's horribly afraid of tropical diseases, though she never says so."

"And you attach importance to her fear?"

"Of course. I count upon it as probably our chief means of catching and fixing her."

"As how?"

She shook her head and quizzed me. "Wait and see. You are a doctor; I, a trained nurse. Before twenty-four hours, I foresee she will ask us. She is sure to ask us, now she has learned that you are Lady Tepping's nephew, and that I am acquainted with several of the Best People."

That evening, about ten o'clock, Sir Ivor strolled up to me in the smoking-room with affected unconcern. He laid his hand on my arm and drew me aside mysteriously. The ship's doctor was there, playing a quiet game of poker with a few of the passengers. "I beg your pardon, Dr. Cumberledge," he began, in an undertone, "could you come outside with me a minute? Lady Meadowcroft has sent me up to you with a message."

I followed him on to the open deck. "It is quite impossible, my dear sir," I said, shaking my head austerely, for I divined his errand. "I can't go and see Lady Meadowcroft. Medical etiquette, you know; the constant and salutary rule of the profession!"

"Why not?" he asked, astonished.

"The ship carries a surgeon," I replied, in my most precise tone. "He is a duly qualified gentleman, very able in his profession, and he ought to inspire your wife with confidence. I regard this vessel as Dr. Boyell's practice, and all on board it as virtually his patients."

Sir Ivor's face fell. "But Lady Meadowcroft is not at all well," he answered, looking piteous; "and—she can't endure the ship's doctor. Such a common man, you know! His loud voice disturbs her. You *must* have noticed that my wife is a lady of exceptionally delicate nervous organisation." He hesitated, beamed on me, and played his trump card. "She dislikes being attended by owt but a *gentleman.*"

"If a gentleman is also a medical man," I answered, "his sense of duty towards his brother practitioners would, of course, prevent him from interfering in their proper sphere, or putting upon them the unmerited slight of letting them see him preferred before them."

"Then you positively refuse?" he asked, wistfully, drawing back. I could see he stood in a certain dread of that imperious little woman.

I conceded a point. "I will go down in twenty minutes," I admitted, looking grave,—"not just now, lest I annoy my colleague,—and I will glance at Lady Meadowcroft in an unprofessional way. If I think her case demands treatment, I will tell Dr. Boyell." And I returned to the smoking-room and took up a novel.

Twenty minutes later I knocked at the door of the lady's private cabin, with my best bedside manner in full play. As I suspected, she was nervous—nothing more—my mere smile reassured her. I observed that she held her thumb fast, doubled under in her fist, all the time I was questioning her, as Hilda had said; and I also noticed that the fingers closed about it convulsively at first, but gradually relaxed as my voice restored confidence. She thanked me profusely, and was really grateful.

On deck next day she was very communicative. They were going to make the regular tour first, she said, but were to go on to the Tibetan frontier at the end, where Sir Ivor had a contract to construct a railway, in a very wild region. Tigers? Natives? Oh, she didn't mind either of *them*; but she was told that that district—what did they call it? the Terai, or something—was terribly unwholesome. Fever was what-you-may-call-it there—yes, "endemic"—that was the word; "oh, thank you, Dr. Cumberledge." She hated the very name of fever. "Now you, Miss Wade, I suppose," with an awestruck smile, "are not in the least afraid of it?"

Hilda looked up at her calmly. "Not in the least," she answered. "I have nursed hundreds of cases."

"Oh, my, how dreadful! And never caught it?"

"Never. I am not afraid, you see."

"I wish *I* wasn't! Hundreds of cases! It makes one ill to think of it! . . . And all successfully?"

"Almost all of them."

"You don't tell your patients stories when they're ill about your other cases who died, do you?" Lady Meadowcroft went on, with a quick little shudder.

Hilda's face by this time was genuinely sympathetic. "Oh, never!" she answered, with truth. "That would be very bad nursing! One's object in treating a case is to make one's patient well; so one naturally avoids any sort of subject that might be distressing or alarming."

"You really mean it?" Her face was pleading.

"Why, of course. I try to make my patients my friends; I talk to them cheerfully; I amuse them and distract them; I get them away, as far as I can, from themselves and their symptoms."

"Oh, what a lovely person to have about one when one's ill!" the languid lady exclaimed, ecstatically. "I *should* like to send for you if I wanted nursing! But there—it's always so, of course, with a real lady; common nurses frighten one so. I wish I could always have a lady to nurse me!"

"A person who sympathises—that is the really important thing," Hilda answered, in her quiet voice. "One must find out first one's patient's temperament. *You* are nervous, I can see." She laid one hand on her new friend's arm. "You need to be kept amused and engaged when you are ill; what *you* require most is—insight—and sympathy."

The little fist doubled up again; the vacant face grew positively sweet. "That's just it! You have hit it! How clever you are! I want all that. I suppose, Miss Wade, *you* never go out for private nursing?"

"Never," Hilda answered. "You see, Lady Meadowcroft, I don't nurse for a livelihood. I have means of my own; I took up this work as an occupation and a sphere in life. I haven't done anything yet but hospital nursing."

Lady Meadowcroft drew a slight sigh. "What a pity!" she murmured, slowly. "It does seem hard that your sympathies should all be thrown away, so to speak, on a horrid lot of wretched poor people, instead of being spent on your own equals—who would so greatly appreciate them."

"I think I can venture to say the poor appreciate them, too," Hilda answered, bridling up a little—for there was nothing she hated so much as class-prejudices. "Besides, they need sympathy more; they have fewer comforts. I should not care to give up attending my poor people for the sake of the idle rich."

The set phraseology of the country rectory recurred to Lady Meadowcroft—"our poorer brethren," and so forth. "Oh, of course," she answered, with the mechanical acquiescence such women always give to moral platitudes. "One must do one's best for the poor, I know—for conscience' sake and all that; it's our duty, and we all try hard to do it. But they're so terribly ungrateful! Don't you think so? Do you know, Miss Wade, in my father's parish—"

Hilda cut her short with a sunny smile—half contemptuous toleration, half genuine pity. "We are all ungrateful," she said; "but the poor, I think, the least so. I'm sure the gratitude I've often had from my poor women at St. Nathaniel's has made me sometimes feel really ashamed of myself. I had done so little—and they thanked me so much for it."

"Which only shows," Lady Meadowcroft broke in, "that one ought always to have a *lady* to nurse one."

"*Ça marche!*" Hilda said to me, with a quiet smile, a few minutes after, when her ladyship had disappeared in her fluffy robe down the companion-ladder.

"Yes, *ça marche*," I answered. "In an hour or two you will have succeeded in landing your chaperon. And what is most amusing, landed her, too, Hilda, just by being yourself—letting her see frankly the actual truth of what you think and feel about her and about everyone!"

"I could not do otherwise," Hilda answered, growing grave. "I must be myself, or die for it. My method of angling consists in showing myself just as I am. You call me an actress, but I am not really one; I am only a woman who can use her personality for her own purposes. If I go with Lady Meadowcroft, it will be a mutual advantage. I shall really sympathise with her for I can see the poor thing is devoured with nervousness."

"But do you think you will be able to stand her?" I asked.

"Oh, dear, yes. She's not a bad little thing, *au fond*, when you get to know her. It is society that has spoilt her. She would have made a nice, helpful, motherly body if she'd married the curate."

As we neared Bombay, conversation grew gradually more and more Indian; it always does under similar circumstances. A sea voyage is half retrospect, half prospect; it has no personal identity.

You leave Liverpool for New York at the English standpoint, and
are full of what you did in London or Manchester; half-way over,
you begin to discuss American custom-houses and New York hotels;
by the time you reach Sandy Hook, the talk is all of quick trains
west and the shortest route from Philadelphia to New Orleans. You
grow by slow stages into the new attitude; at Malta you are still
regretting Europe; after Aden, your mind dwells most on the hire
of punkah-wallahs and the proverbial toughness of the dak-bungalow chicken.

"How's the plague at Bombay now?" an inquisitive passenger
inquired of the Captain at dinner our last night out. "Getting any
better?"

Lady Meadowcroft's thumb dived between her fingers again.
"What! is there plague in Bombay?" she asked, innocently, in her
nervous fashion.

"Plague in Bombay!" the Captain burst out, his burly voice re-
sounding down the saloon. "Why, bless your soul, ma'am, where
else would you expect it? Plague in Bombay! It's been there these
five years. Better? Not quite. Going ahead like mad. They're dying
by thousands."

"A microbe, I believe, Dr. Boyell," the inquisitive passenger
observed deferentially, with due respect for medical science.

"Yes," the ship's doctor answered, helping himself to an olive.
"Forty million microbes to each square inch of the Bombay atmosphere."

"And we are going to Bombay!" Lady Meadowcroft exclaimed,
aghast.

"You must have known there was plague there, my dear," Sir
Ivor put in, soothingly, with a deprecating glance. "It's been in all
the papers. But only the natives get it."

The thumb uncovered itself a little. "Oh, only the natives!" Lady
Meadowcroft echoed, relieved; as if a few thousand Hindus more
or less would hardly be missed among the blessings of British rule in
India. "You know, Ivor, I never read those *dreadful* things in the
papers. *I* read the Society news, and Our Social Diary, and columns
that are headed 'Mainly About People.' I don't care for anything

but the *Morning Post* and the *World* and *Truth*. I hate horrors. . . .
But it's a blessing to think it's only the natives."

"Plenty of Europeans, too, bless your heart," the Captain thundered out unfeelingly. "Why, last time I was in port, a nurse died
at the hospital."

"Oh, only a nurse—" Lady Meadowcroft began, and then
coloured up deeply, with a side glance at Hilda.

"And lots besides nurses," the Captain continued, positively
delighted at the terror he was inspiring. "Pucka Englishmen and
Englishwomen. Bad business this plague, Dr. Cumberledge!
Catches particularly those who are most afraid of it."

"But it's only in Bombay?" Lady Meadowcroft cried, clutching
at the last straw. I could see she was registering a mental determination to go straight up-country the moment she landed.

"Not a bit of it!" the Captain answered, with provoking cheerfulness. "Rampaging about like a roaring lion all over India!"

Lady Meadowcroft's thumb must have suffered severely. The
nails dug into it as if it were someone else's.

Half an hour later, as we were on deck in the cool of the evening,
the thing was settled. "My wife," Sir Ivor said, coming up to us
with a serious face, "has delivered her ultimatum. Positively her
ultimatum. I've had a mort o' trouble with her, and now she's
settled. *Either*, she goes back from Bombay by the return steamer;
or else—you and Miss Wade must name your own terms to accompany us on our tour, in case of emergencies." He glanced wistfully
at Hilda. "*Do* you think you can help us?"

Hilda made no hypocritical pretence of hanging back. Her nature was transparent. "If you wish it, yes," she answered, shaking
hands upon the bargain. "I only want to go about and see India; I
can see it quite as well with Lady Meadowcroft as without her—
and even better. It is unpleasant for a woman to travel unattached.
I require a chaperon, and am glad to find one. I will join your party,
paying my own hotel and travelling expenses, and considering
myself as engaged in case your wife should need my services. For
that, you can pay me, if you like, some nominal retaining fee—five
pounds or anything. The money is immaterial to me. I like to be

useful, and I sympathise with nerves; but it may make your wife feel she is really keeping a hold over me if we put the arrangement on a business basis. As a matter of fact, whatever sum she chooses to pay, I shall hand it over at once to the Bombay Plague Hospital."

Sir Ivor looked relieved. "Thank you ever so much!" he said, wringing her hand warmly. "I thowt you were a brick, and now I know it. My wife says your face inspires confidence, and your voice sympathy. She *must* have you with her. And you, Dr. Cumberledge?"

"I follow Miss Wade's lead," I answered, in my most solemn tone, with an impressive bow. "I, too, am travelling for instruction and amusement only; and if it would give Lady Meadowcroft a greater sense of security to have a duly qualified practitioner in her suite, I shall be glad on the same terms to swell your party. I will pay my own way; and I will allow you to name any nominal sum you please for your claim on my medical attendance, if necessary. I hope and believe, however, that our presence will so far reassure our prospective patient as to make our post in both cases a sinecure."

Three minutes later Lady Meadowcroft rushed on deck and flung her arms impulsively round Hilda. "You dear, good girl!" she cried; "how sweet and kind of you! I really *couldn't* have landed if you hadn't promised to come with us. And Dr. Cumberledge, too! So nice and friendly of you both. But there, it *is* so much pleasanter to deal with ladies and gentlemen!"

So Hilda won her point; and what was best, won it fairly.

THE EPISODE OF THE GUIDE
WHO KNEW THE COUNTRY

We toured all round India with the Meadowcrofts; and really the lady who was "so very exclusive" turned out not a bad little thing, when once one had succeeded in breaking through the ring-fence with which she surrounded herself. She had an endless, quenchless restlessness, it is true; her eyes wandered aimlessly; she never was happy for two minutes together, unless she was surrounded by friends, and was seeing something. What she saw did not interest her much; certainly her tastes were on the level with those of a very young child. An odd-looking house, a queerly dressed man, a tree cut into shape to look like a peacock, delighted her far more than the most glorious view of the quaintest old temple. Still, she must be seeing. She could no more sit still than a fidgety child or a monkey at the Zoo. To be up and doing was her nature—doing nothing, to be sure; but still, doing it strenuously.

So we went the regulation round of Delhi and Agra, the Taj Mahal, and the Ghats at Benares, at railroad speed, fulfilling the whole duty of the modern globe-trotter. Lady Meadowcroft looked at everything—for ten minutes at a stretch; then she wanted to be off, to visit the next thing set down for her in her guide-book. As we left each town she murmured mechanically: "Well, we've seen *that*, thank Heaven!" and straightway went on, with equal eagerness, and equal boredom, to see the one after it.

The only thing that did *not* bore her, indeed, was Hilda's bright talk.

"Oh, Miss Wade," she would say, clasping her hands, and looking up into Hilda's eyes with her own empty blue ones, "you *are* so funny! So original, don't you know! You never talk or think of anything like other people. I can't imagine how such ideas come up in your mind. If *I* were to try all day, I'm sure I should never hit upon them!" Which was so perfectly true as to be a trifle obvious.

Sir Ivor, not being interested in temples, but in steel rails, had gone on at once to his concession, or contract, or whatever else it was, on the north-east frontier, leaving his wife to follow and rejoin him in the Himalayas as soon as she had exhausted the sights of India. So, after a few dusty weeks of wear and tear on the Indian railways, we met him once more in the recesses of Nepaul, where he was busy constructing a light local line for the reigning Maharajah.

If Lady Meadowcroft had been bored at Allahabad and Ajmere, she was immensely more bored in a rough bungalow among the trackless depths of the Himalayan valleys. To anybody with eyes in his head, indeed, Toloo, where Sir Ivor had pitched his headquarters, was lovely enough to keep one interested for a twelvemonth. Snow-clad needles of rock hemmed it in on either side; great deodars rose like huge tapers on the hillsides; the plants and flowers were a joy to look at. But Lady Meadowcroft did not care for flowers which one could not wear in one's hair; and what was the good of dressing here, with no one but Ivor and Dr. Cumberledge to see one? She yawned till she was tired; then she began to grow peevish.

"Why Ivor should want to build a railway at all in this stupid, silly place," she said, as we sat in the veranda in the cool of evening, "I'm sure *I* can't imagine. We *must* go somewhere. This is maddening, maddening! Miss Wade—Dr. Cumberledge—I count upon you to discover *something* for me to do. If I vegetate like this, seeing nothing all day long but those eternal hills"—she clenched her little fist—"I shall go *mad* with ennui."

Hilda had a happy thought. "I have a fancy to see some of these Buddhist monasteries," she said, smiling as one smiles at a tiresome child whom one likes in spite of everything. "You remember,

I was reading that book of Mr. Simpson's on the steamer—coming out—a curious book about the Buddhist Praying Wheels; and it made me want to see one of their temples immensely. What do you say to camping out? A few weeks in the hills? It would be an adventure, at any rate."

"Camping out?" Lady Meadowcroft exclaimed, half roused from her languor by the idea of a change. "Oh, do you think that would be fun? Should we sleep on the ground? But, wouldn't it be dreadfully, horribly uncomfortable?"

"Not half so uncomfortable as you'll find yourself here at Toloo in a few days, Emmie," her husband put in, grimly. "The rains will soon be on, lass; and when the rains are on, by all accounts, they're precious heavy hereabouts—rare fine rains, so that a man's half-flooded out of his bed o' nights—which won't suit *you*, my lady."

The poor little woman clasped her twitching hands in feeble agony. "Oh, Ivor, how dreadful! Is it what they call the mongoose, or monsoon, or something? But if they're so bad here, surely they'll be worse in the hills—and camping out, too—won't they?"

"Not if you go the right way to work. Ah'm told it never rains t'other side o' the hills. The mountains stop the clouds, and once you're over, you're safe enough. Only, you must take care to keep well in the Maharajah's territory. Cross the frontier t'other side into Tibet, an' they'll skin thee alive as soon as look at thee. They don't like strangers in Tibet; prejudiced against them, somehow; they pretty well skinned that young chap Landor who tried to go there a year ago."

"But, Ivor, I don't want to be skinned alive! I'm not an eel, please!"

"That's all right, lass. Leave that to me. I can get thee a guide, a man that's very well acquainted with the mountains. I was talking to a scientific explorer here t'other day, and he knows of a good guide who can take you anywhere. He'll get you the chance of seeing the inside of a Buddhist monastery, if you like, Miss Wade. He's hand in glove with all the religion they've got in this part o' the country. They've got noan much, but at what there is, he's a rare devout one."

We discussed the matter fully for two or three days before we made up our minds. Lady Meadowcroft was undecided between her hatred of dulness and her haunting fear that scorpions and snakes would intrude upon our tents and beds while we were camping. In the end, however, the desire for change carried the day. She decided to dodge the rainy season by getting behind the Himalayan-passes, in the dry region to the north of the great range, where rain seldom falls, the country being watered only by the melting of the snows on the high summits.

This decision delighted Hilda, who, since she came to India, had fallen a prey to the fashionable vice of amateur photography. She took to it enthusiastically. She had bought herself a first-rate camera of the latest scientific pattern at Bombay, and ever since had spent all her time and spoiled her pretty hands in "developing." She was also seized with a craze for Buddhism. The objects that everywhere particularly attracted her were the old Buddhist temples and tombs and sculptures with which India is studded. Of these she had taken some hundreds of views, all printed by herself with the greatest care and precision. But in India, after all, Buddhism is a dead creed. Its monuments alone remain; she was anxious to see the Buddhist religion in its living state; and that she could only do in these remote outlying Himalayan valleys.

Our outfit, therefore, included a dark tent for Hilda's photographic apparatus; a couple of roomy tents to live and sleep in; a small cooking-stove; a cook to look after it; half-a-dozen bearers; and the highly recommended guide who knew his way about the country. In three days we were ready, to Sir Ivor's great delight. He was fond of his pretty wife, and proud of her, I believe; but when once she was away from the whirl and bustle of the London that she loved, it was a relief to him, I fancy, to pursue his work alone, unhampered by her restless and querulous childishness.

On the morning when we were to make our start, the guide who was "well acquainted with the mountains" turned up—as villainous-looking a person as I have ever set eyes on. He was sullen and furtive. I judged him at sight to be half Hindu, half Tibetan. He had a dark complexion, between brown and tawny; narrow slant eyes, very small and beady-black, with a cunning leer in their oblique corners; a flat nose much broadened at the wings; a cruel, thick, sensuous mouth, and high cheek-bones; the whole surmounted by a comprehensive scowl and an abundant crop of lank black hair, tied up in a knot at the nape of the neck with a yellow ribbon. His face was shifty; his short, stout form looked well adapted to mountain climbing, and also to wriggling. A deep scar on his left cheek did not help to inspire confidence. But he was polite and civil-spoken. Altogether a clever, unscrupulous, wide-awake soul, who would serve you well if he thought he could make by it, and would betray you at a pinch to the highest bidder.

We set out, in merry mood, prepared to solve all the abstruse problems of the Buddhist religion. Our spoilt child stood the camping out better than I expected. She was fretful, of course, and worried about trifles; she missed her maid and her accustomed comforts; but she minded the roughing it less, on the whole, than she had minded the boredom of inaction in the bungalow; and, being cast on Hilda and myself for resources, she suddenly evolved an unexpected taste for producing, developing, and printing photographs. We took dozens, as we went along, of little villages on our route, wood-built villages with quaint houses and turrets; and as Hilda had brought her collection of prints with her, for comparison of the Indian and Nepaulese monuments, we spent the evenings after our short day's march each day in arranging and collating them. We had planned to be away six weeks, at least. In that time the monsoon would have burst and passed. Our guide thought we might see all that was worth seeing of the Buddhist monasteries, and Sir Ivor thought we should have fairly escaped the dreaded wet season.

"What do you make of our guide?" I asked of Hilda on our fourth day out. I began somehow to distrust him.

"Oh, he seems all right," Hilda answered, carelessly—and her voice reassured me. "He's a rogue, of course; all guides and interpreters, and dragomans and the like, in out-of-the-way places, always *are* rogues. If they were honest men, they would share the ordinary prejudices of their countrymen, and would have nothing to do with the hated stranger. But in this case our friend, Ram Das, has no end to gain by getting us into mischief. If he had, he wouldn't scruple for a second to cut our throats; but then, there are too many of us. He will probably try to cheat us by making preposterous charges when he gets us back to Toloo; but that's Lady Meadow-croft's business. I don't doubt Sir Ivor will be more than a match for him there. I'll back one shrewd Yorkshireman against any three Tibetan half-castes, any day."

"You're right that he would cut our throats if it served his pur-pose," I answered. "He's servile, and servility goes hand in hand with treachery. The more I watch him, the more I see 'scoundrel' written in large type on every bend of the fellow's oily shoulders."

"Oh, yes, he's a bad lot, I know. The cook, who can speak a little English and a little Tibetan, as well as Hindustani, tells me Ram Das has the worst reputation of any man in the mountains. But he says he's a very good guide to the passes, for all that, and if he's well paid will do what he's paid for."

Next day but one we approached at last, after several short marches, the neighbourhood of what our guide assured us was a Buddhist monastery. I was glad when he told us of it, giving the place the name of a well-known Nepaulese village; for, to say the truth, I was beginning to get frightened. Judging by the sun, for I had brought no compass, it struck me that we seemed to have been marching almost due north ever since we left Toloo; and I fancied such a line of march must have brought us by this time suspiciously near the Tibetan frontier. Now, I had no desire to be "skinned alive," as Sir Ivor put it. I did not wish to emulate St. Bartholomew and others of the early Christian martyrs; so I was pleased to learn that we were really drawing near to Kulak, the first of the Nepaulese Buddhist monasteries to which our well-informed guide, himself a Buddhist, had promised to introduce us.

We were tramping up a beautiful high mountain valley, closed round on every side by snowy peaks. A brawling river ran over a rocky bed in cataracts down its midst. Crags rose abruptly a little in front of us. Half-way up the slope to the left, on a ledge of rock, rose a long, low building with curious, pyramid-like roofs, crowned at either end by a sort of minaret, which resembled more than anything else a huge earthenware oil-jar. This was the monastery or lamasery we had come so far to see. Honestly, at first sight, I did not feel sure it was worth the trouble.

Our guide called a halt, and turned to us with a sudden peremptory air. His servility had vanished. "You stoppee here," he said, slowly, in broken English, "while me-a go on to see whether Lama-sahibs ready to take you. Must ask leave from Lama-sahibs to visit village; if no ask leave"—he drew his hand across his throat with a significant gesture—"Lama-sahibs cuttee head off Eulopean."

"Goodness gracious!" Lady Meadowcroft cried, clinging tight to Hilda. "Miss Wade, this is dreadful! Where on earth have you brought us to?"

"Oh, that's all right," Hilda answered, trying to soothe her, though she herself began to look a trifle anxious. "That's only Ram Das's graphic way of putting things."

We sat down on a bank of trailing club-moss by the side of the rough track, for it was nothing more, and let our guide go on to negotiate with the Lamas. "Well, to-night, anyhow," I exclaimed, looking up, "we shall sleep on our own mattresses with a roof over our heads. These monks will find us quarters. That's always something."

We got out our basket and made tea. In all moments of doubt, your Englishwoman makes tea. As Hilda said, she will boil her Etna on Vesuvius. We waited and drank our tea; we drank our tea and waited. A full hour passed away. Ram Das never came back. I began to get frightened.

At last something stirred. A group of excited men in yellow robes issued forth from the monastery, wound their way down the hill, and approached us, shouting. They gesticulated as they came. I could see they looked angry. All at once Hilda clutched my arm: "Hubert," she cried, in an undertone, "we are betrayed! I see it all now. These are Tibetans, not Nepaulese." She paused a second, then went on: "I see it all—all, all. Our guide—Ram Das—he *had* a reason, after all, for getting us into mischief. Sebastian must have tracked us; he was bribed by Sebastian! It was *he* who recommended Ram Das to Sir Ivor!"

"Why do you think so?" I asked, low.

"Because—look for yourself; these men who come are dressed in yellow. That means Tibetans. Red is the colour of the Lamas in Nepaul; yellow in Tibet and all other Buddhist countries. I read it in the book—*The Buddhist Praying Wheel*, you know. These are Tibetan fanatics, and, as Ram Das said, they will probably cut our throats for us."

I was thankful that Hilda's marvellous memory gave us even that moment for preparation and facing the difficulty. I saw in a flash that she was quite right: we had been inveigled across the frontier. These moutis were Tibetans—Buddhist inquisitors—enemies. Tibet is the most jealous country on earth; it allows no stranger to intrude upon its borders. I had to meet the worst. I stood there, a single white man, armed only with one revolver, answerable for the lives of two English ladies, and accompanied by a cringing out-caste Ghoorka cook and half-a-dozen doubtful Nepaulese bearers. To fly was impossible. We were fairly trapped. There was nothing for it but to wait and put a bold face on our utter helplessness.

I turned to our spoilt child. "Lady Meadowcroft," I said, very seriously, "this is danger; real danger. Now, listen to me. You must do as you are bid. No crying; no cowardice. Your life and ours depend upon it. We must none of us give way. We must pretend to be brave. Show one sign of fear, and these people will probably cut our throats on the spot here."

To my immense surprise, Lady Meadowcroft rose to the height of the situation. "Oh, as long as it isn't disease," she answered, resignedly; "I'm not much afraid of anything. I should mind the plague a great deal more than I mind a set of howling savages."

By that time the men in yellow robes had almost come up to us. It was clear they were boiling over with indignation; but they still did everything decently and in order. One, who was dressed in finer vestments than the rest—a portly person, with the fat, greasy cheeks and drooping flesh of a celibate church dignitary, whom I therefore judged to be the abbot, or chief Lama of the monastery— gave orders to his subordinates in a language which we did not understand. His men obeyed him. In a second they had closed us round, as in a ring or cordon.

Then the chief Lama stepped forward, with an authoritative air, like Pooh-Bah in the play, and said something in the same tongue to the cook, who spoke a little Tibetan. It was obvious from his manner that Ram Das had told them all about us; for the Lama selected the cook as interpreter at once, without taking any notice of myself, the ostensible head of the petty expedition.

"What does he, say?" I asked, as soon as he had finished speaking.

The cook, who had been salaaming all the time, at the risk of a broken back, in his most utterly abject and grovelling attitude, made answer tremulously in his broken English: "This is priest-sahib of the temple. He very angry, because why? Eulopean-sahib and mem-sahibs come into Tibet-land. No Eulopean, no Hindu, must come into Tibet-land. Priest-sahib say, cut all Eulopean throats. Let Nepaul man go back like him come, to him own country."

I looked as if the message were purely indifferent to me. "Tell him," I said, smiling—though at some little effort—"we were not trying to enter Tibet. Our rascally guide misled us. We were going to Kulak, in the Maharajah's territory. We will turn back quietly to the Maharajah's land if the priest-sahib will allow us to camp out for the night here."

I glanced at Hilda and Lady Meadowcroft. I must say their bearing under these trying circumstances was thoroughly worthy of two English ladies. They stood erect, looking as though all Tibet might come, and they would smile at it scornfully.

The cook interpreted my remarks as well as he was able—his Tibetan being probably about equal in quality to his English. But the chief Lama made a reply which I could see for myself was by no means friendly.

"What is his answer?" I asked the cook, in my haughtiest voice. I am haughty with difficulty.

Our interpreter salaamed once more, shaking in his shoes, if he wore any. "Priest-sahib say, that all lies. That all dam-lies. You is Eulopean missionary, very bad man; you want to go to Lhasa. But no white sahib must go to Lhasa. Holy city, Lhasa; for Buddhists only. This is not the way to Kulak; this not Maharajah's land. This place belong-a Dalai-Lama, head of all Lamas; have house at Lhasa. But priest-sahib know you Eulopean missionary, want to go Lhasa, convert Buddhists, because . . . Ram Das tell him so."

"Ram Das!" I exclaimed, thoroughly angry by this time. "The rogue! The scoundrel! He has not only deserted us, but betrayed us as well. He has told this lie on purpose to set the Tibetans against us. We must face the worst now. Our one chance is to cajole these people."

The fat priest spoke again. "What does he say this time?" I asked.

"He say, Ram Das tell him all this because Ram Das good man— very good man: Ram Das converted Buddhist. You pay Ram Das to guidee you to Lhasa. But Ram Das good man, not want to let Eulopean see holy city; bring you here instead; then tell priest-sahib about it." And he chuckled inwardly.

"What will they do to us?" Lady Meadowcroft asked, her face very white, though her manner was more courageous than I could easily have believed of her.

"I don't know," I answered, biting my lip. "But we must not give way. We must put a bold face upon it. Their bark, after all, may be worse than their bite. We may still persuade them to let us go back again."

The men in yellow robes motioned us to move on towards the village and monastery. We were their prisoners, and it was useless to resist. So I ordered the bearers to take up the tents and baggage. Lady Meadowcroft resigned herself to the inevitable. We mounted the path in a long line, the Lamas in yellow closely guarding our draggled little procession. I tried my best to preserve my composure, and above all else not to look dejected.

As we approached the village, with its squalid and fetid huts, we caught the sound of bells, innumerable bells, tinkling at regular intervals. Many people trooped out from their houses to look at us, all flat-faced, all with oblique eyes, all stolidly, sullenly, stupidly passive. They seemed curious as to our dress and appearance, but not apparently hostile. We walked on to the low line of the monastery with its pyramidal roof and its queer, flower-vase minarets. After a moment's discussion they ushered us into the temple or chapel, which was evidently also their communal council-room and place of deliberation. We entered, trembling. We had no great certainty that we would ever get out of it alive again.

The temple was a large, oblong hall, with a great figure of Buddha, cross-legged, imperturbable, enthroned in a niche at its further end, like the apse or recess in a church in Italy. Before it stood an altar. The Buddha sat and smiled on us with his eternal smile. A complacent deity, carved out of white stone, and gaudily painted; a yellow robe, like the Lamas', dangled across his shoulders. The air seemed close with incense and also with bad ventilation. The centre of the nave, if I may so call it, was occupied by a huge wooden cylinder, a sort of overgrown drum, painted in bright colours, with ornamental designs and Tibetan letters. It was much taller than a man, some nine feet high, I should say, and it revolved above and below on an iron spindle. Looking closer, I saw it had a crank attached to it, with a string tied to the crank. A solitary monk, absorbed in his devotions, was pulling this string as we entered, and making the cylinder revolve with a jerk as he pulled it. At each revolution, a bell above rang once. The monk seemed as if his whole soul was bound up in the huge revolving drum and the bell worked by it.

We took this all in at a glance, somewhat vaguely at first, for our lives were at stake, and we were scarcely in a mood for ethnological observations. But the moment Hilda saw the cylinder her eye lighted up. I could see at once an idea had struck her. "This is a praying-wheel!" she cried, in quite a delighted voice. "I know where I am now, Hubert—Lady Meadowcroft—I see a way out of this! Do exactly as you see me do, and all may yet go well. Don't show surprise at anything. I think we can work upon these people's religious feelings."

Without a moment's hesitation she prostrated herself thrice on the ground before the figure of Buddha, knocking her head ostentatiously in the dust as she did so. We followed suit instantly. Then

Hilda rose and began walking slowly round the big drum in the nave, saying aloud at each step, in a sort of monotonous chant, like a priest intoning, the four mystic words, "Aum, mani, padme, hum," "Aum, mani, padme, hum," many times over. We repeated the sacred formula after her, as if we had always been brought up to it. I noticed that Hilda walked the way of the sun. It is an important point in all these mysterious, half-magical ceremonies.

At last, after about ten or twelve such rounds, she paused, with an absorbed air of devotion, and knocked her head three times on the ground once more, doing poojah, before the ever-smiling Buddha.

By this time, however, the lessons of St. Alphege's rectory began to recur to Lady Meadowcroft's mind. "Oh, Miss Wade," she murmured in an awestruck voice, "*ought* we to do like this? Isn't it clear idolatry?"

Hilda's common sense waved her aside at once. "Idolatry or not, it is the only way to save our lives," she answered, in her firmest voice.

"But—*ought* we to save our lives? Oughtn't we to be . . . well, Christian martyrs?"

Hilda was patience itself. "I think not, dear," she replied, gently but decisively. "You are not called upon to be a martyr. The danger of idolatry is scarcely so great among Europeans of our time that we need feel it a duty to protest with our lives against it. I have better uses to which to put my life myself. I don't mind being a martyr—where a sufficient cause demands it. But I don't think such a sacrifice is required of us now in a Tibetan monastery. Life was not given us to waste on gratuitous martyrdoms."

"But . . . really . . . I'm afraid . . ."

"Don't be afraid of anything, dear, or you will risk all. Follow my lead; *I* will answer for your conduct. Surely, if Naaman, in the midst of idolaters, was permitted to bow down in the house of Rimmon, to save his place at court, you may blamelessly bow down to save your life in a Buddhist temple. Now, no more casuistry, but do as I tell you! 'Aum, mani, padme, hum,' again! Once more round the drum there!"

We followed her a second time, Lady Meadowcroft giving in after a feeble protest. The priests in yellow looked on, profoundly impressed by our circumnavigation. It was clear they began to reconsider the question of our nefarious designs on their holy city.

After we had finished our second tour round the drum, with the utmost solemnity, one of the monks approached Hilda, whom he seemed to take now for an important priestess. He said something to her in Tibetan, which, of course, we did not understand; but, as he pointed at the same time to the brother on the floor who was turning the wheel, Hilda nodded acquiescence. "If you wish it," she said in English—and he appeared to comprehend. "He wants to know whether I would like to take a turn at the cylinder."

She knelt down in front of it, before the little stool where the brother in yellow had been kneeling till that moment, and took the string in her hand, as if she were well accustomed to it. I could see that the abbot gave the cylinder a surreptitious push with his left hand, before she began, so as to make it revolve in the opposite direction from that in which the monk had just been moving it. This was obviously to try her. But Hilda let the string drop, with a little cry of horror. That was the wrong way round—the unlucky, uncanonical direction; the evil way, widdershins, the opposite of sunwise. With an awed air she stopped short, repeated once more the four mystic words, or mantra, and bowed thrice with well-assumed reverence to the Buddha. Then she set the cylinder turning of her own accord, with her right hand, in the propitious direction, and sent it round seven times with the utmost gravity.

At this point, encouraged by Hilda's example, I too became possessed of a brilliant inspiration. I opened my purse and took out of it four brand-new silver rupees of the Indian coinage. They were very handsome and shiny coins, each impressed with an excellent design of the head of the Queen as Empress of India. Holding them up before me, I approached the Buddha, and laid the four in a row submissively at his feet, uttering at the same time an appropriate formula. But as I did not know the proper mantra for use upon such an occasion, I supplied one from memory, saying, in a hushed voice, "Hokey—pokey—winky—wum," as I laid each one before the benignly-smiling statue. I have no doubt from their faces the priests imagined I was uttering a most powerful spell or prayer in my own language.

As soon as I retreated, with my face towards the image, the chief Lama glided up and examined the coins carefully. It was clear he had never seen anything of the sort before, for he gazed at them for some minutes, and then showed them round to his monks with an air of deep reverence. I do not doubt he took the image of her gracious Majesty for a very mighty and potent goddess. As soon as all had inspected them, with many cries of admiration, he opened a little secret drawer or relic-holder in the pedestal of the statue, and deposited them in it with a muttered prayer, as precious offerings from a European Buddhist.

By this time, we could easily see we were beginning to produce a most favourable impression. Hilda's study of Buddhism had stood us in good stead. The chief Lama or abbot motioned to us to be seated, in a much politer mood; after which he and his principal monks held a long and animated conversation together. I gathered from their looks and gestures that the head Lama inclined to regard us as orthodox Buddhists, but that some of his followers had grave doubts of their own as to the depth and reality of our religious convictions.

While they debated and hesitated, Hilda had another splendid idea. She undid her portfolio, and took out of it the photographs of ancient Buddhist topes and temples which she had taken in India. These she produced triumphantly. At once the priests and monks crowded round us to look at them. In a moment, when they recognised the meaning of the pictures, their excitement grew quite intense. The photographs were passed round from hand to hand, amid loud exclamations of joy and surprise. One brother would point out with astonishment to another some familiar symbol or some ancient text; two or three of them, in their devout enthusiasm, fell down on their knees and kissed the pictures.

We had played a trump card! The monks could see for themselves by this time that we were deeply interested in Buddhism. Now, minds of that calibre never understand a disinterested interest; the moment they saw we were collectors of Buddhist pictures, they jumped at once to the conclusion that we must also, of course, be devout believers. So far did they carry their sense of fraternity, indeed, that they insisted upon embracing us. That was a hard trial to Lady Meadowcroft, for the brethren were not conspicuous for personal cleanliness. She suspected germs, and she dreaded typhoid far more than she dreaded the Tibetan cutthroat.

The brethren asked, through the medium of our interpreter, the cook, where these pictures had been made. We explained as well as we could by means of the same mouthpiece, a very earthen vessel, that they came from ancient Buddhist buildings in India. This delighted them still more, though I know not in what form our Ghoorka retainer may have conveyed the information. At any rate, they insisted on embracing us again; after which the chief Lama said something very solemnly to our amateur interpreter.

The cook interpreted. "Priest-sahib say, he too got very sacred thing, come from India. Sacred Buddhist poojah-thing. Go to show it to you."

We waited, breathless. The chief Lama approached the altar before the recess, in front of the great cross-legged, vapidly smiling Buddha. He bowed himself to the ground three times over, as well as his portly frame would permit him, knocking his forehead against the floor, just as Hilda had done; then he proceeded, almost awestruck, to take from the altar an object wrapped round with gold brocade, and very carefully guarded. Two acolytes accompanied him. In the most reverent way, he slowly unwound the folds of gold cloth, and released from its hiding-place the highly sacred deposit. He held it up before our eyes with an air of triumph. It was an English bottle!

The label on it shone with gold and bright colours. I could see it was figured. The figure represented a cat, squatting on its haunches. The sacred inscription ran, in our own tongue, "Old Tom Gin, Unsweetened."

The monks bowed their heads in profound silence as the sacred thing was produced. I caught Hilda's eye. "For Heaven's sake," I murmured low, "don't either of you laugh! If you do, it's all up with us."

They kept their countenances with admirable decorum.

Another idea struck me. "Tell them," I said to the cook, "that we, too, have a similar and very powerful god, but much more lively." He interpreted my words to them.

Then I opened our stores, and drew out with a flourish—our last remaining bottle of Simla soda-water.

Very solemnly and seriously I unwired the cork, as if performing an almost sacrosanct ceremony. The monks crowded round, with the deepest curiosity. I held the cork down for a second with my thumb, while I uttered once more, in my most awesome tone, the mystic words: "Hokey—pokey—winky—wum!" then I let it fly suddenly. The soda-water was well up. The cork bounded to the ceiling; the contents of the bottle spurted out over the place in the most impressive fashion.

For a minute the Lamas drew back alarmed. The thing seemed almost devilish. Then slowly, reassured by our composure, they crept back and looked. With a glance of inquiry at the abbot, I took out my pocket corkscrew, and drew the cork of the gin-bottle, which had never been opened. I signed for a cup. They brought me one, reverently. I poured out a little gin, to which I added some soda-water, and drank first of it myself, to show them it was not poison. After that, I handed it to the chief Lama, who sipped at it, sipped again, and emptied the cup at the third trial. Evidently the sacred drink was very much to his taste, for he smacked his lips after it, and turned with exclamations of surprised delight to his inquisitive companions.

The rest of the soda-water, duly mixed with gin, soon went the round of the expectant monks. It was greatly approved of. Unhappily, there was not quite enough soda water to supply a drink for all of them; but those who tasted it were deeply impressed. I could see that they took the bite of carbonic-acid gas for evidence of a most powerful and present deity.

That settled our position. We were instantly regarded, not only as Buddhists, but as mighty magicians from a far country. The monks made haste to show us rooms destined for our use in the monastery. They were not unbearably filthy, and we had our own bedding. We had to spend the night there, that was certain. We had, at least, escaped the worst and most pressing danger. I may add that I believe our cook to have been a most arrant liar—which was a lucky circumstance. Once the wretched creature saw the tide turn, I have reason to infer that he supported our cause by telling the chief Lama the most incredible stories about our holiness and power. At any rate, it is certain that we were regarded with the utmost respect, and treated thenceforth with the affectionate deference due to acknowledged and certified sainthood.

It began to strike us now, however, that we had almost overshot the mark in this matter of sanctity. We had made ourselves quite too holy. The monks, who were eager at first to cut our throats, thought so much of us now that we grew a little anxious as to whether they would not wish to keep such devout souls in their midst for ever. As a matter of fact, we spent a whole week against our wills in the monastery, being very well fed and treated meanwhile, yet virtually captives. It was the camera that did it. The Lamas had never seen any photographs before. They asked how these miraculous pictures were produced; and Hilda, to keep up the good impression, showed them how she operated. When a full-length portrait of the chief Lama, in his sacrificial robes, was actually printed off and exhibited before their eyes, their delight knew no bounds. The picture was handed about among the astonished brethren, and received with loud shouts of joy and wonder. Nothing would satisfy them then but that we must photograph every individual monk in the place. Even the Buddha himself, cross-legged and imperturbable, had to sit for his portrait. As he was used to sitting—never, indeed, having done anything else—he came out admirably.

Day after day passed; suns rose and suns set; and it was clear that the monks did not mean to let us leave their precincts in a hurry. Lady Meadowcroft, having recovered by this time from her first fright, began to grow bored. The Buddhists' ritual ceased to interest her. To vary the monotony, I hit upon an expedient for killing time till our too pressing hosts saw fit to let us depart. They were fond of religious processions of the most protracted sort—

dances before the altar, with animal masks or heads, and other weird ceremonial orgies. Hilda, who had read herself up in Buddhist ideas, assured me that all these things were done in order to heap up Karma.

"What is Karma?" I asked, listlessly.

"Karma is good works, or merit. The more praying-wheels you turn, the more bells you ring, the greater the merit. One of the monks is always at work turning the big wheel that moves the bell, so as to heap up merit night and day for the monastery."

This set me thinking. I soon discovered that, no matter how the wheel is turned, the Karma or merit is equal. It is the turning it that counts, not the personal exertion. There were wheels and bells in convenient situations all over the village, and whoever passed one gave it a twist as he went by, thus piling up Karma for all the inhabitants. Reflecting upon these facts, I was seized with an idea. I got Hilda to take instantaneous photographs of all the monks during a sacred procession, at rapid intervals. In that sunny climate we had no difficulty at all in printing off from the plates as soon as developed. Then I took a small wheel, about the size of an oyster-barrel—the monks had dozens of them—and pasted the photographs inside in successive order, like what is called a zoetrope, or wheel of life. By cutting holes in the side, and arranging a mirror from Lady Meadowcroft's dressing-bag, I completed my machine, so that, when it was turned round rapidly, one saw the procession actually taking place as if the figures were moving. The thing, in short, made a living picture like a cinematograph. A mountain stream ran past the monastery, and supplied it with water. I had a second inspiration. I was always mechanical. I fixed a water-wheel in the stream, where it made a petty cataract, and connected it by means of a small crank with the barrel of photographs. My zoetrope thus worked off itself, and piled up Karma for all the village whether anyone happened to be looking at it or not.

The monks, who were really excellent fellows when not engaged in cutting throats in the interest of the faith, regarded this device as a great and glorious religious invention. They went down on their knees to it, and were profoundly respectful. They also bowed to me so deeply, when I first exhibited it, that I began to be puffed up with spiritual pride. Lady Meadowcroft recalled me to my better self by murmuring, with a sigh: "I suppose we really can't draw a line now; but it *does* seem to me like encouraging idolatry!"

"Purely mechanical encouragement," I answered, gazing at my handicraft with an inventor's pardonable pride. "You see, it is the turning itself that does good, not any prayers attached to it. I divert the idolatry from human worshippers to an unconscious stream—which must surely be meritorious." Then I thought of the mystic sentence, "Aum, mani, padme, hum." "What a pity it is," I cried, "I couldn't make them a phonograph to repeat their mantra! If I could, they might fulfil all their religious duties together by machinery!"

Hilda reflected a second. "There is a great future," she said at last, "for the man who first introduces smoke-jacks into Tibet! Every household will buy one, as an automatic means of acquiring Karma."

"Don't publish that idea in England!" I exclaimed, hastily—"if ever we get there. As sure as you do, somebody will see in it an opening for British trade; and we shall spend twenty millions on conquering Tibet, in the interests of civilisation and a smoke-jack syndicate."

How long we might have stopped at the monastery I cannot say, had it not been for the intervention of an unexpected episode which occurred just a week after our first arrival. We were comfortable enough in a rough way, with our Ghoorka cook to prepare our food for us, and our bearers to wait; but to the end I never felt quite sure of our hosts, who, after all, were entertaining us under false pretences. We had told them, truly enough, that Buddhist missionaries had now penetrated to England; and though they had not the slightest conception where England might be, and knew not the name of Madame Blavatsky, this news interested them. Regarding us as promising neophytes, they were anxious now that we should go on to Lhasa, in order to receive full instruction in the faith from the chief fountainhead, the Grand Lama in person. To this we demurred. Mr. Landor's experiences did not encourage us

to follow his lead. The monks, for their part, could not understand
our reluctance. They thought that every well-intentioned convert
must wish to make the pilgrimage to Lhasa, the Mecca of their
creed. Our hesitation threw some doubt on the reality of our con-
version. A proselyte, above all men, should never be lukewarm.
They expected us to embrace the opportunity with fervour. We
might be massacred on the way, to be sure; but what did that matter? We should be dying for the faith, and ought to be charmed at
so splendid a prospect.

On the day-week after our arrival time chief Lama came to me
at nightfall. His face was serious. He spoke to me through our ac-
credited interpreter, the cook. "Priest-sahib say, very important;
the sahib and mem-sahibs must go away from here before sun get
up to-morrow morning."

"Why so?" I asked, as astonished as I was pleased.

"Priest-sahib say, he like you very much; oh, very, very much;
no want to see village people kill you."

"Kill us! But I thought they believed we were saints!"

"Priest say, that just it; too much saint altogether. People here-
about all telling that the sahib and the mem-sahibs very great
saints; much holy, like Buddha. Make picture; work miracles.
People think, if them kill you, and have your tomb here, very holy
place; very great Karma; very good for trade; plenty Tibetan man
hear you holy men, come here on pilgrimage. Pilgrimage make fair,
make market, very good for village. So people want to kill you, build
shrine over your body."

This was a view of the advantages of sanctity which had never
before struck me. Now, I had not been eager even for the distinction of being a Christian martyr; as to being a Buddhist martyr,
that was quite out of the question. "Then what does the Lama advise us to do?" I asked.

"Priest-sahib say he love you; no want to see village people kill
you. He give you guide—very good guide—know mountains well;
take you back straight to Maharajah's country."

"Not Ram Das?" I asked, suspiciously.

"No, not Ram Das. Very good man—Tibetan."

I saw at once this was a genuine crisis. All was hastily arranged. I went in and told Hilda and Lady Meadowcroft. Our spoilt child cried a little, of course, at the idea of being enshrined; but on the whole behaved admirably. At early dawn next morning, before the village was awake, we crept with stealthy steps out of the monastery, whose inmates were friendly. Our new guide accompanied us. We avoided the village, on whose outskirts the lamasery lay, and made straight for the valley. By six o'clock, we were well out of sight of the clustered houses and the pyramidal spires. But I did not breathe freely till late in the afternoon, when we found ourselves once more under British protection in the first hamlet of the Maharajah's territory.

As for that scoundrel, Ram Das, we heard nothing more of him. He disappeared into space from the moment he deserted us at the door of the trap into which he had led us. The chief Lama told me he had gone back at once by another route to his own country.

THE EPISODE OF THE OFFICER
WHO UNDERSTOOD PERFECTLY

After our fortunate escape from the clutches of our too-admiring Tibetan hosts, we wound our way slowly back through the Maharajah's territory towards Sir Ivor's headquarters. On the third day out from the lamasery we camped in a romantic Himalayan valley—a narrow, green glen, with a brawling stream running in white cataracts and rapids down its midst. We were able to breathe freely now; we could enjoy the great tapering deodars that rose in ranks on the hillsides, the snow-clad needles of ramping rock that bounded the view to north and south, the feathery bamboo-jungle that fringed and half-obscured the mountain torrent, whose cool music—alas, fallaciously cool—was borne to us through the dense screen of waving foliage. Lady Meadowcroft was so delighted at having got clear away from those murderous and saintly Tibetans that for a while she almost forgot to grumble. She even condescended to admire the deep-cleft ravine in which we bivouacked for the night, and to admit that the orchids which hung from the tall trees were as fine as any at her florist's in Piccadilly. "Though how they can have got them out here already, in this outlandish place—the most fashionable kinds—when we in England have to grow them with such care in expensive hot-houses," she said, "really passes my comprehension."

She seemed to think that orchids originated in Covent Garden.

Early next morning I was engaged with one of my native men in lighting the fire to boil our kettle—for in spite of all misfortunes we still made tea with creditable punctuality—when a tall and good-looking Nepaulese approached us from the hills, with cat-like tread, and stood before me in an attitude of profound supplication. He was a well-dressed young man, like a superior native servant; his face was broad and flat, but kindly and good-humoured. He salaamed many times, but still said nothing.

"Ask him what he wants," I cried, turning to our fair-weather friend, the cook.

The deferential Nepaulese did not wait to be asked. "Salaam, sahib," he said, bowing again very low till his forehead almost touched the ground. "You are Eulopean doctor, sahib?"

"I am," I answered, taken aback at being thus recognised in the forests of Nepaul. "But how in wonder did you come to know it?"

"You camp near here when you pass dis way before, and you doctor little native girl, who got sore eyes. All de country here tell you is very great physician. So I come and to see if you will turn aside to my village to help us."

"Where did you learn English?" I exclaimed, more and more astonished.

"I is servant one time at British Lesident's at de Maharajah's city. Pick up English dere. Also pick up plenty lupee. Velly good business at British Lesident's. Now gone back home to my own village, letired gentleman." And he drew himself up with conscious dignity.

I surveyed the retired gentleman from head to foot. He had an air of distinction, which not even his bare toes could altogether mar. He was evidently a person of local importance. "And what did you want me to visit your village for?" I inquired, dubiously.

"White traveller sahib ill dere, sir. Velly ill; got plague. Great first-class sahib, all same like Governor. Ill, fit to die; send me out all times to try find Eulopean doctor."

"Plague?" I repeated, startled. He nodded.

"Yes, plague; all same like dem hab him so bad down Bombay way."

"Do you know his name?" I asked; for though one does not like to desert a fellow-creature in distress, I did not care to turn aside from my road on such an errand, with Hilda and Lady Meadowcroft, unless for some amply sufficient reason.

The retired gentleman shook his head in the most emphatic fashion. "How me know?" he answered, opening the palms of his hands as if to show he had nothing concealed in them. "Forget Eulopean name all times so easily. And traveller sahib name very hard to lemember. Not got English name. Him Eulopean foleigner."

"A European foreigner!" I repeated. "And you say he is seriously ill? Plague is no trifle. Well, wait a minute; I'll see what the ladies say about it. How far off is your village?"

He pointed with his hand, somewhat vaguely, to the hillside. "Two hours' walk," he answered, with the mountaineer's habit of reckoning distance by time, which extends, under the like circumstances, the whole world over.

I went back to the tents, and consulted Hilda and Lady Meadowcroft. Our spoilt child pouted, and was utterly averse to any detour of any sort. "Let's get back straight to Ivor," she said, petulantly. "I've had enough of camping out. It's all very well in its way for a week but when they begin to talk about cutting your throat and all that, it ceases to be a joke and becomes a wee bit uncomfortable. I want my feather bed. I object to their villages."

"But consider, dear," Hilda said, gently. "This traveller is ill, all alone in a strange land. How can Hubert desert him? It is a doctor's duty to do what he can to alleviate pain and to cure the sick. What would we have thought ourselves, when we were at the lamasery, if a body of European travellers had known we were there, imprisoned and in danger of our lives, and had passed by on the other side without attempting to rescue us?"

Lady Meadowcroft knit her forehead. "That was us," she said, with an impatient nod, after a pause—"and this is another person. You can't turn aside for everybody who's ill in all Nepaul. And plague, too!—so horrid! Besides, how do we know this isn't another plan of these hateful people to lead us into danger?"

"Lady Meadowcroft is quite right," I said, hastily. "I never thought about that. There may be no plague, no patient at all. I will go up with this man alone, Hilda, and find out the truth. It will only take me five hours at most. By noon I shall be back with you."

"What? And leave us here unprotected among the wild beasts and the savages?" Lady Meadowcroft cried, horrified. "In the midst of the forest! Dr. Cumberledge, how can you?"

"You are *not* unprotected," I answered, soothing her. "You have Hilda with you. She is worth ten men. And besides, our Nepaulese are fairly trustworthy."

Hilda bore me out in my resolve. She was too much of a nurse, and had imbibed too much of the true medical sentiment, to let me desert a man in peril of his life in a tropical jungle. So, in spite of Lady Meadowcroft, I was soon winding my way up a steep mountain track, overgrown with creeping Indian weeds, on my road to the still problematical village graced by the residence of the retired gentleman.

After two hours' hard climbing we reached it at last. The retired gentleman led the way to a house in a street of the little wooden hamlet. The door was low; I had to stoop to enter it. I saw in a moment this was indeed no trick. On a native bed, in a corner of the one room, a man lay desperately ill; a European, with white hair and with a skin well bronzed by exposure to the tropics. Ominous dark spots beneath the epidermis showed the nature of the disease. He tossed restlessly as he lay, but did not raise his fevered head or look at my conductor. "Well, any news of Ram Das?" he asked at last, in a parched and feeble voice. Parched and feeble as it was, I recognised it instantly. The man on the bed was Sebastian— no other!

"No news of Lam Das," the retired gentleman replied, with an unexpected display of womanly tenderness. "Lam Das clean gone; not come any more. But I bling you back Eulopean doctor, sahib."

Sebastian did not look up from his bed even then. I could see he was more anxious about a message from his scout than about his own condition. "The rascal!" he moaned, with his eyes closed tight. "The rascal! he has betrayed me." And he tossed uneasily.

I looked at him and said nothing. Then I seated myself on a low stool by the bedside and took his hand in mine to feel his pulse.

The wrist was thin and wasted. The face, too, I noticed, had fallen away greatly. It was clear that the malignant fever which accompanies the disease had wreaked its worst on him. So weak and ill was he, indeed, that he let me hold his hand, with my fingers on his pulse, for half a minute or more without ever opening his eyes or displaying the slightest curiosity at my presence. One might have thought that European doctors abounded in Nepaul, and that I had been attending him for a week, with "the mixture as before" at every visit.

"Your pulse is weak and very rapid," I said slowly, in a professional tone. "You seem to me to have fallen into a perilous condition."

At the sound of my voice, he gave a sudden start. Yet even so, for a second, he did not open his eyes. The revelation of my presence seemed to come upon him as in a dream. "Like Cumberledge's," he muttered to himself, gasping. "Exactly like Cumberledge's. . . . But Cumberledge is dead . . . I must be delirious. . . . If I didn't *know* to the contrary, I could have sworn it was Cumberledge's!"

I spoke again, bending over him. "How long have the glandular swellings been present, Professor?" I asked, with quiet deliberativeness.

This time he opened his eyes sharply, and looked up in my face. He swallowed a great gulp of surprise. His breath came and went. He raised himself on his elbows and stared at me with a fixed stare. "Cumberledge!" he cried; "Cumberledge! Come back to life, then! They told me you were dead! And here you are, Cumberledge!"

"*Who* told you I was dead?" I asked, sternly.

He stared at me, still in a dazed way. He was more than half comatose. "Your guide, Ram Das," he answered at last, half incoherently. "He came back by himself. Came back without you. He swore to me he had seen all your throats cut in Tibet. He alone had escaped. The Buddhists had massacred you."

"He told you a lie," I said, shortly.

"I thought so. I thought so. And I sent him back for confirmatory evidence. But the rogue has never brought it." He let his head drop on his rude pillow heavily. "Never, never brought it!"

I gazed at him, full of horror. The man was too ill to hear me, too ill to reason, too ill to recognise the meaning of his own words, almost. Otherwise, perhaps, he would hardly have expressed himself quite so frankly. Though to be sure he had said nothing to criminate himself in any way; his action might have been due to anxiety for our safety.

I fixed my glance on him long and dubiously. What ought I to do next? As for Sebastian, he lay with his eyes closed, half oblivious of my presence. The fever had gripped him hard. He shivered, and looked helpless as a child. In such circumstances, the instincts of my profession rose imperative within me. I could not nurse a case properly in this wretched hut. The one thing to be done was to carry the patient down to our camp in the valley. There, at least, we had air and pure running water.

I asked a few questions from the retired gentleman as to the possibility of obtaining sufficient bearers in the village. As I supposed, any number were forthcoming immediately. Your Nepaulese is by nature a beast of burden; he can carry anything up and down the mountains, and spends his life in the act of carrying.

I pulled out my pencil, tore a leaf from my note-book, and scribbled a hasty note to Hilda: "The invalid is—whom do you think?—Sebastian! He is dangerously ill with some malignant fever. I am bringing him down into camp to nurse. Get everything ready for him." Then I handed it over to a messenger, found for me by the retired gentleman, to carry to Hilda. My host himself I could not spare, as he was my only interpreter.

In a couple of hours we had improvised a rough, woven-grass hammock as an ambulance couch, had engaged our bearers, and had got Sebastian under way for the camp by the river.

When I arrived at our tents, I found Hilda had prepared everything for our patient with her usual cleverness. Not only had she got a bed ready for Sebastian, who was now almost insensible, but she had even cooked some arrowroot from our stores beforehand, so that he might have a little food, with a dash of brandy in it, to recover him after the fatigue of the journey down the mountain. By the time we had laid him out on a mattress in a cool tent, with the fresh air blowing about him, and had made him eat the meal prepared for him, he really began to look comparatively comfortable.

Lady Meadowcroft was now our chief trouble. We did not dare to tell her it was really plague; but she had got near enough back to civilisation to have recovered her faculty for profuse grumbling; and the idea of the delay that Sebastian would cause us drove her wild with annoyance. "Only two days off from Ivor," she cried, "and that comfortable bungalow! And now to think we must stop here in the woods a week or ten days for this horrid old Professor! Why can't he get worse at once and die like a gentleman? But, there! with *you* to nurse him, Hilda, he'll never get worse. He couldn't die if he tried. He'll linger on and on for weeks and weeks through a beastly convalescence!"

"Hubert," Hilda said to me, when we were alone once more; "we mustn't keep her here. She will be a hindrance, not a help. One way or another we must manage to get rid of her."

"How can we?" I asked. "We can't turn her loose upon the mountain roads with a Nepaulese escort. She isn't fit for it. She would be frantic with terror."

"I've thought of that, and I see only one thing possible. I must go on with her myself as fast as we can push to Sir Ivor's place, and then return to help you nurse the Professor."

I saw she was right. It was the sole plan open to us. And I had no fear of letting Hilda go off alone with Lady Meadowcroft and the bearers. She was a host in herself, and could manage a party of native servants at least as well as I could.

So Hilda went, and came back again. Meanwhile, I took charge of the nursing of Sebastian. Fortunately, I had brought with me a good stock of jungle-medicines in my little travelling-case, including plenty of quinine; and under my careful treatment the Professor passed the crisis and began to mend slowly. The first question he asked me when he felt himself able to talk once more was, "Nurse Wade—what has become of her?"—for he had not yet seen her. I feared the shock for him.

"She is here with me," I answered, in a very measured voice. "She is waiting to be allowed to come and help me in taking care of you."

He shuddered and turned away. His face buried itself in the pillow. I could see some twinge of remorse had seized upon him. At last he spoke. "Cumberledge," he said, in a very low and almost frightened tone, "don't let her come near me! I can't bear it. I can't bear it."

Ill as he was, I did not mean to let him think I was ignorant of his motive. "You can't bear a woman whose life you have attempted," I said, in my coldest and most deliberate way, "to have a hand in nursing you! You can't bear to let her heap coals of fire on your head! In that you are right. But, remember, you have attempted *my* life too; you have twice done your best to get me murdered."

He did not pretend to deny it. He was too weak for subterfuges. He only writhed as he lay. "You are a man," he said, shortly, "and she is a woman. That is all the difference." Then he paused for a minute or two. "Don't let her come near me," he moaned once more, in a piteous voice. "Don't let her come near me!"

"I will not," I answered. "She shall not come near you. I spare you that. But you will have to eat the food she prepares; and you know *she* will not poison you. You will have to be tended by the servants she chooses; and you know *they* will not murder you. She can heap coals of fire on your head without coming into your tent. Consider that you sought to take her life—and she seeks to save yours! She is as anxious to keep you alive as you are anxious to kill her."

He lay as in a reverie. His long white hair made his clear-cut, thin face look more unearthly than ever, with the hectic flush of fever upon it. At last he turned to me. "We each work for our own ends," he said, in a weary way. "We pursue our own objects. It suits *me* to get rid of *her*: it suits *her* to keep *me* alive. I am no good to her dead; living, she expects to wring a confession out of me. But she shall not have it. Tenacity of purpose is the one thing I admire in life. She has the tenacity of purpose—and so have I. Cumberledge, don't you see it is a mere duel of endurance between us?"

"And may the just side win," I answered, solemnly.

It was several days later before he spoke to me of it again. Hilda had brought some food to the door of the tent and passed it in to me for our patient. "How is he now?" she whispered.

Sebastian overheard her voice, and, cowering within himself, still managed to answer: "Better, getting better. I shall soon be well now. You have carried your point. You have cured your enemy."

"Thank God for that!" Hilda said, and glided away silently.

Sebastian ate his cup of arrowroot in silence; then he looked at me with wistful, musing eyes. "Cumberledge," he murmured at last; "after all, I can't help admiring that woman. She is the only person who has ever checkmated me. She checkmates me every time. Steadfastness is what I love. Her steadfastness of purpose and her determination move me."

"I wish they would move you to tell the truth," I answered.

He mused again. "To tell the truth!" he muttered, moving his head up and down. "I have lived for science. Shall I wreck all now? There are truths which it is better to hide than to proclaim. Uncomfortable truths—truths that never should have been—truths which help to make greater truths incredible. But, all the same, I cannot help admiring that woman. She has Yorke-Bannerman's intellect, with a great deal more than Yorke-Bannerman's force of will. Such firmness! such energy! such resolute patience! She is a wonderful creature. I can't help admiring her!"

I said no more to him just then. I thought it better to let nascent remorse and nascent admiration work out their own natural effects unimpeded. For I could see our enemy was beginning to feel some sting of remorse. Some men are below it. Sebastian thought himself above it. I felt sure he was mistaken.

Yet even in the midst of these personal preoccupations, I saw that our great teacher was still, as ever, the pure man of science. He noted every symptom and every change of the disease with professional accuracy. He observed his own case, whenever his mind was clear enough, as impartially as he would have observed any outside patient's. "This is a rare chance, Cumberledge," he whispered to me once, in an interval of delirium. "So few Europeans have ever had the complaint, and probably none who were competent to describe the specific subjective and psychological symptoms. The delusions one gets as one sinks into the coma, for example, are of quite a peculiar type—delusions of wealth and of absolute power, most exhilarating and magnificent. I think myself a millionaire or a Prime Minister. Be sure you make a note of that—in case I die. If I recover, of course I can write an exhaustive monograph on the whole history of the disease in the *British Medical Journal*. But if I die, the task of chronicling these interesting observations will devolve upon you. A most exceptional chance! You are much to be congratulated."

"You *must* not die, Professor," I cried, thinking more, I will confess, of Hilda Wade than of himself. "You must live . . . to report this case for science." I used what I thought the strongest lever I knew for him.

He closed his eyes dreamily. "For science! Yes, for science! There you strike the right chord! What have I not dared and done for science? But, in case I die, Cumberledge, be sure you collect the notes I took as I was sickening—they are most important for the history and etiology of the disease. I made them hourly. And don't forget the main points to be observed as I am dying. You know what they are. This is a rare, rare chance! I congratulate you on being the man who has the first opportunity ever afforded us of questioning an intelligent European case, a case where the patient is fully capable of describing with accuracy his symptoms and his sensations in medical phraseology."

He did not die, however. In about another week he was well enough to move. We carried him down to Mozufferpoor, the first large town in the plains thereabouts, and handed him over for the stage of convalescence to the care of the able and efficient station doctor, to whom my thanks are due for much courteous assistance.

"And now, what do you mean to do?" I asked Hilda, when our patient was placed in other hands, and all was over.

She answered me without one second's hesitation: "Go straight to Bombay, and wait there till Sebastian takes passage for England."

"He will go home, you think, as soon as he is well enough?"

"Undoubtedly. He has now nothing more to stop in India for."

"Why not as much as ever?"

She looked at me curiously. "It is so hard to explain," she replied, after a moment's pause, during which she had been drumming her little forefinger on the table. "I feel it rather than reason it. But don't you see that a certain change has lately come over Sebastian's attitude? He no longer desires to follow me; he wants to avoid me. That is why I wish more than ever to dog his steps. I feel the beginning of the end has come. I am gaining my point. Sebastian is wavering."

"Then when he engages a berth, you propose to go by the same steamer?"

"Yes. It makes all the difference. When he tries to follow we, he is dangerous; when he tries to avoid me, it becomes my work in life to follow him. I must keep him in sight every minute now. I must quicken his conscience. I must make him *feel* his own desperate wickedness. He is afraid to face me: that means remorse. The more I compel him to face me, the more the remorse is sure to deepen."

I saw she was right. We took the train to Bombay. I found rooms at the hospitable club, by a member's invitation, while Hilda went to stop with some friends of Lady Meadowcroft's on the Malabar Hill. We waited for Sebastian to come down from the interior and take his passage. Hilda, with her intuitive certainty, felt sure he would come.

A steamer, two steamers, three steamers, sailed, and still no Sebastian. I began to think he must have made up his mind to go back some other way. But Hilda was confident, so I waited patiently. At last one morning I dropped in, as I had often done before, at the office of one of the chief steamship companies. It was the very morning when a packet was to sail. "Can I see the list of passengers on the *Vindhya?*" I asked of the clerk, a sandy-haired Englishman, tall, thin, and sallow.

The clerk produced it.

I scanned it in haste. To my surprise and delight, a pencilled entry half-way down the list gave the name, "Professor Sebastian."

"Oh, Sebastian is going by this steamer?" I murmured, looking up.

The sandy-haired clerk hummed and hesitated. "Well, I believe he's going, sir," he answered at last; "but it's a bit uncertain. He's a fidgety man, the Professor. He came down here this morning and asked to see the list, the same as you have done. Then he engaged a berth provisionally—'mind, provisionally,' he said—that's why his name is only put in on the list in pencil. I take it he's waiting to know whether a party of friends he wishes to meet are going also."

"Or wishes to avoid," I thought to myself, inwardly; but I did not say so. I asked instead, "Is he coming again?"

"Yes, I think so: at 5.30."

"And she sails at seven?"

"At seven, punctually. Passengers must be aboard by half-past six at latest."

"Very good," I answered, making up my mind promptly. "I only called to know the Professor's movements. Don't mention to him that I came. I may look in again myself an hour or two later."

"You don't want a passage, sir? You may be the friend he's expecting."

"No, I don't want a passage—not at present certainly." Then I ventured on a bold stroke. "Look here," I said, leaning across towards him, and assuming a confidential tone: "I am a private detective"—which was perfectly true in essence—"and I'm dogging the Professor, who, for all his eminence, is gravely suspected of a great crime. If you will help me, I will make it worth your while. Let us understand one another. I offer you a five-pound note to say nothing of all this to him."

The sallow clerk's fishy eye glistened. "You can depend upon me," he answered, with an acquiescent nod. I judged that he did not often get the chance of earning some eighty rupees so easily.

I scribbled a hasty note and sent it round to Hilda: "Pack your boxes at once, and hold yourself in readiness to embark on the *Vindhya* at six o'clock precisely." Then I put my own things straight; and waited at the club till a quarter to six. At that time I strolled on unconcernedly into the office. A cab outside held Hilda and our luggage. I had arranged it all meanwhile by letter.

"Professor Sebastian been here again?" I asked.

"Yes, sir; he's been here; and he looked over the list again; and he's taken his passage. But he muttered something about eavesdroppers, and said that if he wasn't satisfied when he got on board, he would return at once and ask for a cabin in exchange by the next steamer."

"That will do," I answered, slipping the promised five-pound note into the clerk's open palm, which closed over it convulsively. "Talked about eavesdroppers, did he? Then he knows he's been shadowed. It may console you to learn that you are instrumental in furthering the aims of justice and unmasking a cruel and wicked conspiracy. Now, the next thing is this: I want two berths at once by this very steamer—one for myself—name of Cumberledge; one for a lady—name of Wade; and look sharp about it."

The sandy-haired man did look sharp; and within three minutes we were driving off with our tickets to Prince's Dock landing-stage.

We slipped on board unobtrusively, and instantly took refuge in our respective staterooms till the steamer was well under way, and fairly out of sight of Kolaba Island. Only after all chance of Sebastian's avoiding us was gone for ever did we venture up on deck, on purpose to confront him.

It was one of those delicious balmy evenings which one gets only at sea and in the warmer latitudes. The sky was alive with myriads of twinkling and palpitating stars, which seemed to come and go, like sparks on a fire-back, as one gazed upward into the vast depths and tried to place them. They played hide-and-seek with one another and with the innumerable meteors which shot recklessly every now and again across the field of the firmament, leaving momentary furrows of light behind them. Beneath, the sea sparkled almost like the sky, for every turn of the screw churned up the scintillating phosphorescence in the water, so that countless little jets of living fire seemed to flash and die away at the summit of every wavelet. A tall, spare man in a picturesque cloak, and with long, lank, white hair, leant over the taffrail, gazing at the numberless flashing lights of the surface. As he gazed, he talked on in his clear, rapt voice to a stranger by his side. The voice and the ring of enthusiasm were unmistakable. "Oh, no," he was saying, as we stole up behind him, "that hypothesis, I venture to assert, is no longer tenable by the light of recent researches. Death and decay have nothing to do directly with the phosphorescence of the sea, though they have a little indirectly. The light is due in the main to numerous minute living organisms, most of them bacilli, on which I once made several close observations and crucial experiments. They possess organs which may be regarded as miniature bull's-eye lanterns. And these organs—"

"What a lovely evening, Hubert!" Hilda said to me, in an apparently unconcerned voice, as the Professor reached this point in his exposition.

Sebastian's voice quavered and stammered for a moment. He tried just at first to continue and complete his sentence: "And these organs," he went on, aimlessly, "these bull's-eyes that I spoke about, are so arranged—so arranged—I was speaking on the subject of crustaceans, I think—crustaceans so arranged—" then he broke down utterly and turned sharply round to me. He did not look at Hilda—I think he did not dare; but he faced me with his head down and his long, thin neck protruded, eyeing me from under those overhanging, penthouse brows of his. "You sneak!" he cried, passionately. "You sneak! You have dogged me by false pretences. You have lied to bring this about! You have come aboard under a false name—you and your accomplice!"

I faced him in turn, erect and unflinching. "Professor Sebastian," I answered, in my coldest and calmest tone, "you say what is not true. If you consult the list of passengers by the *Vindhya*, now posted near the companion-ladder, you will find the names of Hilda Wade and Hubert Cumberledge duly entered. We took our passage *after* you inspected the list at the office to see whether our names were there—in order to avoid us. But you cannot avoid us. We do not mean that you shall avoid us. We will dog you now through life—not by lies or subterfuges, as you say, but openly and honestly. It is *you* who need to slink and cower, not we. The prosecutor need not descend to the sordid shifts of the criminal."

The other passenger had sidled away quietly the moment he saw our conversation was likely to be private; and I spoke in a low voice, though clearly and impressively, because I did not wish for a scene. I was only endeavouring to keep alive the slow, smouldering

fire of remorse in the man's bosom. And I saw I had touched him
on a spot that hurt. Sebastian drew himself up and answered nothing. For a minute or two he stood erect, with folded arms, gazing
moodily before him. Then he said, as if to himself: "I owe the man
my life. He nursed me through the plague. If it had not been for
that—if he had not tended me so carefully in that valley in Nepaul—
I would throw him overboard now—catch him in my arms and throw
him overboard! I would—and be hanged for it!"

He walked past us as if he saw us not, silent, erect, moody. Hilda
stepped aside and let him pass. He never even looked at her. I knew
why; he dared not. Every day now, remorse for the evil part he had
played in her life, respect for the woman who had unmasked and
outwitted him, made it more and more impossible for Sebastian to
face her. During the whole of that voyage, though he dined in the
same saloon and paced the same deck, he never spoke to her, he
never so much as looked at her. Once or twice their eyes met by
accident, and Hilda stared him down; Sebastian's eyelids dropped,
and he stole away uneasily. In public, we gave no overt sign of our
differences; but it was understood on board that relations were
strained: that Professor Sebastian and Dr. Cumberledge had been
working at the same hospital in London together; and that owing
to some disagreement between them Dr. Cumberledge had resigned—which made it most awkward for them to be travelling together by the same steamer.

We passed through the Suez Canal and down the Mediterranean. All the time, Sebastian never again spoke to us. The passengers, indeed, held aloof from the solitary, gloomy old man, who
strode along the quarter-deck with his long, slow stride, absorbed
in his own thoughts, and intent only on avoiding Hilda and myself. His mood was unsociable. As for Hilda, her helpful, winning
ways made her a favourite with all the women, as her pretty face
did with all the men. For the first time in his life, Sebastian seemed
to be aware that he was shunned. He retired more and more within
himself for company; his keen eye began to lose in some degree its
extraordinary fire, his expression to forget its magnetic attractiveness.
Indeed, it was only young men of scientific tastes that Sebastian

could ever attract. Among them, his eager zeal, his single-minded devotion to the cause of science, awoke always a responsive chord
which vibrated powerfully.

Day after day passed, and we steamed through the Straits and
neared the Channel. Our thoughts began to assume a home complexion. Everybody was full of schemes as to what he would do
when he reached England. Old Bradshaws were overhauled and
trains looked out, on the supposition that we would get in by such
an hour on Tuesday. We were steaming along the French coast, off
the western promontory of Brittany. The evening was fine, and
though, of course, less warm than we had experienced of late, yet
pleasant and summer-like. We watched the distant cliffs of the
Finistere mainland and the numerous little islands that lie off the
shore, all basking in the unreal glow of a deep red sunset. The first
officer was in charge, a very cock-sure and careless young man,
handsome and dark-haired; the sort of young man who thought
more of creating an impression upon the minds of the lady passengers than of the duties of his position.

"Aren't you going down to your berth?" I asked of Hilda, about
half-past ten that night; "the air is so much colder here than you
have been feeling it of late, that I'm afraid of your chilling yourself."

She looked up at me with a smile, and drew her little fluffy,
white woollen wrap closer about her shoulders. "Am I so very valuable to you, then?" she asked—for I suppose my glance had been a
trifle too tender for a mere acquaintance's. "No, thank you, Hubert;
I don't think I'll go down, and, if you're wise, you won't go down
either. I distrust this first officer. He's a careless navigator, and
to-night his head's too full of that pretty Mrs. Ogilvy. He has been
flirting with her desperately ever since we left Bombay, and to-
morrow he knows he will lose her for ever. His mind isn't occupied with the navigation at all; what *he* is thinking of is how soon
his watch will be over, so that he may come down off the bridge on
to the quarter-deck to talk to her. Don't you see she's lurking over
yonder, looking up at the stars and waiting for him by the compass?
Poor child! she has a bad husband, and now she has let herself get

too much entangled with this empty young fellow. I shall be glad for her sake to see her safely landed and out of the man's clutches."

As she spoke, the first officer glanced down towards Mrs. Ogilvy, and held out his chronometer with an encouraging smile which seemed to say, "Only an hour and a half more now! At twelve, I shall be with you!"

"Perhaps you're right, Hilda," I answered, taking a seat beside her and throwing away my cigar. "This is one of the worst bits on the French coast that we're approaching. We're not far off Ushant. I wish the captain were on the bridge instead of this helter-skelter, self-conceited young fellow. He's too cock-sure. He knows so much about seamanship that he could take a ship through any rocks on his course, blindfold—in his own opinion. I always doubt a man who is so much at home in his subject that he never has to think about it. Most things in this world are done by thinking."

"We can't see the Ushant light," Hilda remarked, looking ahead.

"No; there's a little haze about on the horizon, I fancy. See, the stars are fading away. It begins to feel damp. Sea mist in the Channel."

Hilda sat uneasily in her deck-chair. "That's bad," she answered; "for the first officer is taking no more heed of Ushant than of his latter end. He has forgotten the existence of the Breton coast. His head is just stuffed with Mrs. Ogilvy's eyelashes. Very pretty, long eyelashes, too; I don't deny it; but they won't help him to get through the narrow channel. They say it's dangerous."

"Dangerous!" I answered. "Not a bit of it—with reasonable care. Nothing at sea is dangerous—except the inexplicable recklessness of navigators. There's always plenty of sea-room—if they care to take it. Collisions and icebergs, to be sure, are dangers that can't be avoided at times, especially if there's fog about. But I've been enough at sea in my time to know this much at least—that no coast in the world is dangerous except by dint of reckless corner-cutting. Captains of great ships behave exactly like two hansom-drivers in the streets of London; they think they can just shave past without grazing; and they *do* shave past nine times out of ten. The tenth time they run on the rocks through sheer recklessness, and lose their vessel; and then, the newspapers always ask the same solemn question—in childish good faith—how did so experienced and able a navigator come to make such a mistake in his reckoning? He made *no* mistake; he simply tried to cut it fine, and cut it too fine for once, with the result that he usually loses his own life and his passengers. That's all. We who have been at sea understand that perfectly."

Just at that moment another passenger strolled up and joined us—a Bengal Civil servant. He drew his chair over by Hilda's, and began discussing Mrs. Ogilvy's eyes and the first officer's flirtations. Hilda hated gossip, and took refuge in generalities. In three minutes the talk had wandered off to Ibsen's influence on the English drama, and we had forgotten the very existence of the Isle of Ushant.

"The English public will never understand Ibsen," the newcomer said, reflectively, with the omniscient air of the Indian civilian. "He is too purely Scandinavian. He represents that part of the Continental mind which is farthest removed from the English temperament. To him, respectability—our god—is not only no fetish, it is the unspeakable thing, the Moabitish abomination. He will not bow down to the golden image which our British Nebuchadnezzar, King Demos, has made, and which he asks us to worship. And the British Nebuchadnezzar will never get beyond the worship of his Vishnu, respectability, the deity of the pure and blameless ratepayer. So Ibsen must always remain a sealed book to the vast majority of the English people."

"That is true," Hilda answered, "as to his direct influence; but don't you think, indirectly, he is leavening England? A man so wholly out of tune with the prevailing note of English life could only affect it, of course, by means of disciples and popularisers—often even popularisers who but dimly and distantly apprehend his meaning. He must be interpreted to the English by English intermediaries, half Philistine themselves, who speak his language ill, and who miss the greater part of his message. Yet only by such half-hints—Why, what was that? I think I saw something!"

Even as she uttered the words, a terrible jar ran fiercely through the ship from stem to stern—a jar that made one clench one's teeth and hold one's jaws tight—the jar of a prow that shattered against a rock. I took it all in at a glance. We had forgotten Ushant, but Ushant had not forgotten us. It had revenged itself upon us by revealing its existence.

In a moment all was turmoil and confusion on deck. I cannot describe the scene that followed. Sailors rushed to and fro, unfastening ropes and lowering boats, with admirable discipline. Women shrieked and cried aloud in helpless terror. The voice of the first officer could be heard above the din, endeavouring to atone by courage and coolness in the actual disaster for his recklessness in causing it. Passengers rushed on deck half clad, and waited for their turn to take places in the boats. It was a time of terror, turmoil, and hubbub. But, in the midst of it all, Hilda turned to me with infinite calm in her voice. "Where is Sebastian?" she asked, in a perfectly collected tone. "Whatever happens, we must not lose sight of him."

"I am here," another voice, equally calm, responded beside her. "You are a brave woman. Whether I sink or swim, I admire your courage, your steadfastness of purpose." It was the only time he had addressed a word to her during the entire voyage.

They put the women and children into the first boats lowered. Mothers and little ones went first; single women and widows after. "Now, Miss Wade," the first officer said, taking her gently by the shoulders when her turn arrived. "Make haste; don't keep us waiting!"

But Hilda held back. "No, no," she said, firmly. "I won't go yet. I am waiting for the men's boat. I must not leave Professor Sebastian."

The first officer shrugged his shoulders. There was no time for protest. "Next, then," he said, quickly. "Miss Martin—Miss Weatherly!"

Sebastian took her hand and tried to force her in. "You *must* go," he said, in a low, persuasive tone. "You must not wait for me!"

He hated to see her, I knew. But I imagined in his voice—for I noted it even then—there rang some undertone of genuine desire to save her.

Hilda loosened his grasp resolutely. "No, no," she answered, "I cannot fly. I shall never leave you."

"Not even if I promise—"

She shook her head and closed her lips hard. "Certainly not," she said again, after a pause. "I cannot trust you. Besides, I must stop by your side and do my best to save you. Your life is all in all to me. I dare not risk it."

His gaze was now pure admiration. "As you will," he answered. "For he that loseth his life shall gain it."

"If ever we land alive," Hilda answered, glowing red in spite of the danger, "I shall remind you of that word. I shall call upon you to fulfil it."

The boat was lowered, and still Hilda stood by my side. One second later, another shock shook us. The *Vindhya* parted amidships, and we found ourselves struggling and choking in the cold sea water.

It was a miracle that every soul of us was not drowned that moment, as many of us were. The swirling eddy which followed as the *Vindhya* sank swamped two of the boats, and carried down not a few of those who were standing on the deck with us. The last I saw of the first officer was a writhing form whirled about in the water; before he sank, he shouted aloud, with a seaman's frank courage, "Say it was all my fault; I accept the responsibility. I ran her too close. I am the only one to blame for it." Then he disappeared in the whirlpool caused by the sinking ship, and we were left still struggling.

One of the life-rafts, hastily rigged by the sailors, floated our way. Hilda struck out a stroke or two and caught it. She dragged herself on to it, and beckoned me to follow. I could see she was holding on to something tightly. I struck out in turn and reached the raft, which was composed of two seats, fastened together in haste at the first note of danger. I hauled myself up by Hilda's side. "Help me to pull him aboard!" she cried, in an agonised voice. "I am afraid he has lost consciousness!" Then I looked at the object she was clutching in her hands. It was Sebastian's white head, apparently quite lifeless.

I pulled him up with her and laid him out on the raft. A very faint breeze from the south-west had sprung up; that and a strong seaward current that sets round the rocks were carrying us straight out from the Breton coast and all chance of rescue, towards the open channel.

But Hilda thought nothing of such physical danger. "We have saved him, Hubert!" she cried, clasping her hands. "We have saved him! But do you think he is alive? For unless he is, *my* chance, *our* chance, is gone forever!"

I bent over and felt his pulse. As far as I could make out, it still beat feebly.

THE EPISODE OF THE
DEAD MAN WHO SPOKE

I will not trouble you with details of those three terrible days and nights when we drifted helplessly about at the mercy of the currents on our improvised life-raft up and down the English Channel. The first night was the worst. Slowly after that we grew used to the danger, the cold, the hunger, and the thirst. Our senses were numbed; we passed whole hours together in a sort of torpor, just vaguely wondering whether a ship would come in sight to save us, obeying the merciful law that those who are utterly exhausted are incapable of acute fear, and acquiescing in the probability of our own extinction. But however slender the chance—and as the hours stole on it seemed slender enough—Hilda still kept her hopes fixed mainly on Sebastian. No daughter could have watched the father she loved more eagerly and closely than Hilda watched her life-long enemy—the man who had wrought such evil upon her and hers. To save our own lives without him would be useless. At all hazards, she must keep him alive, on the bare chance of a rescue. If he died, there died with him the last hope of justice and redress.

As for Sebastian, after the first half-hour, during which he lay white and unconscious, he opened his eyes faintly, as we could see by the moonlight, and gazed around him with a strange, puzzled state of inquiry. Then his senses returned to him by degrees. "What! you, Cumberledge?" he murmured, measuring me with his eye; "and you, Nurse Wade? Well, I thought you would manage it." There was a tone almost of amusement in his voice, a half-ironical tone which had been familiar to us in the old hospital days. He raised himself on one arm and gazed at the water all round. Then he was silent for some minutes. At last he spoke again. "Do you know what I ought to do if I were consistent?" he asked, with a tinge of pathos in his words. "Jump off this raft, and deprive you of your last chance of triumph—the triumph which you have worked for so hard. You want to save my life for your own ends, not for mine. Why should I help you to my own undoing?"

Hilda's voice was tenderer and softer than usual as she answered: "No, not for my own ends alone, and not for your undoing, but to give you one last chance of unburdening your conscience. Some men are too small to be capable of remorse; their little souls have no room for such a feeling. You are great enough to feel it and to try to crush it down. But you *cannot* crush it down; it crops up in spite of you. You have tried to bury it in your soul, and you have failed. It is your remorse that has driven you to make so many attempts against the only living souls who knew and understood. If ever we get safely to land once more—and God knows it is not likely—I give you still the chance of repairing the mischief you have done, and of clearing my father's memory from the cruel stain which you and only you can wipe away."

Sebastian lay long, silent once more, gazing up at her fixedly, with the foggy, white moonlight shining upon his bright, inscrutable eyes. "You are a brave woman, Maisie Yorke-Bannerman," he said, at last, slowly; "a very brave woman. I will try to live—I too—for a purpose of my own. I say it again: he that loseth his life shall gain it."

Incredible as it may sound, in half an hour more he was lying fast asleep on that wave-tossed raft, and Hilda and I were watching him tenderly. And it seemed to us as we watched him that a change had come over those stern and impassive features. They had softened and melted until his face was that of a gentler and better type. It was as if some inward change of soul was moulding the fierce old Professor into a nobler and more venerable man.

Day after day we drifted on, without food or water. The agony was terrible; I will not attempt to describe it, for to do so is to bring it back too clearly to my memory. Hilda and I, being younger and stronger, bore up against it well; but Sebastian, old and worn, and still weak from the plague, grew daily weaker. His pulse just beat, and sometimes I could hardly feel it thrill under my finger. He became delirious, and murmured much about Yorke-Bannerman's daughter. Sometimes he forgot all, and spoke to me in the friendly terms of our old acquaintance at Nathaniel's, giving me directions and advice about imaginary operations. Hour after hour we watched for a sail, and no sail appeared. One could hardly believe we could toss about so long in the main highway of traffic without seeing a ship or spying more than the smoke-trail of some passing steamer.

As far as I could judge, during those days and nights, the wind veered from south-west to south-east, and carried us steadily and surely towards the open Atlantic. On the third evening out, about five o'clock, I saw a dark object on the horizon. Was it moving towards us? We strained our eyes in breathless suspense. A minute passed, and then another. Yes, there could be no doubt. It grew larger and larger. It was a ship—a steamer. We made all the signs of distress we could manage. I stood up and waved Hilda's white shawl frantically in the air. There was half an hour of suspense, and our hearts sank as we thought that they were about to pass us. Then the steamer hove to a little and seemed to notice us. Next instant we dropped upon our knees, for we saw they were lowering a boat. They were coming to our aid. They would be in time to save us.

Hilda watched our rescuers with parted lips and agonised eyes. Then she felt Sebastian's pulse. "Thank Heaven," she cried, "he still lives! They will be here before he is quite past confession."

Sebastian opened his eyes dreamily. "A boat?" he asked.

"Yes, a boat!"

"Then you have gained your point, child. I am able to collect myself. Give me a few hours' more life, and what I can do to make amends to you shall be done."

I don't know why, but it seemed longer between the time when the boat was lowered and the moment when it reached us than it had seemed during the three days and nights we lay tossing about helplessly on the open Atlantic. There were times when we could hardly believe it was really moving. At last, however, it reached us, and we saw the kindly faces and outstretched hands of our rescuers. Hilda clung to Sebastian with a wild clasp as the men reached out for her.

"No, take *him* first!" she cried, when the sailors, after the custom of men, tried to help her into the gig before attempting to save us; "his life is worth more to me than my own. Take him—and for God's sake lift him gently, for he is nearly gone!"

They took him aboard and laid him down in the stern. Then, and then only, Hilda stepped into the boat, and I staggered after her. The officer in charge, a kind young Irishman, had had the foresight to bring brandy and a little beef essence. We ate and drank what we dared as they rowed us back to the steamer. Sebastian lay back, with his white eyelashes closed over the lids, and the livid hue of death upon his emaciated cheeks; but he drank a teaspoonful or two of brandy, and swallowed the beef essence with which Hilda fed him.

"Your father is the most exhausted of the party," the officer said, in a low undertone. "Poor fellow, he is too old for such adventures. He seems to have hardly a spark of life left in him."

Hilda shuddered with evident horror. "He is not my father— thank Heaven!" she cried, leaning over him and supporting his drooping head, in spite of her own fatigue and the cold that chilled our very bones. "But I think he will live. I mean him to live. He is my best friend now—and my bitterest enemy!"

The officer looked at her in surprise, and then touched his forehead, inquiringly, with a quick glance at me. He evidently thought cold and hunger had affected her reason. I shook my head. "It is a peculiar case," I whispered. "What the lady says is right. Everything depends for us upon our keeping him alive till we reach England."

They rowed us to the boat, and we were handed tenderly up the side. There, the ship's surgeon and everybody else on board did their best to restore us after our terrible experience. The ship was the Don, of the Royal Mail Steamship Company's West Indian line; and nothing could exceed the kindness with which we were treated by every soul on board, from the captain to the stewardess and the junior cabin-boy. Sebastian's great name carried weight even here. As soon as it was generally understood on board that we had brought with us the famous physiologist and pathologist, the man whose name was famous throughout Europe, we might have asked for anything that the ship contained without fear of a refusal. But, indeed, Hilda's sweet face was enough in itself to win the interest and sympathy of all who saw it.

By eleven next morning we were off Plymouth Sound; and by midday we had landed at the Mill Bay Docks, and were on our way to a comfortable hotel in the neighbourhood.

Hilda was too good a nurse to bother Sebastian at once about his implied promise. She had him put to bed, and kept him there carefully.

"What do you think of his condition?" she asked me, after the second day was over. I could see by her own grave face that she had already formed her own conclusions.

"He cannot recover," I answered. "His constitution, shattered by the plague and by his incessant exertions, has received too severe a shock in this shipwreck. He is doomed."

"So I think. The change is but temporary. He will not last out three days more, I fancy."

"He has rallied wonderfully to-day," I said; "but 'tis a passing rally; a flicker—no more. If you wish to do anything, now is the moment. If you delay, you will be too late."

"I will go in and see him," Hilda answered. "I have said nothing more to him, but I think he is moved. I think he means to keep his promise. He has shown a strange tenderness to me these last few days. I almost believe he is at last remorseful, and ready to undo the evil which he has done."

She stole softly into the sick room. I followed her on tip-toe, and stood near the door behind the screen which shut off the draught from the patient. Sebastian stretched his arms out to her. "Ah, Maisie, my child," he cried, addressing her by the name she had borne in her childhood—both were her own—"don't leave me any more! Stay with me always, Maisie! I can't get on without you."

"But you hated once to see me!"

"Because I have so wronged you."

"And now? Will you do nothing to repair the wrong?"

"My child, I can never undo that wrong. It is irreparable, for the past can never be recalled; but I will try my best to minimise it. Call Cumberledge in. I am quite sensible now, quite conscious. You will be my witness, Cumberledge, that my pulse is normal and that my brain is clear. I will confess it all. Maisie, your constancy and your firmness have conquered me. And your devotion to your father. If only I had had a daughter like you, my girl, one whom I could have loved and trusted, I might have been a better man. I might even have done better work for science—though on that side, at least, I have little with which to reproach myself."

Hilda bent over him. "Hubert and I are here," she said, slowly, in a strangely calm voice; "but that is not enough. I want a public, an attested, confession. It must be given before witnesses, and signed and sworn to. Somebody might throw doubt upon my word and Hubert's."

Sebastian shrank back. "Given before witnesses, and signed and sworn to! Maisie, is this humiliation necessary; do you exact it?"

Hilda was inexorable. "You know yourself how you are situated. You have only a day or two to live," she said, in an impressive voice. "You must do it at once, or never. You have postponed it all your life. Now, at this last moment, you must make up for it. Will you die with an act of injustice unconfessed on your conscience?"

He paused and struggled. "I could—if it were not for you," he answered.

"Then do it for me," Hilda cried. "Do it for me! I ask it of you not as a favour, but as a right. I *demand* it!" She stood, white, stern, inexorable, by his couch, and laid her hand upon his shoulder.

He paused once more. Then he murmured feebly, in a querulous tone, "What witnesses? Whom do you wish to be present?"

Hilda spoke clearly and distinctly. She had thought it all out with herself beforehand. "Such witnesses as will carry absolute conviction to the mind of all the world; irreproachable, disinterested witnesses; official witnesses. In the first place, a commissioner of oaths. Then a Plymouth doctor, to show that you are in a fit state of mind to make a confession. Next, Mr. Horace Mayfield, who defended my father. Lastly, Dr. Blake Crawford, who watched the case on your behalf at the trial."

"But, Hilda," I interposed, "we may possibly find that they cannot come away from London just now. They are busy men, and likely to be engaged."

"They will come if I pay their fees. I do not mind how much this costs me. What is money compared to this one great object of my life?"

"And then—the delay! Suppose that we are too late?"

"He will live some days yet. I can telegraph up at once. I want no hole-and-corner confession, which may afterwards be useless, but an open avowal before the most approved witnesses. If he will make it, well and good; if not, my life-work will have failed. But I had rather it failed than draw back one inch from the course which I have laid down for myself."

I looked at the worn face of Sebastian. He nodded his head slowly. "She has conquered," he answered, turning upon the pillow. "Let her have her own way. I hid it for years, for science' sake. That was my motive, Cumberledge, and I am too near death to lie. Science has now nothing more to gain or lose by me. I have served her well, but I am worn out in her service. Maisie may do as she will. I accept her ultimatum."

We telegraphed up, at once. Fortunately, both men were disengaged, and both keenly interested in the case. By that evening, Horace Mayfield was talking it all over with me in the hotel at Southampton. "Well, Hubert, my boy," he said, "a woman, we know, can do a great deal"; he smiled his familiar smile, like a genial fat toad; "but if your Yorke-Bannerman succeeds in getting a confession out of Sebastian, she'll extort my admiration." He paused a moment, then he added, in an afterthought: "I say that she'll extort my admiration; but, mind you, I don't know that I shall feel inclined to believe it. The facts have always appeared to me—strictly between ourselves, you know—to admit of only one explanation."

"Wait and see," I answered. "You think it more likely that Miss Wade will have persuaded Sebastian to confess to things that never happened than that he will convince you of Yorke-Bannerman's innocence?"

The great Q.C. fingered his cigarette-holder affectionately.

"You hit it first time," he answered. "That is precisely my attitude. The evidence against our poor friend was so peculiarly black. It would take a great deal to make me disbelieve it."

"But surely a confession—"

"Ah, well, let me hear the confession, and then I shall be better able to judge."

Even as he spoke Hilda had entered the room.

"There will be no difficulty about that, Mr. Mayfield. You shall hear it, and I trust that it will make you repent for taking so black a view of the case of your own client."

"Without prejudice, Miss Bannerman, without prejudice," said the lawyer, with some confusion. "Our conversation is entirely between ourselves, and to the world I have always upheld that your father was an innocent man."

But such distinctions are too subtle for a loving woman.

"He *was* an innocent man," said she, angrily. "It was your business not only to believe it, but to prove it. You have neither believed it nor proved it; but if you will come upstairs with me, I will show you that I have done both."

Mayfield glanced at me and shrugged his fat shoulders. Hilda had led the way, and we both followed her. In the room of the sick man our other witnesses were waiting: a tall, dark, austere man who was introduced to me as Dr. Blake Crawford, whose name I had heard as having watched the case for Sebastian at the time of the investigation. There were present also a commissioner of oaths, and Dr. Mayby, a small local practitioner, whose attitude towards the great scientist was almost absurdly reverential. The three men were grouped at the foot of the bed, and Mayfield and I joined them. Hilda stood beside the dying man, and rearranged the pillow against which he was propped. Then she held some brandy to his lips. "Now!" said she.

The stimulant brought a shade of colour into his ghastly cheeks, and the old quick, intelligent gleam came back into his deep sunk eyes.

"A remarkable woman, gentlemen," said he, "a very noteworthy woman. I had prided myself that my willpower was the most powerful in the country—I had never met any to match it—but I do not mind admitting that, for firmness and tenacity, this lady is my equal. She was anxious that I should adopt one course of action. I was determined to adopt another. Your presence here is a proof that she has prevailed."

He paused for breath, and she gave him another small sip of the brandy.

"I execute her will ungrudgingly and with the conviction that it is the right and proper course for me to take," he continued. "You will forgive me some of the ill which I have done you, Maisie, when I tell you that I really died this morning—all unknown to Cumberledge and you—and that nothing but my will force has sufficed to keep spirit and body together until I should carry out your will in the manner which you suggested. I shall be glad when I have finished, for the effort is a painful one, and I long for the peace of dissolution. It is now a quarter to seven. I have every hope that I may be able to leave before eight."

It was strange to hear the perfect coolness with which he discussed his own approaching dissolution. Calm, pale, and impassive, his manner was that of a professor addressing his class. I had seen him speak so to a ring of dressers in the old days at Nathaniel's.

"The circumstances which led up to the death of Admiral Scott Prideaux, and the suspicions which caused the arrest of Doctor Yorke-Bannerman, have never yet been fully explained, although they were by no means so profound that they might not have been unravelled at the time had a man of intellect concentrated his attention upon them. The police, however, were incompetent and the legal advisers of Dr. Bannerman hardly less so, and a woman only has had the wit to see that a gross injustice has been done. The true facts I will now lay before you."

Mayfield's broad face had reddened with indignation; but now his curiosity drove out every other emotion, and he leaned forward with the rest of us to hear the old man's story.

"In the first place, I must tell you that both Dr. Bannerman and myself were engaged at the time in an investigation upon the nature and properties of the vegetable alkaloids, and especially of aconitine. We hoped for the very greatest results from this drug, and we were both equally enthusiastic in our research. Especially, we had reason to believe that it might have a most successful action in the case of a certain rare but deadly disease, into the nature of which I need not enter. Reasoning by analogy, we were convinced that we had a certain cure for this particular ailment.

"Our investigation, however, was somewhat hampered by the fact that the condition in question is rare out of tropical countries, and that in our hospital wards we had not, at that time, any example of it. So serious was this obstacle, that it seemed that we must leave other men more favourably situated to reap the benefit of our work and enjoy the credit of our discovery, but a curious chance gave us exactly what we were in search of, at the instant when we were about to despair. It was Yorke-Bannerman who came to me in my laboratory one day to tell me that he had in his private practice the very condition of which we were in search.

"'The patient,' said he, 'is my uncle, Admiral Scott Prideaux.'

"'Your uncle!' I cried, in amazement. 'But how came he to develop such a condition?'

"'His last commission in the Navy was spent upon the Malabar Coast, where the disease is endemic. There can be do doubt that it has been latent in his system ever since, and that the irritability of temper and indecision of character, of which his family have so often had to complain, were really among the symptoms of his complaint.'

"I examined the Admiral in consultation with my colleague, and I confirmed his diagnosis. But, to my surprise, Yorke-Bannerman showed the most invincible and reprehensible objection to experiment upon his relative. In vain I assured him that he must place his duty to science high above all other considerations. It was only after great pressure that I could persuade him to add an infinitesimal portion of aconitine to his prescriptions. The drug was a deadly one, he said, and the toxic dose was still to be determined. He could not push it in the case of a relative who trusted himself to his care. I tried to shake him in what I regarded as his absurd squeamishness—but in vain.

"But I had another resource. Bannerman's prescriptions were made up by a fellow named Barclay, who had been dispenser at Nathaniel's and afterwards set up as a chemist in Sackville Street. This man was absolutely in my power. I had discovered him at Nathaniel's in dishonest practices, and I held evidence which would have sent him to gaol. I held this over him now, and I made him, unknown to Bannerman, increase the doses of aconitine in the medicine until they were sufficient for my experimental purposes. I will not enter into figures, but suffice it that Bannerman was giving more than ten times what he imagined.

"You know the sequel. I was called in, and suddenly found that I had Bannerman in my power. There had been a very keen rivalry between us in science. He was the only man in England whose career might impinge upon mine. I had this supreme chance of putting him out of my way. He could not deny that he had been giving his uncle aconitine. I could prove that his uncle had died of aconitine. He could not himself account for the facts—he was absolutely in my power. I did not wish him to be condemned, Maisie. I only hoped that he would leave the court discredited and ruined. I give you my word that my evidence would have saved him from the scaffold."

Hilda was listening, with a set, white face.

"Proceed!" said she, and held out the brandy once more.

"I did not give the Admiral any more aconitine after I had taken over the case. But what was already in his system was enough. It was evident that we had seriously under-estimated the lethal dose.

As to your father, Maisie, you have done me an injustice. You have always thought that I killed him."

"Proceed!" said she.

"I speak now from the brink of the grave, and I tell you that I did not. His heart was always weak, and it broke down under the strain. Indirectly I was the cause—I do not seek to excuse anything; but it was the sorrow and the shame that killed him. As to Barclay, the chemist, that is another matter. I will not deny that I was concerned in that mysterious disappearance, which was a seven days' wonder in the Press. I could not permit my scientific calm to be interrupted by the blackmailing visits of so insignificant a person. And then after many years you came, Maisie. You also got between me and that work which was life to me. You also showed that you would rake up this old matter and bring dishonour upon a name which has stood for something in science. You also—but you will forgive me. I have held on to life for your sake as an atonement for my sins. Now, I go! Cumberledge—your notebook. Subjective sensations, swimming in the head, light flashes before the eyes, soothing torpor, some touch of coldness, constriction of the temples, humming in the ears, a sense of sinking—sinking—sinking!"

It was an hour later, and Hilda and I were alone in the chamber of death. As Sebastian lay there, a marble figure, with his keen eyes closed and his pinched, thin face whiter and serener than ever, I could not help gazing at him with some pangs of recollection. I could not avoid recalling the time when his very name was to me a word of power, and when the thought of him roused on my cheek a red flush of enthusiasm. As I looked I murmured two lines from Browning's *Grammarian's Funeral*:

> This is our Master, famous, calm, and dead,
> Borne on our shoulders.

Hilda Wade, standing beside me, with an awestruck air, added a stanza from the same great poem:

> Lofty designs must close in like effects:
> Loftily lying,

Leave him—still loftier than the world suspects,
Living and dying.

I gazed at her with admiration. "And it is *you*, Hilda, who pay him this generous tribute!" I cried, "*you*, of all women!"

"Yes, it is I," she answered. "He was a great man, after all, Hubert. Not good, but great. And greatness by itself extorts our unwilling homage."

"Hilda," I cried, "you are a great woman; and a good woman, too. It makes me proud to think you will soon be my wife. For there is now no longer any just cause or impediment."

Beside the dead master, she laid her hand solemnly and calmly in mine. "No impediment," she answered. "I have vindicated and cleared my father's memory. And now, I can live. 'Actual life comes next.' We have much to do, Hubert."

COACHWHIP PUBLICATIONS

COACHWHIPBOOKS.COM

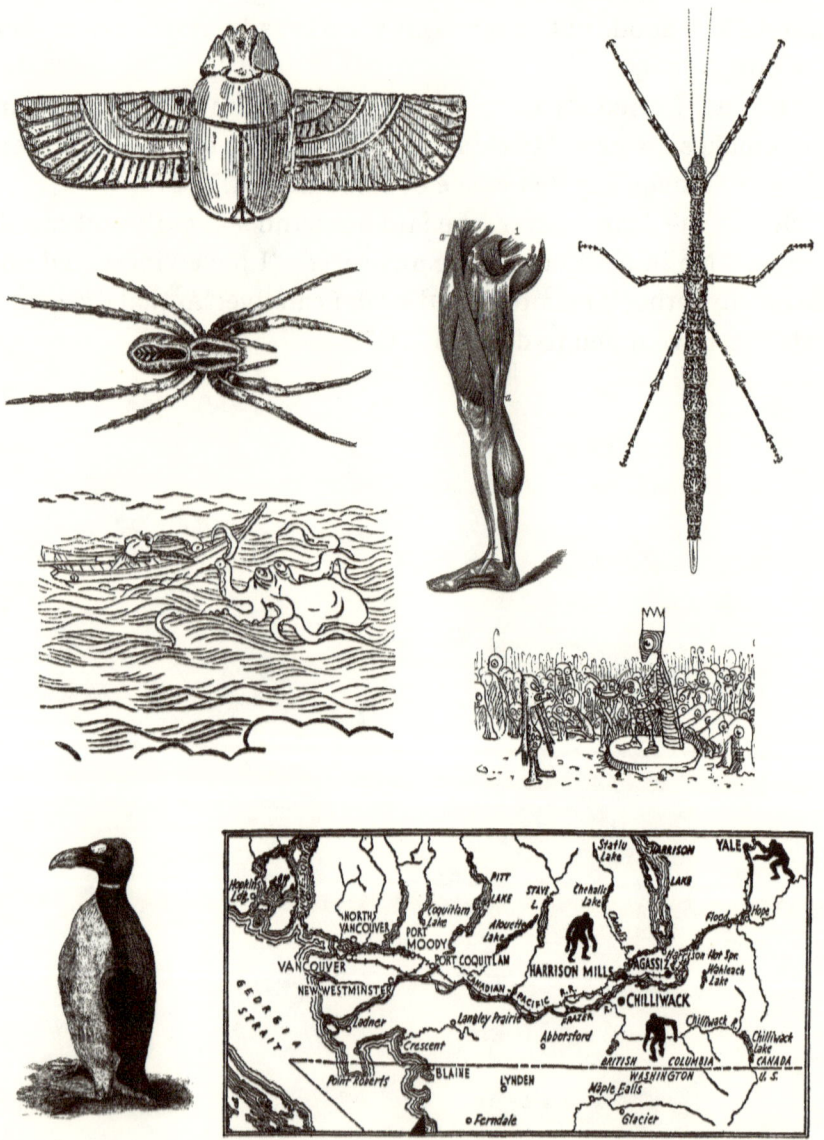

THE CHRONICLES OF ADDINGTON PEACE /
LUTHER TRANT, PSYCHOLOGICAL DETECTIVE

ISBN 1-61646-097-0

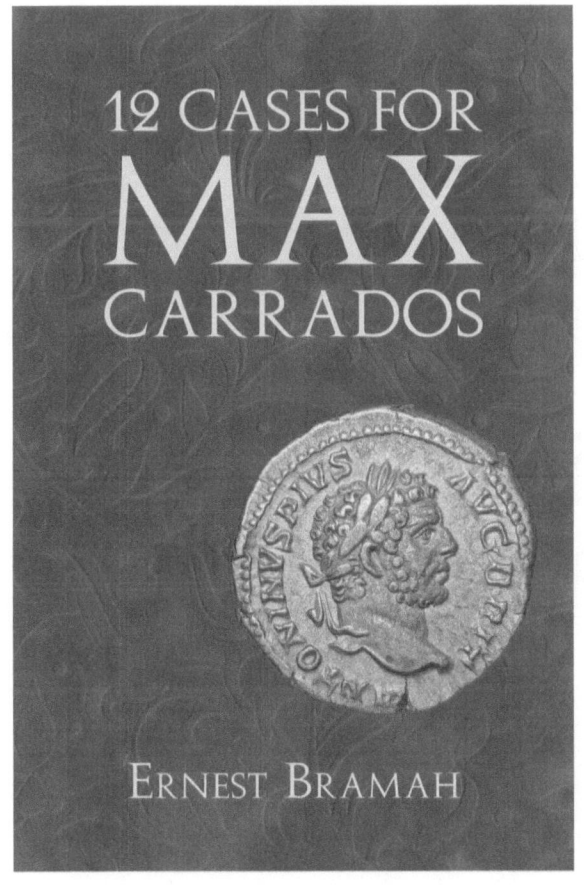

12 CASES FOR
MAX
CARRADOS

ERNEST BRAMAH

12 Cases for Max Carrados
ISBN 1-61646-018-0

THE COMPLETE ADVENTURES OF

ROMNEY PRINGLE

R. AUSTIN FREEMAN &
JOHN J. PITCAIRN

(AS BY *CLIFFORD ASHDOWN*)

THE COMPLETE ADVENTURES OF
ROMNEY PRINGLE

ISBN 1-61646-090-3